PENGUIN BOOKS

FINDING HOSEYN

Colin MacKinnon is a Washington journalist who
writes on the Middle East. He lived in Iran for six
years, first working with the Peace Corps, and last
as director of the Teheran office of the American
Institute of Iranian Studies. He has a Ph.D. in Near
Eastern Languages and is editor of *Middle East
Executive Reports*.

FINDING
HOSEYN

A novel by
Colin MacKinnon

PENGUIN BOOKS

PENGUIN BOOKS
Published by the Penguin Group
Viking Penguin Inc., 40 West 23rd Street,
New York, New York 10010, U.S.A.
Penguin Books Ltd, 27 Wrights Lane, London W8 5TZ, England
Penguin Books Australia Ltd, Ringwood,
Victoria, Australia
Penguin Books Canada Limited, 2801 John Street,
Markham, Ontario, Canada L3R 1B4
Penguin Books (N.Z.) Ltd, 182–190 Wairau Road,
Auckland 10, New Zealand

Penguin Books Ltd, Registered Offices: Harmondsworth,
Middlesex, England

First published in the United States of America by
Arbor House Publishing Company 1986
Published in Penguin Books 1988

LIBRARY OF CONGRESS CATALOGING IN PUBLICATION DATA
MacKinnon, Colin.
Finding Hoseyn: a novel/by Colin MacKinnon.
p.   cm.
ISBN 0 14 01.0453 4
I. Title.
PS3563.A3176F5   1988
813'.54—dc19   87-20724
CIP

Printed in the United States of America by
Offset Paperback Mfrs., Inc., Dallas, Pennsylvania
Set in Trump

Contents

Finding Hoseyn

Prologue:

Givon and
Haj Ali the Bearded

The hour approaches and the moon is rent
asunder . . .

—*The Glorious Koran*
Sura of the Moon, Verse 1

They all hold swords, being expert in war: every
man hath his sword upon his thigh because of fear in
the night.

—*Song of Sol. 3:8*

Tehran. The two were waiting in Sheikh Hadi, in the Jewish quarter, south of Shah Street. One sat crouched behind the wheel of a parked Volkswagen, and the other, a young man, stood some forty meters up the street in a doorway, in shadows, away from the streetlamps.

He had a mat of reeds slung under his arm, and rolled in it, at the very center, was a 9-mm Tokagypt, its safety catch on. He put his hand in the roll and felt the gun, running his thumb over the seven ridges on the butt, pausing on the hammer, and bringing his thumb down again over the ridges to the safety. The pistol was heavy, almost a kilogram. He liked that; it felt serious, and he liked the familiar touch of the gun. It was like shaking hands with an old friend.

There was a row of shops on his side of the street. Metal grating, down and locked for the night, covered the shop windows and what lay behind them: cheap shoes, cheap luggage, cheap sporting goods, cheap calculators. It's that kind of street. Across the way, a wall of rough bricks and untrimmed mortar, the back of a girls' school, ran the full length of Sheikh Hadi up to Shah. That end of the street was deserted.

Givon would come from the other way. Down there, red, green, and white fluorescent lights, some winking from a bad connection, marked the entrance to a government hospital. Givon would pass them. The young man could see figures sleeping on the sidewalk down there, stretched on quilt pallets, low-paid workers of the neighborhood, who had fled the stuffiness of their shops and workrooms. They would be no obstacle.

It was hot. Pale gilt haloes of dust glimmered around the streetlamps. In the summer, dust chokes Tehran. Hanging in the dry air, it drifts in from the plains around the city and lies soft on the pavements; coating the trees, the rooftops, the walls of buildings, it insinuates itself under doors and past windows. The young man's throat was dry with it.

"It is arranged," they had said in Munich. "The man will come and you will commit a revolutionary act. We kiss you and commend you to God."

Arranged by whom? the young man wondered. How? An Israeli—how could he be tricked? "He will arrive," they had said. "We know."

Day would soon break and the man had not yet appeared. Was it off? The Israelis are clever. Had they learned?

From somewhere came the dawn call to prayer. The young man smiled. The call was forbidden in public, had been for years under the American shah, but someone somewhere was playing a tape cassette of a priest singing the call. The priest's voice rang from a loudspeaker through the neighborhoods and over the rooftops in the night, and this, too, was a revolutionary act.

"God is most great," the priest sang in defiance. "*Allaho akbar.*" The man's voice was pitched low and throaty as he pronounced the name of God, then rose to a high staccato "*akbar*," "most great." He sang slowly and with grace, "I attest that there is no God but God. I attest that Mohammad is the Messenger of God. I attest that Ali, Leader of the Faithful, is the Regent of God." The young man recited the same words under his breath, trembling a bit, all the while looking down Sheikh Hadi. "He will arrive."

"Why?" the young man had asked, "why this man?"

"Because he is an obstacle," they told him. "He is an obstacle and yet a key of incalculable importance and opportunity." And they would say no more.

The young man pressed hard against the doorway where he was standing and concentrated only on the glow of red, green, and white down by the hospital. It was a way he had of controlling himself: to watch and not to think. A year before to the month he had driven the red VW and pulled in front of those American technicians. He concentrated then solely on their front fender and left off thinking. Then the minibus slammed into their car from the rear and four more men came over a wall nearby.

It had been perfect. One man went to the front of the Americans' car and told the driver to lie down, and they shot one American and he fell out of the car and sprawled in the street, his hand moving back and forth slowly on the asphalt, skinned and bleeding from the fall; blood trickled from his mouth. Then the young man came up and put a pistol in the American's face and shot, and the shot went in cleanly. The American's eyes went blank, like those of a sheep whose throat has been slit.

They sprayed the backseat through the rear window and blew it in, then tore open the doors and shot each man there in the face from inches away. The young man had never seen powder burns before. One of the pistols had been stolen from the American mission; the other was a Browning; the machine guns had been made in Poland. They left forty-three empty cartridges on the ground.

It had been Ramazan then, and it was Ramazan now, the month when the faithful fast during the day. Both years the fasting fell in the long, light days of midsummer, which increased the burden. The young man fasted, not even taking water. He actually liked the weakness his hunger and thirst induced during the day. It cleared his mind, he thought, and he could be more deliberate and attentive, which made him feel independent of the body. Breaking the fast at sundown, he rebuilt his physical strength.

The call to prayer had ended. The young man left the doorway and crossed Sheikh Hadi into the light of the streetlamps and spread the reed mat on the sidewalk by the high wall. Putting the Tokagypt under a corner of the mat, he knelt there, facing south toward Mecca the Blessed and gazing down at the fluorescent lights.

"*Bismillah, ar-Rahman, ar-Rahim,*" he said in Arabic. "In the name of God, the Clement, the Forgiving." He wore a plain, tight shirt, open at the neck, and a gold chain necklace, which carried a religious medal, a portrait of Ali, Leader of the Faithful, son-in-law and cousin of the Prophet. The young man's hair and beard were trimmed close. He had removed his snub-nosed Persian shoes for the prayer, placing them to the side.

It is late, he thought. Why has the man not come? What if

they have learned? The orders were to wait until dawn. "If he does not come, if something happens, you will leave and go your separate ways," they had said.

The young man looked up and down the street and badly wanted a cigarette, though he knew not to smoke. The police, would they trap them in the narrow street? Or follow them, each his separate way, for the kill?

They caught Ashraf at the airport . . . Ashraf, who had driven the white minibus that time. He had gotten as far as the lounge. They were very gentle. They just tapped him on the shoulder as he stood staring out at the planes shifting slowly on the tarmac. A mistake with the exit tax, they had told him, and brought him in to an office marked Iran Air and then, as a taste of what was to come, knocked four of his teeth in. By that evening he had no fingernails, and a week later he was dead, his legs broken, his buttocks and anus burned black and charred like hamburger with the heating coil of a toaster. Word had come from prison; these things were known in the way such things are known. At the time, they were not conducting trials.

The young man glanced at the car. He could not see the driver, who called himself Ali. Ali would recognize Givon. Ali had been set upon him, had watched him for weeks. Givon, they hoped, would not see Ali either and would not recognize the young man, on whom he had never laid eyes. With luck, Givon would never understand what hit him. If he comes, the young man thought.

A woman passed alone. She had long, black hair done up simply in a ponytail. Her lipstick was thick and carelessly applied, but she was young and had fine features. A simple purse hung over her shoulder, and she wore a light red dress that showed her body, her hips sexy and tight. She had white sandals on her feet. A whore. Setting out? Returning? Out whoring during Ramazan, she was taking a chance. A Jewess or an Armenian. She had put bits of hashish in her cigarette, and the sweet smell drifted behind her. She took no notice of the young man. She stepped around a clutter of building materials and trash, the sort that crowds all Tehran sidewalks, and back again on the walk; she slipped once on the irregular paving

6

tiles. He watched her drift up to Shah Street and disappear. From an open window somewhere—where? the girl's apartment?—an old song of Ramesh's played faintly, her throaty alto pulsating. "And it'll be hard to find a love like me," she sang.

When the young man turned to look back down the street, Shlomo Givon had appeared around the corner, alone, silhouetted against the colored fluorescent lights. He was a large man and he, too, was in shirtsleeves. He had a newspaper rolled under his arm.

A pen light in the Volkswagen flashed on and off twice.

He has come, the young man thought. Givon has come.

By a coincidence it never afterward occurred to him to think about, Jim Morgan was awake and stirring at just that moment, could have heard the same mullah's call to prayer if he had paid any attention to it, which he did not. He'd been lying on his back and staring, sometimes at the ceiling, sometimes at Pari, who lay naked on her side, the sheet down and tangled at her feet. Altogether—her body smell and the long black hair and those round hips, graceful and soft and smooth, her belly sloping downward and the gentle folds there and delicate wisps of black—altogether, Jim found the effect enlivening.

But cursing regretfully, he slid from the bed. There was too much heat and, worse, not enough news, not by Jim's lights anyway, a nightmare for a man who is supposed to write it, one that now and then, like this morning, kept Jim awake and staring at the ceiling.

So, feeling the gritty tile floor under his bare feet, he stepped over to his prized *zilu*, a thin woven cotton mat that he thought he'd picked up for a song (he'd been cheated doubly or trebly on it, of course), and put on a pair of shorts and sandals. He looked back at Pari—the Pear, he called her—the best of the girl friends.

He'd seen her first behind a desk in a bank managed by pink, plump wheezing Brits, who put her up front, prim in tweed and granny glasses on her Persian nose and her long, black hair done up in a bun. He noticed she spoke English like a Brit and thought he wouldn't mind leaving a deposit with *her* and asked her how it happened she spoke English like the queen. She said she'd been in England forever. Where it rains, Jim thought, even on schoolgirls in Kensington who wear uniforms and giggle. Later she told him her father had been exiled in '53 and had chosen London, a haven for old Mosaddeqists even though England—with America—had contrived their ouster.

Later, too, when she told him, "It's permitted, you're allowed to love," Jim knew she meant it two ways, knew it even before she unbuttoned her blouse as he ran his hand back through her hair. The grace of her in that cool night. And this hot one. He padded out of the room to the kitchen and made coffee.

Though the windows were wide open all over the house, the heat weighed down like an anvil, and there was not the whisper of a breeze in the whole city. As it always is in Tehran, the night was hushed, for in the East humanity sleeps when it's supposed to, even on numbingly hot nights.

The air conditioners sat silent (they ordinarily rumbled like trucks) because the power was off just then in Jim's part of town (power failures rolled from neighborhood to neighborhood according to a plan Jim never made sense of). The Iranians blamed the overpaid French experts for the failures and the French experts blamed the corrupt Iranians, and Jim figured both were right.

It was four in the morning. Or something. Jim still had a sour taste of bourbon in his mouth, and at times like this (they seemed to occur more and more often), he wondered what in hell he was doing there.

Tehran was indeed a pisser. Prices had doubled. Power was off. The breweries were down. Nothing worked. Traffic jams were astounding. All the phone numbers in town had been changed, leading journalists a merry chase, and there was no news save a cabinet shuffle brought on by the power failures. Jim had written up the shuffle till he and his editors were sick of it.

Tehran, let us be fair, was not Jim Morgan's idea. His editors had pulled him out of Beirut when the stringer they had in

Tehran, a besotted and paranoic Englishman, filed one lie too many.

Beirut in 1977, they had concluded, was becoming a sideshow; the real action would be in the Gulf. The Persians called it the Persian Gulf and the Arabs called it the Arab Gulf, and that promised bright copy. Much potential in Tehran, and from there Jim could cover Beirut or whatever else went up in flames.

So, one bitterly cold midnight, Jim and wife of the time rattled in from the airport in a dirty and foul-tempered Land Rover. The neighborhood spy, old Ali Aqa, was spending that part of the evening loafing around a nearby construction site, warming himself at a ten-liter cooking-oil can. He had thrown a bit of kerosene and wood scraps into it and set them aflame, and the flickering light played over his hands and face as the wind and snow cut through the exposed girders and whipped around the piled bricks.

Ali Aqa had watched the tall foreigner and his blond *khanom* disembark from the machine and struggle with their bags into their courtyard, the man grunting, the *khanom* silent with a highly displeased look on her face, while Jim's soon-to-exit predecessor—Garrison was his name—fiddled with the Rover's engine. Garrison was a classical scholar manqué and, dubbing the Rover Bucephalus, had written the name in Greek just past the metal grapples that hold Rover hoods to Rover bodies. The Greek reminded Garrison of his lost youth, which he mourned when he was in his cups, which was often. This night Bucephalus's radiator had sprung a leak, and Garrison, stone sober, was cursing the cold and his scalded hand as rusty water passed all too rapidly down the engine block to the street.

Well, Garrison departed, and days went on, and spring followed winter, and Ali Aqa went about his work, ostensibly as night watchman here and there in the streets. From Habib the Street Cleaner and Zari Khanom, the cleaning lady Jim had inherited, and a dozen other minor characters of the streets, Jim's life became pretty well known to Ali Aqa.

Jim had no great urge to be conspicuous—far from it—but in Iran he was the most visible of creatures. The country is enormously observant, and no one, certainly no blond *khareji*, no foreigner, can avoid its scrutiny. If high walls define Persian space, and behind them all seems hidden, beyond them, out there in the streets and *kuchehs*—back alleys—Iran is the most public and open of societies. Neighborhood intelligence is gathered and sifted by the storekeeper (there's one on every corner and he knows everyone), the knickknack seller sitting behind his blue stand at all hours in all weather (he that sells cigarettes and matches and candy and prophylactics in gleaming golden foil wrappers), the locksmith, the metalsmith, the carpenter, the footrunners for hire, the hangabouts who do nothing; and they share it in gossip as they conduct business or sit in the *chaikhaneh* nursing glasses of tea. And Ali Aqa, circulating in the neighborhood, or hanging around the *chaikhaneh*, or perhaps sitting on the ground outside the lunch kitchen, a regular haunt of his, one foot curled beneath him, the other trailing off into the *joob* (an open watercourse), Ali Aqa would listen.

Once a week and sometimes more, Ali Aqa in his cast-off army coat made his way far down Simetri Street and into a *kucheh* or two, where they twist in the natural, old way and where the donkey manure lies golden. There, hard by the Mosque of Emam Zaman, a crumbling old building with a white fluorescent *Allah* on its single unused minaret, was a drab office where Ali Aqa told what he knew, of course with Persian embroidery, to a thin, bilious little man with a horse-like face, who sat behind a desk and took notes.

"By God, sir," Ali Aqa would say in his high, wheedling voice, investing Jim's doings with a significance Jim would have been astonished to hear of, "the goings and comings, sir, the goings and comings are an uproar, *ey, dad o bidad!*" Which was true. Jim and Eleanor—the blond *khanom*—had a hopelessly varied and highly suspicious parade of Persians and foreigners, many of them loud and obstreperous, running in and out at all hours, impossible for Ali Aqa to keep track of; unlike Garrison, who sat alone of an evening and whose closetful of empty bottles, mostly former containers of cheap vodka, tumbled out on Eleanor that very first cold night.

"And, sir, Mr. Jim, the spy"—in Iran all foreign journalists

10

were and are spies—"the *jasoos,* he goes and returns after weeks. Weeks! Dirt on my head, it's a mystery where, sir. *Qorbunet beram,* I'm your sacrifice, I try to learn of these things, but he is very clever and laughs in our beards."

True enough. Jim did travel. But it was mostly on Persian government-paid jaunts to the shah's showcase factories and the empress's orphanages. The traveling did Jim little good; it ingratiated him with functionaries Jim hoped would sometime tell him the truth and who never did.

"And the drinking is a scandal, sir. Snake poison! How these foreigners drink! They cannot be satisfied." That was a canard. In fact, Garrison had set some kind of record in Ali Aqa's observations. Ali Aqa had a general of the army down the street under watch who was no mean toper, but the general's wife controlled things and the general never matched Garrison's prodigies, and compared with those two, Jim, truth to tell, was a disappointment, as Zari Khanom and Habib, who hauled away the empties, could attest. The horse-faced man, nonetheless, made a note.

"The man with the big bones" is how Ali Aqa described Jim, and that was about right. Jim was tall and had broader shoulders than the fine-boned Iranians. But he moved with a lightness that didn't fit his big frame, and Ali Aqa, to his credit, noted that. There was also a look on Jim's face, a sharpness somewhere in the eyes, that Ali Aqa detected. Not all foreign spies were clever, not by a long shot. But this one was.

Jim had a manner in the neighborhood, too, with *salaams* all around to the shopkeepers and workmen, whom he came to know quickly, though *salaam* was about all the Persian he knew. (Ali Aqa reported Jim to be fluent as a nightingale, a *bolbol.*)

Of course, they snickered at him at first, the tall foreigner with the red-blond beard, when he would go by. He was utterly unearthly to them. The shoemaker took to calling him Haji, and they found that funny. Then the tinsmith changed that to Haj Ali, which was even better. And someone in the *chaikhaneh,* where a great samovar of tea for the neighborhood hissed and burbled—it was still winter then and the workmen gathered there against the cold outside—someone in the

11

chaikhaneh changed that to Haj Ali Rishu: Haj Ali the Bearded, which stuck. And that's what they called him ever after: Haj Ali the Bearded.

The snickering stopped after a time, though, because Jim, unlike Garrison, paid his bills, and he had a grin they managed to like. In the end they simply got used to him, red beard and all.

On the clothing side, as Ali Aqa related it, well, Jim was the wrong sort, favoring untidy jackets and shirts and scuffed boots, and was seldom seen in an honest suit. Not respectable, by Ali Aqa's high standards, who thought *kharejis* should dress like bankers. A decided failing.

In this manner, Ali Aqa made his reports and the horse-faced man took his notes, and it was all very routine.

Then, it happened (and here Ali Aqa spoke as a storyteller, a *naqqal*, coming to the sad, inevitable conclusion of a cautionary tale): the blond *khanom* left. It was the beginning of springtime, when Iran, between winter snow and summer desiccation, flowers briefly, and the blond *khanom*, with her hair like the sun and bare young arms, departed, never to return.

"She was a bouquet of flowers, Aqa-ye Ahmadi"—that was the name the horse-faced man used with Ali Aqa, who never learned his real one. "A bouquet, sir! When the *khanom* left, by God, his days became black." Now, that was an exaggeration: Jim's days most certainly did not become black when Eleanor left.

Eleanor was in fact responsible for most of the alcohol consumption Ali Aqa professed to be so shocked at, and it was best all around that she did leave, but Ali Aqa had his own way of seeing things, and Aqa-ye Ahmadi made a note.

Then, Ali Aqa reported—this was most interesting and he related it in some detail—a succession of girls, all of them foreign whores, who made brief entrances and exits (Ali Aqa numbered the whores at forty, which was his way of saying a lot) until finally one remained, who was a dark and pretty heart stealer and—another scandal, this one worse than the drinking—a Persian.

"*Ajab donya-i e!* What a world, Aqa-ye Ahmadi, what a

world!" Ali Aqa said, swatting the back of his left hand with the palm of his right, the Persian gesture of consternation. *"Ey, dad o bidad!* An uproar, sir, an uproar!"

So Ali Aqa. And it was mostly true, if you make allowances. But the horse-faced man down Simetri didn't get the whole story.

Jim had gotten his start as a newshound in Vietnam, and that was the governing factor: it made him an inveterate war watcher. He was twenty-two when he went. There were a lot of them out there in the dying sixties, and when it was over, he, like the rest of them, wondered what else there was. He told Pari that once, when they had just become lovers and she wanted to learn about her green-eyed man. They were in her bed in her small apartment talking in whispers at night, as if someone else were around who shouldn't be awakened, moonlight filtering through ivy over the windows and the city dead silent. She found it astonishing.

"You like war? You actually like it?"

"I love it. There's nothing better. There's nothing more exciting than someone trying to kill you. Once you've felt that kind of fear, you wonder if there's anything more to learn."

"Is there?"

He looked at her, the light falling over her, breast to thighs. She smelled of jasmin. *Yas,* they call it here, she had told him, which sounds like "yes."

"I don't know."

"That's crazy."

"Yeah." It was, and he knew it. But he had long ago given up feeling guilty or wondering much about it.

He still had his press card, encased in ten-year-old plastic that was beginning to yellow, some kind of souvenir of the good old days. It was dated June 1967. "Noncombatant's Certificate of Identity," it read. "Property of U.S. Government. DD Form 489 1 May 51." And under his name, "Last name, first name, middle name last." An absurdly puffy young face, just barely recognizable and looking, Jim thought, pretty stupid, stared out at him whenever he looked at it.

Pari giggled when he showed it to her. "Short-haired and beardless. You look like a boy. It makes me want to take a boy for a lover, all small and cuddly and not much hair there." She ran her finger down his belly. "Very perverted."

"That's you, Pear. Pear the Pervert."

None of which alters the fact that now it was past four in the morning and Jim was sleepless and tired and sitting at his typewriter. You will arrange the notes, sport, and you will bang them out.

AIR COMMANDER GENERAL FAZEL TADAYON KILLED IN HELICOPTER CRASH NORTHEAST OF THE CAPITAL. That was yesterday. Foul play? You get conspiratorial here. Foul piloting much more likely. Highly routine. Two paragraphs at the most, which Jim pounded out nicely despite the hour.

Then he tried to finish an essay on military spending ("Iran's Sweeping Reappraisal of Its Vast and Controversial Arms Purchase Program"), complete with an interview with General Toufanian, known to the press as Too-Funny-For-Words. The general's interview conjured up an ache in Jim, for he had learned once that the old soldier's son had gotten admitted to medical school in Texas thanks to a friend of dad's on the boards of Grumman Aircraft and the University of Texas. Young Dr. Toufanian was to specialize in OB/GYN, and Jim wished him bluebirds, because as far as Jim was concerned, the story was unprintable over his by-line out of Tehran. So he had sat on it, and when the *Wall Street Journal* broke it, the editors got upset. It was all very sad.

Jim dawdled over the Toufanian interview, dull stuff doomed to the inside of the business section. The sun would soon come up, fast, the way it does in the summer in Iran, and Jim tasted coffee and bourbon and morning in his mouth. The day, he felt, should be ending, not beginning. He had nothing on the docket. No conferences, no trips, no nothing. He would drop by Reuters that day to shoot the stuff off and gas with whoever else turned up. And that, basically, is what got Jim into the whole mess.

As Givon turned the corner and the pen light flashed on and off, the young man bent forward on the mat and slipped off the Tokagypt safety. Givon passed through the flickering lights at the hospital entrance. The young man, alert, his hands

14

resting on his thighs, was kneeling south and Givon would pass him face on. As Givon moved toward him, the young man prostrated himself, all the while keeping Givon in sight. The Israeli was heavyset, he could see, and was wearing a white shirt. His face was round. He had a beard. "In the name of God, the Clement, the Forgiving," recited the young man. "Show us the straight path, not the path of those who earn Thine anger or go astray." The man was past the Volkswagen now. He had not crossed the street. He was coming straight toward him. They had been correct.

As Shlomo Givon brushed by the figure praying in the street, it seemed to him that someone hit him hard in the middle of the back, between his shoulder blades. The second bullet caught him in the base of his skull as he lurched forward; bits of shattered bone and brain exploded skyward and arced down again in the yellow lamplight.

The Volkswagen with two men in it now careered north onto Shah Street, then turned left without stopping and was gone in the night.

After a few moments, when the police arrived, Ramesh had stopped singing and people in the neighborhood, speaking Armenian or Persian in singsong Jewish accents, had gathered in the street. Givon had almost reached the girls' school. He lay in his own blood on the sidewalk, one arm flung forward, one pinned under his body.

Ali, the driver of the Volkswagen, was alone. He had dropped the young man and had ditched the car and was walking cautiously through the geometrically regular streets and gardens of Shahr Ara.

Then he saw the SAVAKi, a secret policeman. The man was dressed in a suit and tie, but had an American helmet on his head. He carried an Israeli Uzi and brought its muzzle sharply up. Ali could see the thing in the faint light of dawn, snub-nosed and pointing at him. The man's face was thick and wide like a dog's, and his eyes had no emotion.

"*Ist!*" he shouted. "Halt!" and it cut through Ali like a bullet. Without thought, without sound, Ali ran, plain, simple terror pitching him forward. Ali simply dashed, and the

SAVAKi dashed after him, like a beater on a royal hunt flushing game to the king's pavilion. Rounding the *kucheh*, Ali saw two more ahead and a third on the well-tended lawn behind his own apartment building. They all wore the same civilian suits and ties, absurd on their heavy bodies, and the same helmets.

The grenade was out, and Ali, fumbling, was trying to pull the safety, then pop the pin and hold it to his heart, when a burst of fire knocked his feet from under him and the grenade skipped from his grasp as unspeakable pain tore through his ankle and splintered his leg.

As the young man stood in the visa clearance line, gun oil and the smell of exploded powder clung to the very right hand in which he held his passport. *"Empire de l'Iran"* was embossed on the red document, with the Lion and Sun under the title, the symbol of His Imperial Majesty. The clerk hardly looked at him.

He moved calmly to the departure lounge, eyeing the office doors, wondering which one they had taken Ashraf through.

They announced flights in a surge of static, four at once, his one of them: Lufthansa 301 direct to Munich. He moved to the gate. So far so good. The pretty girl smiling there, demure with her black ponytail and blue and white Iran Air uniform, took his boarding card. Then he was onto the long bus with its flexible middle, which snaked through 747s to the Lufthansa plane, dark blue, white, and gold. At the top of the stairs, Germany began: hot towels for each passenger and a crisp blond stewardess saying a crisp *"Guten Morgen,"* and that was it.

The plane taxied far to build up speed for lift in Tehran's thin air, and it edged up finally over the scorched land west of the city, over mud buildings with multiple domes growing tiny and receding, the rusty, denuded Alborz Mountains to the right.

He was free, though a prisoner of the land still.

I.

The Cave

Think not of those who are slain in the path of God as dead. Nay they are living. With their Lord they have provision.

—*The Glorious Koran*
  Sura of the House of Imran, Verse 169

Praise ye the Lord for the avenging of Israel . . .

—*Judg. 5:2*

1

Word of Givon's killing had reached Ariel Netzer by phone. A spotter in Sheikh Hadi had called and they spoke quickly in coded Hebrew, hoping the tap was asleep.

Netzer arrived at the legation on the run—he lived nearby—and he wanted to bash in the steel door when he got there. The legation was a huge old house, its windows fitted with steel slats like venetian blinds, tightly sealed everywhere from eyes, ears, flying bricks, bullets. The tenants there on Kakh Street considered themselves strangers in a strange land and took the appropriate measures.

The guard appeared uncharacteristically quickly, and Netzer rushed up the front stairs past the assorted goons on the first floor, no-nonsense types with Uzis, up the central staircase to his own office and flung his coat at his chair (direct hit, but the coat fell to the floor in a rumpled green pile).

Avraham Meir was there already, glummer than usual, sitting stiffly at the conference table and looking ghastly in the fluorescent light. They were the only two on the second floor.

"Maroz is in Sheikh Hadi," said Meir, "with Bahrami." Dan Maroz was police liaison and Jamshid Bahrami was the neighborhood spotter. "I've sent word to Jerusalem."

"Reply?" Netzer knew it was too early.

"Not yet."

Netzer couldn't sit still like Meir. He paced ferociously, clenching and opening his fists and striking his hands together, not looking at Meir, who sat in a kind of dazed stolidity. "I can't believe it, Avram. I can't *believe* it. He's the first principal we've lost here."

"I know."

19

"Why *him?* It makes me numb. How *can* they have known?" He paused. "Any word yet from Maroz?"

"Just that he's there."

And nothing more.

Netzer felt things slipping away from them, gone out of their grasp now. Givon's operation—whatever it was—was doomed, dead as Givon, he thought, and it made him ill. Five in the morning. A man dead and an operation blown to hell.

"It's always like this," Netzer said. "I've seen it before. When you least expect it, the dybbuks come in and do their work, and then foolish men sit alone in the dawn and try to understand what happened."

Netzer halted abruptly, facing away from Meir, his shoulders up and his arms pulled tightly to his body. "It was perfect," he said blankly to the wall, and Meir mightn't have been there at all. "How could they have known? How? But they knew. They must have. But how? *How?*"

Netzer walked to the table. A manila folder, Givon's dossier, lay open there, with Givon's name and number, ALERT/5/J201, on the edge. Meir had already been through it. Netzer pushed the contents around on the table, as if rummaging in the stuff would do some good. It consisted of copies of Givon's passport, residence and work permits, a few old letters, a photograph showing Givon younger, a light beard around his face. An honest face. Perhaps for an honest man? It's possible. So why was he in this trade? Netzer wondered about that, too, staring at Givon's eyes. One was very alert, the other smaller and empty, a curious asymmetry in Givon's face that Netzer had never noticed before. Odd how you see things, Netzer thought.

He shoved the documents together and scooped them back into the folder. They had purposely kept the paper on Givon scanty, and Netzer knew there was nothing of use there. Everything was in Jerusalem and Tel Aviv.

Netzer stood for a moment at the table, subdued, leaning on his fists, his arms straight as posts, his head bent down and shoulders hunched, then looked up into Meir's face. "We won't get instructions for some time, and when we do, it'll just be 'Do as you want.' So we'll do what we want starting now. Let's

20

get to his apartment before the police. When they check with SAVAK, it'll be a three-ring circus there. And have someone arrange for a truck. I want a truck there, too." His voice was as expressionless as his face.

In the Kiton Restaurant in Tel Aviv, with its funny great visitors' album—there are sketches in it by Tumarkin and Yossl Bergner—Lifschitz has done a caricature of Netzer (you can see it even today) staring mournfully, round spectacles slipping down over his nose, bald head all shiny dome, and a frizzle of hair running around it like a fur piece around a collar or cuff. Meir found it funny when he first saw it.

But it was all vastly exaggerated (Lifschitz was good at that). In fact, people who knew Netzer—who were few, since Netzer kept his own company pretty much—remarked that one of the man's salient features was his being almost unnoticeable. He was short, but not awfully. A bit overweight, but not a lot. Quiet. The sort who never dominated a room. Sometimes you weren't sure he had been there. People forgot his name, too, or if they remembered the name, couldn't connect it with his face. He had no wife, no private life, no interests. He was a blank, most people thought. It was a great advantage.

Why Lifschitz did the sketch is a mystery. He had run into Netzer somehow through mutual friends, probably out drinking coffee in one of those cafés on Dizengoff Street, and perhaps he thought Netzer was droll. Anyway, when Netzer saw the sketch, he wanted to charge Lifschitz with a violation of the Security Act, and when he heard about it, Meir found that funny, too. The whole thing cooled down, finally, long before Netzer was assigned to Iran.

Meir had seen a younger version of the man, a photo that Netzer had kept for whatever reason, taken on some kibbutz in the forties. It showed a group of workers. Netzer is sitting on the stony ground in the first row, his legs drawn up. He's a boy in shorts, thin and wiry and brown in the sun. He's staring at the camera with a white handkerchief knotted in four corners over his head. He's smiling, but his nearsightedness makes him seem to be asking, What the hell are you doing looking at me? He had that same smile, those same eyes, even then. His eyes were flat and had just a hint of madness in them.

Death for Ariel Netzer always had the smell of wet stone. He had shot that British corporal in a back street in Jerusalem after a winter rain. It was cold. Netzer had pressed himself against a wall, his whole body flat against it; he could see the British boy through a crevice. The boy was Netzer's first kill. From the corner of his eye he watched him pick his way carefully down an incline of wet cobblestones. The boy's boots and the cobblestones glistened in the winter light, and when Netzer squeezed the trigger, the Brit tripped forward, almost dancing on the slippery cobbles. The dragnet was set up within an hour, but Netzer was well out of it, and the Brits never learned whether the killer was Jew or Arab.

Yonah Lavi, the driver, was taking Netzer and his colleagues Avraham Meir and Itzak Lanir through Tehran's still dark and empty streets. Netzer had told Meir the story of the British boy long ago in Palestine. "And now Givon is dead," Netzer said, and that sense of being pressed against cold, wet stone had come on him, even the smell of it.

Reclining in Lavi's Impala, Netzer stared dully out the window at the closed shops. Who killed you, Shlomo? he wondered as the shops passed. Who? Why? Were you set up, Shlomo? Yes? Who set you up?

Lavi, an Iranian Jew, kept the headlights off, the usual local technique for night driving in the city, and Meir, out of habit more than anything, looked for tails. It would have been easy to spot them: Tehran's boulevards, wide, long, and straight, are almost deserted at night. Netzer had once told Meir of black nights of patrol, long ago back in Palestine, when they would mount automobile taillights on the hoods of their jeeps, trick courtesy of the British army. That baffled the Arabs. Oh, yes.

Meir glanced at Netzer sitting silently in the backseat. Meir was too young to remember much of the Mandate days, and good Sabra that he was, he found Europeans difficult. Especially the old ones.

No cars followed them.

Lavi drove quickly, but circled a block anyway and turned into an alley just for routine's sake, and coming back out on Shah Reza Avenue, went down to Shah Street, then down to Jami. No tails.

He turned into Sheikh Hadi from the south (it's a one-way street) and then off left into Kucheh Qabus. The *kucheh*, lined by high brick walls and wide metal gates, looked deserted in the brilliant moonlight. Givon's apartment house was there on the corner, three stories, newly built and falling apart already. A small food store and a carpenter's workshop across the alley were shut down tight.

Lavi pulled toward the building. An open gutter, a foot wide and a foot deep, ran up the middle of the alley, and every so often a concrete bridge covered it over. To navigate the alley in a car you had to cross a bridge diagonally, make a smart turn when halfway over, and straddle the gutter to the end. Lavi, born in Iran, was adept at this technique and brought the car twenty meters up the alley from Givon's apartment house and stopped.

The four of them—Netzer, Meir, Lanir, and Lavi—sat in the car briefly, looking and waiting. They saw no one outside. They saw no movement, no tails.

Netzer, with keys from the legation, tried the front gate. The first wouldn't go in. The second did, but wouldn't turn. And the third worked. Three times turning, each necessary to slide the lock, and Netzer clinked open the steel door to the courtyard. The sound seemed magnified in the early morning stillness. They closed it behind them as silently as possible.

No one was awake on the lower floors. Blue light from the streetlamp shone through the stairwell windows as they padded to the third floor and entered.

"All right," said Netzer softly, "we'll make this quick." They would empty the place. The material would go to Israel.

Netzer drifted through the apartment as Lavi and Lanir brought Givon's papers, books, and electronic gear into the entrance hall and piled them there. They had pulled back the curtains and worked in the light of the streetlamp and the moon.

Netzer paced off the length of the front room, an enormous

rectangle designed for a Persian family, not a lone spy. Givon had not bothered much with it. There was a spare wooden table with a bottle of whiskey on it, half gone, a glass by the bottle, a couple of ashtrays. Full. At the table were stiff-backed chairs made of metal tubing and plastic, a couple of cheap carpets underfoot. There were no pictures on the wall. The room was much like Givon.

Netzer walked back to the bathroom, an inner room, closed the door, and turned on the light. Givon had converted the yellow-tiled room into a stronghold. The door was of thick metal and a steel bar could be placed across it. He had installed a medicine chest with splints, tourniquets, bottles of water, penicillin, and tetracycline. There was a walkie-talkie, as well as a two-way radio that Netzer noted was *not* tuned to legation frequencies. Givon readjusted frequency after communicating, Netzer concluded—a nice touch. Again, like the man.

The window opened onto a blind airshaft and Netzer pushed at it. Just how thorough was Givon? Netzer wondered. He saw a chain ladder neatly rolled up, hanging just below the sill. Tug on a silk cord and a quick trip to the ground floor and rear courtyard is right in front of you. An alternate way out. Just in case.

Netzer sighed. There were rules, Shlomo, and you followed them. How, then did this happen?

Netzer returned to the front room, past Lavi and Lanir, who were sweating and panting by now. Givon's front window was all glass and ran the whole length of the south wall to capture the sun in winter. The window gave Givon a good view of the alley, east and west, and he had chosen the apartment for that.

Netzer saw the truck pull into the *kucheh* below. He left Lanir and Lavi—and Meir, entranced with the paper—and went down. With a gesture, he sent the driver and assistant to Givon's apartment. In the courtyard he checked Givon's car, a drab Peykan, slightly battered like most cars in Tehran. Without touching it, Netzer looked closely at the hood and—ah, yes, of course—almost invisible, a bit of cellophane tape connected fender and hood on the passenger side. If the cellophane is broken, someone has opened the hood to put who knows what inside. It wasn't. A conscientious professional, Shlomo, that you were.

It was a kind of procession of boxes. The crew of young men worked quickly and silently, loading them into an unmarked truck. They all left as the day was just beginning to lighten. The truck went one way and the car another. They did it very quickly. They didn't notice a form standing in the shadows of the carpenter's shop, just up Kucheh Qabus.

As the car left Kucheh Qabus for Pahlavi, they saw a large American automobile turning in. When the two cars passed at the entrance to the narrow alley, four Israelis and four Iranians stared at each other briefly through open windows in the early heat.

"Strangers in the night," said Netzer in English to Meir. "Those were security people. They've gotten here quickly."

"Yes," said Meir absently.

Lavi drove straight to the legation. Lanir and Lavi went their own ways; Meir disappeared into his office and Netzer spent the dawn in his own, waiting for Jerusalem and the Iranians to wake up, lying on a decrepit couch covered in black vinyl whose uneven innards poked and jabbed him through a fitful sleep.

2

Jim dropped his stories off at Reuters. Nobody was there but Vahik Ajamian, the office manager, a pile of dispatches in his in-basket to telex out. Jim's stories—if anybody wanted them, which he strongly doubted—would make the U.S. afternoon editions in his syndicate and his own paper next morning, exactly the wrong way around. Jim put his stuff in with the rest and leisurely went through his competitors' copy in a disinterested search for truth.

What have we here, now? A backgrounder on the shah's trip to Poland. Boring. An interview with Ms. Afkhami, minister for women's affairs (and one sweet knockout), plus a feature entitled "Women's Lot in New Iran," both by a goofy, slightly cross-eyed lady anthropologist from Utah who had been in pestering Vahik the day before. No surprises. Stuff on the Tadayon accident (no surprises), stuff on a delegation of visiting congressmen (whose leader had glided through five countries in a drunken stupor, but that didn't get in). No surprises.

Then Jim saw the story. A killing. Terrorists in Tehran. Done by Jerry Tobin, the Weird Brit. Jim skimmed through it, flipping the cheap yellow triple-spaced pages, and thought he might just pretty it up a bit, correct some of Jerry's sloppy usage.

Jim sat down at a spare typewriter, an evil old clunker made in England and missing a *w* key, and banged out a short. Israeli resident of Tehran. Gets head blown off at four-thirty in the morning. *This* morning, no less. Good Christ, Jerry's fast. No suspects taken. Hit and run. Probably from a passing motorcycle, the usual method.

How'd Jerry get this? Jim wondered in admiration as he typed. A stunner. British embassy, no doubt. They'd been listening in on the police radios and old Jerry had gotten there bright and early. The sun never sets on the *Guardian*. All Brit journalists are MI6 anyhow. He put Jerry's piece back in the pile and continued under his own steam.

Islamic terrorist group likely behind this, Jim wrote, then added a short threnody on underlying anti-Semitism in Iran, discouraged by the government. Shah cultivates excellent relations with Israel. Jim threw in a final top-o'-the-header about the Christians and the Bahais and came up with a nice 800 words, a little color for a dull day. He congratulated himself on splendid sleuthing. Deserve a raise for this sort of work, he told himself. I'll put in for it. Buy the Pear something nice.

Jim took the story home to check on it out of earshot of anyone else, one Jerry Tobin in particular. He tried phoning a few friends at the British embassy, but they were out or referred everything—the usual way of it—to Hastings, a whey-faced, thin-haired time server in the cultural office, whose wife had buck teeth and taught English, and who had long given up on everything. Hastings knew nothing.

The five or six Americans Jim called knew nothing either—or said they didn't—and no one was taking calls from reporters at the Israeli legation, a strong but not conclusive point. Jim called Reuters and had a reluctant Vahik phone Central Police, whose operator ridiculed him for the attempt.

So there we are, thought Jim. Fly it? Wing it out? Just on Jerry's testimony? Or kill it? Stomp it in the dust and walk away from it? Jim figured he'd go back to Reuters, wait around for Jerry, and ask the bastard.

Jerry was fury. Jerry was rage. Jerry was at the top of his lungs. Jerry Tobin's face was as red as his crazy hair and his Genghis Khan mustache, and his eyes were blazing with blue heat (Jerry had the pigmentation of Persian mythological monsters and in Iranian eyes was uglier than Jim in the best of times), but just now, when Jim walked in on him at Reuters, the tall and skinny Jerry had young Vahik by the collar, towering over him, half lifting him out of his chair and yelling into his face. "You little turd, how could that happen? Hey? Come on, you shit! Give me an answer! Give me a bloody *answer!*" And noticing Jim, without taking his eyes off the hapless Vahik, he growled, "The little bastard lost all my copy."

"I am sorree," said Vahik, more or less expecting Jerry, who was unpredictable and had large, bony hands, to knock his teeth down his throat. Vahik had been most impressed the time Jerry threw an ashtray at a particularly obnoxious German free-lancer in to pick brains, then packed the German, a son of a bitch who was working for *Stern* at the time and actually proud of it, out the door. "They came and took eet."

"*Who* came, you dog's ball?"

"I *don't* know. They took eet. I am sorree."

"*Fuckers!* You can't work in this city. *Oh*, the shits!"

"What's up, Jerry?" asked Jim, knowing full well what.

"Ah, don't you wish you *knew*," Jerry yelled. "Don't you *wish*." Still holding Vahik, Jerry swept his free arm aloft in a grand arc above his head, across Her Majesty's portrait on the wall behind, and down to his own nearby desk covered with the detritus journalists in the East knock loose: a *Who's Who in Iran* hanging together by a thread, a battered portable typewriter, a wide-brimmed straw hat, notes, clips, beer mug, pencil stubs—all dull—and a pile of editions of his paper, sea-freighted in and all of them older than ancient.

"There is no cause for concern, mates, none at all. None! Is that clear? Hey? Clear? Jerry Tobin is in charge here, and the message will get through, sports. The Word, I say, the living Word of God, what was in the beginning, miluds, and then became flesh." Jerry released Vahik. "Oh, yes, we strike back, gents, we avenge, we show no mercy, not to SAVAK, no, not to anyone." And Jerry stormed out, probably to the nearest phone.

Vahik, being Armenian and thus used to being put upon, sat rubbing his neck, not looking at Jim.

So they actually came in here. Not even in Saigon was it like this. Just a spot check? Or were they after something?

"I am sorree," said Vahik again, mournfully, still not looking at Jim. "They took eet."

"Okay, sport." Jim walked out, hands in his pockets and head down. He figured the Israeli thing was the source of Jerry's troubles, but he called it in from home anyway. Good old Jerry would take the heat, right? And the story once out—

well, it's out. The telephone connection to the States was direct dial and always sounded better than phoning down the block. Then he had lunch.

The sun beat down on dusty, deserted streets, and waves of heat rose from the pavement, as Jim went out, logy from lunch but sniffing a front-pager. He got a taxi to Jerry's place up on Abbasabad to pump him on the story. It was an hour when sensible people slept, and the bleary-eyed driver was happy for the customer.

Jerry's gate was open, and as Jim went up the stairs to his place, he passed moving men coming down, and when Jerry's frizzy-haired girl friend, Lisa, saw Jim, she glowered down the stairs at him and more or less spat the words, " 'Pay, pack, and follow.' Oh, what a jerk!"

"Hey, hey, what's up, Lisa? Hey, come on, Jim's here. Everything's okay," he said, easing up the stairs past a bookcase coming down.

Workmen were packing. Some government agency must have sent them scurrying to Jerry's place, and there they were, emptying the rooms and Lisa standing glaring at the show in a sack dress, arms crossed tightly across her chest, hunching her breasts up and fuming. She would have been giving off smoke even if there hadn't been a cigarette in her mouth.

"Bastards!"

"Hey, Lisa, bird, tell old Jim."

"He's out. We're out. Back to Yukay. Oh, the *rotter!*"

So. Jim learned they had grabbed Jerry and packed him onto a plane, having dumped a pink-faced German named Roentgen, who protested feebly but took his orders. They chose Lufthansa because that was the flight that was leaving when they had hustled old Jerry out to Mehrabad, and, though Jim didn't know it, good, old Jerry was even now enraged and stomping around Frankfurt Airport.

A joke.

"And now here they're throwing me out, too, bloody, bloody *bastards!* I have a job. A *job!*"

Jim whistled a little di-da and danced around avoiding the workmen, who were hustling all of Ms. Lisa's earthly belongings down the stairs. One gentleman on the lower landing, the beefy sort in a conservative business suit that would not have fit him even if he hadn't been packing heat on his left side, was discussing the matter with the landlord's family, who, wife in housedress and scarf, and three kids of varying height, stared wide-eyed first at him, then at the packers, then up at Jim and Lisa. The story's being told, Jim knew. They're doing it now. How to bust a lease in five short seconds. Watch the foreigners scramble.

And why?

Lisa hadn't the slightest, no notion, but by God, Jerry and his weirdness were at the root of it, she knew, and she'd get Jerry when she found him, she would, and bash his head in if he's lucky, *lucky*, mind. Lisa paced and fumed, scattering cigarette ashes on the tile flooring (the carpets were being rolled up.)

Jim stayed long enough to be decent, but the beginning of a worry was poking him in the ribs—that story he'd phoned in had his name on it—and the more he thought about it, not listening to Lisa's metallic British yammer, the more he worried. It had to be the Israeli thing.

Muttering something he knew was stupid about keeping in touch and working things out and all's well and not to worry, Jim eased down the stairs as the beefy type disappeared into the landlord's apartment and the packers formed a chain bringing the stuff down into the courtyard, then from courtyard to pickup truck.

An object lesson, thought Jim out in the *kucheh*. You mind your *p*'s and *q*'s in the Great Civilization or you'll find yourself elsewhere. It was pretty obvious. Somebody got too free at the British embassy, and old Jerry figured he'd gotten an exclusive. A hot tip. Well, he had, by God. It must have been hot. And now old Jerry's out in the cold and they're throwing Lisa out for good measure. Fast.

When Jim got home, he made another call to his paper just in time to kill the story on the wires and sat in his cluttered office thinking about Truth, a commodity he wasn't used to seeing much of in Tehran.

The Brits, he considered, are not so stupid. They couldn't have thought the matter would be so sensitive—unless they wanted to sandbag old Jerry, which was possible, understandable even, but not likely. No, they couldn't have known. And Jerry couldn't have known. And Lisa sure as hell didn't. But then the question came up in Jim's mind, and it really was the germ of the whole business, and that question was, Couldn't have known what?

The affair became known as Tobin's Retreat to the committee of foreign journalists, the Intercontinental Hounds, who convened late that afternoon as usual at the Intercontinental Hotel. The Intercontinental had a long, low, well-lighted bar and much table space and was perfect for editorial sessions and conferences on journalistic ethics.

The Hounds marveled at the unheard-of efficiency of the police. A very fast, creditable job, all agreed: ejection of Jerry in the morning, Lisa in the afternoon.

"Blotted his copybook," said busty Alice Cochrane of the *Financial Times*. "Got somebody mad. How many votes for SAVAK?" Alice was doyenne of the Tehran correspondents. She'd been there since Xerxes, they said, and was deferred to in bar and at conference. When Alice talked, they also said, the bartenders listened.

The show of hands at the press end of the bar was unanimous. At the other, a couple of Russians were hogging the dartboard, throwing their missiles clumsily like stones and generally missing.

"Scythian barbarians," Alice sniffed, whether at SAVAK or the Russians no one knew.

"SAVAK?" said some unidentifiable member of the press. "Who said SAVAK? Bloody bastards is what *they* are"—and as if they hadn't been discussing it—"Shipped old Jerry out, you know. Shipped 'im out. Swine."

Derek Race, the *Times* man, American, ginger-haired and thin-faced and Jim's closest competitor, thought old Jerry had found out something about the royal family. "He'd been talking about Ass Rash"—the common term in Hound parlance for Princess Ashraf, the shah's twin sister. "He had something on her. I would suggest a royal liaison that went sour, but he's not young enough for the princess's tastes."

"Or pretty enough," said Alice in her husky alto. "Jerry's got the wrong sort of mug. Now, *you're* her type," she said, smiling erotically over her half-moon glasses at Bob Harrigan of the *Post*. "You'll do."

"Not her, I won't. It's you I want, Alice. I love you."

"Would you kill for me?"

"Sure."

"Get thrown out?"

"Well . . ."

The talk went on until Alice finally and peremptorily banged her glass on the bar and said, "Tobin's Retreat is not unprecedented, gents. Think, I urge you, gentlemen, think. I give you the Affaire Modarresi." (Acknowledging grunts ran around the bar here.) "Did we not laugh about, and then with, old Reza Modarresi, whose absence from this watering hole on that sad occasion was so keenly felt."

A point. Reza Modarresi had been writing for AP. One time he filed a workmanlike story with that esteemed organization in New York about heavy snows that had isolated certain Iranian villages. His editor in New York, a man of whimsy, jazzed up the language throughout and at the end tossed in the fateful line, "And while several Iranian villages struggled to dig their way out of heavy snows, the shah was enjoying himself on the ski slopes of St. Moritz." It took a phone call from Ardeshir Zahedi himself to the shah (still in St. Moritz and still, presumably, enjoying himself) to get poor Reza sprung from Evin Prison. "And he was welcomed back to the Intercontinental Bar," said Alice, "and someone bought drinks and it was great fun. He had committed the great sin of writing for AP and he paid for it appropriately. The question is, gentlemen, the crimes of Jerry Tobin being legion, just which one—or ones—led to his rapid departure?"

Jim, quiet and meditative in his cups, just listened and watched and nodded sagely as the theories were spun. Alice caught once what she thought was a fishy look on his face and wondered (she was good on people's faces), but decided to let it go for the time being, she being the soul of discretion and regarding highly other people's secretiveness. She was an open book herself.

Brian Brompton of the *Tehran Journal* thought it was financial scandal. Eric LeBon of the *Journal de Téhéran* thought it was dope. Either Jerry's or Ass Rash's. "She raises it here, she cooks it in Marseilles, she sells it in New York. Jerry, he learns the connection. Or it is possible he is in on it himself, in on the tricks," was Eric's considered opinion, but he left off talking, and drifted away in the afternoon, muttering to himself.

"They just pinged him—persona non grata."

"Gone like a flash."

"Shot out of a cannon."

"Damn!"

And Jim wondered. Lisa hadn't said a thing on the stairs that afternoon, seemed to have no real idea, and then *she* got chucked on an afternoon flight. It turned out later the two of them, Jerry and Lisa, had had a hell of a time catching up with each other in Europe, he in Frankfurt, she in Paris. They found each other via Jerry's home office in Manchester, and Jerry got to Paris the next morning. Flights out of Frankfurt had been booked till the A.M., of course, and Jerry showed up, cursing and demented.

Jerry's paper, which considered itself part of the British government, was much put out, and the editorial board demanded *en masse* that Whitehall lodge a protest with the appropriate authorities in Tehran. The ambassador in Tehran, a scholarly little man with thick horn-rimmed glasses, "and the soul of a newt," claimed Jerry thereafter, advised "a quiet approach," and there the matter stopped. Even before all that, though, the Hounds accused Her Majesty's government of complicity in poor Jerry's ejection.

"They certainly didn't burn up the cables, *did* they, the rotters!"

"Hand in glove with SAVAK."

"Whatever Jerry did, Whitehall didn't care for it either, that's obvious."

"Right."

"Right."

"Damn!"

And still Jim wondered. Jerry'd been poking around at a lot

of things, his newspaper being liberal and not wholly in the shah's camp. Jerry had done a series giving more or less irrefutable proof that the shah's modernization was an expensive joke. That had ruffled feathers.

He'd followed the do-gooders around, too—Amnesty International, the International Council of Jurists—as they collected evidence on the shah's murderers and torturers, and he wrote that up, albeit discreetly. And he followed with relish the misdeeds of the foreigners, especially the Americans, and had a sideline in urban terrorism. Jerry wasn't liked. No, not liked at all. So there were many fine reasons to eject him, all of them worth pondering.

But still, Jim thought, that shooting. It had to be that. But same day service? Strange. It's way too fast, even for the SAVAK brethren. Jim just kept quiet and listened and finally slipped home. The Hounds, gathering later, much later, when it was all over, would be as wrong about Jim as they were about Jerry. But except for Alice, they never knew the truth about either. Never came close.

Jim told Pari that night at dinner. They met at Leon's Grill Room.

"Gosh. They don't do this *often!*"

"Kill people, Pear, or throw out reporters? They haven't thrown out a reporter in living memory. Kill people? I'm not sure there *was* a killing. Or if the killing had anything to do with Jerry and Lisa. Lots of reasons for kicking Jerry out."

"And Jerry and Lisa are gone. Just like that."

"Just like that."

"Pity. I liked him. Not her."

Jim grinned. "Just the opposite for me."

A flash of black eyes, then: "What are you going to do?"

"Look around. I'll track Jerry down tomorrow. Phone his paper, anyway. I want to know about the Israeli. *Was* there an Israeli? If there was, he got hit for some reason. And they hushed it up. I want to know why. Cut it any way you want, Pear, it's a story. Maybe a good one. The Israelis. The Iranians. Who knows, maybe the Arabs? If an Israeli gets killed, can an

Arab be far behind? It's a war story, Pear, the best kind there is."

They decided to be expensive and ordered caviar and blinis and sturgeon and ate in the courtyard as an army of cats prowled through the jungle of table and chair legs.

The Armenian waiters, all with sad, drooping faces, brought in splits of good Iranian vodka frozen in wine buckets. The buckets came off and just the round ice stayed there stuck to the bottles. It made the vodka viscous and gave it a cold crackling taste, and Pari said it was super with the lemon and grated onion and caviar.

Jim kept thinking of Jerry and his story. The maybe killing, Jerry's very real departure. Jim had the newsman's usual aching sense that something somewhere was going on even as he sat at table, and he thanked God he had only daily deadlines.

He thought, too, about young Vahik Ajamian, telex operator, who was—this was universally acknowledged—very much in the pay of SAVAK and God only knew who else.

Later that night, Pari lay beside him, warm body against his, leg up his front and her arm over his chest, her hand tracing the outline of his face.

"You are *zerang*, Jim."

"What's that?"

"'Clever,' I suppose, but it's harder than that. It also means 'fast on your feet' and 'lithe.' "

"That's me."

"And also too clever by half."

"True."

Pari smiled. "You're always on a quest. Jim the Quester. Looking for this and that. Will you ever settle down?"

Jim shrugged and put his hands under his head. "Something happened, Pear. Think about it." He looked up into her face and dark eyes. The first time they had kissed he thought of those Vietnamese girls, light and delicate as butterflies, who would sit on his belly and smile fondly and had the finest of black eyes that in the end were empty—just open, bottomless wells.

He first realized he was in love with her on a spring evening. She had a light dress on and she was standing by a mirror all absorbed, with Jim watching from behind. She lifted her hair and let it fall back on her shoulders. The dress was white and her hair black, and she shook her head and the dress rose and rested again on the curve of those soft hips.

"Ah, watch out for the *paris*, then, luv," Alice had said in her crackly voice when she learned her name.

"The whats?"

"The *paris*. Supernatural females in Persian lore, James. Got to watch them. They are of surpassingly malicious character."

"Not this one."

"They'll do you down, they will." Alice smiled. "Beguile you with blandishments and witchcraft, then bingo! You're under their control. Their powers are greatest at night."

"You can say that again, Alice."

Alice nodded sagely. "They take on human form, James, and make themselves enchantingly beautiful."

Pari was slender and she moved easily, and other women envied her. Jim never knew what she saw in him and his general untidiness of manner and dress, always looking, she said, like a package that wasn't quite properly wrapped.

He ran the back of his hand over Pari's cheek and cleared her hair from her eyes. "Wasted time before you, Pear. That's what it was."

"Um. Me fancy man." He like her Brit way of saying "um."

She stretched in that languorous, feline way he loved, arms out, hands arched back.

"I discovered you in a bank, Pear."

"Um. A full-service bank, it turns out. Like your nose. Like your eyes. Like you next to me."

Her long, slender fingers moved over his forehead, her straight black hair trailed into his face, her above him looking down. She liked his green eyes, she said.

She had smallish breasts, like a girl's, and she brushed his face with them lying on top of him, his hands on the soft curve of her back. The scent of late summer blossoms from the

36

courtyard drifted in, and her smile turned to a filmy concentration and her eyes closed. The archetype of the Pear.

The next day, the Ministry of Information spokesman, a cadaverous bureaucrat with green skin and no flesh between it and his bones, who chain-smoked and had a voice like a barrel of nails, accused Jerry, on derisory evidence, of crimes against state security, cooperating with Black Reaction and terrorists, and spreading false reports. And, a new development, Marie Sidki of Agence France-Presse got her walking papers the day after Jerry. Taking photos, the cadaver said, of some of the wrong barracks (at the wrong time, Jim thought, in the wrong light, with the wrong camera, wrong focus, wrong look on her face, and last, but not least, wrong fucking country for anything approaching an honest journalist).

Jim duly reported the expulsions, adding at the end of the story, which was short, "This is the first time authorities in Tehran have taken steps against accredited foreign journalists." Jim wasn't completely sure of that, but kept it in and, on consideration, crossed out: "The move reflects increasing anxiety over the internal security situation in Iran." We'll just let that one slide, Ace, he decided.

3

They filed into Netzer's office in the early morning like a troop of schoolboys and had to go around the table, Netzer sitting there quietly watching them: Avraham Meir, Dan Maroz, David ben Zion—the latter two were police liaisons—and Nathan Levine, who ran intelligence in the Jewish community.

Meir's head ached; he'd had no breakfast and about as much sleep as Netzer, which was little. What struck Meir was the absurdity of the whole thing. The morning was clear and bright; you could hear the cries of the hawkers in the streets, you could see the same lines of workers waiting for the same buses, the same shopkeepers opening the same shops. Meir found the banality of it all grotesquely inappropriate. Disasters should be bathed in gloom and darkness. The world should not go about its business. The world should stop. But it didn't. Not for Shlomo Givon.

Young Shmuel Ettehadian, born in Iran, like Lavi, brought them sandwiches and tea and long pale green slices of melon, trying very hard not to rattle cups and saucers and plates as he tiptoed up and down the long stairs of the legation, not knowing a blessed thing about the "incident" except that there had been one.

The meeting was a sham and Meir knew it, put on more for appearances than anything, which made things even more surreal. Meir watched Netzer sitting stiffly, as if he'd been shot himself. Netzer's voice was as dry as tinder. It was almost funny.

"Have you seen him?" Netzer asked Maroz.

"Not yet. I will this morning."

Maroz had clever eyes. He was a Moroccan, whose trilled Hebrew r's came from the ghetto of Casablanca. He was listed as cultural affairs officer in the legation directory and he actually had some claim to the title. He recited Arabic verse in the shower, anyway.

"Have you seen him," Netzer had asked. Givon was still a person, thought Meir. When would they shift to "the body" or some such?

"Weapon?" asked Netzer.

"It's too early," Maroz said.

"Any guesses?"

"Could be anything."

Netzer grunted.

Netzer's air conditioner rumbled off to the side, water trickling through the straw filter to humidify the air. The straw was filthy; it hadn't been changed for the whole of the summer.

The room was central top floor in the legation. Its roof had sensors—for thieves, for SAVAK, for anyone. Cats should set them off and did periodically. Netzer had just had the walls swept for listening devices. They were clean. A gulley ran around the wall where the backs of chairs had gouged away the soft plaster. To that, Netzer paid no attention.

"And the police reports, Ari, are guaranteed to be incomplete," Maroz said. "They will not tell the whole story. We've seen it again and again the way they deal with the Americans. They tell half truths very well; whole lies they tell better. They cover their asses. The whole of the police code is written for this purpose." Maroz had a browned, wizened face, like an apple left out too long in the sun, Meir thought. It made his words sound old and dried out. "We might as well establish our own crime lab for all the good theirs is."

Maroz, in short, knew nothing, as Netzer expected; Halperin and Levine knew nothing, as expected; and the spotter, the effete Jamshid Bahrami (Meir called him the Soprano), who arrived late in the morning traffic, was voluble but ignorant, too. As expected. Bahrami had large, soft eyes and was still slightly nauseated from the sight of blood. He'd known Givon to see him.

"The neighborhood is confused, Ari," Bahrami piped, holding his slender hands open on the table to show he had nothing. "People say this, people say that. Everything's contradictory, Ari. It's all fluid. There was a car. There wasn't a car. There was one shot. There were two shots. It's like that, Ari. You can't be sure of a thing." Bahrami shook his head in the Persian way—it seemed to rock on his neck—and clicked his tongue, producing sad, liquid tsks. "Givon, Givon," he said finally. "Poor man."

Netzer let the desultory talk go on for a time (sad, they all agreed . . . robbery no motive . . . terrorists . . . innocent blood . . . it goes to show you) and then ended it. He kept Meir behind; the rest trooped out as they had trooped in, and Netzer felt well rid of them. Some meeting.

The Givon Operation was never called that, was almost never called anything around the legation. It was mostly Givon and some unknown, shadowy figures lurking in the more obscure corners of Mossad and Military Intelligence in Tel Aviv and Jerusalem. Netzer and Meir knew nothing at all. That was the way they ran it. Fair enough. It was the way they ran a lot of things.

Meir was sprawled at the table, staring now at Netzer, now at the gouge around Netzer's wall. "Ari . . ." It was the hopelessness.

Netzer waved his hand limply. "I know."

"So . . ."

"So? So, take it as axiom that however we react to this, however we pursue things, what we do will be usable information, grist for their mills. For the terrorists, the Iranians. Is this not so?"

Meir nodded.

"So. We make inquiries. We play it this way: Shlomo Givon was an Israeli national. He was murdered. We are deeply interested. So." Netzer spread his hands.

"We treat Givon as nonembassy?"

"Of course. And that includes the"—Netzer searched for the words—"the *exterior* aspects of our investigation here." He looked up at Meir. "Watch the cable traffic, Avram. I want the traffic coordinated. No one sends anything unless I initial it. Also, I want nothing in the absolute clear, but I want a few references to this in low-level radio. An atmosphere of . . . call it *concern*. That's what we want. We're *concerned*, you see, yes? But only to a point, Avram. Not beyond. Givon was a national. He was involved in sales to the government. We assumed he was approved by Tel Aviv."

"Ari, they must know a few things."

"Yes, of course. That's all right. We'll play the game this way. It's what they expect anyway."

"And the Americans?"

The Americans. Well. Netzer, and Meir too, admired the immense, worldwide net the Americans had established, far beyond the needs or capacity of their own small country. And their computerization, of course. "But," Netzer had told Meir once, "these American businessmen—they wear their cloaks and daggers like Brooks Brothers suits and club ties. They should be restructuring corporations, not playing *this* game."

Netzer had once been present at a meeting of American intelligence types. It was a regional thing, in Athens. One attendee was the sort the Americans call a hot dog, or so Meir assured Netzer. The hot dog, or whatever they called him, chaired the meeting and was obviously a most impressive fellow, to himself especially. He had lists of "options" memorized, and he would tick them off on his fingers—one, two, three, four—speaking rapidly. He had metal-rimmed glasses, and his haircut must have been enormously expensive. Netzer tried to get to know him out of professional curiosity, for he seemed a dominant type in America. He had degrees in management as well as politics. But he had never seen a dead man, not outside a funeral parlor anyhow, not put that way in, as it were, the line of duty, and this troubled Netzer. Netzer had seen many—close up, killed in various ways. He had himself dispatched a few, and they still lay in his memory, awkward, twisted shapes in Palestine and North Africa.

"The Americans," Netzer said. He blew through his lips. "We will inform them. They know of the death, of course. They must, but we will tell them anyway. Let Zeigerman do it. Or Lanir. It doesn't matter. No extreme acts, though, Avram, no frenzy, no yells or wailing. So. And perhaps we'll see what the Americans know, Avram. Yes? Perhaps?" Netzer grinned and stared at Meir in that way he had. Though Netzer's teeth

41

were irregular, the grin always made Meir think of a shark. Something about Netzer's eyes, maybe, the flatness in them. Then Netzer said, finally and quietly, "We'll win. Oh, we will."

Listeners in the legation had gotten the first scraps the same day, the very morning Givon was killed, though they hadn't the slightest idea what the scraps meant. Very fine electronic eavesdropping, Netzer thought. Pity for the reason.

Presiding over the operation was a glassy-eyed communications specialist named Rafael Frank—they called him Raful—who at age fifteen had written his first paper on encryption theory (Mossad immediately classified it) and now at the age of twenty-eight had the same clearance level as Netzer, who didn't give a damn.

First came a batch of police surveillance orders—the train station, the airport, border crossings, neighborhoods to keep a sharp watch in. There had been an action. That was obvious. Then from the same office and same scrambler and in the same code as the surveillance orders, and spurred almost certainly by the same incident, came:

> V(OICE) I(NTERCEPT) T(RAFFIC) NS 130 5:16 AM 17 RAMA-
> ZAN TEXT: 10-ALERT. SUSPECT SHOHADA ACTION.
> ARMED. DANGEROUS.

They had picked it up on a high-gain omnidirectional antenna that looked like a camera tripod, which young Raful had installed on the roof of an office building a block north of the legation; as far as Netzer could tell, nobody in the whole Iranian world was aware of its existence. Occasionally life was sweet.

Then, via Raful's wizardry again:

> 331 VIT NS 127 17 RAMAZAN 6:21 AM FIELD CAR TRANS-
> MISSION. TEXT: CAPTURE REPORT. OFFICER GILANI.
> SHAHR ARA SECTION. BELOW PARK. APPREHENDED SUS-
> PECT. ONE ESCAPE. CONFIRM SHOHADA GROUP.

On the second day, a police operative, one of the very few around the country, slipped the first report on Givon's death out of Kalantari Four, the police station down by Sheikh Hadi that had sent the first carload of officers. There were copies in Central as well, and these turned up later, of no more use, of course, than the first, which read simply, "Israeli national, resident Tehran, shot and killed 17 Ramazan 4:30 A.M., Sheikh Hadi Street, south of Shah Street. No witnesses."

It was like the October War, like a siege, like doom. They agreed on that, Netzer and Meir did, drinking whiskey in Netzer's dingy apartment late on the second day. They were both exhausted. Neither had slept the night before, and the heat was suffocating. They kept Netzer's thick curtains drawn back for air, and the dim light, fading in the evening, made the gray bare walls drearier than usual. They took their drinks and sat on the balcony, watching the sun go down, and it seemed a fitting symbol for the whole business.

They kept coming back to it, the unavoidable fact: "They knew just when and where to hit him," said Meir. "But he wasn't a creature of regular habits. He was set up."

Netzer seemed to listen as if the thought were new and original. He nodded. "It's likely. Certain, even," he said and sank back in his chair, a wooden frame with dusty cloth webbing stretched over it.

The view from Netzer's balcony was over a vacant lot sealed off by a brick wall. On one side, part of the wall had collapsed, probably been pushed down, Netzer figured, and a mound of trash, deposited by garbage men who dumped it there rather than haul it to the pickup, lay against it like a stile—square cooking-oil cans, plastic bags, and smashed bottles. The wind had blown wastepaper all through the lot. Beyond, the traffic jam was cacophonous.

Meir studied Netzer in the dusk. He felt as old as Netzer, whose face, doughy and empty as they sat there, was past registering emotion. Now, as the sun went down, Meir was getting drunk. Royally. He stared at his hands as if he had just acquired them and wondered what they were for. They were stubby and rough, and he held them palms up in his lap. The whiskey had mixed with his fatigue to make everything, even his own hands, seem unearthly.

In his general daze, and poor Shlomo Givon notwithstanding, Meir thought, too, of Dvorah Lavi and felt vague genital warmings even as the sun went down and Netzer puzzled over Givon. A daughter of Jerusalem, a lily among thorns. My beloved spake, Meir thought, smiling giddily and drunkenly, and said unto me, Yonah is on duty tonight. Dvorah's soft form in dim evenings with Yonah Lavi elsewhere. He thought of the smell of her breasts on those evenings and her warm legs. Where is she now? Meir wondered. No doubt with Lavi. His mind drifted in stupor. The joints of thy thighs are like jewels. The roof of thy mouth like the best wine.

Netzer was moving his lips, talking to himself, staring, a way he had. He suddenly turned to Meir. "They knew, Avram. They knew. But how? Avram, did someone out in the networks get turned? Yes? It's easy enough to do—with money, with a hand on the throat. With a bit of both. How could they have known? Who were they?"

He sighed and ran his hand over his bald head. "This will go to SAVAK, of course. They'll handle it, that collection of buffoons and terrorists; it will go to them. But how will they play it?" Netzer shook his scotch. Too much ice had melted for the glass to rattle.

"Avram, when you cross the border"—Netzer hunched forward in his chair—"and you enter Iran"—he smiled—"you are in a land of dreams and illusions. Reality as we know it is bent around here, like the light in those mirror-encrusted halls of the old shahs. Everything's broken, Avram, shattered, and you can't see the outlines of things. All you see is the blur, just the blur, Avram—brilliant, but vague."

Netzer sipped at his whiskey. Then he closed his eyes deliberately and fell asleep. The sleep of the dead.

4

The first time Jim met him, in the embassy in Saigon, Pete Fiscarelli put a burst of .38 bullets into a stack of reports, though he had nothing against the reports. Three bursts and the plastic covers—looseleaf binders—trembled and tore themselves into a snowstorm of vinyl, but the stack, a foot thick, held together. A crisp spurt of shells came out of the gun like ice from an ice machine.

It was a real sweet gun, Fiscarelli thought, an Ingram M-10 he had smuggled into the country (old-fashioned types forced that on him, men of little vision, Fiscarelli told Jim, who disliked innovation). Jim couldn't hear a thing over the air conditioning, just a *phut* sound, and some torn paper popped into the air.

"Noise suppressor speeds up the bullets," said Fiscarelli, "makes them meaner." The thing was made of blue metal and was no bigger than a service pistol. Fiscarelli, smiling, screwed off the suppressor and put it in a little leather case with embossed gold lettering—his initials P. F. X. F.—on it.

The gun was designated LISP—Lightweight, Individual Special-Purpose. As the user's manual said, and Fiscarelli had this memorized, the gun was for "offensive-defensive covert missions requiring positive kill engagement of point-fire targets." Fiscarelli loved it, loved to demonstrate it.

When Jim met him, Fiscarelli had spent a year or so selecting Vietnamese for disposal. Due process was a brief chat with a villager or two. The defendant was not so likely to be arrested as plinked from 500 yards.

At that range on a quiet night, according to Fiscarelli, you could just barely hear the impact. "You take an M-10 hunting, Jimmy, it barely makes a sound. Get your man in the head and it sounds like thumping a watermelon. That's what we call it: melon thumping."

Fiscarelli looked at Jim blandly. "Very fast muzzle velocity with very little kick. Very straight shot. Only starts to dip a couple hundred yards out."

A sweet little gun. Fiscarelli was an expert, had been sent here and there to demonstrate it. Argentina, Israel, Uganda. There was a black sergeant in Uganda with a round, thoughtful face who grinned when he saw the shells spurt so quickly into the air and heard that very soft, muffled burst of fire. Fiscarelli rather liked him in his British uniform with the plain epaulets. Fiscarelli would chuckle in Saigon when he told the story. Idi Amin. My friend Idi, Fiscarelli would say, and Jim thought it was pretty funny, too.

"Go out at night in Kampala and all you see is eyes and teeth and blades. My kind of town."

There is a film sequence of Fiscarelli—one of the networks is proud owner—bulky in a flowery silk shirt, inching along the embassy inner wall with the Ingram during the Tet offensive. It shows him putting the thing over the wall and squeezing off three good bursts. He is grinning through the whole thing. Fiscarelli enjoyed Tet.

Jim was with Fiscarelli now in the American embassy. It was 10:00 A.M. Fiscarelli was drunk.

"So how'd you hear about our Hebrew friend?" Fiscarelli asked, his voice as soft and easy as Tennessee whiskey.

"I heard."

"When?"

"About when it happened."

"Well, aren't you just a fast mother. How?"

"Hey."

"Just thought I'd ask. Why didn't you put the word out, Jimmy? How come? The Brits ran something, why didn't you?" Jerry Tobin's paper had done a minor thing on it.

"Bad luck, no space, not enough info."

"Uh-huh. Too little, too late." Fiscarelli smiled. "We'll miss you around here. Your editors tell you to look for another job yet?"

"Any day now."

Fiscarelli had a face like a pig and a head like a cleaning brush and he didn't like anybody. He was not chief of station and never would be. There were no photos on his desk. Two wives, long gone, had been driven off into charitable work, then Mexico. He had no children.

"Nobody seems to know anything, Pete. We're dealing with a well of ignorance here. How come? When they got the Rockwell technicians, it was front page everywhere. Here, the States, European funny papers. Why the difference?"

Fiscarelli shrugged. "They were U.S. civilians, Jimmy. Everybody knew them. It would have come out anyhow. So we controlled what came out. You were had. What else is new?"

"This guy wasn't a civilian?"

"He wasn't an American, Jimmy. Was he civilian? How the hell should I know?"

"Don't make it your business?"

"Fuck you. Ask the Israelis."

"Somebody wasted him, Pete. There was a reason."

"Maybe he had curls down his cheeks and wore funny black hats. Maybe they didn't like that."

"Did you know him?"

Fiscarelli didn't answer. He was playing with a couple of .38 slugs. They were stubby and short-range and low-kick so the pistol would stay steady and under control for the second and third shots, and Jim could see where Fiscarelli had made crosscuts over the ends of the lead slugs to they would mushroom out with ragged edges and be about the size of a quarter when they connected with flesh. A short-range weapon. Fiscarelli noticed Jim looking at the slugs.

"You hit right, you take an arm off. Put one in the chest, man has no heart left." He lined them up on his desk like little soldiers. "And they're lively mothers," he said, gazing at the bullets. "Always have a funny spin on them. Put one in a man's stomach, it may come out the top of his head."

"War, huh?"

"Fucking A."

Fiscarelli had an accent from the swamps around Newark and a laconic way of speaking. In Vietnam Jim had believed most of what Fiscarelli said because it had the ring of conviction. But in Iran things got funny. Fiscarelli had functioned all his adult life among peoples and races not his own, but he couldn't hack the locals here, who had ways of getting under his skin that had never occurred to the Viet Cong, and he drank more than ever. When Jim ran into him, he was a case.

His office smelled like a distillery. He *did* hold it well, that was admitted. He began holding it well—whiskey usually—at 8:30 A.M., on entering the office. In the long afternoons, he liked tequila, which he would drink from glass tumblers with a salt crust ringing the rim, and he kept a little tray and a box of salt in a desk drawer for the purpose.

Fiscarelli rubbed his eyes. "Shit, I want action, Jimmy. You never believed in body counts, but I sure did and I still do. Even here. Hell, *especially* here. Pile 'em up, you're bound to hit an enemy."

Fiscarelli was a good killer. "There are only two ways to die," he used to say. "If you stop breathing or if your heart stops pumping blood. Everything else is practical application."

He was thirty-five when he arrived in Thailand. The Vietnam War was just hints and whispers at that point, but Fiscarelli was set to surveying the northeast mountains, ferreting through bush on slopes of forty-five-degree angles, recording Thai mountaineer villages.

He disappeared from Thailand (the Bangkok chief of station knew where to, but no one else did) and turned up later married to a Meo chieftain's daughter in Laos.

Vientiane C of S never liked him—nothing in principle, just chemistry—and began to claim that Fiscarelli was doctoring the reports of Pathet Lao kills. So one day Fiscarelli drove into that lovely, soft city with a gunnysack full of human ears and dumped them on the C of S's desk, and after that the C of S had very positive things to say about Fiscarelli and the personal chemistry seemed to come right. The C of S was not an unsympathetic man and thought the ears were a very fine gesture.

Fiscarelli had graduated to running security in Saigon and had done well, and now he was security in Tehran with a string of bombings and dead Americans—Jim didn't realize how many or how bad the scene really was. Now a dead Israeli. Maybe Israeli Intelligence?

"Was he Mossad?"

Fiscarelli ignored Jim. "You know," he said, "we never got the mothers that did the Rockwell shooting."

"The Iranians say they did."

"Man, that was a whole army that did that. Don't make me laugh. Maybe the same mothers were in on this one. Be nice to chop them up."

"Maybe want to ask questions first?"

"Sure, tie the little bastards down to tables and get a piece of rubber hose yea long and yea thick"—Fiscarelli, sitting at his desk, gestured in tight little motions, not moving his upper arms; it was part of his inertness—"and just go to work on them. Find out what they're made of. Take a couple of days at it and do it right."

Jim declined the whiskey Fiscarelli offered him the second time. Fiscarelli poured himself a small glass. By Fiscarelli's desk, Jim knew, were a pair of crutches, the metal kind you slip your arms into. Fiscarelli had acquired them in Saigon on a busy day. McGovern was in town, they blew up a nightclub just down from the Caravelle on Tu Do Street, and Fiscarelli got hit by a taxi sailing along like an airplane.

Jim had done all three stories for his paper, which printed the one on McGovern. When they finally flew Fiscarelli out one hot night, a spray of tracer bullets floated up after him. The bullets didn't come near the plane. Just Charlie's way of saying good-bye.

Fiscarelli was silent for a time, eyeing Jim. Then he said, "We're doing nothing on it."

"Come on."

"God's truth. It's one of *those* things."

" '*Those* things'?"

"Far side of the moon, Jimmy. Frozen out."

"Ambassador?"

Fiscarelli shrugged.

"The Israelis?"

Fiscarelli stared at Jim. His blue eyes were blank. Jim

knew Fiscarelli's way of looking sideways at someone when he was being serious.

"Who was he?"

"A pants presser."

"Who *was* he?"

"Want to solve the crime?"

"Wouldn't mind. He was Mossad, wasn't he?"

Fiscarelli fingered one of the slugs again. "We of Henderson High"—he stood the slug end-up on his desk, paused, poked it with his index finger, and gently tipped it over—"don't know shit about this."

"Henderson High" was a favored term of opprobrium, and Fiscarelli pronounced it in his "candy-assed State Department" accent. The U.S. embassy in Tehran, built in the days of Truman's ambassador Loy Henderson, is a dull, red brick oblong building with rows of windows on both stories and a gently sloping roof. "Henderson High" is what some who worked there called the place.

With a funny, tight little smile on his face he looked up at Jim. "Okay. You don't know this," he said. "Get that straight. This isn't for background, Jimmy. This isn't for anything. You never heard this anywhere. You just take it and run with it. Got that?"

Jim was careful not to move forward in his chair (you never want to be eager, Jim always felt; reluctant virgin's the best way). It didn't matter, though. Fiscarelli was concentrating on the slug he was rolling slowly back and forth on his desktop.

"Joint Government Committee on Terrorism meets. A special session. Israelis convene it. They're grieving, see, real somber, and they can't figure it, can't figure why some nonembassy type, just this engineer, gets gunned down. His name's Givon, Shlomo Givon, and he's just a poor fuck on a two-year contract out of Tel Aviv. They're worried, they say. Maybe this is the beginning of a campaign, they say. Maybe 'the terrorists'—that's how they always talk, 'the terrorists'—maybe the terrorists are going after private individuals. Very ominous if true, right? They want to share information, and they give us a short, little bio on Givon. He was forty-five, a bachelor, electrical engineer. Not much else. Then they tell everybody—the Yankees, the Brits, the Iranians—that Givon was with Datatron, which *we* knew anyway."

"Datatron. Who's—"

"Hey, hey." Fiscarelli waved his hand languidly in the air. "You'll just listen, Jimmy. You'll just be ears, okay? No mouth." Fiscarelli was studying Jim now with a quizzical expression on his face, and Jim thought he looked like a man about to borrow money, but Fiscarelli just talked.

"Datatron's a company, Jimmy. A funny company. Run by Israelis, right? No publicity, no ads in the paper. A little shit two-bit office off Takht-e Tavoos. Low profile, right? Okay, Datatron supplies the Iranian government. That's all they do, Jimmy. The Iranian government. Electrical stuff. Generators, distribution lines, relays. That kind of stuff. And radios. They did communication for Khuzistan Water and Power. And they're in with the Krauts on another power project down on the Gulf."

"Power transmission? Mossad into that?"

"Jimmy, Jimmy, I said you'll just listen, so why don't you listen better, okay? I said they do radios, right? Radios. That means they do black boxes. We figure some of them are real black, black as you get." Fiscarelli paused. "We figure maybe SAVAK radio equipment. Maybe the whole SAVAK network, you know?"

"Christ, Pete! Oh, shit!"

"Yeah."

"SAVAK! Shit, who else? Was Datatron connected with Rockwell? Hey? People at Rockwell know this Givon?"

"That's privileged."

"Come on, for God's sake!"

Fiscarelli waved his hand.

"Pete, who else? He supply Defense? Foreign contractors?"

"Maybe."

"Holy shit! Hey, look, Pete, we've got a war here, right? This Israeli supplies foreign contractors who've done deals with the Defense Ministry, right? And one of those contractors loses three guys a year ago, wiped out in the street. Now this *Israeli* gets wasted. Hey, war! Right? Super!"

Fiscarelli licked at his upper lip. "We don't know shit, Jimmy. I told you, we don't even know the man's name. Maybe it was Givon. Maybe it was Moshe Dayan. We don't know who he was really with or what the hell he was doing here or why he was doing it. We don't know why he got whacked or who whacked him. We don't know shit." Fiscarelli looked away for a time, then with disgust on his face, took the slug from his desk and threw it into his in-box. "Frozen out," he said.

5

Word arrived: Netzer was to come to Jerusalem. It was a summons more than anything. Netzer had been expecting it. He was on the carpet now and not liking it.

He caught a military flight out, an empty 707 with El Al markings that had just dropped off a stupendous supply of American-designed and Israeli-produced air-to-air rockets, drone guidance devices, and jeep-portable radar stations. Netzer, with a sour look on his face, got aboard way down where Mehrabad Airport trails off into something that looks like the Sahara and only a couple of Quonset huts sit by the barbed wire. No Iranians saw him board. It was well past midnight.

The whole interior of these planes—Israeli military air transport had up to six of them at any one time—were gutted to hold cargo. Netzer sat on a canvas and metal contrivance that ran the length of the plane on one side. There were other passengers, military types out of Israel and returning, and they took great care to ignore him, and that was just fine with Netzer, who pretended to be interested in the contents of his briefcase, then tried to sleep and couldn't.

Two Iranian F-5s escorted the plane halfway to Turkey, where it heeled south toward the Mediterranean and hours later banged and bounced down at Lod, tires squealing briefly.

Netzer sat with the defense minister, the director of Army Intelligence and his own superior, the director of Mossad, the three of them at once, seemingly very informal, in easy chairs in the minister's house in Rehavia, a lemon tree in the garden by the window, the heights of Jerusalem, white and pastel, beyond the garden wall.

"How could it have happened?" asked the minister simply

and directly, looking at Netzer guilelessly, though known to his political opponents as a very tricky fellow.

"It was arranged. He was set up," said Netzer. "What else can we conclude?"

"All right. And what does that imply?"

"It means," said Army Intelligence, "that someone was onto Givon."

"We can't know that," said Netzer. "His cover alone was tempting enough for some people."

"Perhaps," said the minister. He looked at Mossad. "Perhaps then his cover was *too* good?"

Yes, they seemed to agree, the three of them.

Then they looked at Netzer and he knew they wouldn't bring him in on it. Not really. He'd felt it when he first walked into the room, something in the atmosphere.

Givon's operation had been beautifully concealed from everyone. From the legation. From his superiors, even. It had been perfect. Until he was killed.

Then they started. It was like a police grilling. They could have been shining lights in his face and sweating him for information. He had little.

Givon's connection with the embassy?

Almost nonexistent.

The way he lived his life?

Quietly. Middle-class neighborhood. Jewish. He was inconspicuous there.

Chances of hostile Moslem surveillance?

Little. The people in these neighborhoods, they're like schools of fish, Netzer told them. When strange fish intrude, fish that don't belong, they're noticed, they're seen, and it doesn't take an ichthyologist to spot them.

Then how? Traitors? Cowards? Who?

They looked at one another glumly. There were no explanations. No ideas.

"One further unknown is the Americans," said Mossad. "What did they know of Givon?"

A good question.

"We've tried to sound them out in various ways," he said.

"They are opaque. I'm very uneasy. Nothing of this Givon business must reach them."

They all knew the American problem on this operation. It consisted of the question, What do the Americans know? and there was no answering it.

"Now, what action?" said the minister. "Retaliation?"

"Of course," said Mossad. "In the end, we will get information. We will be able to draw certain conclusions. We will draw them."

Netzer found that last remark wildly hilarious. So typical of his superior. We know all, we Mossadniks, we do, was the man's manner. Splendid image building on the part of this *Mensch*, whose very identity is illegal to print in Israel. It was good for appropriations, of course, come secret budget time. It was good for *amour propre*, too. Just lovely for that. And last but not least, it was good for a laugh. "Draw certain conclusions," indeed! Netzer didn't crack a smile.

"Punishment is all well and good," said Army Intelligence, "but to restore the operation—that is essential." That was agreed, too.

The meeting broke up with no real conclusion, as Netzer had expected, cursing the lost time and bad luck. The minister would fret, Netzer knew, about the Americans, about the operation. Army Intelligence and Mossad would fret, too. Netzer, though, would return. He would keep the lid on. He would repair the damage, if they let him. And, if they let him, he would kill someone. He hadn't the least notion who.

The guards started with Ali's hands. They were fine hands, the fingers thin though not long, an intellectual's hands, the hands of a book reader. They used hard rubber truncheons and the truncheons whistled and snapped as they curved with the strokes and then broke against his hands.

They had put him in the inner chamber of the prisoners' bus, where there were no windows, and had bolted the door. They made him stand though he had a wound in one leg. There were others in the bus. The noncom who herded them in was shaking, he was so angry with them.

"You poison little children," he shouted. "You are poisoners, saboteurs. God help our children with bastards like you among us!" His face was red and he was choking with fury. His men—rough, red-skinned peasants from the west—came to hate Ali, too, and they hit him, and as they hit, they hated what they were hitting and struck all the harder.

Ali began to yell. "Islam . . . Imam Reza . . . Brothers, O Brothers. *Baradaran, ya, baradaran* . . ." and left off articulating words, the sound he made eerie and continuous like a siren.

As the bus lurched forward down some unknown road, Ali would stumble and fall to the floor. The bus would jerk forward, then stop, and jerk forward again, and they would pick him up and make him stand and he would fall again. After a time, they let him lie and stopped hitting him.

The bus stopped finally; the noncom checked outside, then ordered Ali to his feet.

Ali's hands were swollen like balloons, and he couldn't keep them at his side. He tried to hold his arms out from his body, but they would brush a seat or hand bar and pain like a knife would shoot up his arms.

The noncom yelled into his face and spat on him. "Hands at your sides, dog! Your balls will burst next!" The red-faced peasant boys started with the truncheons again, their own hands thick and round and hardened with peasant work and cold winters. The truncheons burst on his arms and sides this time, and they pushed him forward to the bus door.

They pulled Ali through the outer chamber and he fell off the bus onto a dry, earthen courtyard. Two soldiers grabbed him under his arms and pulled him toward a brick building. His mind registered the dust of the courtyard as it passed in a blur under his face, the paving stones sliding past, dizzying and out of focus, then he felt himself going up steps, through doors, down corridors, which might have been long or might not, might have twisted or might not, and found himself finally lying on thin straw spread over flagstones. A single lightbulb hung from a wire far above him. As Ali stared at it he heard someone crying. It was someone else.

"I feel sick," Ali said to no one in particular. "I'm falling." But he was already lying on the floor. When he came to, one prisoner was gone, though Ali didn't know it, and the crying had stopped because the prisoner had died.

Ali was pouring sweat. Straw stuck to his face and his clothes. He could not brush it off because he could not move his arms and could touch nothing with his hands. They tried to put handcuffs on him, but the cuffs would not close around his swollen wrists. That was Ali's introduction to Komiteh Prison.

General Forensics had done all it could. A snappish little man named Dr. Bayat was in charge there and very proud of himself with a degree from Germany. He closed his shop on the affair early. He gave all evidence to Dan Maroz at the end of a week and in a polite Persian way told him the case was over as far as his section was concerned. Maroz glumly turned the sum total of it over to Meir and Netzer, back now in Tehran.

"A spray of metal fragments in the head," Meir said. "Only one piece large enough to do anything with. They found it, most of it anyway, sunk in Givon's rib cage, driver's side, front. Unidentifiable type."

"To those stoneheads. Other fragments in the body?"

"Our friend Bayat couldn't find them. At least one exited the front."

"Bayat is all right?"

"Maroz thinks so. Maroz says he's very fine."

"And no other hoofprints."

"No."

Then, nineteen days into it, SAVAK, in the person of a stiff young lieutenant who sat on the edge of his chair in the legation and, refusing tea, eyed Netzer and Meir coldly, told them that the Iranians had picked up a suspect. Meir feigned great astonishment and professed admiration. Netzer sat listening quietly, watching the lieutenant's face. A liar? Probably. Do they know we know? Is all this a charade? Probably.

They had gotten him the very first night, the young lieutenant said, and Netzer, curling his fingers around a pencil, wondered why it took them so long to inform the legation. He wanted to push the pencil into the young lieutenant's stomach. The work, the young lieutenant said, was fast and good.

They had recovered a pistol, too. They took it off the suspect. It was a Tokagypt, made in Hungary. The Tokagypt, said the lieutenant, takes a 9-mm parabellum bullet, ammunition consistent with the wounds Givon sustained and with the lead fragments. Then the young lieutenant put a report on Netzer's desk and left, bowing slightly as he went out the door. He didn't look back.

The report was written in bad English. Meir and Netzer read it, Meir eagerly, Netzer less so, passing the few pages back and forth. Netzer had seen these things before. This one fit the pattern: thin stuff, self-serving, maybe good police work, maybe not. They give what they want to give. Liaison with these people, no matter how good, gets you only so far. "A spirit of close cooperation and mutuality of interests" was the phrase Netzer's superior used to describe the relationship, a phrase Netzer considered consummately stupid. Mutuality of interests? With carpet merchants and cheats, spavined peasants and silky fairies, you have mutuality of interests?

The suspect was named Ali Moftekhar. A picture showed him after capture. His eyes were glassy, as if he couldn't see. His mouth was open, dully, stupidly. They had shaved his head. There were marks across his face. He was looking up as if told to look at the camera; but as if he had missed it, he looked over it, beyond it. Flat light caught his face full on. There was no depth to the face.

A different world, Netzer thought, as he looked at the photograph. Different ethics. You take it as it is, you take *them* as *they* are. There is no other way. Dreamers may stumble through the world as if it's a nice place. It isn't.

Netzer read aloud the dossier, which was brief. " 'Ali Moftekhar. Born Isfahan environs around 1953. Middle class. Member Shohada group, recruited early seventies. Scholarship student Polytechnique. Civil engineering. Family on mother's side related to Ayatollah Morteza Khonsari, with numerous relatives in divinity schools in Qom.' " Netzer scanned the list of suspicious contacts, meetings attended, addresses lived at, demonstrations, code names of informants. " 'Engineer, Karkhaneh-ye Felezat-e Iran.' Translation, please."

"Iran Metalworks," said Meir.

"All right. 'Advanced degree University of Oklahoma, 1975, in metallurgy. Sent abroad on government grant. Iranian Students Organization. Active in Students Confederation of Europe when living in France. Arrested once in Iran for possession of works of Ali Shariati. Highly religious.' "

That was all. Netzer looked at Meir. "Not much. This Moftekhar, where is he being held?"

"Probably Komiteh," said Meir.

Which was more or less right. In Komiteh Prison, down by the barracks in the center of the city, they had wrenched out of Ali Moftekhar all the names and addresses he knew, the titles of all the books he had read and discussed, where he had bought them, how they were circulated. He told them of tape cassettes, polycopied essays on class and revolt and colonialism and dependency, on feudalism, militarism, fascism. Long words whose meanings he no longer knew. He told them who produced the cassettes, who wrote the essays, where the copying machines were kept, who operated them, how the essays were distributed.

Ali had given them everything. SAVAK's "doctors"—men with grade-school educations who wore white surgeons' smocks and carried stethoscopes and actually called one another *doktor*, Dr. Azodi, Dr. Davudi—had "treated" Ali (it was the term they used) with, among other things, the electroshock, silvery probes whose effect ranged from a tickle (they could make prisoners laugh with the thing if they used it in the right place on low current) to something like a rasping buzz saw that would make prisoners shout and snap their heads back and roll their eyes and try to flail the air with their bound arms. Top amperage could produce an external burn or run like white molten lead along a nerve and wither an arm.

After a session with his "doctors," Ali would lie on the floor of his cell as if his arms and legs were unconnected, were just miscellaneous limbs that belonged to others and had nothing to do with him and had somehow gotten tossed there.

Netzer's report also contained interrogation transcripts and a summary and a backgrounder on the investigation.

They had been watching Moftekhar. His apartment had been under surveillance. They picked him up that night. He

59

had been carrying a grenade and the Tokagypt. In his apartment they had found weapons: Czech, Polish, American, the last probably stolen from the Iranian army. The serial numbers were being verified. He belonged to a group. The group was called Shohada (the Martyrs). It was small, SAVAK said, though connected with the larger umbrella group called Mojahedin (the Strugglers). Shohada is shadowy, murderous.

They killed Givon. Givon was an Israeli. He was with the Americans. That's why they had killed him.

The man who pulled the trigger was called Hoseyn Jandaqi. Ali knew nothing of him. The two had been put together just that night for just that purpose by Shohada in Europe. Hoseyn Jandaqi had been sent in for the task. Now he was gone. A phantom.

Where? they had asked.

Ali couldn't answer. France, he guessed. Or Germany.

Ali gave them names of others he knew in the group. Saqafi, Seyfinezhad, Eskandari. Some names they recognized, some were new; some, they thought, were in Iran, some not.

Then they shot Ali Moftekhar.

"Word from Shomer," Ehud Cohen said, "in Aden. Chemissa's made a run. He's left Aden. He's in Beirut now and he's scheduled for Munich. That's all we know. He should be there in ten days, maybe two weeks."

"Can we tag him in Beirut?" asked Yekutiel Shomron. It was their weekly session in Tel Aviv. Cohen was director of Collection. Shomron was director of Political Action and Liaison.

They were walking in the Atzmaut Gardens among tourists and fir trees. Cohen, dapper in white seersucker trousers and straw hat (very wide-brimmed), towered over Shomron, somber in khaki.

"If he's there, he's gone way under," said Cohen. "He hasn't been sighted yet. I don't think we'll ever see him."

"I wonder. You know, if he does go to Munich, those Iranians will be on the schedule."

"Yes."

"And if so . . ." Shomron spread his hands, lifting his shoulders.

Cohen nodded. "Yes."

"Like the old days, you know? Wrath of God, Ehud. We can activate Haruni. If Chemissa shows, we'll teach them a lesson. Really, it's too bloody perfect." Shomron kicked at the sandy path. "Ah . . . communicate this to Tehran?"

Cohen raised his shoulders and ducked his old head, smiling lightly, looking Oriental with his high cheekbones. "Netzer. After the fact. Let him sleep till then."

6

There were two questions and they kept gnawing at Jim. Who got Givon? was one of them. And the other was, Who the hell *was* Givon anyway? Or to put it pragmatically, for Jim had that kind of mind, What the hell was he *doing?*

The Weird Jerry Tobin, reached in London and on the way to Lagos—"cockroaches the size of crocodiles!" he yelled on the phone—was still pissed and demented and convinced the Israelis had arranged his departure and the subsequent cover-up.

"The fuckers are everywhere. It's the Hand of Zion. Keep your back to the wall, you shit, they'll get *you* if you don't look out."

Givon, if that was his name, said Jerry, was in deep on something. Count on it. Electronics? That figures. Israeli machinations, all right. And if it was electronics, look for the Soviets, look for the Iraqis, and look for the Iranians the Soviets and Iraqis run because Mossad and the CIA and SAVAK are thick as thieves. Thicker. It's all in there somewhere, and the Israelis are the goddamnedest fuckers in the universe.

"Lagos, for God's sake. I mean *Lagos.*" To which Lisa might or might not follow.

Jim sympathized.

"Give the Pear a squeeze for me where it counts; come up from behind and reach around," Jerry said finally. "Right. Well, I'm off for a bit of the old malaria. And watch those Israelis."

Jim made other forays into Henderson High on the Givon thing. He banged on doors, sat in waiting rooms, made discreet calls, but in the end got nothing but blank stares from the politicals and the commercials.

At the British embassy, certain silkily loquacious individuals professed great irritation over Jerry Tobin's expulsion, but the embassy, qua embassy, they gave Jim to understand, had done nothing and evidently would not, and that was the end of it.

Jim, thinking of the wisdom of Jerry Tobin, skirted the issue with the Israelis for a time; when he got sick of that and finally mentioned the killing in vague terms—it was at some cocktail function at the French embassy and he was talking with a military attaché named Ramat—the man stared at Jim briefly, turned on his heels, and walked off. Soon thereafter the legation spokesman, the unctuous Uri Gellerman, who hadn't been returning phone calls, got in touch with Jim and on deep background confirmed a terrorist "action" against an Israeli national. What kind of action? Oh, an action, said Uri. And beyond that, the individual involved had had no name, no age, no family, and no occupation. Policy was not to discuss such matters with the press. Jim's interest in the affair was understandable but not helpful. The legation could not cooperate further. Jim would surely understand.

Jim surely did.

Jim found the Datatron distributorship at a fancy address just off Takht-e Tavoos. He wanted to buy up a quantity of decent radios for his company, he told the surprised young gentleman in the dark suit on the display floor. His firm was a small American architectural and engineering outfit working on the new Varamin Autobahn and could he, Jim, talk to the manager?

Well, yes.

The young gentleman in the dark suit brought another, a clone of the first, Jim decided, looking him over. He spoke fine English. He told Jim they did government contracting and, regrettably, didn't supply foreign firms (something about the licensing arrangements), and that pretty much was that. The showroom was empty of customers and the telephone didn't ring once. The whole establishment, Jim thought, was classic. Government contracts, all right. Not much doubt about that.

The manager's name was Ma'loof and the other was named Niknam. Both were Persian; neither had Moslem first names, which was good to know but proved nothing. So Datatron.

Which pretty much ended it. Investigation over. Nothing else to investigate. Givon had left no tracks, the embassies were dead, Jerry was useless, and the whole thing was receding into the past anyway.

Jim went about his chores and put in his time. He covered a convention of foreign archaeologists staged in a glistening conference hall. The archaeologists, wheezing bores most of them, presented endless slides of dusty and incomprehensible test trenches and pottery series, which made no copy. He drifted in and out of cocktail parties and sat in bars in the northern hotels—the Sheraton, the International, the Belair, the Hilton. He followed a Red Cross team sent to inspect prison conditions and got ushered around with them, and, with them, received what he knew was the old Iranian switcheroo. They saw some prisoners who denied being mistreated in any way, shape, or form. Jim duly reported this and felt not very good about it, knew there was a fat chance they had seen the hard political types.

Then he reported Princess Ashraf describing her escape from assassination at Monte Carlo as a miracle wrought by God. The shah always described his various close shaves, five by that time, as miracles, too. A miraculous family, all in all.

And still there were those questions: Who hit Givon? Who *was* Givon? There had been no miracles for Givon.

Jim's stroke of genius was to connect Givon with IBEX. It was another kind of miracle, really, at least as good as Ashraf's. One night Pari was asleep and Jim was in that blurry region between wakefulness and dreaming, which he had never found a good time for ideas except about the Pear, when it hit him like a baseball bat. The electronics. Givon's electronics. Was it the IBEX scandal again, resurfacing, come back to haunt its perpetrators in a stranger guise? IBEX the disaster? IBEX the joke?

Maybe. Jim hoped so, for IBEX had been one hell of a good show.

Jim's paper, a bucket for all of Washington's leaks, had

broken the story, another one of those memories that made Jim ache, for he had had nothing to do with the breaking of it (it was all done stateside) and the envy made him morose.

IBEX, his paper correctly reported, was to be a hyper-sophisticated string of listening posts along the frontiers, especially the borders with Russia and Iraq, to pick up the noises and footfalls of invasion, a microchip Maginot Line: eleven ground monitoring posts, six airborne groups, and numberless mobile ground units. Stupendous contracting at half a billion U.S. at least.

The winning bidder won, as attested by an astounding memo from a CIA in-house investigation of the whole mess that had glittered like a diamond on the paper's front page, the winning bidder won by doing a deal with a Mr. Mahtavi, whose company was a post office box in Bermuda (Reid House, 2280) with an artfully nondescript name (Universal Aero Services Company, Ltd.—as bulls service cows, thought Jim at the time). And Mr. Mahtavi, who knew people in Tehran, would get five to ten percent as sales commission, and on half a billion, that made Mr. Mahtavi a good provider.

IBEX, Jim's paper concluded in a sternly worded editorial, was pure garbage, a congeries of weird ideas that would never work anywhere. There were distant sound analyzers that couldn't tell the difference between a Russian tank and a Russian motorcycle. There were airborne cameras triggered by intercepted communications and radar signals, but they wouldn't take pictures at night or on cloudy days. The computer network was so complex it was unmaintainable stateside. Among the locals? Not a chance, the paper claimed.

IBEX, the editorial said, was a half-billion-dollar dumping ground for all the lunatic ideas that the NSA and CIA and everybody else found too wigged out.

There was more. Deposits were made in mysterious accounts to pay off U.S. government employees, albeit CIA. Auditing the arrangement was a world-class accounting firm of impeccable repute, whose contract contained a clause absolving it from liability for any stealing that might just happen to be going on.

Oh, Jim remembered, it was gaudy.

As the story unfolded, most of the Hounds, Alice Cochrane included, looked for Jim's departure. "MOD"—which is what Alice called the Ministry of Defense—"will strike," she said firmly at the Intercontinental. "MOD does not spare civilian bystanders. No. Especially if they are foreign devils. Young James will go."

But before MOD got around to striking, the leaks stopped. For Jim's editors, that killed the story, and his paper went on to other matters and other leaks. Jim survived; IBEX submerged.

But didn't die. The work, whatever it was, went on.

Then rumors started to go around, first among Iranians, then among Europeans cut out of the contracting. Some of the Hounds took to repeating the talk with knowing looks and in knowing tones. IBEX, they said, was something other than it seemed, something other than Jim's paper reported. IBEX was larger, IBEX was deeper. IBEX was electronic surveillance *inside* Iran, too. Phone taps of a superior sort, not the clumsy old-fashioned kind that Alice swore sounded like wind through the trees when they were listening in ("You can hear the third parties cough," she claimed, "silly bastards"). Intricate bugs of political and religious groups, feeding into computerized data bases. Intercepts of diplomatic communications—radio, telex, telephone—using the latest gathering and deciphering techniques. IBEX, they said, or some nefarious spin-off therefrom, was SAVAK's ultimate control mechanism over foreigners and locals alike. Hence, they said, the deaths of the three Rockwell Americans.

Hence, Jim wondered, the death of Shlomo Givon? Maybe. So why the freeze? SAVAK, Mossad, CIA—they *are* thick as thieves. Why is Fiscarelli frozen out? What's going on here?

Then, in that morning's blurry reverie, it hit him. Lying there in the dark, Pari shifting in her sleep beside him, he figured it out. Or thought he had. And that took Jim to Pete Fiscarelli's office, where he stormed up and down, waving his arms and shouting at Fiscarelli, who told him later he thought the performance was very good and funny.

"Think, goddamn it, Pete, just think! We're Onto Something here." Jim careered around the room and caromed off the walls and filing cabinets.

"One: IBEX is totally fucked up and the Iranians are pissed. Two: The Iranians throw a correspondent out who simply reports some poor bastard got killed. Three: Aforementioned poor bastard being an Israeli electronics guy who supplies U.S. companies the deepest of deep stuff and knows everything the stuff can do. Four: The Israelis drop out of sight into a deep, dark cave somewhere and don't answer their phones. The freeze, Pete, the freeze is for IBEX. Think. Givon was a supplier, right? Maybe Givon was putting in more electronics than they were buying. The stuff's complex. Everything's hush-hush. Everything's need-to-know, right? So maybe you finesse your own stuff in and there's no one to say, 'Stop, this doesn't go here,' right? You get work orders cut. You cut them yourself. So maybe you put in a little extra circuitry, okay? A little extra? Mikes and stuff? Could be all over the place. SAVAK, J2, the Inspectorate. He could have them wired. *Wired.* The army, the navy, the meter maids on Takht-e Jamshid—who knows? Who *knows?* They could be everywhere with this. Think what all they could be doing. What about that Kraut company down on the Gulf?" That firm was none other than United Energy Construction (Vereinigte Energiewerke, SA, when Jim looked it up), biggest of the European big. VE was building two large and expensive nuclear power reactors on the Gulf. Jim had done a thing on the program when VE beat out Westinghouse and Framatome for the contract.

"You said Datatron was doing communications with them, right?"

"So?"

"Let us pause for thought, Pete. A short moment of silent reflection? Nuclear. Now hear this: nuclear. Why would Israelis cooperate on a nuclear plant? They're scared shitless of this stuff, right? Scared shitless someone else in the immediate vicinity might get a bomb, right? They've got their own, so who needs any more, right?"

"No bombs are coming out of that plant."

"Who knows there aren't?"

"Fuck off. Bombs!" Fiscarelli barked a laugh. "You can put that one where the sun don't shine, Jimmy. That's what you can do with that one. No bombs are coming out of there."

"You sure the Israelis know that? Do they? *Do* they? Maybe they're not so sure, maybe they're not such goddamn trusting souls. Maybe they're watching, huh? They know America's angling for power contracts so they don't piss in the wind. Just do a little eavesdropping. And maybe, Pete"—here Jim's voice was at its most horrific—"maybe they're listening in on *you*. Think Mossad wouldn't?"

Jim went on in the same vein—shouts, paranoia, and much arm waving. Datatron was cover, he insisted loudly, and Givon was in deep. Could be anywhere. Including Henderson High. When Givon got killed, the Israelis shut up because they didn't want to blow Datatron. Not to the Iranians, not to Fiscarelli. Jim bent over the front of Fiscarelli's desk finally and yelled, "Givon was on an Israeli operation they don't want you to *know* about. IBEX. They're piggybacking IBEX, for God's sake."

He collapsed, panting and sweating, into a leather contraption made in Tabriz and for some reason called a Beirut chair, hunched down with his neck on the back of the thing, long legs sprawling out in front, hands folded on his chest, idiotic loafers on his feet that seemed to take up half Fiscarelli's office.

Fiscarelli had been staring quietly straight ahead through the whole thing, not following Jim's acrobatics.

"Maybe," he said simply.

"Shlomo Givon," Jim said softly looking up out of the chair. "He died for some good reason."

"Maybe."

Jim's hands were still folded. He was quiet. "How'd they do it, Pete? What's SAVAK saying? Huh? Old times' sake?"

"Want to go out and find me a mullah, Jimmy?"

"Hey?"

"Go out and find me a mullah." Fiscarelli eyed Jim. "State's put the fucking lid on here. You know that. Can't talk to anybody. Leftists, rightists—makes no difference. Anybody we talk to might be SAVAK in disguise, right? Ask a priest about the way things are, he turns out to be an informer. It gets back to the shah, pisses him off. And that's bad for business, right? Might do a little bit less with the Yankees, a little more with the Frogs and the Krauts and the Japs. That's bad for politics, bad for careers. See no evil, speak no evil. The Henderson High motto."

"State run your shop?"

"They're customers for the product. They buy what they like. They don't like a report, they don't buy it." Fiscarelli curled his nose. "Fuck," he said.

Then Fiscarelli paused and Jim watched him. It was the moment, Jim knew. Like taking a girl.

"Ground rules are like before," Fiscarelli said. "You never heard anything. Not here. Not anywhere. You never heard it. Anything I tell you, you develop elsewhere before you run it. Otherwise, you don't run it. And you don't say it belly up at the Intercontinental Bar either. Got that?"

"Sure, swell, super."

Fiscarelli ran his hand over his head. "They got Givon like they got Hawkins."

Colonel Thomas Hawkins had been an adviser with the Finance Ministry.

"Hawkins was careful. Took different routes into town every day and all that. Except he always left his house at seven o'clock in the morning. Never failed." Fiscarelli smiled sadly. "So Hawkins is walking from his house to the street corner—okay?—as his driver's coming to pick him up. Right there Hawkins gets two, maybe three, bullets in the head at close range. The killer gets away on a motorcycle driven by a second person."

"They got Givon the same way?"

"That's what they say. Two shots. One in the head, one in the back, four-thirty A.M."

"Same people? They say they got the guys that killed Hawkins."

"They say a lot of things. The end of the Hawkins case was a shootout, right? In which the party in question, the 'suspect,' and I use the term advisedly, died. Fucking convenient. They also told us the same man had killed General Taheri a couple of months before he got Hawkins. A dead revolutionary and two cases closed. Neat, huh?"

"Think they're lying?"

"No way to tell. You can't get into this stuff. National

pride and independence, they say. Maybe it is, in a way. The sons of bitches don't want us to know how weak they are."

"Yeah."

"But this Givon thing and the Hawkins thing and the Rockwell thing last year—it's all part of one big fucking show, Jimmy. Something's going on."

"Worried?"

"Not officially."

"Unofficially?"

"Fucking A. There's something in the air. Not just a couple of isolated killings. Something else. A shift in the mood. Very subtle. You try to touch it, and it's like smoke in your hand. Just beyond your senses, just under the threshold. I don't like it. It doesn't smell right. Nothing you can put your finger on, but you can feel something here. It's real."

"Anyone else here think that?"

"It's not accepted doctrine. Here's what State turns out." Fiscarelli fished a seventy-page document entitled *Iran: 2000* out of one of his in-boxes and dropped it on Jim's side of the desk. "INR's latest sugar tit. Classified 'Confidential.' You can read it if you want. It's worthless. Greppin brought together a bunch of people and they all decided they didn't know shit. Collected their consultants' fees, though, right?"

Thomas Greppin was at State. Jim had met him once. He was young and from an old tobacco family somewhere in the Carolinas, and he wore half-lens glasses because the secretary of state did. Greppin wouldn't go far, Jim had concluded.

"The authors of *Iran: 2000* assume the shah will be in forever and a day. If by some strange stroke of fortune, he isn't declared immortal and in fact dies, sonny-boy, Prince Reza, will take over with only minor skirmishing and the beloved empress will watch in the wings. What do you think, Jimmy?"

"Horseshit."

"Right. We know nothing, Jimmy. Except what SAVAK tells us, and they're fucking liars."

"I thought SAVAK had a man in every mosque."

"SAVAK *pays* a man in every mosque. Not the same thing. Their stuff is very questionable. And there's human rights. Ma Derian never sleeps." Patricia Derian was assistant secretary of

70

state for human rights and one of Fiscarelli's pet hates. "We can't get close to SAVAK. Ma Derian won't let us. Can't do anything. We can't even sell tear-gas cannisters; the Derian bitch is *sitting* on them. *Tear gas.* Christ Almighty!"

Fiscarelli poured himself a tequila (it was afternoon) and sailed a cable over the clutter on his desk to Jim. "Read this."

Jim read:

> HOSEYN JANDAQI. REAL NAME: NK. BIRTH DATE: NK. EDUCATION: NK, PRESUMED SOME UNIVERSITY. SAID TRAINED IN LEBANON. RELIGIOUS INSTRUCTION AND SMALL ARMS. MEDIUM HEIGHT. GROUP CALLING ITSELF SHOHADA CLAIMED RESPONSIBILITY FOR BOMBING OF USIS LIBRARIES IN TEHRAN, ISFAHAN ON OCCASION OF VISIT OF PRESIDENT NIXON AND SECRETARY KISSINGER IN 1972. HAVE NOT SURFACED SINCE.
>
> COMMENT: INFORMATION PLAUSIBLE, NOT SUBJECT TO CONFIRMATION. EMBOFF BEIRUT COMMENTS SHIITE MOVEMENTS HARBOR IRANIANS. ALSO PLO (SEE AT-TACHED). GROUP CALLED AL-JIHAD IN PARTICULAR. OUT OF MAINSTREAM OF LEBANESE SHIITES. BELIEVE ALI IS THE "MEANING" OF GOD.

"He did it," said Fiscarelli. "The mother that whacked Givon. So they say. Want to copy the man's résumé? Go ahead."

"SAVAK supply this?"

Fiscarelli shrugged.

"They say how they came up with the name?"

"No." Fiscarelli joined his fingertips in a little tent. "We figure they're surveiling. You get a flurry of action, somebody disappears, you put two and two together. That kind of shit."

"Okay, so he disappears. Where to?"

"The Iranians say Europe. So, maybe Europe. Sometimes they're right."

"Think he's still here?"

"Could be."

"Where do they say in Europe?"

"London, Paris, Frankfurt, Rome. Take your pick. The

fuckers are here, they're there, they're everywhere. Every-where."

"And Shohada?"

"Shohada. It means 'the Martyrs.' Liaison claims they're a subgroup of the Mojahedin. For special operations. Claims they don't know much about it."

"Do they?"

"We know what they tell us, Jimmy. Period. And they're not talking."

"Who's this al-Jihad?"

Fiscarelli raised his eyebrows. "They're Lebanese. So they say. Lebanese umbrella group, right? They say they're in Paris. So maybe they're in Paris. They say they're connected with Shohada. So maybe they're connected with Shohada." Fis-carelli smiled. "That's what they say, Jimmy. That's what they say."

"Paris station know anything?"

"Paris station feels it has better things to do than chase fucking Iranian students around."

"French have anything?"

"Nope."

Jim looked out the window. The northern side of Hender-son High, the side away from the street, was less battened down. Tall poplars lined the embassy drives. Jim could see some lawn, a grove of trees, and somewhere in them, he knew, was the ambassador's residence.

"You've got a vacuum here."

"Pretty much." Fiscarelli fished a Xeroxed report from his in-box and pried out the staples. "You can look at part of this. Here's who they are." He gave Jim two pages from about fifteen. They were marked "Secret. No Foreigners."

"Young Hoseyn's in here. Maybe."

Background:

(S) Founded in 1961, the Iranian People's Martyrs (IPM) are one of a number of left-wing terrorist organiza-tions with religious links. They underwent several rein-carnations in the next decade. They adopted the name Shohada in late 1971. In 1972, Ayatollah Ruhollah Khomeyni, the senior Shiite religious figure, declared that it was the duty of all good Moslems to support the IPM and overthrow the shah. This edict gave the IPM legitimacy and enabled it to garner more widespread grassroots support. Ultraconservative bazaar merchants responded most favorably.

(S) After a period of action against Iranian and Western targets, there was a period of decline in the summer of 1973, resulting from security force counterefforts brought on by the first anti-American assassination.

(C/NOFORN) Libya provided weapons and ammunition via Kuwait.

Finances:

(S/NOFORN) After Ayatollah Khomeyni's call to support the Shohada in 1972, bazaar merchants and religiously inclined individuals opposed to secularization channeled funds to Khomeyni via students and pilgrims to Iraqi holy sites. He siphoned off a portion and gave the rest to the IPM.

(S/NOFORN) More direct contributions by the same kinds of Khomeyni adherents may have been given to the IPM.

(S/NOFORN) Libya provided financial assistance to both Khomeyni and the IPM. The Libyan embassy in Beirut allegedly forwarded $100,000 to Shohada every three months.

(S/NOFORN) Active recruitment programs go on among student groups in Europe and USA. IPM has links with foreign, including especially Arab, terrorist groups and is thought part of informal Paris-based umbrella group called al-Jihad (the Struggle, the Holy War). Emboff Paris reports nonconfirmation.

The report listed the activities of Shohada, which, if true, were the stuff of legend, some in the public domain, some not:
   • attempted bombing assassination of a U.S. Air Force general (news to Jim);
   • assassination of a U.S. Army colonel (that was Hawkins, and people knew about it);

• assassination of Iranian agent assigned to the Joint Government Committee on Terrorism (Jim had heard of it, but the report said Shohada had done it with the People's Guerrillas, a communist group, and that was news);

• assassination of two U.S. Air Force officers (well known).

There followed a brisk run of bombings of American and British installations of one stripe or other, and finally, as the report put it, "surveillance of the Jewish Emigration Center, associated with the Israeli legation in Iran."

"The last one," said Fiscarelli, "the Jewish Emigration Center—it's at Shah and Sheikh Hadi. It's close to where they hit Givon."

"Any connection?"

"Who the fuck knows? They're very talented. Better than SAVAK sometimes. Here." Fiscarelli pointed to the bottom of another sheet and held it in front of Jim's face.

(S) The IPM has the capability to monitor SAVAK communications.

"You're kidding! How do we know that?"

"We *don't* know it. We *think* it. There's evidence they monitor some telephone conversations as well."

"And they heard something?"

"Maybe."

"What?"

"Yeah, what?"

7

Munich. It was late afternoon and the sun was just turning golden. Crowds were beginning to build in the shopping streets, and yawning clerks and secretaries in the offices were starting to think of evening.

He walked as if followed, and he was vagueness itself: he could have been a tourist, a student, a drifter. There was no telling. He wore faded American jeans, a cheap navy blue jacket, a gray shirt, a brown knitted cap, an orange book bag over his shoulder. His light reddish hair and beard were cut short. He had a sharp face and colorless eyes, and pointed, almost elfin ears.

They had done the recon for him. They knew everything. The recon was classic and the briefings were complete. But still he would pay a visit himself first, to make sure, to make it come right.

He cut into the beer garden behind the ocher-colored *Justizpalast* under the arc of a trellis and English ivy thick overhead. The perfect dodge. A band of well-scrubbed young people, three boys and a girl, were singing blandly in English. Afternoon customers were sparse at the white metal filigree tables and chairs. Middle-aged waitresses, still unharried, served coffee and pastry and huge seidels of beer, and made change from purses that they carried around their waists and that they closed with a snap. He paused by the back wall, watching the entrance where he had come in. No one had followed him.

He moved out the back gate into the Karlsplatz, walking quickly, hands in his pockets, then down into the Karlsplatz Untergeschoss, an underground shopping area. He emerged into the Kaufingerstrasse under the twin onion domes of the

Frauenkirch, Church of Our Lady, and turned left up the Herzog Wilhelmstrasse to the wealthiest shopping area of the city.

He seemed not to notice the carpet store at first, but then returned to peer through the window at a vast Tabrizi carpet hanging the full length of the showcase, silk, row after row of small, shimmering teardrops of cream and blue and rust. The sign in the window read *Teppichhaus Pars. Grösste Auswahl Besonders Preiswert* ("Pars Carpets. Greatest Selection Especially Well Priced"). Here it is, he thought. It starts here. Inside, carpets lined the walls, blue-gray Nainis, red and white Isfahanis, small and silky pink carpets from Qom, Turkoman prayer rugs from the steppes of Hyrcania.

Young Iranians in blue jeans with long curly hair were lifting and dragging piles of carpets in the direction of a dark, suave salesman in a dark blue pinstripe suit. He stood attentively beside a blond lady, who sat with crossed legs, gesturing with her hand, as the young men peeled back layer after layer of carpet for her personal show, and her husband, his face pink, well shaved, and just beginning to get flabby, deferring to his wife's better judgment.

No one noticed the shape outside. He spent that whole late afternoon hanging around the Herzog Wilhelmstrasse, looking in at the antique stores there, the windows full of art, jewelry, ancient maps.

When the young Iranians left Teppichhaus Pars in the evening, he drifted with them in the crowds, which were now thick, west, past the railway station, and then south. They walked slowly, sometimes pausing by the store windows, and he put them on a long leash.

The apartment house was a faded yellow, five stories high, and shabby. The stucco was cracked like an old man's face, and years of grime and exhaust had bonded to its surface. All the windows were shut and dirty, some with ill-tended plants in them, most not.

The target. So easy and banal. As the young Iranians disappeared inside, he moved to the building. The door at the entrance was a dirty brown, painted over and over. It hung open. The postboxes in the passage were banged up and dented;

only a few showed names, and most of those probably of persons long gone. No phone system or door opener. Part of a newspaper lay in the hall. The address was Mohrstrasse 312.

He could hear them from the ground floor as they went to the second landing, talking loudly, and to the third, he by that time catlike on the second. A door opened. Light came into the stairwell briefly, then he was left in darkness and silence.

He went softly up the stairs and past the doors. There was no name on the buzzer. It was number 5B. He heard no sound from inside, but saw a band of light glowing under the floor as he passed. Fine. Three other apartments on this floor. He didn't break his pace as he moved past 5B. It was the one at the landing, they had told him. And they were right. They always were. From the shape of the building they knew the apartment was small. He went up the next flight of stairs and paused at the landing, waiting in the shadows. The sound of a radio came from somewhere, muffled and heavy. It was music, then speech. He couldn't tell what language. Then music again. He descended the stairs, slipping past apartment 5B, and was out again into a darker evening, where the late summer moon seemed oddly flat.

He returned to Mohrstrasse 312 the next day in the morning rain. Surveillance had watched and had counted the inhabitants all out. Surveillance indicated its belief the apartment was empty by placing an elderly gentleman without a dog (that was the important point) in the sheltered bus stop a few meters from the door. Barely glancing at the elderly man, he entered and went again to 5B. This time he knocked on the door vigorously and forthrightly. If someone answered, he would ask for Herr Kessel. There is no Herr Kessel? But there must be. Here I have the address. Are you sure? He told me himself. . . . But no one answered and there was no need to ask for Herr Kessel.

He looked carefully at the door and felt around the handle, running his fingers up, then down where the door joined. No need even to strip the molding off. He pressed the door slightly and sensed give there. The door would rotate around the bolt, top and bottom both vulnerable. Try the top first. He pushed at the upper part of the door and tried to insert an L-shaped pin of hard steel between it and the molding. But the building was old and the damned door was heavy, and the give wasn't enough. He pushed again, this time straining hard with his shoulder against the door, but it was still no good. He cursed. Try another trick. He put his boot at the base of the door and tested its give there. He felt it yield ever so slightly and spring back when he relaxed the pressure.

He planted his heel firmly on the floor again and pushed hard at the base of the door. It was child's play. He slid the L-shaped pin between molding and door and felt it slide gently upward. It fit. He took a handle from his pocket and screwed it onto the protruding end of the pin, turned it ninety degrees, and slid it up to the lock. It caught the bolt. Child's play, child's play. Another turn and a bit of force and the bolt slid into the lock. The door opened easily. He pulled it shut behind him and with gloves on now, went lightly through the apartment. A quick look. No stealing, they had said.

All right. The apartment was larger than he had thought. Three rooms. A kitchen. A toilet. Pallets on the floor, five of them.

Suitcases, flight bags, knapsacks, were strewn around the room. It looked like an airport. The kitchen was tiny and dirty, and filthy pots and pans had taken over the small table there—an aluminum slum. No furniture.

He went about delicately, looking, leaving nothing disturbed. He found folders, card indexes, photos, identity cards. He took some empty forms and stuffed them into his book bag. Just samples. They wouldn't be missed. Books in Arabic script, which he could not read. Persian. Boxes of pamphlets and tape cassettes. He took some of these, too. Files, typescripts, forms, all unreadable to him. He took photos everywhere, shot as many as possible, all at random.

And then, like heartbeats, he heard the sound: footfalls on the landing. He stopped moving. He stopped breathing. Was it someone? A break in their routine? Were they back? God knows who comes here. Never enough reconnaissance. You can never get enough of that.

He had no gun. He never carried one. It was part of his

vanity. Just a few tricks up his sleeve. So if they came in . . . He was a good liar and a fast runner, and he could use his feet in other ways, too. He had broken a man's shin once with a lovely kick. The man's face paled over, his eyes rolled back white, and he collapsed and puked. They had taught him that. You flex your foot down as your leg comes up fast, then at that sweet instant before contact, which only you can know, you snap your ankle, and the effect, if your ankle is any good, is like a bullwhip with a boot on it. Sends them puking.

He glided to the door like a breeze that never touches ground. He held his hands up, listening. There were no more footfalls, no one passing. No one in the stairwell. Silence. Did they go away? No key at the lock. No motion at the door handle. Sweet. It was someone passing in the hall.

He took more photos and began to pull apart the files. Always one at a time. Like taking apart a machine. Study before grabbing. Arrange things methodically. Then they fit back together. There will be an order. You must respect order, they told him. It talks. Nothing is ever random. Not really. Then he got wide-angle shots of the rooms.

The silence of the building annoyed him. Only the fridge made noise. It was ancient. Tiny condenser coils sat on top, round like a turban. It had a handle that latched. He got more shots of the main room, a kind of hall. In it, against each wall away from the one window, were two bedsteads made of steel tubing; dirty mattresses lay on them. A dormitory for terrorists, he thought. Yellowed gauze curtains blocked the light and the view. They were in two layers, and each gave off dust at the touch of his hand brushing past them. He could hear the traffic outside. Aryans and their automobile horns.

Enough, he thought. Time for the *pièce de résistance*. He looked at the telephone over in the corner.

Then, over the street sounds, he heard it. A kick at the door. *Someone kicked at the door.* You wouldn't call it fear, but his heart pounded.

They *were* here, he thought. They've noticed. They're back.

He glided from the back room, watching the door, stuffing his camera in the book bag, then slipped the bag off his shoulder, resting it softly on the floor, like a feather, like an autumn leaf. The handle moved, and he brought his hand up, stood without thinking, with his body at the angle they had drummed into him. The handle was released. The door remained shut. He moved closer to the door, straining to hear sounds on the landing. Were they there? Would they know? Had they been watching the apartment? Or had someone followed him? Could that have happened? He was supposed to have protection.

If it was one, he would kill. Two, he would escape. Three? Three would be a problem. Initiative they had taught him. Strike with surprise. When you play it right, surprise is another man by your side. That's what they taught him.

Closer to the door. He leaped at it, hands on the lock and the handle, ripped it open, and burst out towering over a stupid kid in shorts. The kid looked at him dumbly.

"Willst du spielen?"

The kid had a beaten-up pink plastic ball, scuffed and half-caved in on one side. He seemed strangely old. His blond hair was mussed and his face dirty; he looked like a thrown-away doll. He *was* too old. The blank look behind his glasses showed that. Yes.

"Willst du spielen? Spielen?" he asked softly, his voice high, just beginning to crack. He held the ball out solemnly in both hands.

To get rid of him: *"Ja, ja. Geh hinunter. Ich komme. Geh hinunter."* The kid's face was too blank to show belief or disbelief, but he turned and, without looking back, went down the stairs, quietly, as he was told.

The man shut the door softly, collected his book bag, and paid a last visit to the telephone on the floor by the bed. He memorized the number.

The kid was waiting in the ground-floor landing, staring out at the rain, silent and motionless. Vehicles sped by, throwing sheets of dirty water onto the sidewalk, and the boy watched. One last look up the stairwell. Nothing. The man passed by the child unrecognized. There was no one else on the landing.

Lousy rain, the man thought. Unseasonable, really. He

walked out into it and crossed the street. When he looked back, the boy was in the doorway with his pink ball.

Later, when they called the number on the phone at 5B, no one answered. They let it ring ten times, but no one lifted the receiver. The second time they called, someone did. They tried to talk with him in German. The voice answered in monosyllabic grunts.

They could not tell whether he understood or not. The one doing the actual calling asked for Herr Kessel. Could he speak with Herr Kessel? The reply was in bad German and hard to understand. But as he spoke, they detonated the device in the telephone handset, and it tore his head off. The young man with the pointed ears was in Salzburg by that time. When he crossed the border, his book bag contained only books and a change of clothing. A Suleyman for a Shlomo, they said, and felt it was no bargain.

8

Jim stood in Jami Street staring north up Sheikh Hadi, not even knowing what to look for. Someone up there toward the end, someone . . . How? Sprang out? Followed him running? Met him head on? Givon had been shot in the back, Fiscarelli said. So was he followed?

Jim walked along the dusty asphalt of Sheikh Hadi, walking where Givon must have walked, and wandered past the dozen points where Givon's killer might have lurked. Jim tried to imagine Hoseyn Jandaqi. What was his age? Jim wondered. What was his face like? His voice? How did he walk?

Jim passed a tailor's shop, its window full of flannel pajamas, shirts, trousers, and, behind them, curtains. A middle-aged woman stood in the door staring out, her arms folded. She watched Jim. A record store blared scratchy songs. A kid stood inside by the counter. He had long hair and wore bell-bottom trousers, adolescent truculence on his face. Jim passed a stationer's, with schoolbooks, writing materials, notebooks, in the window. A shoe store displayed handmade boots and purses. On the side they thought Givon had walked was a school, its playground surrounded by a high brown brick wall.

A couple of boys in shorts kicked a plastic soccer ball around one another in the street, concentrating on the ball as it scuffed and skidded over the pavement, sometimes hitting the wall of the school, sometimes disappearing into a *joob*. They stared briefly at Jim, the foreigner. A poultry store had Hebrew lettering in the window. Scrawny chickens awaiting execution were jammed in cages in the front.

Hebrew always made Jim think maybe there really was a Word, maybe the whole business—burning bush and all—was

82

true. It looked awfully definitive. A people who meant business. As did Yahweh. But Yahweh didn't help Givon.

Just up the street on the corner was the Aliyah, the Israeli Emigration Office. There was always a police guard outside. Even late at night it was under surveillance. It had happened right under their noses.

Jim returned at night to see how the street was lighted. He passed a hospital, whose steel fence was covered with long fluorescent tubes that flickered red, green, and white. Up where Givon was killed, the lamps were infrequent and some weren't working at all.

Jim sent a long report out by courier and persuaded his paper to sit on the story for a time. The implications, he wrote, were vast and astounding and promised front-pagers into the next decade. Jim was particularly happy with the nuclear connection. The Israelis, Jim wrote, were concerned about the VE project. The Israelis, however, were not telling the Americans of said concern or what the hell they intended to do about it. The Israeli Masada complex being well known, Jim figured he might just find some good workable stuff if he got into it.

All Intercontinental Hounds believed passionately without evidence that the shah was developing a bomb. "His nibs wants things," said Alice. "Everything there is. It's his royal nature, luv. He wants to grow up to be a big boy. And what better way? Besides, the region's rather nuclear right now. India's got one. Israel's got one. Iraq's hard at work, the Pakkies are hard at work. *He* won't be left out. Not a chance." The consensus was, the shah would use civilian power plants to do the job. He was buying enough of them, wasn't he? Twenty or something, wasn't it?

It made sense to Jim. In fact, Jim had thought once there might be a story in it and tried the idea out on Robert Korpivaara, the science attaché at Henderson High. Korpivaara was short and pudgy, with blond hair, and was very scholarly and bright and knew his science. He was polite, but he didn't think Jim, to be quite blunt about it, could pass a high school physics course. Which was correct.

"Can't be done," said Korpivaara. "The fuel will be monitored. You count what goes in and you count what goes out. It's simple arithmetic."

"Maybe there'll be another supply."

"We're aware of all this. Want to hear the scenario? Here's the scenario. You take yellow cake. Uranium oxide. You put it in a reactor and bombard it with neutrons, and it turns into plutonium. With plutonium you make a bomb. Boo!" Korpivaara waved his hands and made a demonic face. "That's the scenario, but there are too many problems. The process produces heat. And I mean heat. Most reactors can't handle it. None of the reactors they're building here can."

"Maybe some can. Maybe there's something in the architecture you don't know about."

"VE's a reputable firm. The Federal Republic is a decent state. Forget it."

"We're looking to sign a treaty, right? It'll be a bilateral treaty of cooperation on the peaceful uses of atomic energy. We figure on selling ten billion dollars' worth of reactors in the next few years, right? So maybe there's a little temptation here to look the other way on this stuff? Here in the embassy, I mean. We know the White House is buggy about the problem. So maybe we don't want to stir them up? Huh? Maybe?"

"Nonsense."

"The Persian government is paying one point four billion dollars to MIT to train fifty-four nuclear engineers in a master's program."

"So?"

"Come on! And what is this Kraut firm? Do you trust them?"

"Forget VE. We're in there. We're looking."

"Hard?"

"Hard. It's not there. No nothing. No uranium shipments, even. Those aren't scheduled to begin for a couple of years. The plants don't start up for four more years. No stockpiling."

"University's got a reactor."

"TSPRR? Get serious. It's a toy. You couldn't do a thing with it. It's a pool reactor. No plutonium'll come out of it. It's got a five-megawatt capacity. It's the nuclear equivalent of a training bra. Forget it."

"Could it be modified?"

"We're in and out of it all the time. Believe me, we know. You can't produce anything with it."

"The more reactors, the more likelihood of diversion."

"They're not doing it. We've seen the plans. I've been to the sites. No way you can do it. Everything's very clean. Leaving production aside, you need to be able to separate the stuff. Which is easy, it's a simple chemical process. The difficulty is, the stuff's very dirty, very poisonous, very radioactive. So you need special equipment, equipment that's good for this and this only. So you can get spotted if anybody's watching. We're watching. They're on the up and up."

That's what Korpivaara had said. But if the Israelis are indeed concerned, Jim wrote now, maybe we've got a story.

Jim's editor, who was named Zimmerman, read through the whole thing in his office with the three TV sets that were always on, one for each network. Zimmerman's feet were on his desk. He deposited the sheets one by one on his paunch as he read, and when he finished, he shrugged his shoulders and said something about troops in the field. His nephew worried about long-term damage to the paper if Morgan actually caused an embarrassment.

Zimmerman snorted. "So they throw us out for six months. Six months without coverage from us is their loss. Don't be a baby."

The nephew had tidy, blow-dried hair and sported double-breasted blue blazers and tried carrying a bag once when the fad almost caught on, but was laughed at. "No problem," said Zimmerman, not really sure there wasn't, and went on to other matters.

Jim sat looking down on Tehran through Bucephalus's grimy windshield. He had parked in Elahieh for the view over the city. A light end-of-summer rain pelted the Rover's dusty body briefly, then stopped, leaving streaks in the grime.

The sky was a dusty yellow. Dirt hung in the air, lay on the foliage, coated the trees. The mountains were hidden behind the stuff, and the whole effect was gloom.

What a place. No truth to know.

Jim had arranged it with Fiscarelli.

The word from Fiscarelli was this: SAVAK lies. The Israelis lie. It's IBEX. Or maybe it isn't. Or maybe it's something *like* IBEX—the Iranians may be doing other deals. Things are so tight we'll never know. We can't operate here. We can't talk to the right people even if we can find them, and we can't find them. So, we contract out to the private sector. To wit, one James Donald Morgan.

"Here are the rules," Jim had said in Fiscarelli's office. "If you don't know something, I want you to say, 'I don't know,' and mean it. If you can't tell me something, I want you to say, 'I can't tell you.' No dead ends, no goose chases, no disinformation. We'll have a working arrangement."

Fiscarelli had agreed.

There would be money, too, for there might be costs in this thing that Zimmerman would never dream of. The sums would be untraceable. And Jim, well, Jim was Onto Something, and so the question of money from the embassy came down to: get the news. When you can and how you can, but get it. Jim was a taxpayer, the way he looked at it, and some of that was his anyway, right? Right, he told himself. And in the pit of his stomach he knew he had sinned.

Jim looked over Jordan Boulevard, which shot down like a ski run through the northern suburbs. Sweepers in baggy blue uniforms, peasants just in from the villages, were out cleaning the highway with straw brooms as supercars tear-assed past them. Jim wondered just how many sweepers they lost in a week.

Do it, he thought. You can feel it. It's there. Best thing ever to come your way in these latitudes. If you drop it, you'll never see it again. Stone dead. Like a rock in a pool. Sink right to the bottom, it will. So go after it.

II.

Rubbing
the Lamp

Go forth light-armed and heavy-armed and strive
with your wealth and your lives in the path of God.
—*The Glorious Koran*
Sura of Repentance, Verse 4

If I forget thee, O Jerusalem, let my right hand forget
her cunning.

—*Ps. 137:5*

1

Richard Levesque preferred meeting in noise and behind walls. "You must always have a wall," he would say, "a fence, a barrier. Not so much funny business with the cameras, you know? Lipreading is a profession here." And no rifle-mounted microphones either, he told Jim, filtered to remove everything but the human voice and to amplify that. "Always have a barrier and your troubles will vanish."

They met in the brasserie Grand Zinc because Levesque liked its loud sound system and the three noisy pinball machines off in the corner and its ambience: the Grand Zinc smelled of brandy, dog, and cigar.

The place had a bar of polished wood with brass fittings and a magnificent zinc top. A marble curb ran the length of it and green porcelain panels with black silhouettes of dogs smoking pipes were set in the wood. Portraits of dogs ran around the top of the room, too, and when Jim and Levesque were there, a couple of police dogs lounged on the floor. The bartender, himself looking like a hound to Jim, hunched over the bar and stared off away from Jim and Levesque.

Levesque wore a dark blue jacket; his trousers were a different dark blue. His brown pullover was faded and its collar frayed, and Jim knew without looking that the black shoes Levesque wore were down at the heels. His hair ran straight back from his forehead. His face was thick-featured, and that went with all the rest of him. His eyes were crystal blue and alert and intelligent.

"The blast," Levesque was saying, "was in a telephone handset. Remote-control detonation. Elegant, Morgan, eh, eh, eh, so elegant! And they knew, man, they knew just when to hit. Peff!" he said and smacked a large fist into his meaty palm and laughed.

"You sound envious."

"It would have been nice, you know? To claim the credit? Shit, it was splendid!"

Jim had been bum, stringer, student, and stringer in that order in Paris in the early sixties, an era he remembered as perpetual sunshine, and he had met Levesque while trying to make sense of a scandal years in the running involving a set of unfortunate Moroccans and the French secret service.

The Moroccans, opposition politicians, had gotten ushered into a police car in some Parisian suburb and were never seen again. The scandal spread, underworld connections came to light, and it was all great stuff.

Levesque, late of Algeria and before that Indochina, was then, as now, SDECE Service 7 and was on the outskirts of the affair. One prime mover in the disappearance was a personal enemy of Levesque's (Jim never learned the real reason why—it was a woman or money or both) named Bauldre, and Levesque decided to get him through judicious leaks to the press, including young James Donald Morgan. Bauldre was cashiered finally for culpable negligence, one of the few, and Levesque laughed a lot over it.

Levesque had a jerky way of moving his head and looking around, a kind of omniazimuth search for enemies—Bauldre wasn't the only one—and warily eyed a boy and a girl standing kissing at the end of the bar. The girl had a red dress on that hung down loose and open like a smock and she wore a white sweater.

An explosion in Munich, said Levesque, eyeing the couple, and the art of it was awe-inspiring. As was the German press crackdown.

Levesque was the first break Jim had had in a lonely and, to him, heartrending round of fruitless sessions with assorted scoundrels.

Coming into town, Jim had taken a cab from Les Invalides to the Odéon and got out where a middle-aged long-hair was peddling something called *La Presse Démoniaque* from a bicycle, babbling to himself and yelling at passersby. Jim sensed just for an instant the guy was police, but the glassy look in the man's eyes was real. Sounds like me, Jim thought. Demoniacal press.

Jim caught a second cab, which took him to his hotel on the Right Bank. Journalists just in from the East get followed here, Jim thought, and he wanted no complications. He knew Paris well and was pretty sure it knew him and was watching. Head down and collar up was the way of it, he told himself, for a time anyway.

The Arab parts of town were dry, though, when Jim went through them, just so many Empty Quarters.

He nosed around Belleville and Menilmontant first, scruffy working-class neighborhoods, where he knew some people. In the side streets and alleys and dead ends off rue des Couronnes and rue des Pyrénées, past the tenements and cold-water flats, the smells are falafel and couscous, stuffed vine leaves, and broiling chicken, and the sounds are Sabah and Fairouz and Umm Kulthum, and it could be Algiers or Tunis.

When he passed the mosque on the rue Charonne, the usual young men were there, off work or out of work, and old men sitting in the tiled porticoes reciting and listening.

Jim ran into cross-eyed Rachide there, a Tunisian who ran a lunch counter in what was literally a hole in the wall in the Marché d'Aligre and who was well plugged into *"Les événements,"* as he called them, and who owed Jim a favor or two. Rachide offered few guesses about al-Jihad, not to mention Shohada, and no specifics.

A skinny track tout with a flurry of smallpox scars on his face claimed there never was an al-Jihad. Two men, he said, two men in a phone booth was all it ever was. And a journalist, a useless, garlicky Moroccan named something-or-other Qisus, pumped Jim about the shah's sister, who had survived that machine-gun attack one late night coming home from the casinos in Monte Carlo. But al-Jihad? They come and go, he told Jim. That one went.

Jim checked out the Moslem Students League (Union des Étudiants Musalmans), Section Iranienne. In a third-floor walk-up well south of the university, he found a thin young Iranian in enormous black-rimmed glasses. Jim tried to have a gingerly discussion with him of Iranian links with Arab students of similar stripe, but all he got was talk about Islamic economy and how the basis of production must be Monotheistic Unity. Automobiles, the young man said, must be produced according to the Five Principles. Jim wandered back out into the haze of a September morning.

So it went, wherever Jim went. The story was the same: al-Jihad's gone under. Or died from attrition. Or died of boredom. Or got too bizarre and was disbanded by the Syrians or the Libyans (or whoever) and got kicked out of wherever they were.

All in all, a blank, and Jim started to believe it himself: maybe there was no al-Jihad. But if there wasn't, it didn't mean young Hoseyn was a figment—tell that to Shlomo Givon—and the bullet that hit Givon was no figment either.

Disconsolate, Jim walked along the Seine and listened to the sad water lap at the *quais*. A couple of fishermen were dangling lines into the river. A barge full of sand was moored just up from the Quai de la Mégisserie. The owners had put out their laundry, and the smell of onions cooking in butter lifted from the craft. To be on a boat in quiet water, Jim thought.

He angled back through the rue de la Huchette–rue St-Severin quarter, and when he turned a corner down there, he saw a sign: "We are with you, heroic Arab-Palestinian People, and not with the Dirty, Fat Jews." Hard to tell the fascists from the Reds, in this city of light as the thin haze lifts and the sun comes out.

Jim drifted up to Montmartre late in the day and hung out in Pigalle, which in the daytime is an old hooker without her makeup. The city was dry and dirty after a summer of no rain, and he found it pretty mournful. Grit hung in the air and lay in the streets, and in the gutters dry trash awaited the cleaners. Sad theater bills, parched and flaking off the walls, advertised long-gone delights. A couple of sad whores were in pretty much the same condition.

Then Jim caught sight of him. He had a black cloth jacket loose like a cape over his thin shoulders. His black hair was swept back the way it always had been, and he had no hat on. He wore the same black shoes with the pointy toes. . . . Just the same and in the same old haunts, Jim thought. All alone, though, which struck Jim as funny. Not like him. Getting careless in his old age? Or am I? Jim looked around, but saw no one. He really was alone, and Jim moved in on him from behind, saying "It's been a long time, Hamide."

Hamide Bourachide turned stiffly and showed no surprise when he saw Jim.

"A while," he said. "You been all right?"

"So-so. How's life treating you?"

"*Ça va.* Okay. It goes on. One amuses oneself."

Bourachide had the same voice that Jim remembered, high and hoarse and tense. He allowed Jim to catch up with him at a crossing at rue Fouchot.

No one was around. It was as good a time as any: "Where's al-Jihad these days, Hamide? Everybody says they've gone way under. Deep as you get."

It was good. Bourachide blew through his nose in amusement. "An embarrassing question."

"Come on, Hamide, some friends want to know. What's the story? Not my money."

Bourachide smiled on just the right side of his face. The left was frozen, put out of action long before in a serious legal dispute over half a kilo of sweet white powder. "I don't know."

"*They* want to know. Badly. How about it?"

"Please, please, I'm a man of affairs now." Bourachide stopped and put his hand on his heart. "I have the respect of my acquaintances."

"You always did, Hamide."

"Yes, yes. You know, I've bought Gianni's place." Hamide resumed walking.

"Refresh my memory."

"Gianni's place—Le Sapin—just down the street. But I'm changing the name, I think. Le Boogie sounds better, you know: it's American. Very chic."

Jim dimly remembered Gianni as a puffy-faced Corsican, whose facial tics were variously laid to (a) the ministrations of a team of anatomists (fellow Corsicans), (b) tertiary syphilis, and (c) too close proximity once to a *plastique* charge at the *moment critique*. As evidence for the last, it was noted that one of Gianni's shoulder blades *was* lower than the other. Gianni had disappeared somewhere.

"Your own place. My felicitations. You're doing well."

Bourachide stared into the distance. "All new decor. Whiskey absolutely as labeled." A point of pride here. "Superior sound system. *Son et lumière.*" Hamide gestured, swinging his arms and rotating his hands. "It will be fantastic."

"You going to fumigate the girls?"

Bourachide made a moue of annoyance. "Please, our staff is entirely new. And high class. Very, very high class."

"How long is the shelf life?"

"Please!"

A tour bus eased past Jim and Bourachide and stopped at the corner. Thirty or forty Japanese males, all wearing blue business suits and hissing like geese, piled out with cameras. A guide formed them up and led them platoonlike into a porno emporium.

"So where are they?"

"Al-Jihad? Ah, such questions—who can answer them? Everything on them is idle speculation. Dust, Morgan. Nothing but dust."

Bourachide ran his right hand over his hair and down his neck, his forefinger lingering to scratch at a pimple. Encountering Bourachide was always a treat. What was he doing? Calculating the value of the goods? Or not knowing a thing and trying to come up with something plausible?

Bourachide lowered his eyelids. "Come on, man, we can't talk here."

"So where?"

"I'll get in touch. I'll tell you what. I'll ask a few friends. Perhaps something . . . I don't know. Where are you staying?"

"Le Palmon, rue Maubeuge." Jim gave him the telephone number, and Bourachide turned off into a side street without saying anything—just waved good-bye and ambled downhill through open-air displays of ladies' underwear and cheap dishes and was gone. Like the old days.

A source. Hamide Bourachide had floated up from Algiers as a boy and ran National Liberation Front messages through the streets of Paris and got a mean education among the Arab pack rats of the *bidonvilles*. There's a picture of him from then in his SDECE file. His thin face and his drooping eyelids gave him a world-weary look at sixteen. He had long, tousled hair and just the beginnings of a mustache.

According to Levesque, Hamide learned to use a razor on others about the same time he learned to use it on himself. In the rickety shacks of the *bidonville*—the Arabs called it the *medina*—all tar paper and tin cans, you could tie a straight razor to a pole and stick it through a window or a corner where the walls don't quite come together or down through a hole in the roof. There was a cabaret song some communist or other had written about the technique, called it "action at a distance," and Levesque thought it was funny and would sing it in a music-hall voice. *"Le rasoir dans le soir,"* he would sing. "The razor in the night."

So Hamide learned his tricks, and after independence, his talents were channeled more into commercial ventures than political, and now, as Hamide put it, he was a man of property.

In the Grand Zinc, Jim mentioned seeing him to Levesque.

"Ah, Hamide, Hamide," Levesque said. "The little shit's gone into editorial work, you know? Passports, work permits, residence visas—that kind of thing."

"A fixer."

"A jerk." Levesque brought his shoulders up and watched the young couple—she in the white sweater, her lover in raincoat—leave arm in arm.

"The Arabs love him in the *medina*. The engravers and the printers, they don't know who they're working for, but they love his ass. It gives him power there."

"He says he's bought a bar."

"Why not? Maybe he has. Sure. Hamide has more up his sleeve than his dirty arm." Levesque screwed up his face. "But in the end, Morgan, he's an Arab waif, a boy of the streets until he dies. Which may be soon."

"Oh?"

"Eh, no, no, no—*nothing!*" Levesque put up his hands, smiling. "Eh, it's just the way things are, you know? He has enemies." Levesque looked around.

"He wasn't very talkative."

"The bastard's insolent. It's his nature."

And al-Jihad?

Al-Jihad?

Levesque tapped his wristwatch twice and raised both hands, index fingers pointing to the ceiling, a way he had of indicating serious thought. Al-Jihad, Levesque said grimly, was a major surprise. Al-Jihad's gone under. Packed up. No forwarding address. Operatives gone, no meetings, no pamphlets, no leaflets, no more posters on the *pissoirs*. "What can this mean? I do not like it." Something had happened.

Further: there was news out of Germany. Out of Munich. An explosion. A dead Arab. He was al-Jihad. Maybe. Jim sat fascinated as Levesque talked. "The man's name, they say, was Salih Tarbulsi. Which means nothing. Tarbulsi. A common name. 'The man from Tripoli. Salih of Tripoli.' Sounds phony, unreal, you know? He came in on a Syrian passport. It looks very official; very nice production. Maybe it really *is* Syrian."

"Have you seen the documents?"

"Yes, and also a photo of his ugly mug. I know him. He was an acquaintance of sorts. We knew him as Suleyman Chemissa. The shit ordinarily carried a Jordanian passport. Called himself a trader. Bought luxury goods, sold luxury goods. Offices and agencies in Beirut, Jidda, Kuwait, the Emirates. A capitalist. Wife, family, house in Amman. Strange to see him in this Syrian form. It's new."

"Did he come in alone?"

"Evidently."

"Syrians saying anything?"

"They say they are investigating and will let our German friends know. They will deny citizenship in any case, but it will take them three weeks to do it."

"So who was he?"

"A courier of some sort. A jerk. We don't know. We may never know. Unfortunate." Levesque shrugged his shoulders and glanced at a blond kid operating one of the pinball machines. The kid was skillful and twisted his body like a dancer as the balls bounded around the machine, his cigarette lying on the glass and leaving a brown liquid.

Levesque told the story, *sotto voce*, his sharp blue eyes back on Jim.

When Levesque first heard about it, he paid a quick call on a friend in Bonn. The friend called himself Eilers, Levesque said, but Levesque didn't think Eilers had ever had a real name in his life. Eilers's pale *boche* face never seemed to register an emotion, either, and that was probably a lifelong habit.

Eilers told Levesque the explosion at Mohrstrasse 312 involved Iranians.

"Mohrstrasse 312 was a safe house," said Levesque.

"Some safe house."

"Yes. They must wonder."

"Israelis?"

"Who else? Every now and then I think one of these operations is G-9, you know? But it was Mossad. Certainly."

G-9 was a special paramilitary police section put together in 1972 after the Munich deaths—bloody apartments in Olympic Village and eleven dead young men—and the rotten performance of the German regular *Grenzgeschütz*. Friend Eilers was one of the founding fathers.

Anyway: "Deceased had entered the Federal Republic from Austria. His passport had Austrian, French, Italian, and Lebanese stamps. The Austrian is genuine. The French and Italian are not. The Lebanese we don't know.

"The Iranians have been under surveillance, of course. Up to now, the Germans had nothing on the little shits to speak of except the usual: demonstrations and immigration irregularities. They're all students who don't study." Levesque shrugged. "The usual."

"Now the Germans have something?"

"Ah."

The Iranians, Levesque said, were associated with a carpet joint called Teppichhaus—Levesque couldn't handle the German and pronounced it Tepisho-Pars. Tepisho Pars was wired for sound by at least three intelligence services and that was a laugh. Tepisho Pars had offices in Hamburg, Munich, and Washington, and was run by a Persian family of innumerable members. The establishment had kaleidoscopic permutations and combinations of residents. Interested in religion, they were, and the Moslem Students League, Iranische Abteilung (Iranian Division), congregates of a Friday evening at Tepisho Pars.

"A network of mullahs runs the little bastards with funds from somewhere. Money comes in from lots of places, Tepisho

Pars itself being a prime contributor. Tepisho Pars sells rugs to the rich *boches* and plows the proceeds into the movement. And there's a network. Has to be. They get people in and out of Iran. Messages. Books. Propaganda. Sermons. The heads are priests, after all.

"So far, just Third World jerks, okay? But in the apartment—ah, Morgan, the apartment. Material in Persian. Pamphlets, books, tape cassettes. The stuff is being translated. It should be good. Photos of Mohammadan witch doctors. All with beards. And lists—these in English, German, and Arabic, not Persian—of Jewish and Israeli places, installations, you know? A few American."

And the lists were long. "There are addresses and telephone numbers—Munich, Frankfurt, Hamburg." Israeli banks—Bank Leumi—the Israeli government tourist office, the Zionist Federation, the Joint Israeli Appeal, the synagogues, the chief rabbi, Jewish schools and clubs, Jewish charities, the Institute for Jewish Affairs. A regular directory.

"No explosives, though. No guns. The place was very clean. Which I don't like. Remember the time some young punks pushed a Volkswagen full of dynamite down a hilly street in Heidelberg to the passing shah? It never went off— there was enough to take out a city block—and Tepisho Pars had its dirty mitts in that for sure. But very careful, they are. Nothing to pin on them."

Pictures of the young men were furnished by the Bavarian State Police. Eilers brought out other photos, older ones, other files, other fingerprints for Levesque. They had pictures of the witch doctors, who appeared from time to time at Tepisho Pars.

"So what are they going to do?"

"The Germans? They will make connections. To other groups, perhaps. To Arab groups, the unfortunate Mr. Chemissa being excellent evidence. Then they will make lists, take pictures, round them up and . . . throw them out. Quietly, though, quietly, you know? The press clampdown has been quite good. *Der Spiegel* hasn't heard a word of this."

Levesque tapped his watch and lowered his voice: "I want the Iranian stuff, Morgan. I want what comes out of Iran."

"Munich, Richard. The names, photos, docs, everything. Okay, Richard?"

Levesque looked around. "Hey, Morgan, you were a bum when I first knew you and you're still a bum." Levesque laughed. "Give me the Iranian stuff. Something else: you go back to Hamide, okay? You want something, you talk to him. Go back. He knows this Munich shit. He knows the Iranians maybe. He's stupid. I want the Iranian thing, Morgan. What goes on in Iran, you tell me. But you just go see Hamide."

Munich was cool and damp. The flight had been a Lufthansa milk run, like taking a subway, and Jim checked through an indifferent customs. A blond, long-haired, uncombed guard, his grease gun on the table, sat reading a newspaper, and paid no attention to Jim or anyone else.

Jim's taxi took him over the Isar, a brown river that flows slowly past the old city through a bricked-in channel, then north into the Schwabing District, where Jim checked into the sleek sort of hotel that travel agents like to recommend.

The Iranians had cleared out of Mohrstrasse 312. The door of 5B was locked, sealed by the police, and there was a police guard on the landing. No go. After a time, Jim found Tepichhaus Pars on the Herzog Wilhelmstrasse. The gold lettering on the window was down low and discreet. The place was open. Business as usual. A manager was sitting behind a desk going through papers. A salesman was showing carpets. Everyone seemed to be about his business. Good ones for the business, they are, thought Jim.

The police inspector, of the Bavarian State Police, was a tall, gaunt man, with white hair and high cheekbones who spoke fine English and was hostile to Jim in it as a matter of principle and, having learned what Jim knew about the incident at Mohrstrasse 312, told him to get the hell out of his office.

Jim filed the story. TERRORIST BOMBING IN MUNICH, he wrote, and gave what names and addresses he knew. Iranians with Arab connections. Police close-mouthed. Very mysterious.

Zimmerman loved it. He'd beaten Springer at his own game on his own turf. Jim wanted no by-line on it, though, and Zimmerman more or less guessed why.

Jim caught a cab to the airport in chilly, driving rain. He had a sour stomach and a slight hangover from a bad lunch in a place called the Wienerwald. German drivers bore down on them from behind in the rain, and they all seemed to be driving black Mercedes. The technique was to pull up within a few feet and flash their brights, then speed around.

Jim thought of Givon and of the lights on Sheikh Hadi and the long walk in darkness along that wall. And Chemissa. A connection here? Fast reaction, if so. Israeli efficiency? Maybe. Jim felt tired and he thought of Pari and ached. Then he thought of Hoseyn. He'd disappeared, gone into the slums of Europe's guest workers, and not Jim, not Richard Levesque, not anyone, knew his whereabouts. Vanished from the face of the earth. The cab's heater threw out warmth, but the warmth dissipated quickly. Day was ending, sodden in the low, flat fields.

2

It was evening the next day when Jim returned to Pigalle. Le Sapin was just opening.

"*Le Hadji*," Jim said to the steerer, a young man with hair combed straight back and a blank look on his face, who wore enormous chartreuse suspenders. The light inside was yellow.

"He's not here."

"Just tell him it's Mr. Morgan. He knows me. Really. It's important. See if you can find him."

The steerer whispered to a heavy middle-aged woman behind the bar, who looked at Jim suspiciously for a moment, then left him to study a couple of whores who were sitting at the bar, bored, shooting craps and waiting for customers. A thick wrought-iron screen separated the dance floor from the main room. Ray Charles was on the sound system, but someone changed the music and the speakers hissed for a time and a mambo came on. One of the girls waved her arms above her head to the music.

Jim watched some Japanese, some English, some Germans, come in. A couple of pimps, who really did wear frilly shirts and *borsalino* hats, strayed in and out, all under the yellow lamp. The steerer tolerated Jim, who had come to see the Hadji, but looked at the clock from time to time. A faint smell of disinfectant came from the toilets down the hall.

When the woman came back, she moved her head to the side and down, which meant, Okay, let him through.

The steerer took Jim to the end of a narrow hall back of the dance floor and opened the door with a key. Steps led down to a basement. Cold and the smell of must rose from below, and at the far end, past crates and barrels, was another door, dimly lit.

"*Là bas*," the steerer said.

The door closed behind Jim as he went down. The steps were metal and they shook under his feet. He could feel his way along a pipe banister. The path twisted through crates, but Jim could follow it in the light. Something small scurried over . . . what? Broken glass? Bottle caps? And stopped.

Bourachide clicked the door behind him and stood there for a moment, his hands behind him on the knob as if he were hiding something. The neatness of the office surprised Jim. Metal chairs, a metal desk, filing cabinets, metal draftsmen's lamps. Beige walls. Bourachide himself wore his black cloth jacket and an open cotton shirt with no tie. The light picked up the scars on his face, the one on the left especially, and it made him look like an alley cat who had seen too many fights. They looked at each other, though Hamide's eyes, like Levesque's, stayed fixed on nothing for long. He was used to looking ahead, around, behind.

Even as his eyes darted, there was a sullen look in them.

"How's business?"

"What you want, you make trouble?"

All right, Jim thought. A visitation from Levesque's colleagues. Not a scratch visible, though. A discreet encounter, no doubt.

"Hey, hey, what trouble? Times are good? How are things? You've got a place now. Times are good, Hamide, huh? Aren't times good?"

Hamide just stared at him.

"Not like the old days, right?"

A pair of legs went past the basement window, and though the glass was opaque, Jim could tell they wore high heels.

"Still into things, Hamide?"

"I keep in. You still a paperboy, Morgan. You still sell papers?"

"Yeah."

"Like the old days. Where you keep yourself?"

"Around."

"No, really, Morgan, where? Where you hang out? You not in Saigon these days." He grinned.

"No. I learned to keep moving."

"Yeah? Well, that's good. Yeah, keep moving. That's what I do. Good idea you do it."

Bourachide's English was quick and dirty and hard to follow.

"Ha, Morgan? The old days? They weren't that bad. You come around and we talk? Ha? Operations? Leading personalities? Strategy, grand politics, affairs of state? Yes? I remember you come around after the Israelis. When they got Kubaisi. Remember Kubaisi?"

Jim remembered. Basil Kubaisi, the Israelis said, was with the Popular Front for the Liberation of Palestine, the PFLP, and he'd come from Beirut. "The Israelis say, 'This son of a bitch is going to make sausage from those Russians.' Ha, Morgan? Sausages? Right?" Russian émigrés headed for Israel, stopping off in Austria, was what Hamide meant.

"So Kubaisi. The Israelis shoot him down right in the street here and you come around and ask, 'Who shoots him down?' and I say, 'Goddamn Israelis,' and you say, 'That checks.' "

"Good old days."

"Yeah. Then two months later they get Boudia. A bomb in the car. In front of Faculté des Sciences. And it was very scientific, you know?"

"Technology, Hamide." Mohammad Boudia. They had attached a time fuse to the door of his car. Boudia got in and sat for a few seconds and was blasted to pieces without even turning the ignition.

"So you come around after the Israelis. Like sunshine after bad weather."

"The Israelis got Chemissa?"

"He's dead."

"I thought I'd talk to you about it."

"Sure." Bourachide smiled. "Okay, we talk."

"Somebody got serious. You know who?"

"Ah, Morgan, who knows? Chemissa? Morgan, the man had enemies."

"Obviously."

"No, I mean it, lots, all over."

"Israelis?"

"It looks familiar. Like Boudia."

"What was he up to?"

"He was crazy, Morgan. A crazy man. They all are. You can't say they were up to nothing."

"Must have been something. Think he just moved in rough circles? They blew his head off, Hamide. Nasty trick. They say it left his lower teeth and sent his uppers across the room. Colorful."

"Yeah, a bad group."

"He was with Iranians. What was he doing with them?"

"Hey, Morgan, you just stay clear, okay? You back off. I don't deal with Iranians."

"They dealt with Chemissa. He was a courier, wasn't he? He came out of Beirut? Messenger boy? Money and directions out of Aden?"

Hamide stared. "Who are you working for, Morgan? Who's buying this?"

"My editor."

"Your editor. Why you think Chemissa was a messenger boy? Ha? Why you think?"

"My editor got it in his head. Don't know where from. Never ask."

"No, you never ask." Hamide paused. "Ah, Morgan, look, you remember all that stuff with Boudia? And the goddamn Israelis everywhere? Rome? Norway? I put in on things nobody ever knew. Nobody." Hamide tried a smile on to see if it worked. "Good old days, Morgan, you remember?"

"Sure."

"But this is trouble. The blood's not dry yet, you know?"

Jim was gentle. "What did they want, Hamide?"

In all the time Jim had known him, Bourachide had never given anything away or told the straight truth. Truth was a dangerous and valuable commodity. You had to mix it with something else to cut it, like putting powdered milk in heroin.

"You know too much. Richard's cocksuckers pay me a visit and you know too much."

"So what's going on? Hey, Hamide?" Jim smiled and his

voice was still gentle, almost a caress. "Not my money. Okay? There's bags of it."

Bourachide stared at Jim, and Jim thought he saw that same world-weary look Hamide had when he was sixteen and had that picture taken.

"Young Iranians. Stupids. He comes from Aden. They been in Aden, see?"

"Sure. So why Munich? What's in Munich?"

"It's Germany, Morgan. Crazy Iranians, they're all over the place there. It's a good place. Easy."

"Better than France?"

"Oh, sure. Lots better."

"What was he up to?"

"With a group. A crazy group. I don't know."

"Doing what?"

Hamide lifted his shoulders.

"He wasn't Palestinian, was he? Where was he from, Hamide? Was he Iraqi?"

Bourachide laughed at the ceiling. "Naw, Morgan. Iraqi? It's a joke. Naw, naw, he was Libyan." The smile stayed at the edges of Bourachide's eyes. "A Lib! What you think of that? Does that check, Morgan? Does that check? A Lib plays around with Iranians and someone blows him up. Now, what you think of that?"

A good question, Jim was thinking, even before Hamide asked it.

"Like he was busy all over, you know? He had money. Key to the slush fund. Chemissa pulled the lever and the money ran out. Like you break the bank in a slot machine."

"Libyan money?"

"Oh, sure. Lots of it. All Libyan, all from Qaddafi."

"How much?"

"They say half a billion." Bourachide laughed. "You believe that, Morgan? Half a *billion*! Man, Meheishi said that, you know? Meheishi talked."

Omar Meheishi had been Muammar Qaddafi's minister of planning and had gotten the hell out of Libya and was living at various locations under various names in France and Switzerland. A man in the know who consented to interviews on rare occasions, Meheishi had phoned the Paris correspondent of Jim's paper from somewhere unknown and they had talked for hours and Jim pretty much knew the gist of it. Bourachide was telling him nothing new.

"So Chemissa spent money."

"Like a king, man, like a king."

"Where?"

"Everywhere. Europe. South America. Africa. Everywhere. He financed the Lebanon war. Sure, a hundred million dollars he spent. He did it. Spent it everywhere. Like water."

"So he was a big boy."

"Oh, yeah. So big. Tops. Don't come bigger, man. He got too big."

"Maybe just careless?"

"Naw. No precautions to take when you're that big. You know? Can't be done. He buys weapons. The best. Lots of it. It all goes to Lebanon. Down comes the Holiday Inn and the Phoenicia. You didn't like the Holiday Inn, thank Chemissa it's gone. He did it."

"It was on the west side."

"Makes no difference. He arranged things."

Chemissa, Bourachide claimed, looked over the camps in Libya at places like al-Kufra, Ghudamis, Sinawan, dusty corrals of barbed wire in the south and on the Tunisian and Sudanese borders. Red Brigades and Italian Fascists were shoulder to shoulder down there, and Chemissa ran them in and out. And checked the weapons transfers. Which, according to Hamide, was powerfully funny.

"It goes the other way, man. It goes to Sofia. It goes out of Lebanon and Libya to Bulgaria. Chemissa was running that."

"Bulgaria?"

"Yeah, man, he was doing it. Big stuff. Bazookas, SAM-7s. There's a warehouse there. It all comes in. The Libs got too much, see? So it goes back to Sofia and then here. London, Paris, Munich. It gets used here. That's the idea."

"Launder Libyan stuff through the East bloc into Europe."

"Sure. That's how it works."

"So Chemissa did lots of stuff."

"Oh, yeah. All over."

"So who nailed him, do you think?"

"Could be anybody. I mean *anybody*."

"Israelis logical."

"Sure. And the Americans, the British, the French."

"Maybe an Arab or two would have done it?"

"Maybe."

"The Germans?" Jim thought of G-9.

Bourachide curled his nose as if examining a bad piece of merchandise and rejecting it. "Not in Germany. You crazy? Nah. Germans are too scared."

"Chemissa came out of where, Hamide? Beirut? Or maybe Libya? What was he carrying? This time, I mean? Carrying something for the Libs? To the Iranians?"

"Okay. Sure. He's a traveler. Everybody knows. No sweat. He's everywhere."

"So maybe he checked things out for the Libs and arranged things, right? What do you think?"

Bourachide stared hard at Jim, maybe remembering the telephone book he took by the side of his head the day before.

"He's liaison."

"On what? There's the question, Hamide. On what?"

"It's open. In the clear. It checks. Qaddafi wants to fuck the shah and the shah wants to fuck Qaddafi. It's easy."

"So there's coordinating to do. New recruits to go to Aden. Arrange the trip. Feed them, scrub them, teach them the trade. And Mr. Chemissa oversees all this. That it?"

"That's it." Bourachide crossed his arms confidently, and when he looked at Jim, he knew Jim wasn't all that sure. Bourachide found that strange, but he had staked out a reasonable position and would Jim please fuck off and let's have no more tricks from Richard Levesque, please?

One last point. Jim saw Elias Hamdani, a Shiite turned out of Lebanon by his own kind, who lived precariously in Paris at Levesque's sufferance. Dr. Hamdani, bearded and youngish, not really a doctor if you put great store by formal study, had heard of the man Chemissa. Jim had shuffled his feet in Hamdani's fourth-floor walk-up waiting room, which was full of Algerian women, scarves over their heads, pitch black Senegalese ladies, hacking old men done in by the northern climate, and squalling children in various stages of diarrhea. Hamdani ushered Jim in in place of a largish mother of five from Tunis in a sack dress who coughed disconsolately and significantly when she saw what was happening.

Hamdani, with his narrow rodent's face and spade beard, talked and Jim listened. The Libyans were about, he said, and, the purity of their anti-Zionist motives aside, were shitting the bed. Why, two flew in from Rome just the other day, knocked off a compatriot named Hamide Gharyun (hosed him down really, just outside the Sorbonne law school) right under Giscard's nose, and were off to Amsterdam by car. "And no one seeks or catches them." It was a plot, an intrigue, *une grande histoire*, and the police knew the whole thing.

"They want no Libyans in the jails here. Too hot. They get their weapons via diplomatic pouch in the Libyan embassy— People's Council—although they could probably have carried them in in their pockets if they had felt like it. Oh, just amazing, these people. It made the papers *two* days after the occurrence. *Two*, I say. And only because Mr. Gharyun's comrades-in-arms protested. Otherwise no one would have known. Astounding, no?"

"Yeah. Chemissa connected with this?"

"Of course."

"How?"

"How. You can tell me some day."

And al-Jihad?

"Ah." Hamdani pulled his head back and looked at Jim under heavy eyelids. "They are stronger than anyone thinks. That is the secret of their disappearance. They are finished in Europe because they are strong enough to return to Lebanon." Hamdani sighed.

3

Bienvenue au Liban the sign read in blue neon at the airport, and Jim was back in Beirut, already feeling that empty ache—and excitement—the place always gave him. A few lights in the surrounding hills had come on in the dim evening and, sited around the airport, antiaircraft guns stood out quite uselessly against the sky.

The driver, thin-faced and blasé, took Jim quickly up the Airport Road with its parched center strip, then west through a checkpoint to the Corniche that circled the city. The sun settling into the Mediterranean looked like napalm. Three more checkpoints and they were in the Hamra area.

The streets were jammed with evening shoppers, always the best sign. That meant there wasn't much war. The Syrians had moved in these days, and sniping was pretty much confined to the harbor where Maronite Beirut begins. Shelling and rocketing, the serious stuff, were almost unheard of in the city. The piles of rubble on the sidewalks were familiar, though, and the blasted walls. Jim had known a Beirut that no longer existed. He had watched it die.

He checked in at a good anonymous little hotel he knew, the Staff House, modest and more or less functioning, just off Hamra, but well away from the media and political types. The windows were in place, but taped over. The same blowsy old travel posters of Crusader castles hung in the waiting room and the advertisements for tours of Baalbek and Damascus that never went and the same sweet-assed life-size cutout of an Air France hostess who had stood there for years smiling and gesturing and inviting people to somewhere else, which all in all, Jim thought, was a good idea. The proprietor, a chubby, middle-aged man with mournful eyes, seemed to remember Jim, but Jim didn't care.

Jim knew whom he wanted to talk to and headed for the Commodore Bar, the media watering hole after the St. Georges got blown to hell. The Commodore was a fine hotel. It was up from the beaches, on the other side of Hamra, owned by a family of Palestinian Christians. It had its own water supply and generator; it had its own telex line and an ample supply of *boissons alcoholiques*, as the menu says, and all this made it a hell of a good place to cover a war from. The bar was dark and narrow and, at those hellish moments of mayhem that every journalist dreams of, was a kind of epicenter of bad news. The correspondent density at such times was a gauge of the amperage of the fighting: when it's worst, you can barely see the bottles.

The weather that evening was hot and sticky—Beirut's that way even at summer's end, the mugginess palpable as a hot towel on the face, and they were still burning garbage in the streets, too, which didn't help matters—so the regulars who valued air conditioning and whiskey were at their appointed stations at the bar.

Horst Kremer, the sage of UPI and *Deutsche Welle*, was there, blond, built like a fullback, who'd been in Beirut forever, and Jean Roule of *Le Monde*, in from Paris, tall and paunchy, with his graying hair combed straight back and beard fringing his face. Mohammad Ali Segal was there, too. Segal, Brooklyn-born and once named Norman, had seen the light of Allah in grad school and Cairo and was now in Beirut. The three of them, Kremer, Roule, and Segal, were together, Segal waving his arms and yelling about the Druzes and the Christians.

Listening to them, rapt, was young Greenline Charley, born Charles Kunkelman, who started life in the East in a camper on the beach at Tangier, hanging out in the *souk* and smoking hash. Though it was beneath his talents, Greenline Charley became NBC's telex boy in Cairo, long-haired and very earnest. That's when Jim got to know him. He got his name when M. A. Segal, then in Cairo, too, told him to piss over to Beirut and collect the tapes and films from both sides of the city and not to worry too much about the Green Line, the snipers' paradise that cut south through town. Charley's task was to courier the tapes out to Athens and civilization, even as shells fell on the airport and Middle East Airlines 707s lumbered down the runways. Charley survived.

There were some European TV people, too, with cameras and lights they had parked in the corners and nobody bothered them for it. It's that kind of place.

So Jim gassed with the bunch of them, mostly about the Christians and the Druzes in the hills, who were doing things to each other. That was the news from Beirut these days. Splendid stuff, they told him, stories that wrote themselves.

Then Dave Gordon of the *Post* showed up. The master. The first man on Jim's list. After desultory nods here and there, Gordon went over to the end of the bar, his usual perch, to a chair pretty much reserved for him, and sat there, alone and aloof and more than a little spooky. Some said Gordon sat there to assign grades to the quality of the gossip, since he knew all truth, and the rest of them put together couldn't match him. Some said he liked to keep his back to the wall, that certain unnamed intelligence agencies—the Syrians? the Iraqis?—were gunning for him. Some others, most maybe, said he was just an arrogant prick. Whatever—for Jim he was a man to see.

When Jim went over, Gordon gave him that curt nod of his. "You're back. Couldn't stay away? Beirut's endless fascination?"

"You're still here."

"What else is there? All we need are bigger and better wars."

Gordon ordered a scotch and Jim got a refill. Gordon was tall and thin, with thick-lensed glasses that made his eyes look too big, all dark pupils crowding out the whites to the edges of the rims. They used to say that even when he grinned he was serious about it.

"I saw your stuff on the Shouf. It was good work."

As it was. The Shouf was a mess. Jim remembered it as pretty villages on mountainsides, white houses and red-tiled roofs and terraces and cedar trees. The Christians and the Druzes were mixed all through it, all of them pretty murderous. Gordon had been up there for the most recent carnage while most of the rest of the regulars sat in the Commodore.

"Yeah, I guess. It's very dirty up there. Really stinking, you know? I'm sick of it. Good and sick of it, so I come in here and get shit-faced," Gordon said.

Gordon was always telling people how sick he was of it and they knew what he meant: shapes once human dusted with lime that public health people had sprinkled on them and that didn't do much good and the sweet nauseating smell of rotting meat; collapsed buildings, the dust still hanging in the air; people whose faces were beyond tears. But Gordon always came back. It was part of his craziness.

"So what's Tehran like?"

"Stinking. Dull. You can't do any work, but it doesn't matter because there isn't any work to do. No truth to know."

"You need a war, Jimmy." It was Gordon's cure, like Jim's for everything. "Maybe you'll get one there. They say the place is full of guys from Saigon."

"Yeah. Same guys. Even the salesmen. It's amazing."

"Station chief's a veteran, isn't he?"

"Yes. So are a bunch of the rest."

"None too comforting a thought. They certainly buggered things up in Saigon, didn't they?"

"Oh, yes, nicely."

"Think they'll do it again?"

"They're very consistent people."

Gordon leaned back in the bar chair. "*Al-Anwar* got the shit blown out of it last week. You hear that?"

Jim hadn't. *Al-Anwar*, a daily, was published in the eastern sector. Five journalists had been hurt in the bombing.

"Eddy Boutros works for them, doesn't he?"

"He was there when it happened. Almost got his designer jeans blown off. Nothing hit him, though."

"Cheers to Eddy's health. Know who did it?"

Gordon shrugged. "Maybe Eddy wanted a raise. Maronites say one of the PLO groups. I don't believe it, but nobody knows."

"Nobody ever knows anything here," Jim said. Except you, Dave, except you. And I could stand some help, sport. Jim studied Gordon. Put it to him, he thought. Get moving. "Look, uh, hey, Dave, any chance for a private talk with you?"

Gordon eyed him and grinned. That was expected. Nobody better than Gordon for conspiracy.

"We'll take a little drive, maybe?" Gordon paid the bill and they drove slowly around the Moslem sector in Gordon's VW, both of them way too big for it. Up on Hamra, most of the streetlights were on and people were out, young men watching the girls. The cinemas had just let out, their marquees half lit and almost sullen. The place had gotten cheaper since Jim had been there last. Poorer people with nothing to do, in from the fringes of town and the camps, just wandered there.

"Look, Dave, I'm into a thing on the al-Jihad group. They still around?"

Gordon looked over at Jim. "Yeah."

Something in the way Gordon answered, the tone, how he turned his head, whatever, told Jim he was into one of Gordon's No Trespassing areas. Gordon, everyone really, had these private preserves that no one was allowed to ask about, and Gordon could be prickly when he was onto something.

"Al-Jihad. Yeah, they're around. So you hear. They are accused of all manner of crime. They are said to regularly shoot up the Syrians, the PLO, the Druzes, the Maronites, the Melkites, and, just once in a while to keep their hand in, the Israelis. They're still nice Shiite boys. You know, word is they're the ones that hit *al-Anwar*. Chucked the bomb right through the door."

"Motive?"

"Bust the truce. Syrians and the PLO mainliners want to keep things quiet in the north. Everybody figures the Israelis are going to begin a push in the south—that's why Jean Roule's here, by the way. Probably you, too. A crowd gathering at the scene of a fatal accident. That why you're here, Jimmy? That it?"

Jim didn't answer. He could see Gordon grinning very earnestly.

"So the saner groups want the rear quiet. These guys don't. They want a shit storm wherever they can find one. Shoot everybody, bring in the Millennium."

"They're waiting for the Hidden Imam to come back,"

Alice Cochrane had once said. "He'll be on horseback and dressed in green and he'll lead them to the millennium in the starry firmament and it'll be the End of Time. If they die fighting for Islam, they'll go straight to the Garden of Delight."

"They in with the Israelis?" asked Jim.

"Some would say so. Maybe it suits them. It's pretty bizarre if they are, though. Why blow away Christians? Too bizarre. And count on it, the Christians will blow away somebody here. Count on it. But it's all a sideshow. The big top is down south. Keep your eye on the border."

"Are the Israelis coming in? You think they're going to push?"

"It's about due. Lebanese regulars are supposed to move into the border area, exchange territory with the Christian militia. Fat chance. The American ambassador has assured everyone here the Israelis will stay out of it and that's the usual prelude to an Israeli attack. It's a real tipoff, they're such dumb fucks. The Americans, I mean. Yeah, it's about due. Gemayel's been talking about it and so's Arafat. We'll get our push. So what are you here for, Jimmy? You here for that?"

They stopped for a light. A kid, his head shaven, selling cigarettes, came to the window on Gordon's side. *"Sigayir, missou! Sigayir!"* he said, and Gordon waved him off.

Jim had rehearsed a dozen ways of doing it, of holding back information while extracting it from Gordon, none of them even remotely plausible. Up front is the only way. Gordon is too smart.

"Al-Jihad, Dave. I'm looking for a guy I think's connected. Can we confirm an identity?"

Gordon turned from the kid, who was being persistent. "Probably not. Who is it?"

Right up front. "A young guy. An Iranian."

The light changed and they kept heading east on Hamra, and the kid stood there back in the middle of the street with his box of cigarettes. He was wearing pajamas, dancing in the traffic.

"You're on to an Iranian thing with them?"

"Yeah."

"Well, they've got Iranians. They've got everything."

114

Crowds surrounded the car from the theaters and Gordon had to ease the VW through them, girls with kerchiefs on their heads in the muggy heat, young men alone or in groups. They seemed aimless. Where did they go when the show was over? Jim wondered.

"Where would he be?"

"I don't know. Maybe in town here. Most likely in the south, maybe with the Amal. There are other possibilities, but that's where good Shiite boys mostly go. Down south. Then they go to heaven."

"This guy's in and out of Iran."

"Does stuff there?"

"Yeah."

They stopped again for a light. They were out of the theater row and the crowds had begun to thin. Gordon puffed his cheeks out, staring ahead at the street. "Look, reporting stuff, events, you know, fights, bombings, speeches, whatever, that's one thing. No big problem, okay? But you're going after some *one*, Jim, some *guy*. That's dangerous. I mean, that's positively lethal, you know?"

"I know. I want him."

"And you want me to help out?"

"Yeah."

"Why should I?"

"You're crazy enough." A point. Craziness was one of Gordon's assets when he first set foot in Beirut two years and three or four lifetimes back. It kept him going, and it was all right for a while, but in time Gordon got frazzled and the craziness turned into something bitter and secret. His friends saw it. The craziness . . . or demons—they didn't know which—drove him and kept driving him to know everything. He pretty much did, everybody thought, including Jim, studying Gordon's profile now, dark against the still lighted storefronts, white refrigerators and crystal lamps shimmering in the showrooms.

Gordon had been there for the worst of it in '75 and the Battle of the Hotels, when being thrown out of the Holiday Inn took on real meaning if the wrong people grabbed you on the fifteenth floor. As the smoke rose and the lines shifted, Gordon wanted to watch it and feel it and smell it and know all the players. Not just their names, but their personalities, how they moved and how they used their hands. He shifted from neighborhood to neighborhood to do it. He wanted to watch them as they got sly and evasive and so learn their weaknesses. He wanted to learn why and where the streets dead-ended into sandbags and flying lead, and then out of town, where the hills rise, he wanted to know who was in them and the logic of geography and blood. Jim thought he did know and thought he hated it. But he kept coming back. Gordon always came back.

"Let me think."

"Sure. Yeah."

They had gotten way over toward the edge of the sector.

"Danny Rizq around?"

"Are lizards around? Sure, Danny's around. He gets worse. Why?"

"Want to get the Christian angle. See a few of them."

"Danny was coming into Chez Temporel when I was leaving. Try down there." Gordon paused. "Be careful. This al-Jihad thing's a bomb."

"I know."

Jim had Gordon leave him off and promised to be in touch.

He ambled down through Zeituni, the old whorehouse district just off the harbor, which had gotten the hell blown out of it in two years of shelling. Old whores still worked it, though, mostly Egyptians, trying to look like Cleopatra, with makeup caked around their eyes, fat, winking, and waving, in *minijupes*, with thighs like watermelons. In Zeituni some things are timeless.

Jim headed left through pastel pink and orange apartment blocks, whose balconies were hanging with bougainvilleas, and, avoiding Hamra, turned toward the beach. The militias didn't stop him.

Chez Temporel was unscathed, one perfect restaurant, surrounded by debris and bombed-out buildings. It had been right in the middle of things, preserved they said, because it served as a field kitchen for the combatants on both sides. Everybody called it Chez l'Immortel after that.

Jim found Danny Rizq in characteristic surroundings in the filigreed and tiled archways of the restaurant. Danny was a

116

Greek Catholic and he had pull all over town, and this got him stories and a by-line in a British weekly that covered Middle East business. He wore a gold necklace and sunglasses pushed up on his head nestled in his thick black hair, and next to him he had a very cool-looking blonde. She looked like the same sweet-assed Air France cutout in Jim's hotel, and Jim figured, hell, maybe she was, come back to life for Danny.

"Jim, well, goddamn! Geneviève, an old friend."

Geneviève smiled as if all of Danny's friends deserved lovely, fresh smiles. She made Jim think of lemon sherbet, daffodils. Exquisitely accented blue eyes. Classic type. The best, the very best. Really Air France? Jim wondered. Was she working the hotels? So why with Danny?

Danny slapped Jim on the arm and his teeth flashed white, and he waved his arm at a waiter. He pointed his finger like a pistol at the waiter, then at his scotch, then at Jim. Old Danny had a way.

"Jim is an American reporter, Geni, greatly *distingué*. Very brave. He eats bombs for breakfast. You honor Beirut, Jimmy. What do we owe our good fortune to? It's been so long, you know. Back in the action here?" Danny liked speaking English colloquially and fast. It looked so fine, like wearing fancy clothes or driving a fast car well. Danny moved effortlessly through two worlds—the Arab and the European—and he wanted both to know it.

"You know, there's not much action right now," said Danny, "thank God. So what brings you here? A routine sweep?"

"I guess. Mostly I want to go fishing, Danny, see if anything's around. Anything up?"

Danny flashed his teeth again and Jim knew he believed *that* story. "Nothing much really," Danny said with a look on his face that meant, You say what's up, you bastard.

Jim's scotch arrived, brought by a fast-moving waiter.

"You know, it's amazing how quiet things are in town." Danny pointed at a large hole in the front window. "That's a month old. Think of it. The hundred-percent last shelling around here was a month back. Half-Ass Asad has put the lid on things for a time and the Phalangists are busy being good Christians, it seems. Very strange. You here to cover *that?*"

"Maybe. I'd like to talk to Pierre Habib."

Danny shifted his eyes a bit and rattled his drink. "Pierre's unavailable for comment, Jim. Permanently."

So. Scratch a source. "What got him?"

"Pure bad luck. A 155 landed on him at dinnertime. A stray. Some asshole just let loose with it. Can you believe that? Ruined dinner, of course. He wasn't alone, either. Four others bought it, all blown to *kibbeh*."

"Where?"

"Well over the line—over there." Danny pointed east with a fork.

"A 155's a big shell. It must have come in like a bus."

"Yeah. But that was a month ago."

Jim raised his glass. "Absent friends," he said. Back to Beirut. It was like visiting a cancer ward. Every time Jim came through, someone was missing. A good source, Pierre Habib. A Maronite Christian on the political end, he had run intelligence for the Lebanese Forces. A good source, dead at thirty-one.

"How about Michel Khoury?" Michel was Pierre's second-in-command and just as smart.

"Ah, Jimmy, you're so good. He's replaced Pierre, at least temporarily. You see, Geni, he's *so* good, isn't he?"

She smiled at Jim again with her perfect blue eyes and wide mouth.

"Temporarily?"

"Until the next stray 155."

"Any way to see him?"

"Easy, but not in *this* part of town. You want to cross?"

"Yeah."

"The phone directory isn't worth a shit these days. Neither are the phones, and he has a new address anyway. You go through the Sodeco area. It's a little out of the way, but the Ring gets tense, even these days. The taxi drivers over here will take you. They circulate. No sweat. When you get to Michel's place, you want to be a little calm, you know? No fast moves." Danny wrote the address out with a felt-tip pen on someone else's business card he had collected and gave it to Jim.

Jim left Danny and the blonde (she never became Geni to

118

him), who were sharing a *terrine de canard* and looking out the window at the sea. A few white gulls still circled over the gentle waves, which were dark and capped with incandescent foam. A light in the harbor, some marker buoy, shone right through the shrapnel hole.

Jim memorized the address and tore up the card and threw it away. The driver of the first cab Jim flagged bounced his head backward and gave a sharp tsk with his tongue, the ageless curt refusal in the East. The second agreed, but at a *prix fixe* Jim used to pay for a trip to Damascus. The third asked more or less the same, and Jim figured that was the going rate for this time of night and got in.

He didn't give the exact address at first, just the general area, the Eastern way.

Syrian regulars waved them through two checkpoints, neither of which did much checking. A sergeant at the second gestured across a square at a street angling off. The square was small and empty, and a line of frondless palm trees ran down the center past a couple of metal park benches, chewed and twisted from the shooting. The buildings around the square were two stories high and all of them dark. In the moonlight Jim could see they had been blasted out and gutted. The Green Line.

The sergeant spoke nonchalantly with the driver. All Jim could understand was *"ma'leish,"* "no problem," which, he supposed, was a comfort.

The street opposite was no street. It was an alley, arched over with a second-story passage between two buildings. The arch looked wrecked to Jim, but it still hung there, linking nothing to nothing.

The driver brought the taxi slowly around the square to the alley opposite, and nosing into it, blew his horn and flashed his lights, and moved up to the checkpoint. Sandbags piled neatly cut across half the alley and two 50-caliber machine guns and a recoilless rifle poked out of them. The driver tried to be reassuring, smiling at Jim in the rearview mirror and waving his hand up and down, saying, "Okay, okay."

Five or six young men in fatigues and black undershirts were lounging around looking bored, like armies everywhere when the shooting stops. One was playing a cassette tape. The music was jazzy and electronic and sounded vaguely Italian. A boy with a wooden crucifix around his neck put his head in the window and the crucifix dangled into the car. He checked Jim's passport. American. He smiled and said, "Very good, very good," and waved them through.

Jim became increasingly precise with his directions and he could see the driver get a cagey look on his face. The driver finally stopped the car and pointed down a street to a line of office buildings just on the edge of the Dowrah commercial district.

"You go there," he said, and added, "*C'est par là*," just for good measure. He took Jim's money, folding the various-sized bills dexterously, and backed his Impala away slowly and was gone.

It was quiet. For the first time Jim heard that low rumbling far away in the hills—the Shouf—like distant thunder back home on hot evenings when the weather is set to break and storm. Only here the weather won't break. Jim knew the sound, and knew there wasn't anything like that in Minnesota.

The address on Salib Street was an arcade called Passage Mizraoui, and the entrance was thickly sandbagged. A permanent brick wall stood in the middle of the sidewalk, which you had to go around. Mercury arc lamps lit up the whole street in yellowish blue, their connections buzzing and sputtering from the humidity.

Walk to the side and show your face and hope they think it's too pretty to shoot up, Jim was thinking, and he moved down the street with what he thought was great aplomb, when a voice barked, "*Haut les mains*."

"Hey, sports. Great. Good to see someone. Okay. I was getting lonesome." Jim put his hands in the air and stopped walking. Grin and keep talking English. "Terrific. Anybody home?"

"*Silence!*"

Jim shut up. Two men came out of a doorway on the opposite side of the street. Both had M-16s leveled at Jim's chest, and Jim felt hands grab his belt from behind. Two men on each side behind him, he figured. They pulled him forward and one of the men with the M-16s stood in front of him and stared, holding the gun pointed at his face while someone frisked him from behind and removed his wallet and passport. They stood him up against a wall, feet well out, balanced on his arms, while someone went through his wallet. All the papers were in English: press pass, ID, international driver's license, a couple of hundred Lebanese pounds.

"What you want?"

"I'm a friend of Michel Khoury's and I'd like to see him. How about it?"

"No here. No Michel Khoury."

"Hey, swell. Come on, I'm press. Honest. I mean it's *important*. You know? Like life or death? He won't like it if I don't see him. Honest." Jim kept his smile on though all he could see was wall.

The man hesitated, then disappeared with Jim's papers, and after a time, when Jim's arms had gotten good and stiff, he felt a tap on his shoulder.

"Okay, you come."

They took him into Passage Mizraoui and up four flights of stairs (the elevator was out of commission and the air conditioning was off and everyone was sweating). Michel had the whole floor, Jim figured. Maybe the whole building. They conducted him down a corridor lit only from open doorways, and Jim could see sullen groups of men in the rooms talking in hushed tones, staring out at him as he passed.

No victory celebrations here. Why all the gaiety? Something up? What the hell is it? The warm reception downstairs. Crowds on the fourth floor. Down the hall someone was using a shortwave set, the hissing and static faint, cut off when transmitting. Sentries were standing at windows at each end, but well out of sight from the street. Too close to the Green Line. Bab Idriss was an easy shot away, and Jim noticed the windows had no glass in them. A guard looked at Jim and pointed to an open door. Michel was sitting behind a metal desk.

"*Bon soir*," he said simply. Jim's papers were on his desk.

Michel offered him whiskey with ice from a tiny refrigerator.

"To your health and safe arrival," said Michel and blinked. His eyes were large, and he had a way of closing, then opening them one at a time that made each seem independent of the other. His neck was thick and his head seemed to rest right on his shoulders; he had the general demeanor and build of a frog.

"Yours," said Jim and sipped the whiskey. It tasted fine.

"It's been a long time, Jim. Where have you been?"

"All over the place. In and out of the world."

"It's been too long."

Jim had known Michel back when he was running intelligence in Jounieh port, living in his father's mansion—the Palais, they called it—surrounded by Greco-Roman statuary and Arab miniatures and a regiment of servant boys in white T-shirts. Michel had no women, preferring the servant boys, and his favorites among them, doe-eyed and languid, were shut up like Turkish catamites with the Damascene wood carving and tile arabesques of the Palais.

But Michel had run intelligence in the port with cool efficiency (he had the piloting concession, too), and then went on to bigger things: liaison with the odd groups—Palestinian and Lebanese Moslem splinters that had no use for the PLO. He'd been in and out of Israel, courtesy of Mossad and the Israeli coastal patrol, and back in Lebanon he kept seconded Israeli guerrillas under his wing in the northern mountains. He hated the PLO; he knew them well, their personalities and family ties, their strengths and weaknesses. He knew their order of battle, if you could call it that, north and south.

"Hey, Michel, you're not much different. A little less hair, huh?"

Michel grinned. "Maybe. You're a little fatter?"

"Yeah."

"It means you've led a good life. Please forgive the formalities downstairs. You understand." It was an order. Michel talked that way.

"No problem. Sure. That's the way of it." Jim looked around. The room was almost bare, pretty different from the Palais. A glass-topped metal desk, one old-fashioned black telephone, maps of the city and the country on the wall, with markers stuck in them. A Lebanese flag furled in the corner, a photo of Pierre Gemayel, the Phalangist leader, taken long before age had cut away everything but the man's meanness. A fading poster with the emblem of the Lebanese Forces, green cedar tree on a red field, stuck to the wall with thumbtacks. One corner was loose and curled upward.

"I've shifted quarters. How did you find me?"

"A mutual enemy. He told me about Pierre."

Michel's face didn't react. "A loss. You remember Elie Bashir and Raoule? They were with him."

"They say it was a stray 155. Does anybody believe that?"

"Until we find out who did it, it was a stray 155."

"No luck yet?"

"We'll get them. We know everybody's address." Michel blinked again and wiped his face, and Jim caught the unsteadiness in his hands without even looking for it. Too much whiskey, too much thunder in the hills, too much sleeping in a different place every night because you don't want some stray 155 landing on you. There it was, plain as day.

"Lot going on these days, Michel? You still bringing the stuff into Jounieh?"

"Oh, yes." Jim noticed the hint of a question in Michel's voice. Just a hint.

"Business good, I hope."

Michel smiled. "Never better." So Michel had kept the harbor master concession and collected on everything coming in. Michel was customs as these things are done in Lebanon, and put a tax on everything. The radios, the videotapes, BMWs, spare parts, Moet & Chandon—everything. Some went to Michel, some to the *kitayib*.

"So, what's the party about, Michel?" Jim pointed out to the hall and the men.

Michel paused. "One person made a mistake."

"What happened?"

Michel looked away. "Oh, he was very incompetent. He had an accident. Out in the harbor." He looked back at Jim and winked.

Right. That's the Michel Jim knew.

"Business or politics?" Jim asked, as if there was a difference here.

"Please."

"Poor bastard probably tried to get around the Lebanese Customs Service. What do you think? Am I close?"

Michel waved his hand. It was a kind of agreement.

"Who was it?"

"One of no consequence."

"I won't print it."

"No, you won't," said Michel. "Whiskey?" Michel was being touchy these days. Whoever the unfortunate never-to-be pilot was, old Michel is sure ready for his friends. Expects them to come in here with a battalion by the look of things. Waiting for air strikes and tanks the way they're lined up.

"We can talk about old times," said Michel, "but that's not why you came."

"No."

"What do you want? Exclusive interview? Why did you come here?"

"Editors are on me, Michel. They've given me marching orders. Got to do some things on the groups. Size up the teams, pick the winners. That kind of thing."

Michel was very alert. "Okay, so we're the winners. Figure it. You want anything else?"

"Hey, that's no good. Can't help a friend? Editors are on my ass, Michel, no kidding. May have to buy my own way home. You know? I need copy. Any old thing."

"Go talk to the PLO."

"Sure. But I need the old indigenous angle. The Lebanese internal situation, including the mean ones and the bad ones, like you."

Michel didn't laugh. He always thought Jim was something else besides a journalist, maybe CIA, maybe not, but if not, then *something*, and Jim had sensed it early on, had never done anything to disillusion Michel, which gave him some leverage and seemed to loosen Michel up. Being with a fellow practitioner, he could be clinical about things, so to speak, spook to spook.

"Michel, who's running the al-Jihad group out here these days?"

Jim loved asking questions. It was like dynamiting fish.

You never knew what could float up to the surface. The technique was to keep the questions short. No leading. Don't even nod your head. Ask the question and shut up. Let your victim do the talking. Funny, so many of them really feel obligated to fill up the silence. Even Michel.

Michel smiled that smile of his, which was just a little oily, and his staring frog's eyes never left Jim. "Where did you hear of them? Do you know of this group? How do you have knowledge?"

Caught him, thought Jim. A two-by-four right between the eyes. Banged him and woke him up.

"Hey, Michel . . ." Jim made that what-the-hell-is-this Arab gesture—you hold your hand palm up, point your index finger to the ground and pump your arm up and down.

"They are elusive. They have little protection. They don't enjoy an easy existence. The Syrians or the PLO pick them up now and then. Their ranks are very much thinned, I believe." More whiskey for both of them. Michel splashed it over the ice but didn't freshen the ice, and the drinks were mush now in the heat. His nerves are raw. Whiskey not doing the job.

"Who's running the show here, Michel? What's the leader's name? Must have a name."

"Jim, what is this? What are you doing?"

"Looking around."

"The leader they call Captain Heydar," Michel said slowly, looking closely at Jim. "They're always called Captain Heydar. There may have been a dozen Captain Heydars in the last year. Thanks to the Syrians, as I say, there's been a rapid turnover."

"The old revolving door."

Michel shrugged.

"Where do they get their troops?"

"The south. Of Lebanon, of Beirut. The organization is in place. But even there, you know, their existence is most precarious. They are not like the rest of them."

"What's the difference?"

"They are Shiites, a crazy people. God talks to them through their imams and He tells them pretty crazy stuff. They beat themselves at special times. You know? Times of mourning? Very terrible. Very savage. Blacken their own eyes, bloody

125

their own scalps, with swords." Michel raised his eyebrows and lowered his head and looked benignly at Jim. "They'll bloody yours, too, my friend, if you get too close. They're not nice people."

"Can I find them?"

Michel stared balefully at Jim with his frog's eyes. "They're enemies of the PLO, Jim, and of the Syrians. And they're survivors, you know, they're good at hiding. They fade away. I don't think you'll find them. And if they think you're coming, we might have to ship you home in a box." Michel paused. "What in God's name do you think you're doing? This is very stupid. What do you think you want? Really, what?"

"I want a story, that's all. No secrets in Beirut, Michel. Not between friends." No truth either, thought Jim. That was the other side of it. Everything is public and nothing is certain. "Hey, come on, Michel, I want to make some connections. Honest. Scout the terrain. That's all. Seriously. Might make good reading for the rag."

"You're crazy."

"Michel, you think everybody's crazy?"

"Maybe everybody is."

"Anyhow, I want an introduction."

"From me."

"Just a way in. A little background is all, Michel."

"And for us?"

"For the sake of future business. Scratch each other's backs."

"What will you do with this 'way in'?"

"Have a talk with the troops. Print what they feel like saying—subject to my editors' rotten sense of news, of course." Jim grinned what he thought was an honestly rueful grin and hoped Michel bought it.

"I cannot help."

"Hey, come on. You've done me a lot of favors, Michel. How about another?"

"The best favor would be to put you on a plane. Tie you up"—Michel was laughing now, a soundless and, it looked, mirthless shaking of the shoulders—"drag you out and send you to . . . where? Where? Where are you from these days?"

"Around."

"Yes. Okay, we'd send you out. Where's *my* favor? Newsmen, you always want favors." Michel had stopped laughing. "You know?"

"We're the salt of the earth, Michel. We're not all that inconvenient."

"Information is your business. You buy and sell it. Al-Jihad's sense of insecurity is well founded. Life is dangerous for them. Information gets around and people die as a consequence."

"Not my game, Michel. Best to leave the pieces in place. Might have future business with them, too. All in all, in my trade, best not to be considered lethal."

Michel smiled. "Just the opposite for me. You know, they gave me my first gun when I was six. I was very little and the gun was very big, but I learned to strip it down and put it back together. We love our weapons here."

"Yeah. How about it, Michel?"

Jim could see Michel studying his face and knew there was nothing there to study. Michel shrugged. "For the sake of future business . . ." Michel wrote something on a piece of paper and gave it to Jim. "Don't carry this around. It might explode."

Jim looked at the note.

"What do you want for Christmas, Michel?"

"Just give me tomorrow. Where are you staying?"

Jim told him.

"Call them and tell them that you're stuck over here for the night, because you are." Michel put up his hand. "It's best. You can try if you wish, but believe me it's best. Another thing. If you mention my name, no one will believe you, but I will hear of it. Is that understood?"

Right. Too hot to be subtle tonight.

Michel looked away. "Be careful," he said finally. Interview over.

It was a rotten night on the floor, door locked and hot as blazes. It seemed to Jim that he spent much of his time in Beirut on some floor or other. Once, a couple of years back, when all hell had really broken loose in town, he was camping out with Nigel Stevens—*London Times*—in an apartment with no furniture on the Christian side that Stevens had inherited as the *Times* man. On the floor. There was no water and the electricity had been cut off for days and they both stunk like hell. And that kid—what was her name? Naomi something?—up from Israel on a one-month contract with *Newsweek*, washed their underwear in water she had hauled up five floors. She hung it out overnight on lines between the buildings, and by morning snipers had shot them to shreds— just white cotton tatters hanging from clothespins. They all bought new underwear.

Sweet Naomi from Philadelphia, with her slender legs and motherly bosom, had been on a kibbutz before her *Newsweek* stint, and they made her buy an Uzi there and she was smuggling it back into the States in pieces. "I bought it for a hundred and thirty-five dollars. It's mine and I'm taking it home," was what Naomi said that hot night. She assembled it for Jim's benefit and edification, and it sat on the floor there looking mean and simple and workable. Nigel had disappeared into some cellar, Jim hoped forever, and Naomi was the only thing *Newsweek* ever did for Jim. Old days.

He was hungry as hell on Michel's floor by this time. He'd had no dinner, just whiskey at various points around town, and he kept thinking of the *terrine de canard* Danny Rizq was eating with Geni. And he thought of Geni, who was perfect, and then he thought of the Pear, and wondered why he was such a dope. Bring her a present from old Beirut? A hand grenade or something? She could wear it around her neck. Be the hit of the season.

Jim got rid of Michel's note long before leaving the eastern sector and had a change of clothes and a shower and breakfast at the hotel and felt pretty good.

4

Jim checked in at the *Daily Star* (it was still being published), whose society editor, a lanky poetess with long, straight black hair, and not much society to cover, was stringing for Jim's paper and selling heirlooms to keep alive. Her family was an old one, and large, sad eyes seemed to run in it. From stuff he heard from her, Jim typed up an innocuous color piece on the city and phoned it in.

Greenline Charley, shuttling between various telex transmitters in town, was doing a thing on hash farming in the Bekaa.

"Hey, we're talking agribusiness here. Five hundred mil a year. The PLO taxes it. It comes out in boxes and they put little stamps on it. You believe that?"

"Sure."

Charley wanted to do a thing with Jim. "The shah's sister sells opium, doesn't she? Let's do it. Roundup of the Mideast Drug Trade. Survey of the Capitals. Who's Who in the Smack Business. Like it?"

"Get us all killed, Charley. Count me out. There's no truth to know in Iran anyhow. It's all fuzz."

And Gordon. Jim decided Gordon had had enough time to think about young Hoseyn—twelve hours, by Jim's lights, was more than enough. Gordon had a fancy flat in Ein Mreisseh. It had a French-style telephone of which Gordon was very proud. The curtains were shiny, the windows had glass in them. On one wall hung a watercolor of a caravansary, the sun hot, the camels loaded, water-bearers with full goatskins on their shoulders, brass cups in their hands, palm trees, the works: some local Armenian's fantasy of the days under the Ottomans.

Against his better judgment—he'd told Gordon too much already—Jim told him the address he got from Michel, and even Gordon was surprised.

"I know them," Gordon said slowly, "and life isn't always what it seems." He got up and strode back and forth in his shorts and sandals, with his glass of hot tea, straining to figure it. Did Gordon know too much and so make too many connections? The man was baroque.

"Michel deals with the odd ones, he does," Gordon said. "He gave you Tahrir Islami."

"Does that make sense?"

"Might. They're fuzzy-wuzzies. You know them?"

"No."

"You're out of touch. Greatest thing since Stonehenge for the copy. On a dull afternoon, you do a thing on Tahrir Islami. The home folks"—that's what Gordon called his editors, the home folks, in fact a cabal of humanity-loathing skinflints, to hear him tell it—"the home folks love it."

"So anyway, they're fuzzy-wuzzies. Small, but weird. No telling who they are or who they deal with. Maybe they're a holding company, you know? Or *poste restante* for various and sundry other fuzzy-wuzzies? It might figure. It's that kind of name. It means 'Islamic Liberation.' What is friend Michel telling us?"

Gordon was bobbing his head. "I've been there. My, my, my, things *do* get Byzantine. They're in an eerie little back street down toward the racetrack. Not your high-rent district. You ask around because you can't find the place right off and nobody knows what you're talking about, right? Of if they do, *they're* not talking. Or they tell you it's been shut down. That kind of stuff."

Gordon sat on a bolster and stared off at his painting of the caravansary and Ottoman ease. "You find the place eventually, okay? Over the door, they've got this big green silhouette of the Imam Hoseyn in a V formed from crossed Kalashnikovs in fists. Heavy. He's got a halo, but you wonder about those Kalashnikovs. And there's always a crowd outside, young guys in blue jeans and T-shirts hanging around in the shadows. I mean it's weird. At night, and you get the full effect only at night, there's one light shining down on the picture from above the door, and everything's shadows. It's a one-story building, crummy looking place. No class, Tahrir. The neighborhood's pure Lebanese, though. People moving in from the south, most of them Shiite, and that's where Tahrir gets its troops, I gather." Gordon was nodding now. "Poorest of the poor. Farm boys, mostly."

Michel was saying, Gordon concluded, that al-Jihad had linked up with—or maybe was—the frizzy-haired weirdos that had stationed themselves up and down the museum crossing, the ones that maybe hit Meloy, the American ambassador, in '76.

"And Hoseyn is with them?"

"Well, they're Shiites."

Gordon looked at Jim. "You trust Michel?"

"Sort of."

"Yeah, 'sort of.' That's a problem, Jimmy. Michel's an Israeli operative."

"I know."

"They take everything seriously."

"So does everybody around here. It's a serious place."

Gordon let a moment go by. "Well, you don't want to be on the wrong side of Michel, *comprenez*? They've got reach, even over here, and if you have to go over there . . ." He pointed with his tea eastward and raised his eyebrows. "But who does the reaching for him over here? And why does Michel want Tahrir to get to know you? There's a question, Jimmy. Got an answer?"

"Milk of human kindness?"

"Maybe you'd better watch it? They're not stupid. You come out of Iran. Maybe they know something happened in Iran. Maybe they figure that's what you're after. Maybe that's not so healthy." Gordon poured more tea and stared at his shiny curtains, which were closed for the sake of the glass in the windows.

"So what's the story, Dave? You in?"

"I don't know." Gordon raised his eyebrows. "High risk, Jimmy. I mean high risk all down the line. You, me, everybody. You're going after some *one*."

"I know."

"You've got big ones. I'm surprised you can stand up." Gordon hesitated. "What'd this Hoseyn do?"

There are times, Jim told himself, there are times when we are honest. When it actually pays. This, God help us, is one of those times. Bombs away, sport.

"Killed a guy," he said, and more or less told the truth as he knew it to Gordon, who smiled and nodded and said, "Yeah, yeah," as Jim talked.

"Has he been in al-Jihad? Is he now? Where did he train? To do what? Any friends? A general fix, Dave, a general fix. But very discreet. They can't even know we're asking."

"Shit, you can say that again."

"He'll be just out of Iran. Might not be here. Might be in Europe."

"And he was just in an action."

"Yeah."

"Only one to get out, they figure."

"So they figure. The name's probably a fake, but maybe not. The action wasn't, though."

"It'll cost money."

"It's around."

"Go halves on this?"

"Can't. Just a favor I might never pay back."

"You shit. Tahrir's where we look for brother Hoseyn, Jimmy. And it will take three or four guys. There shouldn't be any tracks. We'll pop it down the line. Everyone'll cost money, but we present it right, it won't cost all that much. It'll take time, though. Might have to go to Aden and back."

"That's okay."

"So we'll start it going and let it percolate."

Gordon didn't even bother to ask what Jim was doing on this. Gordon would go halves in his own way, Jim knew. Gordon figured a thousand U.S. would do it. Jim would scare it up.

Jim stuck around for a week and took a tour of the south with Greenline Charley and Mohammad Ali Segal, hoping for an Israeli raid. Gordon, Roule, Kremer, the others, had vowed to wait in town, specifically the Commodore Bar, till it hit the fan, which was no telling when. They'd been right, Jim concluded, when he filed no story save a thin analytical piece (PLO checkpoints unfriendly and nervous . . . Israeli air force sonic booms . . . Air of expectancy . . . In Sidon, commercial life goes on . . .) plus expenses. No Israelis.

Jim left for Tehran. Gordon would manage the Tahrir thing. From a distance. He caught an early flight and got in by midmorning. Pari met him.

"Hullo, Pear. They fire you at the bank?"

"Ha, ha. Took the day off for the return of James Morgan, Newshound. I read your stuff—exhilarating. I don't think I want your head blown off, though."

"Hey, hey, don't look for it, Pear. I keep my head down."

Pari, who drove Bucephalus back to town, was voluble on the way in, the chief topic of conversation being Devlin the bum-patter, who was going back to Yukay and how everyone was happy about that, but Jim—maybe it was guilt, maybe he was right—sensed the talk was forced.

Jim knew he was away too much and couldn't talk about half the things he did and wouldn't talk a lot about the others. That was a bitch, and he tried to compensate with holidays and knickknacks from around. Pari had collected, among other things, a cedarwood box from Damascus inlaid with camel bone and mother-of-pearl and good for not much, an absurd blue porcelain hippopotamus from Cairo (Eighteenth Dynasty and fabricated in Luxor the week before), black-stained wooden clogs from Kabul with pieces of mirror in the heels. They, at least, had character. These he would turn over with an embarrassed sort of shuffle at the airport, if she met him, or at home, and she was young enough to like them (as well as the embarrassed shuffling) as Eleanor hadn't liked either.

Pari went to André, an Armenian delicatessen, and came back with cold cuts and French bread and beer and cheese.

At lunch they talked of Paris and Beirut, and Pari wondered, "Shall I call you Ace or shall I call you Scoop?" She had an alto voice that made Jim think of burgundy wine and wonder why he ever went to places like Beirut.

"They call me Our Man Morgan at the embassy."

"Good God, you mean they don't respect newsmen?"

"They think the press gets it all wrong."

"Well, it's a good name. I shall call you My Man Morgan. Okay?"

And he told her about Hoseyn. "He's a killer, Pear, but that's not the whole thing. Lots of killers around. More killers than we know what to do with. But he had a reason for hitting Givon. The Israelis are up to something huge, I swear to God. Nobody knows what, and that's the reason. Hoseyn knew what and didn't like it."

"What are you going to do? Interview him?"

"I might. At least profile him. Figure out who he works for and then find out who the hell *they* are. And find the motive. The Israelis are thick with the Iranians. And thick with the Americans. So maybe there's a deal. Maybe something's going on." He shrugged. "Or maybe not. Maybe the Israelis are out there by themselves, all alone. And that's not so unusual, you know. Just about right, really."

"What have you got?"

"Curses, spells, and incantations, Pear. That's about it."

After lunch, they went to bed, waking in the late afternoon. Jim traced the indentation in the side of her slender hip with his fingertip. Whiter than expected at first, and Pari resting on her stomach, looking up at him slyly. The Feminine Principle.

The Pear made sense. He wondered, have a kid? Never got around to it with Eleanor, who might have turned out all right for it really. Had the tits for it. Feed a brigade.

Pari was on her back now, studying his face, arms up under her head, face serious. Pear the Observant.

"Penny for them, Pear."

"You. You want this so badly."

"There's a war on, Pear. And nobody knows about it. That's what makes it so stupendous. Just super."

The room was shaded and she couldn't see his eyes in the dimness, but knew they were open in that stare he had when he was Onto Something, figuring motives, weighing the power of adversaries, divining the outcome of some conflict. Though their bodies were touching, he'd be away from her at those times, as far away as Beirut, as Munich, as the moon.

* * *

The young man from the French embassy was blond and stylishly dressed and had a bright look on his face. He wore shiny, high-topped shoes. He didn't say a word, just walked through the courtyard, around the blue pool, up the five or six steps to Jim's first-floor office, waved hello, deposited the packet, and waved good-bye. Bizarre, Jim thought.

The packet contained Xeroxed deposit slips in Arabic (with translations) for a bank, Banque du Proche Orient et d'Europe, address: Mazraa Avenue, Beirut. Jim was quietly thankful to Richard Levesque and friend Eilers, who had supplied the stuff out of Munich.

A note was attached to the slips: "Banque du Proche Orient et d'Europe (Bank of the Near East and Europe) is part of the Salem Trading and Investment Company, President and General Manager, M. Charles Salem. Telephones: 682900-6. Telex: 22861 SALG LE."

The payments were large, multiples of $10,000 mostly. They had been deposited monthly, more or less, running from autumn of last year to one month back. They had been signed by Suleyman Chemissa.

Jim arranged them in order. The last was dated September 10. Chemissa died on the fifteenth.

The slips showed no balances, only the account number (120101), the date, and the amount. The figures totaled $129,400.

Why to Lebanon? Jim asked himself sitting there in his office in the dark. Because that's where they have assets? A feint through a Christian bank—Charles Salem, being a good Christian name—is very nice. And Mr. Salem doesn't know where it comes from. Probably thinks it's Libyan. As indeed it might well be. And why the Libyan connection? Why Mr. Chemissa? Libs financing al-Jihad? Maybe Shohada? Who else? Tahrir Islami?

Eilers had also supplied a list of names recovered from the sundry documents of Mohrstrasse 312. Hoseyn Jandaqi was one of them.

5

Ariel Netzer strolled down Kakh Street, his limp, which favored his left side, almost unnoticeable. A bullet fragment or rheumatism—or both—had lodged there long ago. Though he despised Iran, he liked the street his legation was on. He liked to walk under the tall poplar trees that line Kakh. He liked the activity he saw on the street, the work, the bustle. Shops here seemed to open halfway onto the sidewalk, where carpenters banged and sawed, making beds, shelves, wardrobes; where shoemakers, greengrocers, locksmiths, plumbers, and florists practiced their trades. The whole bourgeois workaday world of the urban East lay open here.

Two cables had come in. Together, they had sent Netzer out for a nervous walk. One, from Bonn, read,

SUSPECT HOSEYN JANDAQI NO LONGER UNDER SUR-
VEILLANCE OF FEDERAL REPUBLIC POLICE. HAS ELUDED
OUR SPECIAL UNIT SEARCH. POSSIBLE STILL IN FEDERAL
REPUBLIC. RETURN TO IRAN VIEWED UNLIKELY.

They've lost him. The Germans have, we have, Ehud Cohen has. We had everything on him. On all of them. We had their names, whole lists of them. Fingerprints now, whole bales of them. And he's gone.

The cable had a Jerusalem address, as well as a Tehran one, the PM's office almost for sure. Since when did the PM take an interest in tragicomedy?

The other cable was out of Tel Aviv. A report from Beirut, sourced to Lebanese Forces. The informant was NORE-FERENCE (Tel Aviv was sitting on things as usual). An Ameri-can out of Tehran named James Morgan is investigating the terrorist group Shohada, said the report. The American is a reporter. That was all. Just a stray paragraph in a roundup of Ha Qirat gossip, sandwiched between a short note on what some bureaucrat claimed Cy Vance really thought of West Bank settlements and a thing out of Damascus on the Saudi family connections of the Syrian defense minister.

This Morgan, who was he? Netzer had asked Uri Gellerman, who kept a watch on the press, about the man. Gellerman knew Morgan and didn't like him. And yes, Morgan had in fact mentioned something once about Shlomo Givon to a military attaché named Ramat. "We put the fire out."

"You didn't tell me, Uri? Why didn't you tell me? This wasn't right. You should have told me."

Gellerman shrugged. An oversight.

"Sure, fine. An oversight."

Well, thought Netzer, idling on Kakh, an American reporter is asking questions in the wrong places. Netzer had a spy's contempt for persons who tell stories in public. How much more interesting is the private reality, he thought, how superficial the front page.

Was Morgan on it? What did this Morgan know? Were there others? He had asked that, of course. Tel Aviv knew of none. Uri Gellerman knew of none. Or so he said, barring an "oversight," thought Netzer. But if this Morgan is on it, what about the U.S. embassy? Was this Morgan CIA?

And what do *they* know of Givon? Netzer wondered. The Americans. And beyond them, who? How much is out? Then Netzer began to wonder just what his life was worth. To die in Persia?

Netzer stopped and peered into a bakery, his hands clasped behind his back and shoulders hunched in an old Slavic mannerism he'd never lost, and watched flat sheaves of bread bake quickly on white hot beds of pebbles. He'd said to Meir once, "Why, from the legation to the palace"—the Marble Palace, the Kakh-e Marmar, which gave its name to the street—"there are four different kinds of bakery, four different kinds of bread. Extraordinary."

Would they? Netzer moved on. Is this fear, or was he just getting old?

Netzer distinguished age and experience. The former he tried to disregard, but he knew deep down that age finally would take him. He thought he recognized age in moments of caution. He worried about that. Once he caught himself lifting his legs slightly when starting a car. He had seen too many photos of explosions, good, complete police series of course, very clinical, and when he turned the ignition key, he caught his legs moving ever so slightly up and away from the floor. That, he thought, was age, and it troubled him.

Netzer paused by a newsstand. The evening papers were out, with their black and red headlines he could not read. The magazines were done on cheap paper with cheap printing. Singers and actresses on the covers, the ladies with heavy mascara and soulful expressions, the men with spade beards and long pompadours that looked like lion manes.

A Turkoman in from the East with a carpet over his shoulder squatted in the wide *joob*, dry now. The Turkomans, they always look as if they're sizing you up, thought Netzer, looking at you from the edges of their Mongol eyes. These people don't laugh. He had a white turban around his head, not the Khorasani type with the long, trailing tail, but the short cotton kind, from up around Astarabad, and he wore a long gray shirt that came down to his knees. The carpet he carried was simple and geometrical. He ignored Netzer.

Netzer passed a florist's shop, where fancy cars pulled up—BMWs and Mercedes and the like—and fancy people got out to buy flowers, the standard Persian gift of guest to host.

He wandered south in the evening light, under the poplar trees. The days were shorter now, the weather chilly. The smell of roasting beets wafted from a vendor's cart.

To die in Tehran? They may succeed. He walked past high walls, covered with vines that surrounded a *pied à terre* for the shah's idiotic brother, and down the way on the other side, he knew, was another for the shah's whorish sister. Long may they reign. Netzer grimaced in contempt.

When he arrived at Shah Reza Avenue, all the signs of a royal appearance were there. The avenue, a wide east-west boulevard, was cordoned off and the traffic kept off it by police in white gloves and white hats and blue uniforms. Mercedes patrol cars prowled up and down. The drivers had loudspeakers and yelled *"Yallah! Yallah!"* at anyone who dared get in the street. The shah was indeed making an appearance, and traffic was tied up through the western end of the city. The armored Rolls-Royce, gold-colored, rushed through the empty street in silence, in from the airport, the shah lying back, his thin face just visible. Was he bored? Netzer wondered. Did he wave? Did he look at the crowds? No one applauded. Then he was gone, and Shah Reza Avenue returned to its customary chaos. The sidewalk merchants went back to hawking Levi's at three times their American price, and the lottery ticket salesmen, the poorest of Tehran's poor, went back to waving the blue and yellow booklets of tickets, crying, "Winners, winners, get your winners here!"

As Netzer drifted back north, he felt it. It was as if someone had laid a hand on his shoulder. He felt it. Someone in the street, someone behind him. He had a sense of it and it wasn't age. He wondered who they were, his eyes dreamy, seeing but not seeing the street, the shops, the passersby. Is it you, Hoseyn? Are you real, after all? A friend of yours? Who? He walked into the legation without looking back.

They learned of Carmen from Sara Khanom, for old women are grand observers, she whom the schoolchildren teased as she made her way in the *kuchehs*, bent over, her wizened old face working God knew what emotions of her seventy-seven years, eight children, and many deaths.

"*Ho, ho, tariaki!*" the children would yell. "Ho, ho, the opium smoker!"

Sara Khanom lived among numberless relatives on the first floor of Givon's apartment building, and thanks to her, the sharp scent of burning opium regularly wafted up the window well. Her scarf around her old head, her husband long gone, Sara Khanom sat and smoked away her days.

When the men came asking, Sara Khanom said yes, she knew of the whore, and yes, she knew her whereabouts.

The whore was Armenian, Sara Khanom had told them. An Armenian named Carmen, and Givon was with her often.

"That night?"

Oh, yes, that night.

It was enough for them. They had asked many questions, but Sara Khanom had put them off and pretended to be more fuddled than she was, and when she told them of the whore, they went away and left her alone, which was the idea. Sara Khanom was not uncooperative. She had lived her life among Moslems, and she had no hope for Jerusalem, not next year, not ever.

They grabbed Carmen a bit down Iranshahr Street, not far from the Lausanne Hotel. They had pulled the car over and chatted and fixed a price, and after some talk, she had gotten in. She became frightened in the car and had begun to scream, and then they handcuffed her and gagged her, smearing her lipstick. They called her Armenian whore and scared her to death.

She was pretty. She had a thin face, no pockmarks, only a *salak* on her cheek. She had good hips and legs.

SAVAK sent the interrogation transcript via regular liaison to Netzer, who read it carefully alone in his office at night.

"You are a Christian," her interrogator said. "Your name is Carmen. Carmen Hairepetian. You live close to the Sheikh Hadi intersection. You are a whore. You are a whore and a killer."

"No!"

"Yes. And you are political, which is why you are with us."

"No!"

"Who are your accomplices?"

"Please, I beg of you, I beg of you, I do not understand."

"You killed a man."

"I don't understand."

"You understand too well. We deal with the politicals. The ordinary police deal with common criminals. You know the police well enough, though, do you not? For you are a common criminal too, are you not? Who are your accomplices?"

SUBJECT FAINTS.

"We know who you are."

"Yes."

"We have been watching you."

"Yes."

"A man died, Carmen. What was the arrangement? Tell us, Carmen. Only tell us."

INTERRUPTION.

"You are being held because a man died. It was in the month of Ramazan the Auspicious, only a few weeks ago. Think. On Sheikh Hadi, Carmen. You were there, Carmen."

"No, I—"

"Only speak, Carmen. We must know, Carmen. You asked to meet him there. You asked. Why then? Why there? The man you saw. Think, Carmen, it was late. The man you saw. Why then? Why at that time? You know he is dead. You heard. What did you think when you heard? That your accomplices had succeeded?"

"No!"

"You established a regular liaison. In the neighborhood, Carmen, it was known, you were seen. With this foreigner."

INTERRUPTION.

"By God, by God, by God . . . He was nervous. He sent me away."

"When did you see him?"

"I don't know."

"What time?"

"Late. At night. Three o'clock. Late. It was late. It was always late."

"And?"

"I saw him."

"At his apartment?"

"Yes."

"Did you have intercourse?"

"No."

"Why not?"

"He did not desire it."

"Why were you there?"

"We had arranged."

"Before?"

"Yes."

"How long before?"

"We would meet. He would arrange."

"You arranged it at your last meeting?"

"Yes."

"You had intercourse then?"

"Yes."

"He desired it?"

"Yes."

"But not this time? He did not desire this?"

"No."

"Was it ever so before?"

"Sometimes. Yes."

"Did you always meet at his apartment?"

"Yes."

"Did you go out?"

"Sometimes."

"Where?"

"To the cinema, to a restaurant."

"You are political."

"No."

"That's why you are here."

"No."

"You led him out?"

"I left."

"You led him to his death."

"No!"

"Yes."

And then, Netzer saw, they walked her through it, though the girl could hardly talk. Where she and Givon had been, what they had said, where she went afterward. Especially that. Givon had told her to walk north on Sheikh Hadi. A friend would be there, he had said. A friend was to meet her, a good man. "I would tell him my name. We would arrange a meeting." She stood on Shah Street, conspicuous, afraid of the police. She stood and stood, she told them, and the man never came.

"Givon had lied to you?"

"The man did not come."

They blindfolded her, Netzer knew, when they released her. That was the way they did it. They emptied her purse and dropped her with a few bus tickets—flimsy pieces of white paper stamped with purple Achaemenian wings, the symbol of a long-dead god—in Zhaleh Square, far from home and late at night.

It was a drop, Netzer thought. Carmen was the signal. So

obvious. The late hour, even the newspaper he was carrying fit.

They knew of the drop. They had arranged it.

"The man did not come," Carmen had said.

But he wouldn't have come to meet Carmen; he would have come to meet Givon. He was a traitor. And he did not come.

Who was he? Who did not come?

Yoram Kohan sat in his Land Rover on the side away from the pedestrian pavement, watching the cars approach. They reverse the traffic on Kakh during the day; it's one way north for evening rush hour. Kohan's Rover was parked the wrong way, absurdly.

A fuzzy pair of dice, chartreuse with blue dots, hung from the rearview mirror. The leaves had turned and charcoal smoke drifted in the street. It was warm in the car, though, for the afternoon sun, low now behind walls and buildings, had heated it.

Then Netzer walked past as scheduled. He paused far down at a telephone booth and made a call. Kohan detected no change in the flow of pedestrians. Nothing happened. Someone was banging with a coin in his hand on the glass wall of the booth. Was that it?

Netzer came out. He was very cool. He looked the person straight in the face and walked away. Nothing. He disappeared in the crowd and Kohan waited. When Netzer came back up the other side, his face had no emotion. He wore a beret and his green raincoat. Not bad to get rid of that sometime, Kohan thought. He wears it all the time. The only one he owns. A trademark.

It worked, though. They had come. Audaciously, today as yesterday. They double-teamed him. One on each side of the street, one pausing as the other moved ahead. One had been there the day before. One was different. It was good work. The imprint of Moscow on it. Out of where? Kohan wondered. Libya? Lebanon? Aden? Moscow itself? It was how they did it when they were being subtle. A drifter way ahead, with the tail for emergencies. Sometimes they put five men on a route, like post horses or runners in a relay race. Passing on the baton, the first tail leaving off altogether, the second becoming the tail with the third moving beyond. Moscow. Good chess players. Good runners.

Kohan caught both of them full face and got a side shot of one. The photos were good. The one he caught with a side shot was young, of medium height, lithe. Moving with grace, said Kohan when they talked about it later.

He wore a black sweater, a brown jacket, and brown trousers slightly flared at the ankles. He had short hair, beard trimmed neatly. They didn't know him.

They staked out Netzer's place with a parked van on Moshtaq Street, around the corner by the vacant lot. It was driven during the day by one Sioon Babazadeh, a wheeler-dealer in auto spares down on Naser Khosrow, where all the tool and hardware shops are, who lived close to Netzer's flat and by arrangement let the thing be rented occasionally at night and who could be persuaded to park it on Netzer's street.

The light was good from the concrete lampposts, but no one lingered there in the *kucheh* by Netzer's gate or stood in shadows down the way. No one even drifted by the place to pause suspiciously.

They didn't know why. It worried them.

6

Jim was back in Beirut, sleeping on—what else?—the floor at Charley Kunkelman's unfurnished apartment. They were lucky, Charley assured him, to have water.

Gordon had nothing yet but proclaimed sterling prospects. Jean Roule had returned to Paris, Horst Kremer and Charley were spending their days endlessly practicing snooker in an underground game parlor down from the Danish embassy, and Mohammad Ali Segal was incommunicado (he had gone on a heroic bender, for convert though he was, Islam and its injunctions rested on him lightly).

The political officer at the American embassy had a slight Southern accent and he asked no questions about Jim or his motives, and Jim began to realize that Fiscarelli operated far beyond Tehran. His name was Doug Wyndham. His suit was neat. His hair was cut.

The embassy in those days was just off the Corniche, down with the fire-blackened hotels and restaurants, its windows covered over. In the streets and alleys behind, PLO gunmen with *kleshens*—that's how they pronounced Kalashnikov—and dressed in fatigues stood guard protecting the building. They were very casual, and Wyndham found them jolly.

The name Charles Salem was an eyebrow raiser, Jim found, for the man in Jim's absence had acquired a certain local fame.

"I know him. Oh, Lord, do I know him. Just a minute here." Wyndham unlocked a file and rooted through dusty folders with red and white Immediate Attention tags stuck on them God only knew how long ago, his back to Jim, mumbling,

"Where is it, where is it, where is it?" and then in a kind of singsong, muttered, "Aha, aha!" and returned to his desk with a fat manila folder, and fished out cables, his face suddenly weary. "Try Beirut 2839 for starters."

Jim read an account of how one Charles Salem, Lebanese, was wanted in the Federal Republic of Germany for defrauding German companies of some five million deutsche marks and how the Lebanese government refused, by act of parliament, to extradite him.

"Great!"

"There's more. Try Beirut 0981." Wyndham handed over another cable marked "Confidential" and Jim ran his eye down it:

SUSPECTED OF RUNNING A CONFIDENCE OPERATION THROUGH WHICH FOREIGN GOVERNMENTS, COMPANIES, AND CITIZENS ARE INDUCED TO PAY COMMITMENT FEES ON BOGUS LOANS PROMISED AT VERY LOW INTEREST RATES. . . .

PRINCIPAL BUSINESS IS TO RECEIVE AND RETAIN FUNDS FROM WOULD-BE BORROWERS UNDER THE PRETEXT OF ENTERING INTO CREDIT ARRANGEMENTS WITH THEM. . . .

MR. SALEM IS WANTED BY THE GERMAN AUTHORITIES FOR FORGERY, IT WAS REPORTED BY THE LEBANESE OFFICIAL GAZETTE DATED APRIL 13, 1977. . . .

IT HAS COME TO EMBASSY BEIRUT'S ATTENTION THAT THE MOST RECENT KNOWN TRANSACTION BETWEEN AN AMERICAN BUSINESS FIRM AND THE SUBJECT LEBANESE COMPANY APPEARS TO HAVE RESULTED IN A LOSS BY THE AMERICAN SIDE OF DOLLARS 562 THOUSAND UNDER CIRCUMSTANCES SUGGESTING FRAUD. . . .

Wyndham put his middle finger under that last sentence and made a rude noise. " 'Suggesting fraud.' *I* wrote that. State taught me how to talk and write. 'Suggesting fraud'! Charley Salem's a cheap, motherfucking shyster, is what I should have written. There's more. Try Beirut 3094."

SALEM APPARENTLY HAS CLOSE TIES WITH THE LIBYAN GOVERNMENT AS WELL AS PALESTINIAN LIBERATION OR-

Like al-Jihad? Like Shohada?

"Mr. Salem smells like a rose," said Jim.

"That's our boy. Crooked as a dog's hind leg. The FBI wants him, the Germans, the French, the Canadians. Very popular man. In great demand."

"At parties and stuff. Why no extradition?"

"Too many friends, too little law here these days."

"So they pass a *decree?* I mean, the parliament passes a decree?"

"Yep, Ol' Charles knows lots. He deals, you know? Man'll sell anything. A Picasso, a woman, a fighter-bomber. That's his charm."

"Yeah. This stuff about 'Palestinian gunmen,' is that true?"

Wyndham screwed up his face. "Well, the Charles Salem Establishment for Trade and Investment does have armed guards all over the place. Looks like a fire base, in fact. And they are, we believe, Palestinians. But PLO?" Wyndham shook his head. "I don't think so. There was talk about that for a time and it was strange, very strange, because the PLO actually took out an ad in *Mideast Digest* to deny the rumors." Wyndham fished out a Xerox of a quarter-page magazine ad. It had a black border:

SALEM TRADING AND INVESTMENT COMPANY (STIC),
BEIRUT
Please note that neither the Palestine Liberation Organization, nor any of its departments or organi-

zations, have any relationship with Salem Trading and Investment Company (STIC), Beirut.

Faris Ramlawi
London Representative of the PLO

"Wow."

"Extraordinary, really. They claimed all the rumors were Israeli disinformation. Probably were." Wyndham smiled. "Mr. Salem is well connected. No shit. Not like the PLO to take an ad out in a magazine if they don't like you. Ordinarily they have other ways of dealing, you know? The man's got family somewhere in the structure. Maybe all through it. Maybe there are payoffs." Wyndham looked at the ceiling. "Did I say that? Did I say, 'Maybe there are payoffs'? That's thinking from an earlier life. In addition to the payoffs, I meant, there must be something else. We've never been able to figure it, but you know it's there. Has to be."

"He gets Libyan money?"

"That's the rumor. Everything's circumstantial, of course. Nothing on paper."

Jim thought of those deposit slips scattered around a cheap apartment in Munich—dates, amounts, and account number—and thought of Levesque and Hoseyn.

"But the theory makes sense," Wyndham said. "The Libs bring money in here, right? What form it comes in is kind of a question of purpose."

"Yeah?"

"Well, what do you use it for? For one thing you pay off the locals you support. That you do in cash. Best all around. No questions, probably damn few records—maybe somebody's fingerprint on a voucher that goes back to Tripoli, okay? And you buy whatever stuff around town you need, also with cash, also better all around. But, figure. What about other places? Other stuff? Suppose you want to buy stuff in Europe. Big stuff from halfway reputable places. You don't do it out of a bag from the embassy. You do it legit. But you need an account, preferably dummy, with as little paper as possible in the possession of blue-eyed foreign devils. Which is where Beirut comes in. In effect, there are no banking laws here. Hence"—Wyndham sighed—"people like old Charley and his Banque du Proche Orient et d'Europe, SA. Letterheads, telex numbers, post box, board of directors, projects, checks, money orders, letter of credit services—all of it totally bogus, son. Nothing to it. Just paper. Paper and Charley. Plus some money, of course.

"Charley claims to have everything. He's got twenty-eight ships floating on the deep blue waters, but he won't name them. He says he acts as agent for two hundred and fifty foreign companies, but he won't name *them* either, except in phony lists for suckers."

"Figments?"

"Visions of cherry plums." Wyndham coughed gravely with a look on his face that meant everything here is just too weird and then, with a tone in his voice that was the verbal equivalent of a nudge in the ribs, said, "Mr. Salem is reported to have benefited when the banks got knocked over." The Banco di Roma, Jim remembered, and the British Bank of the Middle East were hit by commandos of one stripe or another in '76. Nobody ever figured out who it was. Wyndham thought the event capitalized Banque du Proche Orient et d'Europe.

"Upshot," said Jim, "the Libs launder money through Charley and it goes to Europe to phony companies there, and they buy stuff with it and nobody knows it's Qaddafi."

"There it is," said Wyndham.

Hence the importance of Mr. Chemissa, thought Jim. Delivery boy. And the Iranians. Use a Lib for protective coloration. Only Iranians would think of it. There it is. QED.

Wyndham put Jim at a spare desk with the Salem file and ostentatiously went about his own business. Jim sifted through the stuff, some of it with stratospheric classification levels, and knew that after giving it to him, Wyndham would try to snooker him into playing spook. They all do. It's their nature. Dogs bark, monkeys climb trees. It's their nature. After the trade with Fiscarelli, though . . . what? Maybe he'd lost a little something? But Jim put that thought out of his mind. Let's not get amorous with them all, sport. Save it for marriage. Jim didn't know what Fiscarelli had told Wyndham, but Fiscarelli knew nothing of those deposit slips or Suleyman Chemissa and Jim would keep it that way.

Jim ran through the documents. Newspaper reports, interviews in the local press (bought and paid for by Salem), cable traffic from Washington, a World Traders' Data Report that read:

> Local bank provides following assessment on Salem Trading and Investment Company:
> —Financial situation: confused.
> —Morality: leaves something to be desired.
> —To be avoided.
> Embassy recommends that the U.S. Department of Commerce give wide dissemination to general alert on subject.

In a Xeroxed letter the U.S. Council of Better Business Bureaus (Industry Standards Department) noted that Salem's three U.S. lawyers were of "questionable" status, each having a problem or two with his local bar association and each showing a rare talent for disappearing.

From the U.S. embassy in Paris:

> Economic officer learned that Salem is using the following two individuals to help him work his confidence game: Pierre-Yves Graziani, a Swiss national, apparently involved in banking, whereabouts unknown, and Stefan K. Tupov, 88 rue Clichy, 75012, Paris, tel: 241-51-71, telex: 721426 F, reportedly Bulgarian, who, according to U.S. businessmen, is director of all Salem's activities overseas. Graziani is apparently young (mid-20s) and Tupov is in his 60s and claims to have excellent connections with important American and European business and official personalities.

That was a good one. Jim would wing those two back to Levesque and see what happened.

There was a report on a session held by major Western commercial/econ officers in Beirut solely to discuss the problem of Charles Salem. The Australian section read in part:

It is not certain that Salem was absent from a series of scandals involving Middle East financiers and members of the Australian socialist government in 1973–74. The Australian officer present stated that because the government had fallen partly as a result of scandals in the Middle East, any case such as Salem's carried strong political implications in Australia. The officer then discussed one of a number of frauds that occurred this year in which Salem had swindled real estate developers in Queensland for an amount he estimated as A$300,000. When the Australian victim sought to press his case in Australian courts and had come to Beirut to confront Salem, Salem advised him to forget the whole matter if he wished to leave Beirut alive. The man dropped the case.

Jim found, finally, receipts for cash signed in an uncertain Latin script by Charles Salem himself. The cash had been donated by one Douglas M. Wyndham, Intelloff Beirut. The sums were low, the dates not recent. The politicals and the commercials in the U.S. embassy, Jim was not surprised to note, had different priorities.

"Charley's a bagman?"

Wyndham looked up from his papers. "In his foolish youth. The relationship has soured."

"Somebody scare him?

"That or he's become an honest man. The former, as we say in our reports, is more probable." Wyndham leaned back in his chair. "Everybody's backed into a corner here. Know what I mean? Everybody. Especially guys like Salem. It makes everybody dangerous."

Gordon had said that even though things are quiet, it's still like the old days. Night life pretty much ends at nine. You crawl into your hole and pull the hatch down over you, for in addition to the militias, there are mere gangsters in the streets, thugs pure and simple, except they carry grenade launchers.

Jim thought hard about those gunmen at the Salem Trading and Investment Company.

At Charley Kunkelman's Jim found a package. Gordon on his way to Tripoli on some story of his own had dropped it off.

It contained a photograph of a young man. He had short hair and just the beginnings of a mustache. He was neatly dressed. He wasn't looking directly at the camera. The photograph was commercially taken, a portrait, probably a birthday or graduation photo. The subject looked like a choirboy. It had "Studio Rouhani" stamped in English on it. On the back, Gordon had written, "Hoseyn Jandaqi."

7

The Salem Trading and Investment Company, Charles Salem, president, was a sight. When Jim went there, he saw three white Mercedes with drivers parked outside the flamingo-pink four-story building on Mazraa Avenue. It's there even today, where the avenue bends away from the coast, though the Mercedes have long been liberated.

Guards in military fatigues lazed around on pink plastic chairs on the ground floor. They had Kalashnikovs, but no signs of rank or allegiance, and probably didn't have much of either, Jim guessed. One who sat behind a gray metal desk motioned Jim to the elevator, and they didn't make a search, even out of boredom. Wyndham had made the appointment; Jim was expected.

The elevator stopped on the fourth floor and opened into an empty chamber. A door opposite slid open electronically and a neat young man in white shirtsleeves with little epaulets and a dark blue tie—he looked like an airline steward—showed Jim to an anteroom off the main office area, where Jim fidgeted for half an hour while telexes banged and telephones rang and secretaries typed.

A preposterously beautiful girl brought in tea and smiled as she poured it into a very delicate china cup. Her skin was porcelain white, like the china, and her hair was jet black and her wrists delicate; her long, thin fingers were like finely carved ivory. She had on a white blouse, and her breasts hung forward as she poured the tea. Jim watched with marked interest as she left the room.

On the coffee table were magazines and newspapers—the *Economist*, *Le Monde Arabe*, the *Daily Star*—which Jim thumbed through without looking at them, till finally the door opened: "Ah . . . you come from Doug." It was the great man himself, Charles Salem, industrialist, smiling, standing motionless in the doorway of his inner sanctum.

"Come, come, come," he said and made a kind of pawing gesture in the air with his right hand that meant "approach." "This is a quiet place from troubles of business. We have commerce with the world and the world comes in. No good for thinking."

"Guess not."

Salem brought Jim into his room over thick carpets that bounced back like trampolines to a couch and a chair, both made of rosewood and chrome and leather and money. With his hand gentle on Jim's elbow, he gestured toward the couch, then sat down in the chair. They studied each other's faces for a moment of silence. Jim was the new boy from the embassy and wasn't sure he looked the part.

Salem did, though. He was exquisitely manicured, barbered, and tailored. He wore a cream-colored silk suit and a wide intricate silk tie and too much cologne. His eyes were large and moist, and he would have been handsome with less weight.

"It's too long we haven't seen Doug, Mr. Welles." He pronounced the name "Well-us" in a liquid throaty voice.

Jim declined the Havana cigar. Behind Salem, lamps and ewers that looked Phoenician or Roman stood on open shelves. When Salem saw Jim looking at them, he smiled. "The antiquities, ah, yes. I love the antiquities. The heritage of my country."

On Salem's desk lay a fluted glass bowl. It was cobalt blue and had a rim of teardrops. "Roman!" said Salem, and smiling, passed it to Jim. "The antiquities, they are very beautiful."

"Yes." Jim admired the bowl and wondered how long ago the thing had been made. A month? A year? Two millennia? No way to know, not in Beirut.

One window ran the full length of the room and looked west over the Mediterranean. Jim could see a single white motor launch far away easing slowly around the beaches and out of sight. A fine day.

"So, Mr. Welles, it is good pleasure to see you."

"My pleasure. Doug sends his best."

"Yesssss—you!" said Salem and reached forward and tapped Jim on the hand and laughed. "And is pleasure. How is Doug? Doug is well?"

"Oh, sure, super. Couldn't be better. He hopes things are going well with you. Business good, Mr. Salem?"

"Ah," Salem angled his head down, a man overwhelmed with the weight of things. "Now we are so busy here. We fight for the reconstruction of Lebanon, as every sincere Arab must. Our duty, our duty."

Salem recited his lines like a kid's part in a school play, and Jim's face must have shown the boredom, for Salem shifted his weight in the chair, leaned forward, and raised his voice. "It is our obligation. You ask Doug. We set up the largest number of factories, regardless of personal profit. Right now we are improving Lebanon not with the guns. No, no. That is not the way. We are improving with the capitals."

Jim stared at Salem and thought of Chemissa in Munich and Michel over on the east side in Passage Mizraoui with the windows shot out.

"For example, we establish the cement factory, we set up iron foundry—first in the Middle East—we have license to build cars, prefabricated houses, plastics. The Salem Group does all this, Mr. Welles. Yes, oh, yes. But our cooperation with all the embassies too is correct and good, and we especially appreciate American concern for the well-being of Lebanon, and we always wish to help our friends. And so, we are so busy, Mr. Welles. How can we help Doug? Doug and you? What can we do?"

Jim eyed Salem and figured he pretty much knew how to play him, had that figured sitting in the embassy sifting through the paper on him. Item: The PLO are unhappy with him. Item: He's here thanks to the kindliness of the Syrians. Item: He's been trafficking with the Americans and that can be dangerous. The payoffs, Jim had seen, sitting at that empty desk Wyndham gave him and staring at the police reports, the payoffs came from Wyndham, though the commercials didn't like it. Plain as day. And Wyndham was a certain kind of protection. But now Salem has danced away for whatever

155

reason and he wonders what the Americans have in store for him. And one final item: Chemissa. Who could be the kiss of death for all manner of men, including Charles Salem.

"Well, first of all, Mr. Salem, let me say that Doug has always valued the relationship. He has. That's sincere."

Salem smiled, as expected, and folded his hands on his desk, saying, "That is excellent."

But Jim quickly modulated to a minor key: "There are problems, though, you know?" He squinted at Salem. "Tough ones, sometimes. For him. And in the embassy."

"What sorts problems? We solve. You tell me, we solve the problems." Salem was very expansive, leaning back and blowing cigar smoke at the ceiling.

"Well, not so much for you to solve, see, as for Doug," Jim said, still squinting. "On all sides. You can't believe it. But, still there is the need to know." He paused. "And the need to help friends."

Salem's mouth was a little open and his hands were motionless, and Jim could sense the alertness under the flab. Play it right, sport, he thought.

"Problems can arise. Misunderstandings. You know he doesn't run the whole embassy."

"No, of course not." And smiling again: "It is too bad. It would be a most excellent embassy if he did."

"There are others there. In the embassy, I mean. Military. Other politicals. Police. You know? Not everybody agrees on everything. People in the commercial section, for example, Lebanon being a prime business area even now for sales." Salem's eyes drooped a bit and Jim thought it must be a way Salem had when he was listening carefully.

"Some of the commercial people feel it might be better to restrict some of the advisory contacts. It's crazy. There *are* commercial reasons for doing it, of course, and other reasons." Jim had dropped his voice; Salem hadn't moved. Jim got the sense, though—and this was fine with him—that Salem somehow had stiffened without moving.

"But dropping contacts . . . I mean for a man like Doug, it's crazy. I mean, contacts are *everything* for him. The man *needs* them. Can't go around throwing away valuables, you know? That's what contacts are—valuables. Right?"

Salem was waiting. He didn't even nod.

"It would make life difficult. Doug wants to avoid that."

Salem still didn't react. He just sat there.

"The commercial people are making big trouble. Doug has to have something, you know? He's got to be able to go to them and say, 'Hey, I know this guy,' or 'Hey, I know *that* guy and he's okay, he's helpful. He's a friend, not an enemy. We can't roll this guy up. We can't pull the floor from under him. We've got obligations for good work.' That's what Doug has to have, see?"

Salem nodded, but his face was unreadable, and he spread both pudgy hands on his desk. He wore a wide wedding band.

"Doug, we work together," Salem said.

"Yeah."

"I mean cooperation. Real cooperation. Back when the Syrians move in. So the Syrians know the U.S. viewpoint. And the Syrian informations. They are donkey people. What Doug wants to know, we find, yes? We find. It is not easy. The connections, yes? I have the connections. So what problems in the commercial section?"

"Well, to be blunt, Mr. Salem, allegations that Doug kind of overlooks too many things. In his zeal to know, I mean. Things *do* have to be looked at in the *total* perspective, the big view. How everything fits together."

"Yes, of course. Ah, yes. and *I* say this. It makes the greatest sense, does it not?"

"Sure. Anyway, Mr. Salem, we've got these problems with the commercial section and Doug thought you ought to know."

Salem nodded tightly, and seemed unsure whether to be grateful for the news. The man's on alert, Jim was thinking.

"We are the most helpful. We sincerely appreciate American role in helping the rebuilding of Lebanon. Can we help you? That is what we ask. That is all we ask."

"In fact, yes. We're looking for . . . ah "—Jim moved a little closer to Salem, a between-you-and-me tone in his voice—

"we're looking for a special kind of information."

"Ah, Doug, Doug, he is a man who wants to *know*. I mean *know*. The completest. How he wants the details! But we oblige. We are happy to oblige. He is good friend. The object of your interest, Mr. Welles? The special informations?"

"There is a group here. We thought perhaps someone of your wide contacts, Mr. Salem, might be familiar with some individuals in it."

"Ah."

"The al-Jihad group."

Jim thought it was funny how a face could harden and freeze a smile when you trip the owner. Salem's face was stopped action.

"Very difficult," Salem said quietly. "And very unimportant. They are not of importance. Why is Doug wanting this?"

Jim spread his hands.

"I mean they are small, you see?" Salem said. Jim thought the questioning look on Salem's face was genuine, the puzzlement of an expert.

"Can't really say. Wants to know all the players, I suppose. I'm just an errand boy." And I've got no idea what you're making of this. Not the faintest. He's turning it around, though. Thinking about Doug. Thinking about Chemissa. Which way to go? In or out? Salem is looking very cool. Pity the Krauts. They will never get this man. And then, maybe I won't either.

"Al-Jihad is problem." Salem smiled at Jim, his eyes just so slightly narrowed. "Hard to find. No good here. They move from place to place. They have no place of fixed abode. No, sir, they move."

"There must be some around. Who are they? What does the name mean?"

"The name? It means 'struggle.' The name is meaningless. Everybody struggles. I struggle for Lebanon. We all struggle. And who are they? Who knows?"

"Doug needs to know, Mr. Salem. He needs to know who they are and what they do. Especially in banking. They do their banking here?"

Jim paused again and watched Salem. The man never figured on this, Jim thought. Not from Doug, not from anyone. Stick it in and break it off: "Banking, Mr. Salem?"

"I think this is not possible. Who can know this? Why do you come to me? I am businessman."

"Well, your range of business interests, Mr. Salem, I mean, my God, the activity! The Salem Group is into every major industrial sector in Lebanon. It's amazing. And your contacts must be so wide."

"You are thinking this. How are you knowing, Mr. Welles? How can you know?" Salem's voice was a baritone, and he smiled. And who, Jim wondered, would advance this guy money for a cheap loan?

"Well, Mr. Salem, al-Jihad has an Iranian component. This is not unknown. In fact, much is known of them. Including their international connections." Jim stared at Salem, who was still being very cool. "It's regrettable. These Iranians, they may not last as a viable movement. Let us be frank, Mr. Salem."

Salem was watching him warily now, still smiling vaguely. Jim thought of those Phoenician front-on portrait busts of merchants and their women from Tyre, Sidon, and Berytus, long dead, who stare straight forward with the faintest of smiles worn away by the wind and salt air.

"A man has died in Munich. You know the man." Salem made no sign. He sat motionless.

"It is thought he died by the hand of the Israelis. It would make sense, now, would it not, Mr. Salem?" Jim's voice was rapid now and he showed no feeling; when he thought about it later, he decided he didn't have any at the time. "His name is reported by police to be Tarbulsi. In fact, it was Chemissa, Suleyman Chemissa. His passport was Syrian, but in fact this Chemissa was Libyan. This is known. It is also known he dealt with Iranians. Perhaps connected with the al-Jihad group. Now, the Iranian elements, as I say, will not last long, Mr. Salem. Some have been taken. Ultimately they will lead to others. Perhaps many others.

"Other matters are known. The apartment where Mr. Chemissa died was searched, Mr. Salem. Things were found.

159

Items. Among them were deposit slips from certain Middle East banks. Chemissa was a financial courier of some sort, you see."

"Ah."

And now, the Israeli card, always useful. Drop it on the table. "We figure those who did it knew everything in the apartment. Probably went through it when they placed the bomb. Think so? What do you think, Mr. Salem?"

"Possibly."

Jim shook his head. "Sure thing, Mr. Salem. No 'possibly' to it." Jim put his hand on the cobalt blue bowl and ran his fingers over the fluting. Admission of acquaintance. Score. Should have been a lawyer. Bags of money in the law.

"No, they went through the place, Mr. Salem. Probably turned it upside down and put it back together again, wouldn't you say? That's the way of it, right? The way they work?"

Salem lifted his hands slightly.

"So they know what the police know at least. I mean at *least*. In fact, when you think about it, they might have walked off with stuff the Germans will never see. Right? The Israelis will link Chemissa to anybody they want."

The pitch was simple. The Israelis have long arms. They reach everwhere. They reach right into Beirut when they want to and they hit whoever they want. Think of Ghassan Kanafani, after all. Jim kept his eye on Salem. Palestinian. Poet and novelist. They said he was PFLP. They said he was a dangerous man. Maybe he was, maybe he wasn't. Who knows? But right in Beirut—and they walked right in because the door's wide open—right in Beirut they booby-trap his car and get him and his seventeen-year-old niece in the bargain. And think of Bassam Abou Sharif. Parcel bomb. Blinded him in one eye, and left not much of the other. Right in old Beirut. And then, Mohammad al-Najjar, Kamal Naser, Kamal Adwan, and a hundred others, mostly bystanders of varying grades of innocence, Mr. Salem, got themselves killed in one raid. The Israelis came in in assault boats, left in helicopters. The list goes on. Dangerous place, Beirut.

And Chemissa? Could be the kiss of death.

"We've heard something," was the message. The Israelis

know. They know you. They got Chemissa. Maybe they'll get others. Maybe you're on a list in Tel Aviv? Come through, sport. Stick with us. Doug can be protection. Doug can ease things.

Salem was thinking it over. He's never gotten a message like this from Doug. He must be wondering, Is it from Doug? He must be wondering, period.

Jim glanced away from Salem to the iridescent glass vials and oil lamps on Salem's wall. A bronze dagger with green patina wasted away to only the suggestion of the old shape hung point down over Salem's shoulder. Salem tapped his cigar into a marble ashtray, studied the ash for a time as if bemused by it, and returned his gaze to Jim and stared at him pensively, rubbing his chin with the back of his hand, as if asking, What is in your face? What is this?

Jim thought of those gunmen on the first floor. Wyndham knows enough to get Salem blown up by half a dozen factions and Salem knows it. And the Syrians, if they knew some things, would finish him off in an appropriate manner. Still, Salem had a look on his face that suggested he played for keeps.

Here, Jim thought something else about Salem's protection—was it just friends in the militias?

Salem had once imported 300 night-vision gun scopes from a California electronics company and sold them all around town. You mount one on a rifle and you go hunting in the dark. Wyndham claimed there was a noticeable, measurable, countable increase in accurate night shooting for a time, but since Salem had been so fair-minded in his sales policy, the whole business just quieted down in the end. Everybody was better off, Doug said. And nobody was sure Salem was sole source of the stuff anyhow. But how did Salem get the things out of the States? The sights were high-tech merchandise of great complexity and lethality, and you didn't just sell them to anyone who came along. You needed licenses on your licenses to trade in the stuff.

Jim had asked Wyndham about that. He professed to be mystified by it all, said he was amazed, had no information, thought maybe it could be renegades from the agency, but it sure was hard to figure. That made Jim brood. Renegades from the agency? Are they always renegades? The agency has its parties and factions, about as bad as Beirut, to hear some of them tell it. So maybe, Jim thought, considering who Salem's friends just might be, a threat from a newshound to Salem could be trouble for the newshound? Maybe he's got the whole thing figured already? In that case, was it bad or good that Salem didn't double over in laughter?

"So what you want?"

"Advice. Can you give us some advice? Some help?"

"What advice? What help?"

"What's al-Jihad doing? Who's doing it?"

Salem waved his hand. "It's all nothing. Iranians. Nothing. This Chemissa is dead, yes? It is over, I think."

"Come on. One man dies. The movement goes on. There'll be other Chemissas. Count on it."

"What you want? What does Doug want? We must be clear. It is necessary that we are clear. That is top priority. First rank."

"Okay." Jim bent forward. "Chemissa. For the record."

"Chemissa? Record? We must be clear."

"What did the man bring in? What was he doing? And where did it go?"

"Easy. Chemissa was Libyan. The Libyans bring money in. What else? These groups, they all take money. They are all professionals. They need money."

"They work out of Aden and here."

"Sure. Okay. So Doug knows this. He knows more than I do, by God." Salem pointed his finger skyward and twisted his hand as if rattling a doorknob. "By God, he does."

"What does al-Jihad do here?"

"They hide. They are row of coffins."

"Must be more to it than that. You've worked with Chemissa. What is it?"

"Maybe he was the customer. We have many. Full service. We are full service bank." It sounded like "fool service" the way Salem said it, and Jim agreed with that.

"Yeah."

"But it is best to stay away from Iranians. They are a confused people."

"God talks to them . . ." Michel had said. "He tells them pretty crazy stuff. . . . Not nice people."

"I've heard that. But you've had dealings."

"We are public. I did not 'deal.' This is business." Salem rested his hands on his paunch. "There is difference. With Doug, I deal."

Dealt, sport. "So they're banking here?"

"Yes, sure, okay."

"Out of here to Europe?"

"Okay."

"Or wherever."

"Okay."

Wherever meaning Iran? Is that how they do it? "Aden to Beirut, and from here to the great world, is what it sounds like to me," Jim said. "From here to wherever? And the money comes in here for laundering?"

Salem's face was very serious now.

"Wash it and dry it here, right? Hang it out on the line—best place in the world for a little discreet laundering—and off it goes. From a Libyan account to a Lebanese to a European, right?"

"Maybe. But is mystery. It is all mystery." Salem leaned forward, smiling gently, his hands in a gesture of entreaty. "Mr. Welles, this is not healthy." Salem had a look in his face now—call it solicitude, concern, care for Jim's well-being—that Jim didn't like.

"I keep hearing that."

"Then you should listen. Doug has said this? Has he said so? Then Doug is smart." Salem looked away from Jim. "Do you know someone who needs a loan, Mr. Welles?" he asked wistfully. "We are financiers. We are builders. Producers. We are not for the destruction. No, no." He pushed the air away from him, as if ridding himself of something distasteful. "No, no, no. We believe in the future of humans. The future of *humans.*" He said it with conviction.

"Is al-Jihad headquartered here?"

Salem looked back at Jim. "Office yes, HQ no. HQ is in Aden. They have the HQ, the camps, the supplies, money, guns, lectures, everything." Salem bent forward again, and his

163

wide silk necktie, pink dappled with green, played over his paunch. "How else can I help? Doug knows all I am saying?"

"I guess."

"Then how can I help more?"

"Anything. Names, photos, who leads them, what they're up to, where the money comes from, where it goes. Especially the money."

"Photos? Naw, you crazy? You come back. We talk. Maybe names. A report. No photos."

"Why not?"

"You think they keep albums? Nobody can walk away with the photos. Not possible."

"Just the Iranians, Mr. Salem. They're dead men now. Really. Good as dead, most of them."

"It would not be well to be one to kill them."

"They kill each other. Get us whatever you can. But we need to know the money. Payment and deposit documentation. When and where and how much."

"And Doug . . . Doug wants this? Why Doug wants this?" Jim noticed that searching look again in Salem's face, his mouth open.

"He wants it."

Salem feigned a minor hesitation. "This will involve expenses. Earnest money of a sort." He looked openly at Jim, who wondered how many times and to how many people Salem had said that; maybe it was just force of habit.

"Not up front."

Salem smiled and spread his hands. "What can I do?" He turned his head to the side, still smiling. "The nature of the transaction would require cash up front. There are intermediaries, men who must be encouraged from the outset. It is easy. Doug has account number. We've done all this before. You are new in town."

In the end, Jim agreed. The Israeli threat will never cow Lebanon, he thought. Wyndham will know how much to pay and the arcane modalities of payment.

Salem smiled broadly. "We see. We see soon."

But there was something in Salem's look when Jim left. Salem had stopped asking why Doug really wanted all this stuff. . . . Just a glimmer there in the corners of his eyes hinted that Salem was thinking perhaps, just perhaps, Doug had been taken too. Jim hoped Salem wasn't thinking it.

Jim did a piece on the man that Zimmerman liked. Salem reminded Zimmerman of one of a number of New Jersey pols. He ran it in the Sunday op-ed section. Score, Jim thought. And a double play.

Jim happily established himself at Charley's on a pallet in an unused room. Gordon was still in Tripoli, which pleased Charley immensely, for Gordon was missing the show in Beirut, a fine one even by local standards, and Jim and Charley wrote it up: BOMB EXPLODES IN CENTER OF CITY, THREE KILLED. . . . DRUZE LEADER AMBUSHED AND KILLED IN SHOUF. . . . CHRISTIAN LEADERS OF LEBANESE FRONT GATHER AT IHDEN TO DISCUSS SECURITY MEASURES TO DEAL WITH CONDITIONS IN SHOUF. . . . PALESTINIAN GUERRILLAS BLOW SHIT OUT OF CHRISTIANS MEETING IN IHDEN, LEAVING FOUR DEAD INCLUDING MAYOR OF BINT JUBAYL.

Jim filed lots of copy, and through it all, Charley's scrawny British girl friend, whom Charley insisted on calling his bird, did dishes and played at being domestic.

One afternoon Jim was out on the rue Salaam, and Salem's young man, still looking like an airline steward, pulled up in a taxi and gestured for Jim to get in.

The delivery was fast. On the next corner the young man got out. With any luck, no photos had gotten taken of Jim or the delivery, and there were no tails on the cab. Jim had the car circulate through the business area down toward Arts et Métiers, got out, and immediately hailed another and went around the corner and down a bit to Charley's place. He saw no tails. But then you never do.

The young man had slipped Jim a plain white envelope. It contained a note that read: "Bank Hügen, AG, SA, Claridenstrasse 33, Zürich, Telefon: 201 76 22. Account number 22YW21. Banque POetE account in question is 1151798," which Jim knew already. Salem had come up with one account in one foreign bank.

That night Wyndham's driver, a middle-aged, soft-looking man in short sleeves, came by. Jim recognized him. There was an emergency, he said, and a message from Wyndham. An address down past Jineh, almost to the Khaldeh radio tower, which was a long drive south of town and nobody should be moving down there at this hour. No explanation.

The car had diplomatic plates. They rode in silence, went through the Jineh checkpoint with papers that satisfied the Syrian guards, and pulled through a high chain-link fence surrounding a brick building and a courtyard. Barbed wire looped over the top of the fence. On the far side of the building were railroad tracks, and beyond them an embankment. A few sickly palm and cypress trees competed for space on a hill rising behind that. The yard was lit with mercury lamps from the neighboring area, and the driver's dark skin looked olive green in the light.

The building was a warehouse. It had a loading platform and corrugated iron doors that opened straight up. Gendarmes in red berets and carrying grease guns stood on the platform. Two police cars sat in the yard on either side of another with diplomatic plates. Their lights were off and the motors silent. The driver motioned for Jim to go up.

Wyndham was there with another American, whose name Jim never learned. He had gray crew-cut hair and was thin and wasn't saying anything. He walked around poking at piles of rubbish with his foot. Old newspapers were piled around, and in the far end lay battered hubcaps, automobile bumpers, red plastic taillights, all of them broken, and a couple of chemical-encrusted batteries.

Wyndham looked sick. He motioned with his head and said, "Over there."

Jim looked at a heap lying in the corner. It was a man stripped to his underwear. He looked as if he had been pushed or dragged along a gravel road. Blood had dried and caked, and a pair of ribs cut crazily through his chest like springs bursting through an old sofa.

"Oh, Christ," said Jim. There was enough left of his face. It was Gordon. There were cuts all over him and black circles of charred and blistered skin. The soles of his feet were bloody and lacerated and burned.

"What could they have done?" said Wyndham, more to himself than anything. "Oh, Jesus, what could they have done?"

"Christ."

"We get a call. Comes right through to me. He knows my name and tells me there's been an accident and I'd better haul ass to this address. Very polite on the phone. Good English. Went real slow and nice with the address so I'd get it right. Said it was pretty bad. Then he hung up."

Gordon's right hand was no longer a hand. At the end of Gordon's right arm was a thin claw, pink-colored, without skin or much flesh. A warning to writers. The wire was still around his wrist. Jim hoped they'd killed him first.

The other American with the crew cut had stopped poking around. He shrugged. "Body goes to the morgue. They didn't do it here, and we've seen enough. Let's go."

Jim and Wyndham and the other American got into one car and the two Lebanese drivers into the other. The other one drove.

"Those burns were from cigarettes," the man said. "You don't kill somebody that way. Either they did it for the fun of it or he had something they wanted. So they worked on him. Then they stopped that and beat the living shit out of him. So all in all he died a number of times, but the last time was real recent. The blood's fresh. When they got started, though, is anybody's guess." He looked at Jim. "What do *you* know?"

"He had enemies. He asked questions. He knew stuff."

"Like what? Who's he been bugging lately?"

Jim looked at Wyndham. Wyndham nodded: no secrets from crew cut. "Was he with you?" asked Wyndham.

"Yeah."

"Okay," Wyndham said and sat quietly.

"Political?" said the other to Wyndham.

"Yes."

Jim told them of Gordon and al-Jihad. But not of the photo.

So who did it? I did it, thought Jim as he sat staring at the dark sea, sitting in the park along the Corniche, Wyndham's idea of a safe holding place. The guards were unobtrusive. The boys who sold Coca-Cola and ice-cream from pushcarts had gone home. Long, slow waves lapped the beach below, and behind Jim, the wind blowing through the palm leaves made them crackle.

I did it. Automobiles tore along the Corniche and half of them seemed to be playing "Colonel Bogie" on their horns.

Gordon had his own enemies. Could have been one of his own things.

Sure. Oh, sure. He got too close, got careless. Risky business here. "Pop it down the line," Gordon had said. What line? Who? "Pop it down the line."Al-Jihad is the line. And Charley Salem? "Mr. Well-us, this isn't healthy." No, not at all. Some of Gordon's craziness was in this. Craziness got him in the end. But I did it. That's for sure.

Jim got up from his bench and walked along the Corniche. He could see where the harbor curved around the Bay of St. George and then where the mountains came down abruptly in the east, cutting off Jounieh, where Michel brought his ordnance in from Haifa. Ships were lying in the harbor. Where it sickles around, Jim thought, are the Maronite Christians and here are the Moslems; Michel over there and Salem here, and Dave got wasted for his troubles. Corniche was what they called the thing in Monte Carlo. So Beirut had to have a Corniche. And now Jidda has a Corniche. And Dubai. Corniches all around.

It was the game. It was the way you play it. Crazy Gordon had gone in with his eyes open, hadn't he? Well, hadn't he? Jim thought of those wide, staring eyes of his and the connections he had all over town.

You needed a cutout because going in yourself was too dangerous. So you asked Gordon would he kindly step in. What was that Persian proverb? Better a clever enemy than a foolish friend. Poor Gordon had both.

There was some shapeless slop on the beach, muck washed up by the waves, bilge from somewhere; Jim looked at it and felt the kinship.

That night the crew-cut American and some others pumped Jim further for information. He had none to give them. Whoever did it would get away, they all knew. Happens all the time, Wyndham said. It stinks. Beirut stinks. Lebanon stinks.

Wyndham supplied guards to the airport. The poetess at the *Daily Star* did the story on Gordon for Jim's paper.

8

Jim got back bone-tired. Too much alcohol, too little sleep, and Gordon. He went through customs fast. Pari was there in her raincoat and he ran his finger down her Nefertiti nose, which always astonished him, the blond boy brought up among folk who sported the Anglo-Saxon variety, and down to her full lips, and her eyes fixed on him, not quite sure of herself, and over the curve of her front.

"Hullo, Pear."

"Hullo, Ace. Bad?"

He looked it, he knew. "Indescribable."

Her long arms were thin and warm around his neck, eyes looking up not closed when they kissed. Her tan raincoat and demure dresses were trademarks. So were the arms around his neck.

"They got Gordon, Pear. He's dead."

"Oh, no."

"Yeah."

And at home: "Now what?"

"Find them."

"*Find* them!" Those eyes flashing again. The crying made them shinier. "They'll find *you*, you nitwit. Oh, you bloody nitwit."

Jim sitting on the bed motioned helplessly with his hands up and open and dropped them back on his knees, a glum kind of acknowledgment of the way things are. Rough. Very rough. He thought of Eleanor and how things got bitched up with her. New life with the Pear, he had thought. Sure. Maybe there aren't any new lives. Not ever.

Pari's hair was badly combed.

He followed her with his eyes as she paced.

"They're going to kill you."

"No."

Her eyes flashed. "You don't know. You just say what you want. You talk yourself into anything for your bloody, bloody story."

"I don't even know what the story is, Pear. It must be a good one, though. And I don't know who 'they' are."

"Then why are you doing this?"

"They killed a goddamn friend and I'm the only one who'll do anything about it. Nobody in Beirut will, nobody here will."

"And us?" She stopped pacing and stood looking through the curtains and ivy into the courtyard.

"I've got to, Pear. I haven't a choice. They got Gordon. Killed the man. Why Gordon? Why not me?" And, the newsman in him irrepressible, "What did he get close to?"

No ties, no bonds, she had said once and meant it. But Jim had heard that before and knew that it didn't work at 3:00 A.M. when you're alone and your fancy man's gone and may be with someone else. Or may just never come back because the scene's no good anymore and you're part of the scene and he's dropped everything. Or may have gotten his fool head blown off.

He had bought her a necklace from what was left of the *souk* down toward the Green Line. It had a fine gold chain. An agate rimmed in gold hung at the end. The stone was milky, with a dark green patch at the base; it looked three-dimensional, like some strange plant frozen there for eons, which is why they call that kind of stone a moss agate.

When he gave it to her, he knew it was a mistake. He had never known what to do with women who cry their eyes out.

Salem's list of Iranian clients, courtesy of Doug Wyndham, was a joke. It partook of no reality. Not one of them had any earthly existence Jim could ever discover, and he had grave doubts about the Zürich bank account. He had relayed the latter to Levesque in Paris via the same young gentleman in the French embassy who had brought Chemissa's deposit slips. Maybe the number was a ghost, like Salem's companies.

Things seemed to end. Levesque was silent. Fiscarelli had

nothing more, though he had gotten wind of Jim's interest in Charles Salem.

"Who's this guy when he's at home? What aren't you telling me, Jimmy?"

"Can't tell you."

"Fuck you."

Avoiding the Hounds pretty much, Jim drifted around the city and turned in dutiful copy. GULF WILL REMAIN COUNTRY'S MAJOR OVERSEAS PREOCCUPATION, he wrote. IMPORTS CONTINUE TO RISE. CRITICAL MOOD SPREADING. PROBLEMS IN AUTOMOBILE INDUSTRY.

But Jim's gut wasn't in it. Deflected from a chase, his work got flabby and he knew it. And besides, there wasn't much doing anyway. He hung around the French and British embassies for gossip and got none. As for the Americans, they had put a temporary freeze on political stuff after a series of stupefying financial scandals had broken stateside. A U.S. rear admiral had been indicted for alleged efforts to steer a multimillion-dollar Iranian contract to a private concern that had hired him after retirement. Lovely story, Jim thought, but nothing doing on it in Iran. He checked, but just got denials—"belches and guff," he wired Zimmerman—from a Ministry of Defense spokesman, a sly little man whose uniforms looked British-tailored and who sported a collage of medals and ribbons—fire-engine red, lime green, silver, and gold, the optical effect of which was blinding. The man's singular Anglo-American language was, all Intercontinental Hounds agreed, designed to confuse honest journalists.

Jim had heard, too, that Congressman O'Shaughnessy was doing deals in New York for the Pahlavi Foundation, wangling tax-exempt status for the blessed organization whose primary function was to funnel money out of Iran. The money started as oil money, but soon, though at some unknown stage, became the shah's money and, via the foundation, got invested in real estate and the like. The shah's favorite charity, everyone called it. But again, no soap in Tehran. No truth to know. The U.S. Justice Department was most intrigued, but that was D.C. and New York. The fun was all back home. No truth to be had in Tehran. Nobody talking.

Jim took to sitting silently, staring off somewhere, thinking about Givon and Gordon and wondering where the hell his war was and what the hell he was doing there in Iran, the desert, where there was nothing. A blank place, a blank time.

He and Pari drove Bucephalus to a cabin outside a village called Sharak, up where the mountains hang over the city. The cabin belonged to a friend who used to own the village—"used to own the villagers," Pari said—and Jim and Pari sometimes spent summer nights there, usually alone. "Sharak will be utterly deserted at this time of year, Jim, and I shall get you alone and seduce you. We shall play house."

In Shemran on the way up, they stopped for food and kerosene, and Pari told Jim how years back Aqa *Joon* would take her up in wheezing old buses to Shemran or Pol-e Tajrish. Aqa *Joon*, which is what Persian children call Persian fathers, would buy me ice cream, and the street vendors would call me *Khoshgel Khanom*, 'Miss Pretty,' and we'd walk on the winding back roads up here." She remembered her father's hand, she said, large and rough over hers, and she remembered that the brass button on the cuff of his khaki military tunic was at her eye level.

"The air was cool and clear in the fall then and there was a smell of charcoal braziers and pine. Very fragrant."

"Miss it?"

"Yes," she said and pointed. "Now look, it's all this."

The Shemran circle was clogged with traffic and decrepit Mercedes-Benz taxis and people shoving bundles and themselves into the cars while buses lumbered through the throng and the diesel fumes lifted and hung thickly over the traffic like a bad omen.

On the way up from Shemran, they passed villages and isolated huts, all with yellow guard dogs, big and square-faced, that rose as they passed and growled and lay down again morosely. Jim pointed out the dogs had no ears. He'd seen that before and wondered why.

"The villagers cut them off when they're just little puppies and they make them eat their own ears."

"Jesus."

"It teaches them a little lesson about life."

"I suppose."

"They're very nasty."

"Yeah."

The cabin was squat and square, built against a hill, and a stone fence ran around three sides of it. In the courtyard was a pomegranate tree that somehow survived the altitude. The cabin was whitewashed, and each wall had a single window. The roof was made of young poplar and jutted out to form eaves. The door hung loose on its hinges when Pari tried it, and the latch was a joke.

Inside, the walls were white plaster, some of which had fallen to the floor. A charcoal brazier and a kerosene heater sat in the corner. Two *charpas,* four-sided frames on legs strung for sleeping, lay together.

Pari eyed the *charpas.* "Oh, damn those things. Lovemaking's wretched on them."

"They make interesting patterns on your bottom, Pear, believe me."

Jim banged their one knapsack into a corner and spread sleeping bags on the frames while Pari lit the kerosene heater and the chill finally went out of the cabin. They had brought brandy. Jim pulled out the bottle, and they drank it from coffee cups as the wind whistled through the eaves.

Outside on a wide stony path that led through terraced garden plots, Pari hugged herself in her down jacket in the wind. "It's super up here, Jim. Everything's clean and fresh. You think clearly, see clearly. There's a quality in the light up here. You can see forever, the edges of everything are so sharp. I think that's why the ancient Iranians worshiped the sun in this country."

The path turned steep and ran through a hillside cherry orchard, whose gnarled old trees had whitish banded bark. As they moved from shade to sun to shade again, the shadows from the leaves of the cherry trees dappled Pari's face. The sky was as blue as the lapis lazuli that the miniaturists of Safavid times ground into powder for their painted heavens.

Pari cocked her head to the side, her hair falling over her shoulder, and squinted in the sunlight.

"Where is it now, My Man Morgan?"

Jim had told her of Salem, who was too strange to keep quiet about, of Levesque. "I don't know. They're doing something in Europe, Pear. They're holding hands with the Libyans. Something like that. Chemissa was a Lib. And al-Jihad's folded its tents in Europe and moved back to Beirut. Something's up with them."

"And how do the vile Persians enter the plot?"

"The vile Persians get training. Money. They get a place to run and hide when it gets too hot for them here. Maybe Libya, maybe Lebanon. The Libs fund al-Jihad, so it's one big family. And they're targeting Israelis and Americans, which all makes sense. But there's something more than that, and I can't figure it. Commerce. Business. Something. Wheeling and dealing, anyhow."

"That figures. Find an Iranian, find a dealer."

"Yeah. And you can just catch a glimpse of it, Pear, far off and dim."

"Investments? Killers making a killing?"

"Maybe. And the Israelis are in it somehow. And maybe we'll never figure it. It's endless. Circles and circles and circles. It just gets funnier."

"Some fun. Take me to Beirut?"

"Your ass, Pear. Not a chance. I've got no protection. No helmet, no flak suit. All I've got is a pencil and a notepad. That's it. And sometimes I think they attract bullets."

"But it's so *fascinating*, Jim. All these chaps lurking in *shadows*."

"They're pretty murderous."

"No Beirut?"

"It's grim, Pear."

He helped her over a streamlet, his hands under her arms, and she felt as fragile as a doll.

"Alice says that *paris* are beautiful sprites. You are begotten by fallen spirits and you direct the pure in mind to heaven with your wands."

"You're not so pure in mind."

"Gave it up when I was six."

Snow hung just above them from the mountaintop. Below, they could see villages even smaller than Sharak, clusters of huts, with a teahouse perhaps, nestled in ravines.

At the next streamlet—it was wide and bridged with stones in a pointed Persian arch—water was flowing, apportioned with great exactitude, down through the intricate network of watercourses and spillways and dams up above there; it fell all through the chessboard of landholdings and down the face of the mountain. There was no telling where the water came from.

The bridge led to a gulley, and Pari, her eyes wide in the sun, pointed. "Look down there. You can see the city."

There it was. Through a pass, Jim saw a brown smear stretching away, molded to the contours of the mountainside that Tehran is built on. A dingy canopy of dust and smog hung over it.

"Yeah. The water that starts up here, Pear, flows to the very end. All the way down through it. The hillside and the water—they're a perfect symbol of society here. The shah with his palace up in the mountains, fat cats just below him, and so on down to the very bottom of the hill. The Great Civilization."

Tehran's poor live in the south of town, beyond the city limits, in their *halabiabads*, tin can towns, built with oil cans and scraps of metal, bits of wire, wood, paper, whatever. The whole south of Tehran is a kind of encampment, miles and miles of the displaced and the dispossessed. Jim had seen it; he felt more at home in the Palestinian camps in Lebanon. There was a sullen anger among these people, and you were likely to get stones thrown your way down there. The police pretty much kept nosy reporters out.

Tehran's graveyard and the city's vast garbage dump are down there as well, and between them, its vast collection of poor and angry people. The brick kilns are down there, too, whose tall, yellow smokestacks rise irregularly like the minarets of a ruined city. And an oil refinery and its flare-off. Black greasy smoke from the refinery mingles with the yellow dust from the kilns.

It was Reza Modarresi who had told Jim about an area called the South City Pits. You can't see them from the main roads; they're hidden behind the natural rises of the sandhills below the town. But off Meydan-e Shoosh, an unpaved street leads to the first one, a hollow three hectares wide and ten meters deep and piled with city trash: scrap metal, parts of wrecked machinery, cardboard and bones heaped up in the middle. Outside, along the rim, there is a row of houses and truck-loading docks, and a few teahouses that cater to the thieves, pickpockets, drug dealers, smugglers, and whores of the area.

"You'd think to look at it and smell it that nobody could live in the Pits," Reza had said, "but there you'd be wrong." Reza shook his head in the Intercontinental Bar, beer foam on his mustache. "The people have dug holes, caves, into the sand walls of the pits and they floor them with cardboard and hang cloth over the entrances."

The Pits stretch for acres and acres, Reza told Jim. "The addicts have one area and the whores another and the smugglers another. The addicts don't use their real names. They call each other Abbas Aqa. It's pretty funny. Everybody's called Abbas Aqa down there. And you can smell the opium over the other smells. They sleep. They dream. They have their *keyf*, their contentment. The whores advertise by putting up black cloths on long sticks." Sometimes, Reza said, fires catch in the refuse and blanket the area in bitter smoke: black flags and black smoke, dust perpetually kicked up by the winds, and the stink of rotting garbage and bones.

"It's the way things are, Pear. Purity at the top, muck at the bottom. Rich folks up here, poor folks down there. And the water flows down and down and down and picks up filth, mile after mile of it, till finally when it reaches the south of town, it's an open running sewer. Bad as you get. It's perfect, Pear. Just perfect."

"It's awful, isn't it?"

"You ought to see it. It's worse than that."

"Someday south Tehran will rise up and swallow the north. Two by two they'll come and then four by four and then platoons and regiments and armies."

"Do you believe that?"

"I don't know. I guess not."

Jim and Pari crossed back over the footbridge. Four young men approached from a side path, each with a picnic sack over his shoulder. They wore long thick stockings and alpinists' trousers, and their faces were ruddy from the wind and sun.

They looked at Jim with plain, absolute loathing, and Jim stared coolly at them. Hostility toward foreigners was endemic in Iran, he'd learned long back, and there was no escaping it. The four of them came down and one walked intentionally in front of Pari so that she had to stop. Jim let them go.

"Why this?" he said. "I've been in countries we were more or less at war with and I've never seen anything like it, Pear. How come?"

"They don't much like you, Jim. They blame you for most of their ills. They don't much like me, either, because I'm with you and because I am as I am."

"I didn't do it."

"No." She brushed her hair from her face. "I'm not comfortable here. Let's go."

They passed a teahouse under a pine tree by the side of the path, with a ring of *takhts*—wide low benches—set out and a cage with a mynah bird in it. The stream was dried up here and white, as parched as bones in the desert, and the four young men were there, staring at them sullenly. The bird scratched in the bottom of the cage and was silent.

9

The photograph had started in Shuwayra, a tin-can slum up toward Tripoli. It came down hidden under the spare wheel of a bus into Beirut's central *souk*, got passed on with whispers to a gold dealer in a back room there—neither the driver nor the dealer knowing what it meant—whence it made its way south by delivery boy and gas tanker to Sidon, and there at night over the Litani River and fast to Tel Aviv, and copied, to the clutter on Ariel Netzer's carrel in Ha Qiryat in Tel Aviv's northern suburb.

It was a photo of a young man, a boy really. A school portrait, the face turned slightly away from the camera. The eyes were large and intelligent, the hair trimmed short. The boy had the beginnings of a mustache. You're young, Netzer thought. Are you Hoseyn Jandaqi? Will I kill you?

Netzer was absent from Tehran a total of six weeks and four days. Joel Halperin arranged it. Halperin, director of operational planning and coordination, was an old Irgun man who knew Netzer from those days far back on Kibbutz Kfar Rosenstein. Halperin had his own reasons to be curious about what was coming to be known within the service as the Givon Affair, and, doing an end run around his own director, he managed to clear things with the defense minister. Netzer, though few knew it, had the run of Ha Qiryat, access to the foreign information, their own internal documents.

The photograph of the boy Jandaqi was the only piece of the puzzle to come in from Lebanon. But it was a good one. It was the same boy Yoram Kohan had photographed trailing Netzer in the street.

The rest from the foreign services had come from Germany, mostly from Munich, Mohrstrasse 312, that room where

Ehud Cohen had exploded a telephone: notes, essays, speeches, lectures, tape recordings, letters, pamphlets, names, addresses. A torrent, in its way. The Germans had been generous. Holocaust guilt, Netzer thought. Like pensions to survivors.

Netzer had assembled the German material at the carrel where he had ensconced himself in a room in Ha Qiryat's main Records Division. The room was all welded metal and had doors with combination locks. Though air-conditioned, it smelled to Netzer of humanity.

The best of the German stuff was a book, or a book of sorts, a spiral notepad half filled with tight Persian handwriting. Hoseyn Jandaqi, whose putative photograph lay next to it in Netzer's carrel, called it his *Ketab-e*, his *Secret Book*, a kind of diary. In it, Hoseyn, hiding here and there, on the run in Germany, had written down his experiences, his dreams and visions, scraps of poetry. It was a strange collection.

Netzer could read only the Hebrew translation, but kept the Persian original, his one link with Hoseyn, by his hand in the carrel.

The book began, in a sense, Hoseyn's life began, it seemed to Netzer, at night in the streets under the blue lamps, where students in Iran pace to memorize their lessons, walking up and down, holding their books before them in the dim light, reciting, repeating. They meet, too, and talk in the stillness. Netzer knew that. He'd seen them.

At the Polytechnique down Hafez Street, they must have identified Hoseyn as a prospect. They approached him. Late at night, he wrote, whispered comments, at first freighted with double meaning, then more and more precise on social and economic "conditions," led to meetings in apartments in shabby parts of town—around Zhaleh Square and Baharestan and south of the Hassanabad area.

A man Hoseyn called Rahmani appeared briefly in the pages. Netzer didn't recognize the name. Shin Beth's Central Registry, Non-Arab Affairs had drawn a blank. A cell leader? A cadre? Can we find him?

This Rahmani lectured and Hoseyn listened, even memorized, apparently, some of what he said. "There is only one enemy," Rahmani told them. "Imperialism and its collaborators. When SAVAK shoots, dear friends, it kills Moslems and Marxists. When it tortures, it tortures Moslems and Marxists. And therefore, at present there is a seamless unity between Moslem revolutionaries and Marxist revolutionaries. In truth, O brothers, why do we respect Marxism? Marxism and Islam are not identical. But Islam is closer to Marxism than to Pahlavism. Islam and Marxism teach the same lessons, for they fight against injustice. Islam and Marxism contain the same message, for they inspire martyrdom, struggle, and self-sacrifice. Who is closer to Islam—the Vietnamese, who stood before the bombs and the flames to fight American imperialism, or the shah, who helps Zionism? Islam fights oppression and Islam will work together with Marxism, which also fights oppression. They have the same enemy: reactionary imperialism."

Hoseyn typed for them and ran a German copying machine, then took to leafleting in the working-class districts and spray-painting slogans of mud-brick walls, all the while dodging the police.

It was Rahmani who gave final approval. Hoseyn didn't write why, what Rahmani had looked for, how Rahmani had judged him, but in his twenty-first year Hoseyn Jandaqi, with Rahmani's blessing, went out to Libya, to a dusty camp (barracks, barbed wire, and heat) at an oasis, a caravan crossing down toward the Egyptian border, where the hills of sand rolled away in all directions and forever. Hoseyn didn't identify the place. To Netzer it sounded like al-Kufra. Best guess, anyway.

Some of the teachers were bearded Cubans and they spoke an odd mixture of Arabic and English. Here Hoseyn learned how to drill in urban courtyards and learned why cities are better than the countryside, with its suspicious, fearful peasants. He learned how to blow up bridges, using Dynamon, a compound they told him you can bend and shape to fit your target. He learned how to raise money by appropriating the contents of banks.

From the oasis—al-Kufra or wherever—Hoseyn went on to Lebanon to another camp, this one near the sea, he wrote, where the blue water seemed a road to all the world. Netzer knew a dozen such places, built of cinder blocks, with water

hydrants where the narrow lanes meet, electricity, even telephone lines.

Hoseyn wrote of summer days near a Crusader castle
called Beaufort. It was an early mark of Western imperialism,
they told him, and asked him where now were the men who
had built that castle? Dead Franks pushed beyond the sea.

And after Lebanon, South Yemen, to a camp up-country
called Camp Khayyat (Camp Tailor). Here Hoseyn learned to
strip down a Kalashnikov. He learned to use the Skorpion and
Makarov pistols, too, from a man named Pachito. The Skorpion's light as air, said Pachito, and you can fire it in one hand,
a virtual machine gun. Pachito showed them how to carry it
low—the harder to see—and snap it to the horizontal with a
turn of the body, reducing momentum so the gun steadies just
parallel with the ground a meter at most, maybe a few centi-
meters, from target.

Yes, thought Netzer, no two-handed aim and squeeze,
Yanqui-fashion, for Pachito. Was this how they murdered
Givon? Two shots, close range. In the back, in the head.

Maybe.

Pachito spoke slowly in English and an interpreter translated, sentence by sentence, into Arabic. Hoseyn listened with
the rest of the Iranians, who didn't mix with the other groups,
who were many—thin, dark-featured Dhofaris from Oman,
Turks, Ethiopians, Indonesians, Japanese. There was a red-
headed boy from Ireland and others from Europe—Belgians,
Swedes, Dutch, Italians. There was no mingling save among
the Europeans. The other national groups were kept apart.

A tall, blond, unfriendly European who called himself
Khalid taught explosives and hand-to-hand combat. Netzer
could see them, could imagine it. They'd be sitting cross-
legged on clean stretches of sand under canvas or in the shade
of a palm grove. And Khalid—a German? a Swede?—would tell
them how. The techniques were universal. To grab from behind, you lock the left forearm across the throat to guide the
knife that the right hand jabs through jugular and severs larynx
in one fast sweep. No noise . . . only a gurgle of breath passing
through liquid.

Netzer hoped they'd find Khalid, teach him a final lesson.

In Aden they gave Hoseyn an identity card. Though Hoseyn didn't say, Netzer knew his picture would have been on it. Was it the same picture that Halperin had gotten from Lebanon and now lay in Netzer's carrel? He looked at the photograph again. A boy. He'd be older now. Changed. Too bad they hadn't found his card in Munich.

In Aden, too, they taught Hoseyn to use the Czech version of the AK-47. Netzer knew the weapon and didn't like it, knew its tendency to climb when set on automatic. They train them in everything, East bloc weaponry, West bloc. For whatever turns up.

Hoseyn attended lectures on the psychology of hijacking and hostage holding, where they taught him to craft messages to the authorities so his every nuance would be clear to them, so he could bend them with a clever sequence of threats and demands and finally get his way.

Once Wadi' Haddad himself came and spoke to Hoseyn's group. Netzer thought of Haddad's face, which he knew well from the few pictures they had of him. Haddad's baldness and the small mustache under his protruding nose made his face look rounder than it was. Haddad was in East Germany, Iraq, Aden. Impossible to find. How they wanted Haddad.

Haddad spoke in Arabic, and Hoseyn proudly wrote that after Libya and Lebanon and time now in Yemen, he had learned enough of it to follow a political speech.

Haddad spoke of liberation, not just of Palestine, but of the world, of bonds that would unite all strugglers together over the whole face of the earth. He spoke of capitalism and the Jew, of imperialism and Zionism that went hand in hand. To smash the one was to smash the other.

To his Iranian audience he spoke of the shah and the shah's subservience to imperialism and his cooperation with the Zionists and collaboration in Tehran itself with the Jewish elements.

Hoseyn had encountered few Jews in Iran, he wrote. They lived apart in older sections of the cities. But it was known that much commerce was in their hands: the boutiques, television, cinemas, all the new fads from the West. They had their hands in such businesses. Netzer thought of Givon's neighborhood, and the street Sheikh Hadi, where Givon had died. An older section. Apart. Hoseyn had been there.

From Yemen Hoseyn returned to Iran. He had been in on the Rockwell action. Confirmed. He described the Americans' car and how they had caught it between two vehicles and how they had shot in the rear window and killed the passengers.

"Violent acts," he wrote at the end of his account, "are needed to shatter the illusion that the people are powerless." He'd memorized that from somewhere, some cheap underground pamphlet, Netzer knew.

Here, maddeningly, Hoseyn left off autobiography and copied in bits of verse. Strange stuff, Islamic mysticism. Netzer, on the chance it might mean something, called in a professor from Hebrew University, a young Persian woman named Shadi, thin, dark and a bit homely, who was interested in Sufism, not terrorism. Netzer liked her face. It was broad, with high cheekbones and a long nose, not the sort of face Meir would look twice at. She had a liquid voice, and Netzer looked softly at her as she explained the translations. She read them out for him, first in solemn Persian meters, then, translated, in lackluster Hebrew. One went:

> The Light of the World's Eye lies hidden from men,
> But who sees other than His eye? His Light is in
> Closeness and the Soul.

Netzer had heard this sort of thing before and knew the rhetoric well enough. He'd studied it out of curiosity.

" 'Closeness,' Shadi? What does that mean?"

"Closeness to the Godhead. And God is revealed in the world, in a sense *is* the world and the devotee can merge with Him. It's a kind of pantheism."

"Yes."

She read another verse:

> His love is a Sea and we are drowned in Him. In
> Him is our boundless Sea.
> Ah, we give our lives to the Beloved,
> What are our lives in comparison with the
> Beloved?

" 'Give our lives to the Beloved,' Shadi? The cause is Islam, yes? The Path of God?"

"Yes. There's a strain in Persian sufi verse which if you read it a certain way, you can take as encouragement to self-sacrifice in the political realm, in the everyday world. They do this."

"But still close to the Godhead."

"Yes."

There was more of the same, a page or two, some of it badly memorized, Shadi said, the verse not quite scanning. Mysticism. Netzer listened to it, half-interested. Then, though he had no use for the verse as verse, he went carefully through it all, looking there for Hoseyn, hoping he might find him in the words. He didn't. In the end it was all incomprehensible.

Shadi said the boy's hand was good, said it was clean and graceful, the hand of someone well tutored. Netzer made a note on that.

In a final section Hoseyn wrote of exile and memories. There were times when he would sit alone, he wrote, and choke at the thought of old days gone by, waiting and thinking in shabby quarters somewhere down from a train station perhaps—Munich? Netzer wondered—alone and shut up in a safe house. That touched something in Netzer. Netzer could imagine the dust on the faded curtains of those houses blotting out dirty windows that looked out on numberless slums. He'd seen such places, been in them himself.

Strangely, as Netzer sat there trying to read Hoseyn's notebook, Shadi at his side, a piano tune, unbidden, played through Netzer's mind and wouldn't leave, just a phrase of a short étude by Chopin. It was crazy to think of her, but the tune wouldn't stop. The pianist's fingers were light and she was young and very, very serious. Anna Sobienewska. When she played, she twisted her mouth, though, which young and clumsy Ariel found funny.

In this tableau, her hair is long over her shoulders. He is watching from behind in Dr. Sobienewski's old drawing room in Kraków, up Ulica Bydisci by the old university, where the doctor (of classical philology, not medicine) was still allowed to teach. There are two lamps on the piano. Sheet music lies scattered on the floor. Her waist is slender. Then he comes around and rests his elbow on the piano, she still concentrating. The room has blue flowered wallpaper, and a small Oriental carpet lies on the wood flooring.

Netzer looked at his own hand there in Tel Aviv, at the blunt, stubby fingers and the cracked skin. You pinch it in a bunch, he thought, and it stays in a bunch. Her hands were soft. Her face was thin. She had blond hair.

The tune floated on summer air. It was the tune and the light and especially her hair he remembered, sunlight streaming onto it through the window some golden afternoon, with butterflies in the garden, those pale gossamer graces that are born only to die.

That world was dead; so was the pianist, both destroyed decades back. The thought of that world came to Netzer with aching regularity. He looked down at Hoseyn's cheap spiral notebook, the neat hand, the translation with his own notes in the margin, the boy's photograph. Netzer had been born an exile, he had decided long before, but was one no longer. This Hoseyn, though, if that was his name, would always be one, even in Iran.

Hoseyn wrote of his home in some nameless town on the fringe of the Great Desert. Sitting in Germany, he recalled the smell of vinegar and garlic from the old clay pots of pickled vegetables in the back room and elsewhere the scent of rose water, and everywhere a fine layer of yellow dust from the street, from the plain, from the desert.

He wrote of how they would bring the old kerosene stoves down from the stairwell and clean them and plug them into chimney holes in the walls, one to a room.

Hoseyn would go up on the roof and drop a cord down each chimney pipe. His father down below would tie newspaper to the cord and tug at it, and Hoseyn would pull the wadded paper up through the pipe and clean out the encrusted kerosene soot. The autumn wind caught some of it and carried it off, delicate jet-black filigrees, across the flat rooftops of the city. Hoseyn could still feel the tug on his hands, he wrote. From his father.

Once a month or so a *rowzeh-khan*—a reciter of verse on the martyrdom of Hoseyn ibn Ali, the Prophet's grandson—

would come to Hoseyn's house. She was an elderly lady who would chant old stories of the rightful heir to the caliphate and his death 1,300 years ago in the gardens of Karbala in Iraq.

"They probably have a room," Shadi said, "with a wall draped in black cloth and a chair at one end covered in the same black cloth. It's traditional. That's where the old lady would sing the story."

Netzer knew the story—anyone sent to Iran had to learn it—how Hoseyn ibn Ali brought a small band of followers from Mecca to fight the tyranny of the usurping caliph Yazid. But they were badly outnumbered and were halted in the desert near Karbala. Hoseyn's Bedouin guard fled under threat, and Yazid's commander attacked. All but two of the males of Hoseyn's party were killed, and Hoseyn himself was decapitated. They carried Hoseyn's head to the viceroy in Kufah, and when he turned it over with his stick, the crowd shuddered and someone there cried out, "Be gentle, brother, on that face I have seen the lips of the Prophet of God." A just man dead, fighting injustice. A model.

Hoseyn Jandaqi had dreamed of those riders as a boy. Their robes, he wrote, were green and their horses were white, chestnut, and black. Their pennants were red, and their swords and lance heads flashed in the sun as they rode toward the enemy and their own deaths.

Then it ended. Netzer laid the pages aside and thanked Shadi. There had been no mention of Givon.

Netzer felt vaguely disturbed, as when a traveler awaking on a train finds himself in a strange land, where an incomprehensible language is spoken. *Secret Book*, indeed. He could never know this boy. Never would. But he would kill him.

As for the rest, well, the dead Arab, G-9 confirmed, was Chemissa, Suleyman. Age thirty-seven. An engineer. The trace showed he had been trained in America. University of Texas, the Americans said. Mechanical engineering. The Libyan connection was to be noted. Central Registry had his name. He was connected, they said, with elusive, fugitive groups working out of Aden. They'd surveiled him there. A fixer. They said they had little else on him. A mystery. He had left no traces in Munich, at least none the Germans supplied.

The next day Netzer started on the cassettes. One had been made by a priest named Baharlu. The Germans knew him, had photographs, which they appended.

Hojjatoleslam Mohammad Baharlu was a bear of a man. One photo caught him as he was walking slowly, looking uncomfortable in a badly cut brown suit, out of Munich's railroad station, past the taxi drivers and porters. Another, a portrait they'd gotten from somewhere, showed him dressed as the priest he was, with an *aba*—a light brown cloak—over his shoulders and a turban on his head, a bit of forelock peeping out from under it. His beard was long and black and curly, with sparkles of white on the sides.

In the middle of Baharlu's forehead was a visible *jamohr*— place of the seal—a raised callus an inch in diameter that pious folk develop by constant prayer, touching their foreheads to those ceramic tiles called *mohr*, though some say that these *jamohris* simply rub the tile incessantly on their foreheads to produce the effect.

Baharlu, they knew, traveled throughout Germany, operating from the Shiite Center in Hamburg. He preached everywhere, and cassettes of his speeches were copied, and copied again they made their way to Iran.

Netzer knew no Persian, but wanted to hear Baharlu, hear the inflections, catch if he could the ambience of the room. Shadi came back and together they listened to the tapes. They could tell Baharlu had an audience. They could hear chairs moving and individuals coughing; sometimes the audience would answer Baharlu as he spoke, or break in saying, "*Allaho akbar*. God is most great." Netzer sensed Hoseyn there under the hiss of the tape.

Netzer listened carefully with the translations before him, Shadi turning them for him as Baharlu spoke, slowly and meditatively.

"A Moslem," Baharlu said, "is either a true revolutionary or not a true Moslem. I look upon you brothers here and think of our dead brothers at home and those of Palestine expelled from their land by imperialism."

Shadi pointed out that Baharlu would occasionally repeat in Arabic something he had said to his Iranian audience. "It's a

187

strange Arabic. He learned it in school."

Did that mean there were Arabs present?

Likely.

Netzer smiled. Suleyman Chemissa?

"I know you live today," Baharlu said, "as our blessed Prophet—God's peace be upon him. . . ."

The group repeated, "God's peace be upon him."

"And his blessed Helpers—God's peace be upon them all . . ."

"God's peace be upon them all."

". . . as they lived in the days of the extirpation of ignorance and the breaking of idols. My brothers, in the whole of the Koran there was not a single Moslem who was not a revolutionary. Now it is our time, again a time of ignorance, a time for idols to be broken. Imperialism dominates Iran. It has transformed our society to a bourgeois model, totally dependent on foreign capitalism and capitalist relations. The Pahlavi dynasty is without support beyond the comprador class, and the shah maintains himself with terror, intimidation, and propaganda. We can shatter this atmosphere of terror with heroic acts. Through the examples and militant teachings of Mohammad, Ali, and Hoseyn. Islam is the expression of the toiling masses fighting oppression, and Hoseyn is the supreme symbol of that fight."

The audience sang a prayer here. Netzer hoped Hoseyn Jandaqi's voice was among them.

Other tapes had come to Munich, from the holy cities of Iraq, from Karbala and Najaf. On some of them, an old man's voice, nasal and thin now, but still bearing traces of an old sonority, spoke in his provincial accent. His message was simple and he repeated it constantly in his talks: "The shah must go."

The old man, Netzer knew, had been an exile in a strange land for years, expelled from Iran for instigating riots in the mid-sixties, and feeble now, though in the photographs accompanying the tapes, his body, like his voice, still showed signs of a former robustness. The hands and the arms were thick, and the eyes were sharp and penetrating.

From Iraq the cassettes came to Germany and France and

were copied there by the hundreds, perhaps by the thousands. Students, exiles, employees even of the mosque financed by the Iranian government in Hamburg, helped copy them. Then busloads of folk brought them overland through Munich and Turkey, concealed in the scarves on their women's heads, in hollowed-out books, in traveler's kits, in vest pockets, clothing, electrical appliances, radios. Some were simply mailed.

Thence, many of them, to Qom, that dry white desert city a hundred kilometers south of Tehran, where the caretakers of the Fayziyyeh, the old man's school, shut down since 1975, got them and distributed them.

In the shadow of the golden-domed shrine of Hazrat-e Ma'sumeh, for the Fayziyyeh lies just to the north of that wondrous building, they were passed surreptitiously to others in the back chambers, away from the courtyard paved with the tombstones of the pious (Islamic gravestones are flush with the ground and cover the coffin). They say Qom imports corpses and exports mullahs, but in those days, at least, Qom distributed tapes, too, and they made their way to all the mosques of Iran.

"We must weep for the whole of Iran," the old man said, "that these 'gentlemen' "—he said the word in English—"that these 'gentlemen' go to the universities and don't wish to learn true knowledge, which is Islam, but, no, want to ape the foolishness of the West and of the imperialists.

"The matter of free elections and the shah's promises are all false. And elections, free or not, with this shah and this regime are unlawful. And the promises of the shah, too, are all based on deception. And the nation of Iran will no longer be fooled by these conspiracies. *Shah bayad bera.* The shah must go."

And the crowd—it was somewhere by the shrine of the Imam Hoseyn at Karbala—echoed him and said, *"Allaho akbar, Allaho akbar!"*

"The shah for some time has been busy carrying out his schemes to fool the nation. He's talked with individuals, he's retreated in order to fool the people. But the nation is not willing for the shah to remain shah, however much he may retreat. The shah must go."

189

"*Allaho akbar!*" sang the crowd.

He spoke of the crimes of the shah and the upturning of religion. Did not the state seize the schools, once the province of priests, and teach children foreign ideology? Did not the state seize the courts, also once the province of priests, and substitute injustice for true justice, which is Islam? And did not the traitorous shah sell the birthright of the nation to the foreigners and give them commercial rights—monopolies—unheard of elsewhere? Did not the shah buy arms to oppress the people and reward the imperialists? The so-called land reform, the destruction of the family, the capitulations to the foreign militarists who could commit crimes in Iran, even rape, even murder, and not be tried, but no, could escape justice, infidel criminals, was all this not an abomination? Was it not?

The crowd sang "*Allaho akbar*" at all the appropriate points, and the old man's voice broke with emotion through the sermon. "The definite word, supported by the nation, is that the shah, with all the crimes he has committed against this nation and country, with all the treason he has committed up to now, is not acceptable. Not himself, not his dynasty. This dynasty must be overturned. The shah, must go."

"*Dorud bar Khomeyni*," sang the crowd at the end. "Hail Khomeyni!"

For Netzer they all sounded alike. The printed essays bored him. Through them clumped thudding Marxist phrases like an army of peasants. Class analysis, dependency, toilers, earnest "critiques" of this and that position. Netzer had no patience with such stuff. Social abstractions, even convenient ones, bored him.

And he'd seen the anti-Zionist stuff before: "America monitors and directs the line of events in the Middle East so that the Zionist racist elite that forms the criminal government hierarchy of Israel can control the events of the region in aspects and implement any plot and conspiracy they choose with the aid of the Great Satan. Hence it benefits in this way from the numerous efforts of other puppet Arab regimes that unjustly dominate Islamic countries and serve imperialism. The Islamic Nation is under constant oppression here, an oppression that stems from the deep enmity and hostility of world arrogance against Islam and the Moslems."

To Netzer it was all empty. A few new authors for Central Registry to catalogue and for Operations to try to find. That was all. Rahmani, Chemissa, Baharlu, tapes of an old man's harangue. In all of it Netzer saw only ghosts and phantoms, and, staring at the boy's picture, wondered, Who's running you, Hoseyn? Who are they? Netzer could almost feel the presence behind Hoseyn of a ghostly committee whispering softly, gently nudging Hoseyn forward, lifting Hoseyn's arm for him, sighting down the barrel of Hoseyn's gun, and tapping Hoseyn quietly to signal the moment of firing.

Who *are* they? Netzer wondered.

10

"Account number 22YW21," said Richard Levesque, "is held by a corporation called Allgemeine Produkte."

It was a different bar this time, up near the Gare de l'Est and not nearly so fancy as the Grand Zinc. It had electronic games, though, and the place sounded like World War III.

Levesque had phoned Jim in Tehran. Jim's presence, Levesque said, was required in Paris. No couriers on this one.

Monsieur Charles Salem, said Levesque proudly as whole universes exploded around them, had accomplished a small and neat act of betrayal, better than Monsieur Salem would ever know. There was indeed a Bank Hügen on Claridenstrasse, Zürich. It was not spectral. Bank Hügen was a solid and discreet house at least four hundred years old. Bank Hügen employed a certain Graziani, the very gentleman whose name Jim had pulled out of Wyndham's files in Beirut. And (this was good): they had broken the bank's code.

"It was easy. We make inquiries at Bank Hügen. We find a Graziani, Pierre-Yves. Swiss national, of course." They had watched this Graziani. He was a cheap crook. That he worked for Bank Hügen was shocking, but there it was. When Graziani made the mistake of crossing the border, Levesque had him arrested on a bogus currency violation charge and sweated him for two days. (Tupov, incidentally, the other name in the Salem file, was nowhere to be found, for there was no Tupov, and the U.S. businessmen had been snookered worse than they thought, but Levesque, policeman that he was, took that all with calm. One sad truth plagued Levesque's life as it did Jim's: most leads are worthless.)

Anyway, said Levesque, they sweated Graziani and they sweated him and they got nowhere. They went through a room he kept in Paris, they went through his car. Finally, perhaps exceeding their legal mandate, they went through his apartment in Zürich. Here was a break: they found a computer printout in code.

Customs had recourse to military cryptographers, who, using computers ordinarily dedicated to breaking diplomatic codes, took a very close look at Mr. Graziani's printout. Which turned out to be Bank Hügen's list of clients.

"Now"—Levesque tapped his wristwatch—"there are at least fifty thousand active accounts held by French citizens in Swiss banks. All are playing the national sport, which is not lovemaking. It is tax evasion." Levesque's face showed a stagy kind of glumness when he said it that led Jim to figure Levesque was one of the 50,000.

"One hundred seventy-five million francs of flight capital is involved here, and Mr. Graziani thought to acquire some of this by threats to disclose. And so, we have the account numbers of Bank Hügen's depositors, the amounts on deposit, and the names of the account holders. Very elegant. Customs is now tracking them down by searching the Finance Ministry's income tax records, which are computerized."

Levesque leaned forward. "Allgemeine Produkte, possessor of account numbered 22YW21, is domiciled in Liechtenstein. It controls these companies." Levesque produced a little list and read it to Jim. "Rochant Frères; Alliance Electronique, SA; Compagnie Weber d'Assurance; Transports Méditerranéens; Ingénieurs Rolands. All have French names and registries. None," Levesque said triumphantly, "are French taxpayers. My friend"—Levesque tapped the table now—"we've got a giant here. Octopus, you know? Banque du Proche Orient et d'Europe transfers money to AP, and AP owns the five French companies—at least five. There may be more."

He leaned still closer to Jim. "But it's a funny octopus, a funny kind of capitalism." He tapped his wristwatch. "They're all phony. All are post office boxes. *All* of them. Now I ask you, why so many post office boxes? It's indecent. Letterhead stationery that is meaningless. Telex numbers that connect to nothing, telephones no one answers. The boards of directors from the Marseilles Book of the Dead. *Étonnant*, really."

193

"Weird, Richard."

"So. And 'Allgemeine Produkte,' the name means 'General Products.' I like that."

"Has a ring to it. Nothing there? Nothing at all?"

"Ah, they're so *sly*, Jim, so clever." Levesque smiled. "Drop AP for the moment. Now, it happens Ingénieurs Rolands turns up on other lists. It is partly foreign-owned and it is nicely registered with the Office of Foreign Assets Control. The company is registered in the name of a French partner called LeGros, who is nowhere to be found. This is mysterious. The Office of Foreign Assets Control lists a Mr. Hushang Razavi, an Iranian, as silent partner in Ingénieurs Rolands. *He* is nowhere to be found, and *this* is mysterious. But six months ago, Ingénieurs Rolands applied for and received an export license to ship overseas current converters manufactured by Calmer Cie, a company headquartered in Lille and one of the world's foremost producers of electromagnetic technology.

"But Calmer Cie doesn't have that many customers. Their equipment is specialized, after all. Fifty to a hundred, tops. Calmer Cie is state-owned. So we find out who the customers are. The list is internal and closely held. But we obtain it." The look on Levesque's face suggested burglary rather than interministerial cooperation. "Possibly these are not all the dealings, but it is a list, yes? We inspect the said list, we see what? All customers are familiar but a handful. We inspect the handful, we find what? Not Ingénieurs Rolands, but a company called Rochant Frères of Marseilles, which, as I say, is owned by AP and is only a post office box and some stationery. Most mysterious, you see? So. Now, these current converters are heavy machines. If Rochant Frères is a post office box, how can you fit them in? Current converters are too big to fit into mailboxes. Too heavy. So where do they go, Morgan? Where do they go?"

"Freight forwarder with a note to the P.O. box."

"Just right. They go to freight forwarder, whom we visit. Who takes his orders from the P.O. box, too, see? It's easy. And what do we find? Rochant Frères buys the motors from Calmer Cie, Ingénieurs Rolands buys them from Rochant Frères, and Pars Imports of Tehran buys them from Ingénieurs Rolands.

Pars Imports says they go to a textile company. It's black and white, open and shut."

"What textile company?"

"Who knows?"

"Who's Pars Imports?"

"Iranians. Who can tell?"

"Port of entry?"

"Into Iran? Bushire, on the Persian Gulf."

"Who's Rochant Frères?"

"Ah, that's hard. I don't know. It's just a post office box. Just a hole in a wall. Just a little door."

"No assets at the post office?"

"Hey, hey, Morgan, that's a good one, that's where we live. Yeah, man, that's a good one. We have breakfast, lunch, and dinner at the post office, you know? No, there are no papers. No records anymore. Funny, no? Gone."

"So other people have breakfast at the post office?"

"That's it. It's bad. It's open city, Morgan, no tracks. Not by anybody."

"Isn't this a little involved?"

"Surely. That's why we follow it. The sure signal of thievery."

Levesque told Jim he wanted the Iranian connection and left abruptly. Through the window, Jim watched him buy flowers and disappear into the rue Sebastopol. The flower seller, an old lady, stood in the chill by her green pushcart. The pushcart had thick red wheels, and asters covered it.

Current converters, Jim thought. Sounds like Datatron. To Bushire on the Gulf. Sounds like the VE project. Put it together, sport, and it sounds like Shlomo Givon.

Jim had taken down the name of the Iranian partner in Ingénieurs Rolands: Razavi. Hushang Razavi.

When Jim came back to Beirut again he said no hellos at the Commodore. His visa was multiple entry, and he hoped it generated no attention.

Michel, when Jim found him, was alert, still with the whiskey in his hand. Might have been the same glass.

"Was it you?"

"No."

"Who?"

Michel stared at Jim for a moment, and Jim saw no guile in his face. "When in a game of chance," Michel said finally, "look about to see who is the fool. If you do not see him"— Michel smiled sadly—"you're the fool."

"Who did it?"

Michel put his whiskey glass down. "A photograph was involved yes?"

Jim sat quietly. All right, he thought. All right.

"It was passed down a chain, yes? A chain is of great advantage sometimes. For concealment of the source, it is excellent. But the chains sometimes have weak links. It is their great defect. This one did. The photograph came into the wrong hands. That fact became known. The weak link, Jim, was very weak. And with encouragement informed of the person who first inquired after the photograph."

Right. The fool.

"A word, Jim," Michel said, again looking straight at him. "I could threaten to kill you and it would mean nothing. Here, when someone looks you in the eye and says that, you both forget it. But when you hear it, Jim . . . indirectly, that's different. Have you heard anything? Any bad talk? Any at all?"

"Am I hearing it now?"

"In a manner."

"Your opinion?"

"Leave."

11

"This group, Joel, these martyrs—where are they?" Netzer was with Halperin in Ha Qiryat. "One dead Arab. One. And the rest slink away."

"It was a fine operation."

"I don't question the fineness. But they struck too soon. No consultation, not even a mention to the rest of us. Yes?"

"Security."

"Sure, Joel, security. Did you know of this operation?" Halperin shrugged.

"And now they're all gone."

Netzer started on their own Givon material.

The classifications of all Givon's documents were Top Secret and Secret, so all had been hand-carried out of Tehran by courier and only in double envelopes. Two receipts were required for the stuff—one for the outer package, one for the inner. The documents were logged out, then in, by date, number, title, and accepting office. Netzer checked the inventories, bored, just to be sure. These were done three times a year, and on Givon's documents they all came up right: no apparent losses. He got the printouts, too, listing all Top Secret material for which each receiving unit was responsible. There were three units for Givon's stuff. Technology (under that, Electronics and Services), Coordination (Methodology, Central Registry, Non-Arab), and Protective Security. All came out clean. The documents logged out of Tehran were all logged nicely into Tel Aviv. They'd had clean handlers. Some documents were listed as destroyed, and Netzer wondered about *them*, but he tracked them down and they turned out to be insignificant—books, newspaper articles, and the like. But what there was he called in, every scrap of Givon material he could access, every folder, chart, photograph, dossier, situation analysis, map, diagram, memorandum, note, conversation report that Givon had ever produced out of Tehran.

Rafael Frank had been put in charge of a bank of listeners and transcribers in Tehran and himself had been run out of Tel Aviv, unbeknownst to Netzer, who smiled when he learned. The quantities were enormous. Netzer thought they must have had regiments of translators working eight-hour shifts, like coal miners.

Givon and company had been everywhere. They had covered SAVAK (six offices in Tehran, several in the provinces), and via SAVAK they had gotten here and there into Military Intelligence, the Inspectorate, the Special Office, the Plan Organization, the Atomic Energy Organization, the National Iranian Oil Consortium (eleventh floor, director's office, no less). They had managed to piggyback SAVAK surveillance of foreigners, too, first and foremost themselves, of course, then the Americans, the British, the Russians.

They covered the OPEC office, municipal police units in Tehran, the military police, the gendarmerie headquarters in the capital and the Gulf provinces.

They hadn't neglected the private sector. They had made surprising and altogether admirable inroads into banks (Bank Omran, Bank Tehran), investment companies (Iranshahr Finance), insurance companies (Bimeh Melli), industrial ventures (directors' room, Fars and Khuzistan Cement Company), the Pahlavi Foundation. Netzer turned the pages with wonder, something close to awe.

Givon and team had also supplied disinformation of a high artistic quality, messages for SAVAK prepared in Tel Aviv: phony Israeli negotiating positions over oil barter arrangements, overestimations of Iraqi military strength (to frighten His Imperial Majesty into higher preparedness on the western frontier, which in point of fact probably hadn't been necessary); and once, daringly, Netzer noticed, they had manufactured references to a certain anti-Israeli journalist in the pay of the Syrians, seeming evidence that he was in fact an Israeli agent. (It had no effect, though, Givon noted. The man, owlish and professorial, continued to appear on the more serious television talk shows. Pity.) The tricks ran on and on, and Netzer studied them approvingly.

It was beautiful, as easy as walking in the door.

But then, going through all of it—the cables, the yellowing papers, the dull plastic folders—Netzer wondered. He thought of the young man and that picture out of Shuwayra. Just a name, a photo or two, and a spiral notepad. That was all he had.

Hoseyn, Hoseyn, Hoseyn, he thought, rubbing the red patches on his nose where his rimless glasses had cut in, bringing his hand over his forehead and temples, which were beginning to ache chronically, working his mouth as if drawing the saliva would draw out the secret of the documents and the death. Hoseyn, he wondered, where are you now? What is your connection with these people? Who's behind you?

Meir in Tehran thought Netzer was malingering, but it wasn't so, and Meir should have known. Netzer, in fact, spent his days and nights poring over the material. It took weeks. He wanted Givon's contacts. The secret lay with them, men suborned, bought, and paid for. Their signatures and thumbprints on receipts for cash would be on file in Tehran and Tel Aviv. Was one a double? Did one get turned? Did one betray? How to tell?

The names of Givon's informants, of cooperative individuals, were coded, and Givon, it seemed, had kept half the code in his head half the time; they were lacking in the files, or if present, then inconsistent. Maddening.

At the end of a long day a few weeks into it, Netzer would feel a ubiquitous pain from his neck to his forehead. Sometimes the pain localized itself and crept from, say, just in front of his right ear up into his temple and around into his eyesocket. Sometimes it was in the back of his neck, pushing insistently at the base of his skull, sometimes in the hinge of his jaw. He would bring his hand, its fingers thick and stubby, to his eyes and rub them.

Netzer, alone and morose, took to talking to himself. "We kept the material file on Givon's contacts meager on purpose," he said late one night (he thought it was afternoon), "to protect the network. To protect them! It's a joke. Get it? We protected them, all right. From ourselves!"

Netzer sometimes felt that life was a cosmic mistake and that misunderstandings were the basis of it. God has played a trick on us, he thought. This is part of the trick. A minor piece of comedy, of course, just a bit of business, like one of those little steps Ophir makes on the stage when he imitates a bicycle or some such. In the end, not funny. Like this.

He went on and on, hour running into hour, days merging, documents he was attempting to collate acquiring feet and wandering off and hiding somewhere when he needed them most, leading him on mad chases among the piles.

After a time, he felt like a Talmudic scholar, his back bent and aching and his ears ringing with study. Netzer smiled at the thought, for he had no faith, not in monotheism anyway. Netzer thought the universe was full of devils, in fact, and that nothing transcended anything.

When he'd gone through all the material again and again— he lost track of the times—he had lists and his own diagrams, painstakingly drawn. The lists were long, the diagrams complex. Names, places, access routes to buildings. Some of the equipment had been sold outright, some of it installed clandestinely. Netzer had noted the cooperative personnel. They never knew, most of them. That's what Givon had thought.

Givon. He kept to himself, they all knew. He'd drifted away. Gotten strange. Was he crazy? Possibly. What did he get close to?

As he worked, Netzer sensed something. A pattern. The way dates and offices fell together. You could tell, he thought, if you put it in order by date, by location, even by receiving office in Tel Aviv. A word from here, a word from there seemed to suggest a third location. Then with the third location and a fourth, Givon would find a fifth. Had Givon been triangulating with the material? Netzer thought he saw something more than scientific serendipity spin out before his eyes. The process seemed methodical. Was Givon going after something? Or someone? Someone so deep he was on the other side of the earth?

In Tehran, with Netzer gone, Meir wandered around town aimlessly. There *was* Dvorah. Her face was round, her hair cut

200

short, her eyes dark and flashing. She liked it when Meir recited poetry she could not understand. She liked, he thought, having her lips bruised.

But Netzer? Where was he? Meir envied him being in Tel Aviv with the food there. Meir remembered the Lieber Gott on Allenby Street and Lily the chef, the *kashrut* certificate there on the window. You walk through the door and then down the three steps and encounter the insane waiters, aging, all of them from Poland, shuffling in and out, afflicted with tunnel vision. They never see you unless they look straight at you and they don't do that unless they choose. Ah, but the *cholent*, the knishes. And Batia's up on Dizengoff and Arlosoroff streets, the cheese blintzes there, Meir thought, the goulash, the *kishke*. Nothing like that in Tehran.

The November rains chilled and darkened the landscape and Meir, despondent, pottered around at routine legation duties and wondered if the energy had gone out of the search.

In Tel Aviv, amid the files he'd unearthed, the puzzling diagrams, incomplete and suggestive timetables he'd constructed, the lists of names, some phony, some real, Ariel Netzer had come across a cable, Classification Gold, the highest of the high. It was perhaps just by chance they'd accessed it for him and it was certainly just by chance he'd noticed the brief paragraph. It was attached to the end of a situation report Givon had sent. It referred to an operation in Tehran. Netzer hadn't heard of it before, not a whisper, and neither had Halperin, the latter said, when Netzer confronted him with it. "More security, huh, Joel? Like the Chemissa operation, right?"

A special team had come in and gone out, the two of them concluded. Had to have been that way. The paragraph read in entirety: "EAGLE operation via Confident2. Termination as planned. Placed 9 Feb."

Someone had killed someone, Netzer and Halperin both knew. The language was typical and the sense obvious. There was no other paper on the action that Netzer could discover, and that was typical, too, and indicative. There had been a killing. Givon was connected, perhaps had arranged it.

* * *

Who were they? Netzer sat in his locked vault and stared at the paragraph, reading it repeatedly. "Termination as planned." More ghosts, more phantoms. "EAGLE." What was EAGLE? Why did Givon die? He switched off the fluorescent lamp in his carrel. He knew where to look in Tehran.

12

Meydun-e Shoosh, the Square of Susa, lies far to the south even of Reza Khan's great railroad station. It is in a part of the city where people washed up when the villages decayed and agriculture died during the Great Civilization. Enormous trucks from the southern ports roar through the place and head for the freight yards and warehouses down there, pushing their way through wheezing, half-broken-down buses, vans, and cars, all of them coughing smoke.

Here, Reza Modarresi drifted amiably through the stream of the jostling folk that fill the *kuchehs* and the byways off the *meydun*. Women with tins of water balanced on their heads, and children under their arms, their chadors clenched in their teeth against the gaze of men. The vegetable sellers and their braying donkeys, the kerosene man pushing his cart of fifty-liter cans down the street, his clothes permeated with the stuff, a cigarette dangling from the side of his mouth. *"Nafti, hoy, nafti!"* he shouts and his cart rumbles over the pavement and is gone. And the salt man—the *namaki*—returning home from the upper parts of the city, his pushcart piled with stale bits of bread, hard as rocks, that he's gotten in those wealthy neighborhoods in exchange for the salt he starts out with in the morning, taking the dry crusts to kitchens off the *meydun*, where they're boiled into soup, keening, *"Namak! Namaki!"*

Reza Modarresi's roots went back to dusty villages in the east, in Khorasan, which means "Land of the Rising Sun," he told Jim once, where peaches and pistachios grow and where Reza had a tangled network of family and clan, many of whose members were mullahs of a certain dignity, and one of the latter, ill-humored and stern, a *hojjatoleslam* in the holy city of Mashhad.

Reza had a Reuters card and wrote for an American news magazine. Every press bureau in the East has someone like Reza, and they attain an odd savvy. Reza was, among other things, contact point for the foreign journalists, the ones who came and went, who called him "Ray" and punched him in his ribs jovially and got enough information out of him to write their articles. He tolerated them; they were occasionally useful. He drove a fancy car, had long hair, wore jazzy clothing, and had married an emancipated woman, who wore her hair short and who had, in Jim's considered opinion, a sweet little body.

Reza had an innocent face, boyish, with a child's eyes, and a way of holding his head that made him look ingenuous and forthright. Which he was not.

The foreign journalists never began to know what he knew. Reza knew everyone in the Pahlavi scheme of things, starting with the leaders of the *zurkhanehs* (houses of strength), and the toughs of the fruit and vegetable bazaars, the *chaqukeshan* (knife wielders) of the south of town, who dressed in black—black trousers, black shirts, black belts, and wide-brimmed black hats—*araq*-drinking wild men. He knew the directors of the labor guilds and syndicates and unions, owned and operated by the Pahlavis. He knew, of course, the journalists of preference who got by-lines and royal subsidies, and who were so good they didn't have to be told what to write; he knew the lawyers, doctors, engineers, the leaders of the Rotary Club, the Lions Club, the Tehran Club, the Gorgan Club, the Freemasons. He knew the *majles* members and committee chairmen, and he watched them, for the independent legislation they introduced was the clearest possible indication of royal thought.

He knew their secretaries, aides, whores, adjutants, and lovers. He knew ex-prime ministers and why they had gotten cashiered (some of them for peculation, some for honesty, for circumstances constantly ebbed and flowed in the Great Civilization).

He knew the particulars of the assassinations of generals, whose murders were thought political (and were, at least,

204

halfway), but whose deaths occurred in moonlit alleys on assignations of one sort or another.

Reza's mind was an infinitely complex tableau of these personalities and their interlocking interests, duties, and enmities, all looking upward to the apex, where the Light of the Aryans shone forth as a blazing sun.

And so, of course, Reza knew the royal family and its factions and feuds, and the strain of lunacy that ran through them.

Reza's world was the world of these persons—and being a provincial from the east and an outsider to them all, he moved through them all with a certain nonchalance, a detachment—wherein a *chaqukesh* who lurked about Naser Khosrow or Sabzi Meydun, he with the sharpened belt buckle fashioned for the neck of a foe (his or someone else's), was not, in Reza's eyes, much different from a sleek and fatted industrialist lazing in a palace in the far north of the city. Reza's eager eyes took them all in in a kind of wonderment. Life, for Reza, was a vast show, all of it instructive.

Jim had come to know him well, recognized he was an encyclopedia, erratic sometimes, uncooperative at others, but an encyclopedia nonetheless. The name "Hushang Razavi" meant nothing to Reza when Jim asked in an offhand way if he might, just might recognize it. They were in the Marmar Hotel, whose dark, circular bar made it a reasonable place to ask such questions. But Reza got a funny look on his face at the mention of Pars Imports. Jim knew him well enough to recognize it. Onto Something.

"It's a Pahlavi business."

"Yeah? What isn't?"

"Not much. It's touchy, Jim. I mean real touchy." Reza had been on other business. His informant, a kid with an honest face who leafletted the university students with Third World, and third-rate, Marxist tracts, had told him about a flap down off Meydun-e Shoosh. "There was a major thing there once. It's a truck yard in the south of town. It was hushed up, but the government—that's what people called it; it was Tehran municipality—came in one day and cleared out the squatters' shacks around the place. Everybody out, clean. The army helped. Didn't leave a house within a hundred meters of the place in all directions. The government said it was putting up public housing, but the project has yet to start. Made a few of the radical leaflets.

"You can imagine it. Homeless people, most of them owning nothing. Old women with bundles on their heads left sitting outside the quarter, feet in the *joobs* as army trucks roar by. Kids yelling. The young men would have hightailed it out of the area when they heard the army was coming in. These operations happen. It's known. There'd be no mullahs around just then either. But they would come back. And so would the young men."

As Reza looked at Jim, he knew Jim was on to the Pars Imports thing in some strange way Reza didn't fathom, for Jim, try as he might, couldn't hide the hungry, calculating look on his face.

Reza didn't want to. He really didn't. House and wife and kid, Reza thought. And he thought it again and said the words to himself: house and wife and kid. Then he wondered what Jim knew and how he knew it and stared at his hands again. House and wife and kid. And even as he said those words and told himself, Don't do it, don't even think about doing it, he was wondering if he'd get away with it.

In the byways off Meydun-e Shoosh, Reza drifted. It could have been a purposeless stroll. With no sign of interest, Reza managed to wander past one truck yard in particular, with its great gate closed. A truck parked in front, Reza guessed—correctly—was a watchpoint. Reza took it all in in a glance, not batting an eye at the single lamp by the door, the tower on one end, the clearing in front of the place strewn with rubble, the empty houses across the clearing. Behind it, it looked as if there was a vacant lot, but he didn't go to see. The dirty brown gate with the words "Pars Imports" painted across it and the No Parking sign and the closed shops—those were what he looked at. It was an easy run past it, and to Reza's eye it was enough. The crowds were curiously thin here—there were no shops and no houses—and Reza didn't care for the feeling that gave him and passed beyond to more humane scenes.

While buying a pack of Winstons, manufactured in Israel,

all firmly believed, at the odds-and-ends seller's blue stall, Reza learned that the onetime owner of said unprepossessing truck garage now known as Pars Imports was an old man, a billionaire many times over, named Haj Amin Golpayegani, a fat hajji of many pilgrimages and drenched in sanctity.

And while making a purchase of sweets from a corner grocery, the *kharbarforushi*, he heard that the place, when this Haj Amin owned it, was called Says Bar (Says Trucking).

They told him Haj Amin dwelt in the upper part of the city, and Reza knew this was true; the name Haj Amin Golpayegani had rung all sorts of bells in Reza's capacious and talented mind.

A quick trip from Meydun-e Shoosh to the upper reaches of the city is never possible. On the way Reza had a passable plate of rice and kabab with ground sumac, raw egg, and broiled tomato and a fine bottle of the soda water and yoghurt drink called *doogh*, well away from the Pars Imports neighborhood, whose food kitchens are dangerous to the health. He snoozed in the Reuters office till the late afternoon, when the city reawakened, and then made his way up to the environs of the house of Haj Amin Golpayegani.

The person of Haj Amin was not the object of Reza's attention. Not just then. Reza set that problem aside for the time being, for he had a hunch—he deserved his Reuters card for this—that Haj Amin was the sort who would do business in the neighborhood of Haj Amin, not in the neighborhood of Says Bar. And in the immediate neighborhood of Haj Amin's old house, there was but one *mahzar*. A *mahzar* is a kind of notary public's office, where Persians record their affairs: marriages, divorces, rents, sales of property, writs of various kinds, tax depositions, powers of attorney, deaths, loans—in short, all the business of life.

Reza entered Mahzar No. 4 of the *nahiyyeh* of Shemran. The obligatory wait in the main hall gave Reza time to size up the lines of authority. After a short discussion with the blue-smocked teaboy, made interesting to the latter by some small change, Reza found himself in an alcove off the main office, where the subdirector of the *mahzar*, a man of well-trimmed beard and portly belly, brought Reza four large, thick volumes of the land and improved property records of the third year past. The neighborhood of Meydun-e Shoosh had let Reza know that the company was indeed only in its third year of operation, newcomers they were, under the protection of the shadow of the shah, may his life be long.

Reza Modarresi, nothing if not patient, with great care ran his eye down the long pages of the white blue-ruled paper and the purple seals and the orange and green stamps and the signatures and addresses they contained, searching. The smell of kerosene heaters was now in the *mahzar*, for high above the city a chill comes on early in the season when the sun declines. In the fading light, Reza looked for the signature of Haj Amin and the name "Says Bar," and he cursed himself for taking on the task and for the waste of money. The charge for a sight of the books was outrageous, and Reza had no real right to inspect public records save what he could purchase. But the very expenditure kept him at it and prodded him on. In the adjoining hall, young clerks, some in mullah's *aba* and turban, busied themselves stamping books, copying out contracts, issuing marriage licenses, and paid Reza no mind. Reza, tired, looked up occasionally from his labor to see from the window the tin roofs of the surrounding houses and tall fir trees and, on Tochal Mountain, the snow, orange now in the fading day, creeping lower as the season turned.

A melancholy time. Reza tried to exorcise the gloom by humming and by thinking of verses of spring, of which he knew many. "Now returns the rose," he sang under his breath, paging through the *daftars*, "to the meadow, from Nothingness to Being. The violet now at the rose's foot in obeisance bows." And, taking up another volume, "At dawn went I to the garden, roses to pluck, when of a sudden heard I the nightingale's trill." Long before he'd gotten through volumes three, four, and now a fifth, he'd run out of verses and his voice had trailed off in weariness. It hadn't worked. Reza shivered in the chill and gloom, thinking of winter coming on, and paging through the dusty, leather-bound record books, cold to the touch.

The teaboy had circulated quietly as afternoon became evening and turned on lights all through the *mahzar*. Outside, too, Reza saw lights shining here and there on the mountainside in the night, white points in the barren darkness.

The yelp of triumph he made was audible to the clerks nearby, though they had no idea what it was about. Looking down wearily once again at the *daftar*, eyes aching, Reza had seen it. Haj Amin, in the month of Dey, in the year 1352, had signed his property in the *nahiyyeh* of Meydun-e Shoosh, in the *ku* of Nosrat, over to the company Pars Imports of such and such a registration in such and such a *mahzar* for such and such a consideration. There followed the signature of the attorney for the company Pars Imports, a man unknown to Reza. Reza duly took notes.

So, Reza—he came to think of himself as Reza the traveler—found himself once again in the area of Meydun-e Shoosh, at Mahzar No. 49, a dusty, tumbled-down building, with crumbling stairs and peeling paint not far off the *meydun*. The employees here were all mullahs, and the one in charge, elderly and bilious, sat at the very end of the one long room on the second floor in turban and robe, his collar smudged and buttoned high around his throat, his beard of the three-day species. He had a sharp eye and a low voice, and from his face, Reza knew him as one not well-disposed toward inquirers. Every rose has a thorn, thought Reza as he approached, remembering the words of an old poet, wherever royal pearls are found, man-devouring sharks must be also, and—standing now directly before the mullah—all treasures are guarded by snakes. And so this mullah shakes the chain of enmity toward me.

The mullah grunted acknowledgment of Reza's existence, poor though he considered it, and with a flinty gaze listened as Reza attempted to perforate his stony heart with the diamond tears of a sad story.

There was a man, Reza intimated, whose name must remain unrevealed, whose wife was in her own right an owner of some poor property. The wife, alas, seeks divorce, and the man, fearful he does not know all the circumstances of her property—a settlement would be more auspicious if he did— wishes information of a certain kind that is to be found, it is thought, in a *daftar* of this place.

"Great personages," Reza said, "are marked with charity," and made his offer.

"Get thee gone!" was the mullah's stern and immediate reaction to Reza's absurdly low proposal.

But with the velvet persistence practiced by those who deal with authority in Persia, Reza insinuated darkly that he who sent him on his mission was a personage of not inconsiderable weight, whose rank in the world was to be reckoned with. Which second lie impressed the mullah not one iota, and Reza in the end upped the price. After hesitant consideration, the mullah said simply but with a snarl, "There," and gestured with his eyebrows to a corner of the room and a wooden bench.

Reza, who had in hand the exact registration number of Pars Imports, found the volume quickly and the reference with dispatch. When he did, he felt the very same emotion Jim did when he was Onto Something.

There was indeed a Pars Imports, registered with the proper number, in the proper book, on the proper page, with the proper date. Everything was proper. And who signed as the owner of Pars Imports, Incorporated, with the stamp on the red lion and sun in purple ink affixed thereon, but the president himself, one Engineer Hushang Razavi.

"Holy shit. So what kind of deal was it?" Jim and Reza were in the warm brilliance of the Intercontinental, Reza mellow now on vodka tonics he had left off counting.

"Property transfer. No stock, nothing. It was like buying a house."

"Jesus."

"Yeah. Pretty funny."

And so Jim wondered along with Reza.

Reza knew something of Haj Amin. He was of an ancient family, much courted by the shah (land reform had passed Haj Amin by, though it plagued his neighbors).

"The guy's old, Jim, you know? Really old. And real traditional. From the south. Made his killing selling hides and wool and sugar cane. He's a billionaire, Jim. He swims in it." Reza was wrong on the billions, and Jim knew that in the way you know things in Iran—suspicious surmise—but the man must have money. That was for sure. "And he just lives in this crappy little house, you know? In the north of the city. Really crappy, Jim. First-rank lousy. Villas and palaces all around him and he lives in this place. The main floor is sunk below the street. It's got this courtyard, okay? In which there is nothing. Zero. And across the courtyard is the kichen on one side and the toilet on the other. First-rank lousy and the man's a *billionaire*. There are a lot of these guys. They're not modern. They got no sense. Why live like that? They don't know any better."

For Reza and for Jim, too, the crossing of two stars in the firmament is never without meaning. But also for Reza and Jim, the trick is to divine their meaning. Hushang Razavi and Haj Amin Golpayegani. A conjunction to be noted.

There's never enough room on Naderi, the old shopping street that borders the south wall of the British embassy. Reza walked it slowly, idling in the crowds and the hubbub. He passed a blind man dressed in rags moving jerkily through the commotion, squeezing an accordion. The man's neck was twisted (it looked broken), and he faced up toward a sky he could never see. A boy beating a tambourine led him, their sounds rising above the noise of the traffic and the crowd. The sidewalk was littered with magazine kiosks out toward the street and a dozen kinds of merchandise piled against the walls of the dingy yellow brick buildings—rolls of plastic tablecloth, cheap glass dishes, empty bottles, shelled walnuts piled in little pyramids on aluminum trays, roasting ears of corn the Persians call *balal* and vendors dip in salted water for the customer. Sidewalk salesmen were beginning to pump up and light their hissing Primus lamps, the netting in them glowing so white you can't look at them directly. Tehran was coming properly alive after the torpor of the afternoon. It had scrubbed its face and had its tea and was awake in the evening air, which was chilly and, like the snows on Tochal, hinting of winter. Skewers of kabab sizzled on charcoal braziers along with *kubideh*—chopped lamb mixed with onion and tarragon and formed into patties—and the pungence of the lamb and the onions lifted in the evening air.

Reza bought a bouquet of carnations in pale green waxed paper and turned down Qavam ol-Saltaneh, then into a narrow lane of four-story apartments. He pushed the buzzer of one.

After a time, a soft voice over the intercom asked, *"Ki e?"*

"Yeprim, Khanom," he answered. Reza had a square head and light skin and could put on a believable Armenian accent when he spoke Persian; hence his *nom de guerre* Yeprim— Abraham in less explosive languages—was Armenian. One weighed the odds in these things, as in all others.

When the door buzzed open, Reza entered and went up the stairs. The scents of stewing lamb and lemon and fenugreek were in the air. He passed a motor scooter tethered for safety on the second landing, then on the third floor he found the familiar old door, scuffed and kicked and scratched at the base, and knocked twice. It was the old signal (Reza had other signals for other ladies similarly ensconced), and she let him in.

She was known as Farifteh. Middle Eastern folk call their entertainers by one name for some reason, perhaps out of affection for them and their quirks. She was known to Reza as Farfar Khanom. He had worked her for her scandals and sold them everywhere, for Farfar Khanom sang to him the way she used to sing to her audiences.

She seemed tired to Reza this evening. Her face lit up only briefly at the sight of the carnations. She'd been crying, like the last time; Reza could see the double chin, hair frizzy now and unkempt, the reddened eyes. Her real name was Sediqeh. She'd been raised in the south of Tehran, married at fifteen, divorced at eighteen, with two daughters both gone with the father. Stagestruck, she had slunk around working-class theaters, around the cafés of Lalezar, down by the cloth merchants' bazaar, the shops where they sell the sewing odds and ends, and acquired a second husband, a violinist of some fame, and her star rose, for her voice was rich.

Farfar Khanom had a room and a kitchen, partitioned from the rest of a much larger apartment, the whole owned by an Assyrian widow infamous for her stinginess.

Reza sat at an unsteady wooden table and gazed at Farfar Khanom, who snuffled and blew her nose and wiped at the mascara running down her cheeks. She'd pulled the frills of her dressing gown up around her neck for modesty. A four-poster

212

took up one side of the room. Over it hung an airline calendar a year out of date, showing a coy Japanese miss in kimono peering out from behind a fan. A garderobe stood at the foot of the bed and one of its doors hung open. Silky, ruffly, pink and lavender things hung on the inside. The autumn chill was in the room.

"It's bad, Yeprim. My days are black."

"*Ey*, Farfar Khanom, make them better."

Reza put a roll of opium, wrapped in paper like a brown crayon, near her arm on the table, and Farfar smiled at him.

"How does the song go, Farfar?" Reza hummed one of her tunes, a playful twinkle in his eye, an old song from the old days: " 'You can open my hand, you can dishonor me . . .' Remember the song, Farfar Khanom? Isn't that the song? 'You can make me pour a sea of tears, but you can hardly deny my love, can hardly find a lover like me . . .' Isn't that the song?"

"Yeprim, a song dies, too. Like a human being." She smiled bitterly at him, her eyes tearing.

Talk of death disturbed Reza. No one should talk of death to come. Reza made a small puffing sound as if to dispel any notions of the subject in the room.

"*Ey*, not when *you* sing it, Farfar. When you sing it, it lives forever, or so it seems. Yes."

Her smile told him she knew it was nonsense, but he knew, too, that she could remember being alone in a spotlight at the Chattanooga, the Baccarat, or the Las Vegas, a microphone in her hands, held close to her lips when she sang. The clamor in the club would stop then and the people would listen. She could see the tables near the stage dimly lit with little orange lamps, and around the tables groups of businessmen would sit, or army officers, and she would get them to join her songs, the fast numbers, the slow ones:

> You can tread on my heart
> Forget me with all my sorrow
> Take all your love from me
> Leave my heart alone and lonely
> But you can hardly deny my love
> Can hardly find a lover like me.

213

She even sang in Turkish—"*Sän gözüm sän*," "Thou art my eyes"—and the middle-aged Azerbaijani businessmen would come alive and get up and dance by their tables as the accordions and clarinets played Azeri melodies.

Her records had sold in the sixties, but then stopped. No one knew why. Her ne'er-do-well husband had taken to heroin and playing in cheap cafés back around Lalezar, and died finally of an overdose or an underdose, no one knew, and she herself, between lovers now, took up for brief stints with older men who remembered her records and her pulsating alto: "*Mituni mosht-e mano va bokoni*"—"You can open my hand . . ."

"I have nothing, as you see. What do you want, Yeprim? *Ey, Khoda,* what do you want?"

Reza rested his hand gently on her arm. "You have a wealthy admirer, Farfar Khanom, do you not? Times cannot be all bad."

At first she wondered who Reza could possibly mean. "Soul of my heart, Yeprim . . ." she said with a curious frown.

"Amin Khan, Farfar," Reza said softly and suggestively, his hand still on her arm. "Haj Amin Golpayegani."

Which brought a laugh from Farfar Khanom. "Ay, hoo! A moon! A shining moon, he is, the dog!" She coughed. "May a calamity visit him, spread him on bread and a dog wouldn't eat it, *ey,* Yeprim! May he die young, may his body go into the clay, may the Washer of the Dead seize him! *Ey,* Yeprim, Haj Amin, by thy soul, is as mean as a merchant of Isfahan, he that puts his cheese in a bottle and rubs his bread on the outside for the flavor and the savor. A consummate miser is Haj Amin!"

Reza had known of the man's miserliness, of course. Why, the old man was niggardly even with the opium he enjoyed and rationed it to poor Farfar, when together on Farfar's creaky bed, they smoked in the old way the little clay pots called *vafur* set on the very end of a straight pipe. Both would doze, as the full effect took them, motionless for hours.

Haj Amin's miserliness was a standard theme of Farfar Khanom's, and her current outburst was moderate compared to earlier ones. She quoted the old poet Sa'di of Shiraz to Reza, who nodded recognition of the verse and agreement with the sense:

214

Whatever thou asketh in charity from the base
Profiteth thy body and diminisheth thy soul.

"With Haj Amin," she said, "there is no profit for the body and much diminution of the soul, such is his baseness." She stared sadly into Reza's eyes and fluttered with her dressing gown. Farfar Khanom always wore long sleeves, probably to hide the tracks up her chubby arms.

Reza nudged her arm again with the stick of opium. She sang, and Reza cheered her on like those businessmen and officers at the Chattanooga.

13

Alice Cochrane smoked two pipes. Into one she stuffed tobacco, tamping it down with a metal contrivance whose use she learned to admire from one of her dons at Oxford. The other she reserved for hashish. Alice didn't mix.

"I'm for hash, all right," she once told Jim. "Oh, yes, the divine weed. The Green Parrot, the Mysteries, the Seyyed, are what the Persians call it. A relaxant, James, a sweet fragrance. But," she assured him, "opium only on the rare occasion. No, not often. Just a toke once in a great while. Hash is it: the lineaments of gratified desire," she said smiling.

Alice had produced twenty-five years of good stuff for the *Financial Times*, which the Brits call the *FT* and Jim called the *Futt*. Editors of the *FT* came and went, but Alice stayed in place in Tehran. Her work was unrequited and she got piecework pay, for that's the way of the *FT*. The *FT* spans the world with these folk—in Istanbul, Rabat, Cape Town, Kuala Lumpur, Buenos Aires, some of them blissfully rich in imports-exports or public relations or something else. Alice wasn't.

Alice had come in the early fifties—about when Pari was leaving—as a young lady at the time of Mosaddeq. The Americans at the time were renting crowds and busy reinstalling the shah, and Alice dutifully recorded the dealings. For that's what they were, the buying and selling of opinions and mobs. British brains and American money, Alice remarked at the time, was what Whitehall considered the natural scheme of things.

Just walking the streets then Alice could raise a crowd. Foreigners were rare and Alice was unique. People would stop and stare at the comic *khanom* from *Engelestan*, blond and blue-eyed—*ajab!*—and alone.

Alice acquired a husband at some point, who, flying from Houston to Jidda to Tehran and points en route, never quite put together the deal he dreamed of, and moved in and out on Alice with a certain insouciance. Rumors connected him—his name was Stutely and he had a cockney cleverness—with a little French girl in Tehran.

Alice was a resource. So, one evening Jim made his way down to her place, far to the south of town, off Pahlavi and down a couple of back streets, away from the traffic. She lived in a one-story, ramshackle affair, built around a courtyard with a single light shining down from a concrete lamppost. *Takhts* outside were arranged around a shallow blue pool, and behind them all around the courtyard, rose cypress and persimmon trees. The walls were whitewashed panels of stucco interrupted with brick columns. Here Alice, in her kaftan, held court, now for the Intercontinental Hounds, now for a group of Sufis.

Vajiheh, Alice's *kolfat*, let Jim in, and he found her in her library surrounded with battered Persian editions run off on cheap Russian presses and paper, manuscripts, notes, note cards, a riot of filing folders, a collapsible metal table that served as a desk topped by a squat little typewriter and a samovar bubbling in the corner, tea glasses, sugar cubes, plates, orange peels, clutter on the desk, clutter on the floor. Jim wondered what the servant girl did to earn her keep. Stutely was nowhere to be seen.

"How goes it, luv?" Alice peered over her spectacles.

"Working on a thing, Alice? I can come back."

"Nonsense, luv. It's my honor. What's up?"

"Listen, Alice, I'm doing a thing for the rag. Very hush-hush, okay? Need some help. But it's very, very inside. We can't go yelling it from the housetops."

Alice grinned. "Ah, no, luv, wouldn't *dream!*"

Jim told her at least five percent of what he knew and considered himself generous. Give a little, get a little, he thought, and it set Alice off like a gong, as he knew it would.

"An *Israeli!* Of *course* poor Jerry got chucked for it," she said, and pulled a tea-stained English edition of Marco Polo

217

from a steel bookshelf for a preliminary disquisition on Iranian political murder. A hoary tradition.

"The very word 'assassin' comes from these parts," said Alice, leafing through the book, which she knew well. "Marco tells us of the Old Man of the Mountain, right? Well, the mountain is just north of here, whereon is constructed a fortress, vast and impregnable, at least till the Mongols took an interest in it. You can imagine their bloody Oriental eyes fixed on *that* place."

She found the passage she wanted and read it to Jim: " 'Now no man was allowed to enter the garden, save those he intended to be his *ashishin*,' that is, to be the boys he stoked up with hash, whence our word 'assassin.' For 'when the Old Man would have any prince slain, he would say to such a youth, "Go thou and slay So-and-so, and when thou returnest, my angels shall bear thee into Paradise. And shouldst thou die, nevertheless will I send my angels to carry thee back into the Paradise." So he caused them to believe.' Ah, yes, James, hash, smoke, delirium, mysticism, dreams, and paradise—a heady mixture."

Alice read on: " 'He kept at his court a number of the youths of the country from 12 to 20 years of age, such as had a taste for soldiering, and to these he would tell tales about Paradise, as Mahomet had been wont to do, and they believed in him, just as the Saracens believe in Mahomet. These he would introduce into his garden, four or six at a time, having giving them a certain potion'—that was the hash, you see— 'which cast them into a deep sleep, and when they awoke, they found themselves in a garden, all full of ladies and damsels who dallied with them to their heart's content, so that they had what young men would have.' "

Alice winked here.

" 'And when he wanted any of his *ashishin* to send on any mission, he would cause that potion whereof I spoke to be given to one of the youths of the garden, and they had him carried into his palace. So when the young man awoke, he found himself in the castle, and no longer in the Paradise. Whereat he was not well pleased. He was then conducted to the Old Man's presence and bowed before him in great veneration.'

"That's how they did it, James, how they made assassins, if old Marco's to be trusted. Got 'em drunk on God."

"More like hash."

"Same thing."

"Yeah. So, who's doing it, Alice? Who's the Old Man?"

"Khomeyni, of course. And a bunch of them here and another bunch in Europe. Don't know 'em. Not my cup of tea. But I'll tell you, the bazaaris are behind them. Bazaar's falling apart these days and they blame His Nibs," which is what Alice called the shah. "Inflation, profiteering, price fixing. Your major industrial families, the *nouveaux riches*, they've been pushing out the bazaaris for years. The *nouveaux*, they're the ones in the driver's seat now. They're the ones with the factories, the banks, the insurance companies. They're even getting into the retail trade. Department stores and all that. Cutting into the bazaaris' old markets and old ways. That's the trouble here as far as the bazaaris are concerned.

"All the oil money comes in and sends prices through the roof. His Nibs blames the merchants and organizes goon squads of college students to go round and harass them. When prices keep going up—it's his fault, mind—he jugs tens of thousands of bazaaris. It's a bear garden. The poor don't stand a chance in all this. The country's buried in money and yet times are as hard as *they've* ever known, a lot of them. So some of them think the best way to rid of His Nibs is to blow hell out of very public targets. It'll show he's not all powerful. That's the idea behind all this. When you've shown that, more'll jump on board. Then you've got your revolution. So, assassination and more assassination.

"As for an Israeli, well, there's always been a dash of the anti-semitism here. You know, they brought out a twenty-toman note a couple of months back that had six-pointed stars on it—perfectly good, traditional Islamic design, James—but they had to recall all the notes. Bazaaris didn't like them. Said it was the influence of the Jews, Jews were running the show in the Finance Ministry. So they called them all back, replaced them with eight-pointed jobs."

"People believe this stuff?"

"Nope. Only the dummies, and there aren't that many

219

running the bazaar. No, James, it was just a way of getting at the government. The government knows the bazaaris can raise an army of dummies over just such an issue."

"The usual things aren't what they seem?"

"Just so."

Alice took Jim out to her sitting room, the *otaq-e neshiman*, and they sat together on a *takht*, a worn-out old carpet draped over it. The city had quieted down and a chill hung in the air. By the door, Alice's girl put coals in a metal basket with a wire chain attached and spun the basket, coals and all, around her head; they glowed hot and hissed in the air of the hall. Then she brought them in and put them on the ceramic neck of the *qalyun* and on top of that, the *tutun*, the tobacco. Jim drew in the smoke and it bubbled through the water, a leaf from Alice's lemon tree in the *qalyun's* glass potbelly.

Alice lay back on her elbows. "You know, Mostafa Khomeyni, the old man's son, is dead. In Qom. Killed, some think. And you can feel it, Jim. You walk down a street and there is something subdued there. People look away. A sullenness. The war has escalated."

"Who got him?"

"They say SAVAK. But it's the usual: can't tell. Only thing you know is that his name was written on a leaf." Alice took a puff on the *qalyun*.

"Meaning?"

"On the fifteenth of Sha'ban, the names of the living are written on the Tree of Life. The leaves that fall carry the names of those that will die in the coming year. Poor Mostafa. His leaf fell."

"Another martyr, then. They sure like it. Martyrdom, I mean."

"Oh, yes, lots. And they like things hidden, too. Everything that's worthwhile is. A God unseen, a twelfth imam who is in occultation, unseeable, an inner faith, esoteric doctrine known only to initiates. Perhaps that's why they talk about light so much. There's a story that in the beginning, Mohammad, Adam, and all the one hundred and twenty-four thousand

220

prophets and the twelve imams were created from a ray of divine light."

"Could have fooled me."

"Um. There's another that Fatemeh, the wife of Ali, went bathing one day and when she got out of the water she was pregnant with Hoseyn. Her term was only six months, and her womb glowed with light in that month when Hoseyn was born."

"There's no light, here, Alice. It's all dust. You can't know anything here."

"Yes, you can, but you need a sense of ambiguity to cope. Reality is under the language, not of it. We're too literal-minded."

Alice looked up at Jim. "You know, the Pahlavis will never win, no matter how nasty they are. Not ever."

"Going to be a fight?"

"Yep."

"Which side are you on?" Jim asked. The old union question.

"Truth and Light."

"The light of the hundred twenty-four thousand prophets?"

"I suppose." She gave Jim the *qalyun*.

"Smoke, Alice. That's Iran."

"Right. But it's mesmerizing, isn't it?"

When Reza, who had an Oriental's delight in filigree and conspiracy, talked, Jim always wondered how much was true and how much was Reza. But they weren't drinking in the Intercontinental this time. They were both stone sober in the evening in Jim's chilly office, and Jim needed no sense of ambiguity to grasp the reality in the language. Reza's voice was low and earnest as he spoke of Pars Imports and Farfar Khanom, and Jim decided Reza couldn't be making it up, not much of it anyway. It was too good even for Reza's imagination.

Hushang Razavi was dead, hands and face blown away in a cheap truck yard in the city's southern slums on a freezing day in February. So said Haj Amin Golpayegani in one of his soaring flights on the wings of opium, and Farfar Khanom had been there to hear it.

Haj Amin, she had reported, "would sail through the Seven Heavens, between the *Arsh* and the *Farsh*" (the Empyrean and the World, she meant).

As he sailed he babbled, and as he babbled his talk ranged over all subjects and all times and was scarcely coherent.

He talked now of his youth and cleverness, now how he made his fortune, anticipating scarcity, mostly, or selling contraband in Tehran, when during the war of Hitler, the *Englees* sent stores to the *Roos;* and the Kurds and village Arabs, who knew the value of nothing in the great city, would loot the trucking convoys driving to the northern border, and he, Haj Amin, would repair to Arabestan and Kurdestan and conduct business.

He talked of death, too, his own, that of others, and on occasion he talked of the *shoom,* the bad omen, of Says Bar and of the one that purchased it. When he talked thus, he shuddered.

The name of the man was Razavi. Haj Amin's face became vacant then; his voice died off and he sat in silence, brooding. Farfar knew not much else of the matter, though grateful for the small brown rolls of opium that Reza produced.

What was the connection? Jim and Reza wondered. Old Haj Amin and this Razavi, part owner of a company in France and dead as a doornail in Tehran.

Jim had learned to trust his eye and his memory more than anything else in the world and hated cameras, but he had an old Mamiya-Sekor with a wide-aperture lense and fast film, and sat patiently in the dark behind Bucephalus's dirty windshield for a sight of Haj Amin Golpayegani. The apartment was as Reza had said: two stories, the first halfway underground, and two tall pine trees that towered over the place from inside the courtyard.

Now and then a lone young man or group of young men would pass the Rover, some out in the one suit they owned, jackets cut off short to save on cloth, done in outlandish checked patterns. Some of them sang in the night, wailing down the alley, some sad Persian song of the Absent Friend or the Beloved that Jim couldn't understand. It always sounded like a cry. Saddest place in the world, Iran.

When Haj Amin appeared at the door, Jim caught him. The man's hair was flying in all directions. He was in a bathrobe and striped pajamas—let history record this, thought Jim, as he got shots—white and blue, lengthwise. They were short and showed his skinny calves and plastic sandals. Haj Amin was making fond farewells to a blond lady, blond but Persian, Jim guessed, who lingered at the door, she in her forties maybe, in a black coat, hair pretty much in place, talking pleasantly. Was it Farfar? Leaving, she turned a good aristocratic nose and gave a pat to her hair finally as if to say, There, that's done.

A day or two later—the shots of Haj Amin had turned out fine—Jim was on Amirabad wandering toward Reuters when he felt again what he'd felt before. It had been a hunch at first, just a sense. He'd ducked into a department store, mingled with the crowd there, and then emerged again into the street, wary and curious. Would he see someone there loafing around who had been loafing around somewhere else? Would someone glance into his face and turn away too abruptly? Nothing happened.

Then, once or twice, he'd cut down back alleys, long, straight, and empty in parts of Tehran, and usually deserted, and no one would follow, and he'd come back to the main street a quarter mile down. Was any part of that milling, shoving crowd familiar? Did any part of it appear and then reappear? The noonday rush at Shah and Pahlavi streets—he'd felt it there, too—were all the races and tribes of the East. Dour and loutish Azeri peasants, thin-faced Arabs from the Gulf, dark-skinned Baluchis from down Zahedan way, Afghans in white turbans, and Turkomans from the north—among all that profusion of tribes and nations, Jim looked for the sign, the tip-off.

When it came, it was the wrong kind.

14

It was a mistake. Had been from the first. He never should have done it, never gotten involved. The old one, Netzer, frightened him, though he seldom saw the man. But there was something in his eyes and voice and something about the way Netzer conducted himself that made David Yerushalmi always feel like backing away from him when they were together. David talked a bit too positively with him, was a bit too jovial, he even imitated Netzer's way of laughing now and then to seem . . . seem what? He didn't know why he did it. Something in the old man's eyes. And he should never have gotten involved.

Netzer and Meir were in David's carpet shop. Netzer, his hands clasped behind him, was pacing meditatively along a wall hung ceiling to floor with carpets. He stopped before a pink Qomi *farsh*, reached out and brought his hand softly down the finely knotted silk. "This is so beautiful, David. A prayer carpet. Places for the hands and head. They mark them." They always spoke English with Yerushalmi.

Yerushalmi didn't reply.

"Prayer. How these Moslems pray! It's to their credit, yes? Pious people. We should admire their piety."

Netzer caressed the carpet again. He hadn't taken his eyes off it.

"I have heard, David, that their prayer is a kind of acting out of life, a metaphor for existence. Have you heard that?" Netzer took a step backward, then another, the better to admire the carpet, and cocked his head. "That when they bow first and put their heads to the ground—it signifies birth. It means that they are born of dust, David. They think that. Like us. Then they bring their bodies back up to the kneeling position and when they do that it means that they are in the midst of life, metaphorically speaking, of course." He returned to the carpet, turned over a lower corner as if to count the knots, then let the corner fall. "Then back with their faces in the dust, eh, David?"

Netzer, his eyes flat, turned to Yerushalmi. "That second prostration signifies death. 'To dust we return,' yes? That's what they say. Just like us. Then they rise to their feet after the prostration of death and they stand and that signifies the Resurrection. Life after death for the faithful. A beautiful metaphor isn't it, their prayer?"

"Sure, Ari."

Yerushalmi had a high, nervous voice and he fiddled with his necktie—it was unlike him to wear one—and stroked it as if to soothe it somehow, as if the whole problem would go away if the necktie would only behave. He looked around the room, at Netzer, at Meir, at nothing.

Had he not known Givon? And did he not know Givon's fate? And was not Netzer the reason? Why? Why, oh, why, did he fall in with Netzer and his ilk? Dangerous men.

David Yerushalmi was thin, hawk-faced, and balding. He combed his hair in an elaborate bouffant to cover the ruddy spot on top. Kissed by the sun like a Jaffa orange, thought Meir. Why hide the inevitable? Yerushalmi wore bell-bottom trousers and a tight shirt, and the American embassy ladies loved him. He had a trick of calling himself David when he talked with them. "David recommends this beautiful Isfahanian carpet. For you take. Don't pay. Take home. David knows you. David trusts you. Take. Put it in your best room. Put it in the room you invite your most esteemed guests. David knows you will like it. They will like it. David asks no cash."

He held Friday morning lectures in his carpet shop, and a nephew passed around tea and flat bread and fresh, tangy white cheese as David talked. "And this, friends, David has acquired this just this week. I travel all of Iran. I am looking for the best, I bring only the best. And this is good example, fine example. . . ." Then would follow one of the carpets David had gotten at risible prices out in the countryside—a Qashqai tribal from Abadeh, perhaps, or a thick-knotted, silken, shimmering affair from Kerman.

He is good, thought Meir, who broke the rules and went one morning. The Yerushalmis didn't seem to recognize him. They *were* good. Naturals. The goyim sat there watching the gay colors unfold, a splendid show always. How much of what he gives *us* is show? Meir wondered, watching David fidget there as Netzer talked, the door locked to keep out customers.

One day, long before, the old one had come into the shop and admired all the right carpets. Just like this day, he ran his fingers lovingly over the silk, inspected the knotting from the back like an expert, and then with a nod and a hand lightly caressing David's lapel, brought David to the back room.

A bank account in Tel Aviv, he said. An international account. Easy transfer of funds from Tehran. Iranian rials go to dollars, deutsch marks, Swiss francs, whatever, in the account. No questions. Bank Leumi. The legation would take care of it. No need to go through banks, through Iranian authorities who can be troublesome. They know how much you send. It's not easy to explain everything. And the rate of interest is so favorable.

Just some easy tasks, the man had said. You have a bit of conversation with Monsieur or Madame X, and I have a bit of a chat with you. No difficulty. It will be easy.

And then, one must consider one's security. Really, a bank account in foreign currency—untouchable—in Tel Aviv. Very safe. Among your own kind. No one is pressing you. Consult. We have time, he said. But think: you are in a position to be helpful. It would not be forgotten. And there may come a time when *you* need help, David. The hand on the lapel again. The gates to Jerusalem are always open, of course, but I mean real help, David. Help here. Substantial help.

And David Yerushalmi came to understand: intercession. A good word with authorities can lead to much of import. And if, God forbid, injustice is threatened, then a good word may avert it. And later, perhaps, emigration. Substantial help.

A carpet store in Tel Aviv?

Why not?

Or some other enterprise?

Why not?

To those who are wise, the world lies open, is it not so? "A little one," the old man recited, "shall become a thousand, and a small one a strong nation."

You have the best trade here, David. A superior clientele. The embassies, the top foreign business people, the military advisers. We ask nothing dangerous. Just a word now and then. You keep your ears open, perhaps pass on a word or two to someone. You see? It's easy. It's more—how shall I say?—the *climate* here, David. It's the climate that we want to know. You can help.

David was given an embassy code: Confident2.

"How did they run it, David? How many were there?" Netzer had come back and was standing in front of Yerushalmi. Meir was off to the side. "How many?" Netzer asked again.

"I don't know."

"Was it small? Two men, three men?"

"Ari—"

"How many?"

"I don't know, Ari. It is a long time that they did it. They brought someone."

"Someone?" Netzer's voice was soft. He hadn't reacted. Never did when suddenly he learned everything he wanted to know. "Someone, David?"

"Someone new."

"Only the one?"

"No, no. They stopped here. Givon and this one. There was somebody else. They bring somebody else."

"Ah. So there were two. At least the two, yes, David? Who were these?"

"I don't know."

"But they . . . 'stopped here,' you say."

"Yeah, sure, Ari."

"What do you mean 'stopped here'? What does that mean?"

"Givon and this one, they bring a boy. They say, 'This boy, he works here,' okay? 'Here he works.' "

"Yes, David. And this 'boy,' whom they bring, who works here, was he Iranian?"

"Yeah, Ari, I think."

"You never saw him before?"

"Never."

"Or again?"

"No. Not again."

"In and out, is that right? Is that how you would say it, David, yes?"

"Sure, Ari. In and out. That's just right."

"In and out. Fast." Netzer was looking away from David, down at a pile of carpets. The one on top seemed to fascinate him. The colors? The pattern? It was a garden, a paradise, where arabesques of vegetation looped around grazing deer, and stylized lions with elongated bodies turned their faces and stared flat out at the observer.

"Did he have a name, this boy? What did they call him?"

"They say Reuven. Reuven Eshaqian. That's his name for us. So we call him Reuven."

"Ah, Reuven. Okay, so this boy, this Reuven, he works here how long?"

"Maybe three, four, days, maybe a week. I don't know, Ari. It is a long time."

"Yes, David, it is. What kind of work?"

"He's with the other boys. He lifts. He carries."

"And he sleeps here?"

"Yeah. Here."

"Sleeps on the carpets?"

"Yeah."

"Then goes."

"Yeah."

Netzer looked up into Yerushalmi's face, which seemed to say, These people are asking me because they don't know? Why don't they know? Why are they asking me? and Netzer all the while thinking, A busy street. Full of bearers, who come and go. The boys working in the carpet stores are anonymous, constantly changing, untrackable. Good cover. A good place to hold someone in from abroad, from Israel.

"What was he like, David? How did he act?"

228

"Nervous. He was nervous, Ari. His voice was uncomfortable. But he wouldn't say why. He wanted to leave, Ari. It was written on him. Get the hell out. Run somewhere."

"It's very strange, David." There was a wistful note here, a kind of puzzlement in the way Netzer held his head cocked, as if waiting to hear something that might never be.

Meir stared at Yerushalmi and sensed that it frightened him, and Meir enjoyed that, all the while telling him, "Relax, relax, David, think." Netzer wondered, as he asked the questions, smiling, Did they turn you, David? Were you the one? Did they buy you?

Yerushalmi was a cutout to keep the legation contacts with Givon to a minimum. The routine meetings would come through Yerushalmi. And maybe, thought Netzer, that was a mistake. Levantines. Yerushalmi the Levantine. It was in his gestures, in the way he walked, in his eyes, which were dark, soft, liquid. They're born cowards, Netzer thought.

"David, what did he look like? Can you tell me?"

Yerushalmi's eyes moistened. "Ari." He stared at Netzer and felt the hand on his lapel again, caught Netzer's flat gaze. Intercession, they had said. A Tel Aviv bank account. It would be easy. Just a chat now and then. And now they come here talking of death. Of Givon, who is dead.

"What did he look like, David, this boy?" A pause. "Young?" Netzer stood in silence expectantly, then leaned on an immense carpet rolled like a pillar erected against the wall, all the while staring at Yerushalmi.

"David, David, it's sad. This man dies, this Givon. He was a good man, David, our man. His enemies are the terrorists, killers. The only safe thing is to learn. To know. These people are killers. They killed Givon. We must know everything. The only safe way."

David sighed. Reuven, if that was his name, and it surely wasn't, was dark and Oriental. Reuven wore Levi's—Levi's trousers, a Levi's jacket. That was all. It was long ago.

For Netzer, the boy—Reuven or whoever—was unrecognizable. The other, the one who came with Givon, was unrecognizable, too. Netzer wondered just what protégés of Ehud Cohen's they had been. Netzer knew some of Cohen's people.

There must have been others he didn't. It didn't matter much anyway.

That evening in Netzer's place, the whiskey was warm Johnnie Walker Black.

"Who was Givon, Avram? Did we know him?" Netzer was in uniform: his old gray sweater, patched at the elbows, the seams under the arms parting just slightly, a soft plaid flannel shirt, corduroy trousers, cheap shoes.

"They ran it very closely," Netzer said to Meir, and as he said it, a shimmer of wonderment played over the word "closely." Yes, they certainly did. In fact, it was unprecedented. So, why so closely?

"They ran it around us. Givon did. Cohen did. Out of Tel Aviv. First, this whole operation, all this surveillance. Then the action, this EAGLE, which they hide from us. Then they ask us to find out who killed Givon and why. Do you like that?"

Meir did not. "It's Cohen. He did this."

"Yes. And our investigation, if we can call it that, Avram, is part of the joke. It looks so good, you see. Perfect cover for them and whatever they are doing. We dash here, we dash there. The Iranians observe us dashing all about, oh, so terribly seriously, and they see that we find nothing. We're not bad boys. Not at all."

"No, we're good boys."

"Yes." Netzer caressed the side of his glass. "Think, Avram: Who are the objective killers? Who would have killed Givon? Not 'who could,' Avram, 'who would.' " Netzer grinned that shark's grin of his. And then he said it: "You know, it could be SAVAK."

"Madness."

"No, no." Netzer kept staring at his glass. "Disguise it as a guerrilla operation. When we got Hafez and Salah Mustapha, we disguised it. They thought it was Palestinians. Don't be so sure the people who got Givon weren't SAVAK."

The Egyptian intelligence chief Mustapha Hafez died in Gaza when his jeep hit a land mine. Salah Mustapha, the Egyptian military attaché in Jordan, died in a grenade explosion in Amman. Shin Beth was responsible for both assassinations. Netzer ran control on the latter.

"*Madness.*"

Netzer shook his head. "Not at all."

Things had come clear. Netzer had thought through the implications, which had come logically, one by one, not in a rush, not reluctantly, but in order.

Netzer hadn't gotten to all the Givon material in Ha Qiryat, not by a long shot. That was obvious. It was Ehud Cohen's doing that he hadn't. That was also obvious.

And Hoseyn Jandaqi was a traitor.

"Givon kills someone, yes? Stalks him through the ministries, tracks him down, whoever he is, wherever he is. And kills him, 'termination, as planned.' Then, strangely, Givon dies. What do you think, Avram? Who would kill him?" That smile again. "The Iranian government. They stage a guerrilla theater operation, then they arrest and exterminate the real leftists. Roll them up. It's all very funny, really, just these innocent lambs with their bombs and guns. But you will note this Jandaqi always escapes, yes? The others, Moftekhar and his like, they die, others of the group, but not Hoseyn Jandaqi. Oh, no, *he* remains alive. And why? He's a traitor, Avram. He's an Iranian government agent. And the Iranian government is attacking us."

"Madness, Ari. This material from the Iranians. The reports . . ."

"Of course, Avram. The cooperation, the fine information. Stuff we never ask for, magnificent stuff. Carmen, after all. Good work, that. And the report on Shohada. Wonderful. And Ali Moftekhar and his confession and his betrayals. Yes, yes, all this. And why? Because they're feeding us what they want. Can't you see? They're *feeding* us. Believe none of it, Avram. They're liars and we're fools. And"—his hand gripped Meir's arm—"targets."

Meir stared at Netzer. Was it madness? "A land of dreams and illusions," Netzer had once said. He was right about *that*.

Wind rattled the window. Bare branches of the poplar trees played in the moonlight.

Netzer's eyes hadn't left Meir's, though the words had

231

been said. Netzer was feeling just the first hints of a question, and unease, the sort they say precedes a heart attack, touched him, a feeling almost like sadness or like sundown on a gray day in the dying light. That kind of feeling.

Netzer's voice was soft, almost dreamy. "It was *not* a terrorist attack, no matter what the evidence. They are doing something, and Givon knew it. It was time for them to act. Nothing else makes sense."

"Why insist that things make sense, Ari? Things don't make sense here."

"Yes, they do, Avram. We just don't know what sense."

Netzer laughed soundlessly, but the laughter didn't reach his eyes, which remained open and staring and observant. His glasses were rimless, and he kept them well polished, a curious exception to the man's general untidiness. Netzer's glasses caught the light and gleamed, and it seemed to Meir that his eyes gleamed, too, but that was a trick of the light.

It was cold. It was raining. Jim found Levesque in an Alsatian restaurant on the Right Bank with phony leaded glass windows and waitresses in dirndls and white caps and white aprons who avoided them. They drank bad beer.

Levesque's voice was vacant. The first thing he said was, "I want this public," which was an astonishing statement considering the source, and Jim took it to be the word of a serious man. Not even a preliminary hello. "I want this public." Jim just looked at him thinking. What?

"Allgemeine Produkte—the holding company—they've been active all over Europe. They export to French subsidiaries. The French subsidiaries then sometimes sell to Rochant Frères, which reexports to Iran. Sometimes the French subsidiaries themselves reexport. Again, to Iran. In Iran the receiving entities are: Behnam Industries, Iran Textiles, the Ministry of Defense, Lavand Chemicals."

"Super!"

"Wait." Levesque put up his hand. He looked like a traffic policeman. "It's the material, Morgan. It's the purchases." Levesque paused, but Jim sensed it wasn't for effect. He just paused. "A gasification plant from a little Swiss firm called

MORA based in a little Swiss town called Chur. It's south of
Zürich. It goes to AP to CMB Métallurgie Cie—which is a new
dummy company, a child of AP, of course—to Lavand Chemicals, okay? Okay. Then they buy tubes of all kinds. Tubes of
hardened steel, tubes of special aluminum, tubes of marten-
sitic steel. Very strange. The last is so hard it's used only in jet
engines and ultracentrifuges. AP buys it from a Dutch firm
called Sjollema en Cleef and ships it to the Ministry of Defense, okay?"

"Okay."

"They make these purchases over a period of two years.
Then they buy high-speed metal-cutting machinery. Very high
tech, very top of the line. AP buys from another Swiss firm,
Mels GmbH. AP then sells the machinery to Rochant Frères,
which reexports to Behnam Industries. Air carrier out of
Toulons is Arya Flight, an Iranian charter. Governmental.
Okay?"

"Okay."

"That was four months ago. Now, then"—Levesque grimaced at his bottle of beer—"last month, three weeks ago, AP
buys remote-control handling machinery from a German firm,
Bayern-Seyner in Munich. Rochant Frères buys it from AP. It's
sitting in a warehouse in Toulons. It's going to Lavand Chemicals. Remote control. It's the last that tips us off, Morgan:
remote control. You know the technology we're talking about
here, Morgan? You know?"

Tehran ahead, Jim ordered bourbon from the Air France
stewardess, who was Gallic, blond and lovely, no cardboard
cutout like the lady in the Staff House in Beirut.

It's perfect. The Beirut bank. The phony companies. The
purchasing program in Europe. The airline—Iranian governmental and chartered out of Toulons. Pars Imports, too: a
depot, a warehouse, a stopping-off place. And probably a laundry: they bring stuff in, switch shipments. Perfect.

They are going nuclear.

Engineer Hushang Razavi did the deals. Up and down
Europe.

Then somebody got him. Figure the Israelis. Figure Givon.

Then the Iranians got Givon. Who tried to wire SAVAK. Or the shah. Or everybody. And the Iranians found out. Somehow. And killed him.

Hoseyn Jandaqi?

Jim was bobbing his head like Gordon when Gordon was putting it together. Every time we go looking for revolutionaries, we catch something else. Businessmen. Pahlavi companies. Government airlines.

This makes young Hoseyn a government worker.

Zimmerman will die and go to heaven. His house plants will turn healthy. The bags under his eyes will disappear. Pulitzer here? Oh, yes, we are definitely Onto Something.

III.

The Jinn

And the Jinn did we create aforetime of essential fire.

> —*The Glorious Koran*
> *Sura of Hijr, Verse 27*

He discovereth deep things out of darkness, and bringeth out to light the shadow of death.

> —*Job 12:22*

1

"The best of the stuff was skimmed off, yes, Joel? And that was Ehud Cohen's doing, yes?" Netzer faced Joel Halperin across a table in Halperin's office. He'd been in town for a week this time.

"It was a trick. They kept the best stuff from us."

"Do you blame them?"

"Funny, Joel. That's very funny. They didn't trust us. They didn't even trust you, Joel. Right? *You* didn't know."

Halperin was silent, but it wasn't the pause of a liar. No, the silence said, Halperin hadn't known.

"Was Ehud Cohen's skimming—we'll call it that, yes?—was his 'skimming' in response to my appearance on the scene back then? Should I take it personally? Or was it maybe just a precaution Cohen's people had taken?"

"Precaution maybe, Ari. It's easy enough. There's a code, maybe. You don't put the code in and you access certain materials, and when you do, the rest of the stuff pulls itself in and hides, like a sea anemone. A little pressure here, a passing shadow there maybe, and the information disappears and you don't even know it was there to begin with."

"Where does it go, Joel?"

"Somewhere."

"Sure, Joel, somewhere."

"It's a good way. You don't know the code, you lose half the stuff."

"You do, but they don't, right?"

"Right."

"And it's always the best half you lose, Joel?"

"Sure, and why not? You're surprised?"

"No, no. But, tell me, Joel, when the stuff gets 'accessed,' as you say, and the best of it drops out of sight, what then? Are there warning bells? Alarms? Do lights flash, do steel doors come slamming down?"

"Possibly. Have you seen any?"

"No."

"Nor have I."

A pause. "Not reassuring."

"No, Ari."

Netzer had taken great pains not to avoid Ehud Cohen this time. They greeted each other warmly Netzer's first day back, and after that, they saluted in the halls. Netzer even lunched with him once in the commissary, watching as Cohen, happy and voluble, talked in a thick Russian accent of Syrian adventures (carefully avoiding detail), and had given no hint, not at lunch, not ever, of . . . anything. Cohen was discreet. He must have wondered why Netzer was there in Tel Aviv, but if he did, he asked no one, certainly not Netzer. None of his business, he seemed to have concluded. But, then, Cohen was an old fox from Odessa.

Netzer studied Halperin's bluff face. Halperin was no Cohen, no intriguer. In that group picture from Kibbutz Kfar Rosenstein that Meir had seen once, Halperin is standing behind young Ariel Netzer, who is sitting cross-legged in shorts on the stony ground and has a white handkerchief knotted at the four corners on his head for the sun, which must have been brilliant, for they're all squinting at the camera, Netzer's face thin, burned by the wind, his eyes gleaming even then.

When Wladyslaw Anders's army of bourgeois liberals and freethinkers from Warsaw—that joke of the Soviets, Netzer called it—sent units to Palestine, Netzer came with them. The uniforms they wore, Polish mostly, some British, all seemed slightly different from one another; multiforms they called them, and everyone stood out. Netzer's first campaign cap was Russian, he remembered. At war's end, he left the army for Kibbutz Kfar Rosenstein, then with Halperin went into the same unit in Irgun, and the British became the enemy.

"I remember our unit, Joel, we dropped across the river

once"—Netzer meant the Jordan—"down from Irbid. It was the only time you and I ever saw action over there together. It was night and the moon was bright as a lamp. And each star, each individual one, burned brightly, and they all seemed to hang in the sky, some high, some low. You could make each one out, each like a lamp in a fantastic chandelier. Everything was clear, everything was sharp. Like the times. There was no ambiguity then, Joel. No ambivalence. And a Jordanian patrol came along, remember that? The Arab Legion, they called themselves, the Jordanians. And you could see their faces absolutely clearly. It was like daylight. We got the lead man. He was a noncom, a sergeant-major British-style. He would have been a loss to them. The rest fled. Remember that, Joel? Watching for Arabs? Watching for enemies? We didn't use each other then. The tricks were for the Arabs."

Halperin remembered.

At the end of the week, Netzer brought in Raful Frank and left him briefly in Halperin's anteroom, with its windowless, featureless, khaki-colored walls, standard issue at Ha Qiryat. Young Raful had come with Netzer from Tehran, Raful the wizard, who had caught those early police reports on Givon, Raful, who had run Givon's operation against SAVAK (and around Ariel Netzer).

He sat there staring blankly at the one piece of decoration Halperin, God knows why—Halperin hated ethnic chic—had hung on the anteroom wall. It was a ceramic tile, an Arabic inscription in bold white Kufic lettering on a deep blue background: "*La illaha ill'allah*," it read. "There is no God but God." The Arabic letters, just *alifs* and *lams*, themselves were all vertical strokes, looking to Raful like a string of ones running right to left. God is one, God is one, God is one, they seemed to say. One, one, one.

Raful's short-cropped blond hair, as always, managed to be mussed. His shirt was dirty. He wore gray tennis shoes that were torn and patched. He was acned and he bathed with a soap that smelled of chemicals.

Secretaries found Raful a distasteful article and, when he was around, looked at one another significantly. It was the same look in Tehran, Tel Aviv, or for that matter Oslo. One of Halperin's girls, Tova something, whose army uniform curiously made her look even younger and fresher, sharpened her nails nervously alone with him as Raful sat there staring and motionless and silent, and finally saying, "Akh, akh, akh," she fled to the canteen to get away from him. Raful didn't notice.

It never really came out just how Netzer and Halperin recruited Raful. Some wondered about that. Wasn't he Cohen's man? Wasn't it Cohen's operation?

Some who pondered the point (and it did get raised—in little cafés in Kerem Ha Otanim or along Ben Yahuda Street in Kerem Neve, as well as in spare offices in nameless buildings down unimportant side streets in Tel Aviv and Jerusalem) said Netzer and Halperin must have talked about promotion. Wiser heads considered that unlikely. Some others thought they'd played on the boy's emotions, on the Givon thing, the unavenged death and all that. But the odd birds who actually knew Raful well (like Netzer, he had few friends) and who migrated between cryptographic assignments and dull university posts thought it was Halperin, thought Halperin had offered Raful a shot at something.

Such as? they would be asked.

Well, they would answer, such as the new encryption standard (Elron Industries was to produce the chip). Fantastically powerful. Cracking it would take a million computers a million years. Maybe Halperin was going to bring Raful in on that. It would make sense. Or maybe it was the Russians in Syria. They were doing funny stuff up there with messages broadcast in pseudorandom frequency emissions—a message looked and sounded like white noise, but was in fact one fine Arab gentleman talking to another, with Soviet mediation no less. Maybe Halperin offered Raful a crack at *that*. Maybe.

But they didn't know, not really.

Netzer was in his carrel again, reading a report. The report explained EAGLE.

Getting it had been a piece of cake. Ehud Cohen and his people had set no land mines Raful couldn't deal with. Raful had simply swept the stuff out. Like ashes from a brazier, Netzer said later.

One part of the report detailed a series of meetings held in Israel in the summer between General Hassan Toufanian, the Iranian vice minister of war, and the Israeli defense minister, Ezer Weizman; the foreign minister, Moshe Dayan; Yitzak Lubrani, Netzer's immediate superior; and a number of aides. The discussions were nominally over weapons procurement. But not just that. Weizman was too tricky to let the moment pass.

As he read the report, Netzer could see Weizman sounding Toufanian out, could read Weizman's mind from the text. Toufanian was talking, and Netzer, who knew him well, could almost hear his voice. Toufanian had a way of wheezing the last vowels of a phrase and letting the sound die away.

"We are not Arab," Toufanian said, "but we know Arabs. Lately some people from Iraq were in Tehran. We made some type of agreement together."

All right, thought Netzer. The Iraqis are at ground zero. It makes them think. All they can do is put their fingers in their ears and hope the shah doesn't open fire. Or they can come crawling to Tehran.

Toufanian went on. "The most important thing is really our big neighbor, Russia. Their aim has never changed. This is to come to all these waters. We are obliged to develop some type of deterrent force."

There it is, thought Netzer. Plain as day, "Deterrent force."

Weizman answered him: "You will see the thing tomorrow." Weizman was talking here about the Flower, a very big, very accurate missile with a 750-kilogram payload and a range of 200 kilometers. Netzer barked a laugh when he read Dayan's comment.

"General Dayan raised the problem of the Americans' sensitivity to the introduction of the kind of missiles envisaged in the joint project. He added that the ground-to-ground missile which is part of the joint project can be regarded also as a missile with a nuclear head, because with a head of 750 kilograms, it can be a double-purpose one.

"General Dayan remarked that at some stage, this problem will have to be raised with the Americans and that he intends to raise the subject with his Imperial Majesty during their next meeting."

What a man, thought Netzer. Not an honest bone in his body. Then an aide named Ben Yosef brings it in. Had they orchestrated this before? Netzer wondered—who should say what. Or did they just improvise a little tune on the piano?

Mr. Ben Yosef: "We have something about the French and the Iraqis."

General Toufanian: "Do you think the French will start with Iraq in this field?"

Mr. Ben Yosef: "It is a possibility."

Dr. Suzman (another aide): "They will start with anyone that will pay them."

Then Weizman picks it up and Netzer could almost see his face and hear his voice—warm, Mediterranean, open—and under it all, cunning. "We have information that they are going over there to build a reactor."

General Toufanian: "Atomic, yes. But in principle the family of ground-to-ground missiles that they have is the Pluton."

Netzer detected censorship here. The sentences weren't connected, the language didn't work, and he cursed Ehud Cohen—was Cohen even now haunting him?—and read on.

Mr. Ben Yosef: "It is a possibility that we must take into account."

Poor Toufanian, thought Netzer. They're all over him. How will he handle it?

Then in comes Weizman: "All missiles can carry an atomic head. All missiles can carry a conventional head. They can carry all sorts of peculiar heads. Ours is 750 kilograms."

General Toufanian: "And the Indians started to make something with a 600-kilogram head."

General Weizman: "Fair enough. That will carry a conventional head."

Dr. Suzman: "It will probably also carry nuclear weapons."

General Weizman: "The worst thing that can happen to this area is when everyone starts playing with atomic weapons: the Iraqis"—a dig here, thought Netzer, and maybe too obvious—"Qaddafi, the Egyptians . . . and this can be in less than ten years. And the French will sell anything to anybody."

Toufanian ends it: "Yes, they will sell anything, but it will not work in the end."

Suzman tries to pick it up: "I wouldn't count on it. It may work, and if it does, it's very dangerous."

But Toufanian drops it for a time. The talk goes on to Israeli missiles, then Toufanian steers it back to the French and their projects. It's a little dance, Netzer thought. He's dancing around them. "I think the French started the same thing with you and Pakistan."

General Weizman: "We started it when Abdel Nasser fired his Zaphar."

Mr. Ben Yosef: "He didn't fire it. He demonstrated it, but without firing."

General Toufanian: "I don't think those Egyptian missiles ever flew."

General Weizman: "No, but this helped develop the missile you are going to see tomorrow. You must have a ground-to-ground missile. A country like yours, with F-14s, with the problems surrounding you, needs a good missile force, a clever and wise one."

The sales pitch, thought Netzer. Weizman was sounding him out and hustling him in the same conversation. Amazing.

General Toufanian: "I think we are the only two countries in the region that can depend on each other."

Netzer smiled at that one. Yes, Lord of Hosts, yes. The fine Iranians. The Land of Israel and the Persian Empire. Why don't they talk of Cyrus and the Temple?

"Because look at Pakistan. And this morning I landed in Ankara, and there is still no government there. And Iraq, we know what they're doing, an arsenal of Russia. You have two Russian arsenals—Qaddafi and Iraq. And we have Iraq as an arsenal of Russia and not only an arsenal. They are coming down. They want to come to the Persian Gulf."

General Weizman: "Any intelligence you want, let me know. You want us to start looking into the subject of India?"

General Toufanian: "That was a subject His Majesty

raised. He mentioned that the Indians have developed or are going to develop a surface-to-surface missile with a 600-kilogram warhead."

Mr. Lubrani: "With the French."

General Toufanian: "Yes, with the French."

General Weizman: "Good, General, anything you want, ask these gentlemen."

You can tell, Netzer thought. It was there in everything Toufanian had said. His dodges and feints couldn't hide it. "Deterrent." They want a bomb. But Toufanian doesn't know how to read us. He doesn't know what we want.

Then there were cables.

PARIS 3872. GOLD LEVEL. TEL AVIV 260, JERUSALEM 24, TEHRAN 140. REFTEL TEL AVIV 3540. SUBJECT: EAGLE.

CONFIRM HOTBOX PRODUCTION. CALMER CIE. USED PLUTONIUM SEPARATION FROM SPENT URANIUM. OS-TENSIBLE SALE TO ITALIAN FIRM ENERGIA NAZIONALE SEMIGOVERNMENTAL UNIT IN MILAN. QUERY: WHO IN EN IS HANDLING ORDER? (COMMENT: ROME AND PARIS STATIONS CAN HANDLE. INDIVIDUAL TO BE MARKED AND ALL PARTICULARS.)

And another:

PARIS 3954. GOLD LEVEL. TEL AVIV 260, JERUSALEM 24, TEHRAN 140. REFTEL TEL AVIV 3872. SUBJECT: EAGLE.

LIKELY SHIPMENT MARSEILLES. DESTINATION BUSHIRE. METHOD UNKNOWN TO SUBJECT. ROCHANT FRÈRES PURCHASER. CALMER CIE MANUFACTURER. INFORM-ANT CLAIMS CLEARANCE FROM TOP LEVEL OF FRENCH GOVERNMENT (COMMENT: SUBJECT NOT PRIVY TO UP-PER-LEVEL FRENCH DELIBERATIONS.)

The cables had gone out over the ambassador's signature, but Netzer knew he was ignorant of the whole affair. Who's doing the transmission in Paris? Who of Cohen's protégés?

Raful found other cables. Disposition of the reactor. Hotbox plans. Waste storage. European firms involved. Dates, places. Other branches of Persian government involved. Names.

Finally, in from Paris, and this very recent:

PARIS 4703. REFTELS TEL AVIV 3954, 3872. GOLD LEVEL.
HOTBOX NO LONGER WITH CALMER CIE. MOVED TO UN-
KNOWN LOCATION.

They've let it go, Netzer thought. They've bungled it. Lost it. If they can't find it . . . Was it Ehud Cohen or just bad luck? Well, Netzer would learn where to place the blame later. For now, he wondered, where is the hotbox? Coming my way?

From a file in Central Registry, Non-Arab, a bio-trace. It started: "The shah's link with the aviation establishment is through one of his oldest friends, General Hoseyn Kiani. He was one of those chosen to be educated with Mohammad Reza in the special elementary school established for that purpose."

Kiani, the accompanying report said, was EAGLE. Project head. He would work with Toufanian, they thought. Toufanian would handle the open contracting, Kiani the deep stuff.

"Little is known of Kiani's family backround," the bio-trace read. "His father was a sergeant—later promoted to captain—who probably was associated with Reza Shah in his premonarchical days; he might have been Reza Shah's orderly. Except for a brief period, he has always held important positions and had great authority even though his military promotions have been at or near normal rate. Mohammad Reza may have used him as early as 1941 as a go-between with the German embassy. Kiani is unofficial head of the 'Iranian Aviation Mafia.' In addition to his rank in the Imperial Iranian Air Force, he holds positions on the board of Iran Air, Air Taxi, and Iran Helicopters, and is silent partner in Iran Aircraft Industries.

"The Aviation Mafia controls all aviation activities in Iran. Even though a Directorate General of Civil Aviation exists as part of the Ministry of Roads, the function of this Directorate General is essentially to carry out instructions issued to it by the Mafia.

"Kiani is quiet, unassuming, and meticulous in carrying out his duties. He is well off financially thanks to his civilian posts. In his own words, 'Whatever I have, I have through the grace of the Palace.' "

The study contained one full-face photo of Kiani (he was smiling) and another taken at a Pahlavi gathering. The shah was entertaining close family and was dressed like a pimp, in a crazy dark silk jacket with arabesques of light cording. They were all standing around a roulette wheel. Kiani was in the background looking straight on at the camera. A good shot of the man, one of the very, very few. He was short, like the Pahlavis. He had receding hair. His face was broad. His eyes were flat and expressionless. There was a curious hook in the eyebrows, as if he were surprised, but the eyes registered no emotion. He seemed bored.

This man Kiani was EAGLE. Givon had found him. He had killed Givon, they figured. At a safe distance, that is. Netzer's stomach was churning.

Givon had tracked this Kiani through the ministries, tracing his footfalls through a labyrinth of cutouts, front men, phony companies, through communications (some meant to confuse), through Iran, through Europe. Givon hadn't been fooled by the evasions of a careful man who, methodically and logically, had constructed a network of laboratories, storage depots, research institutes, commercial ventures, and military offices, all dual-purpose, all linked through himself, the central node.

Behind Hoseyn Jandaqi is another Hoseyn, Hoseyn Kiani. No end of Hoseyns in these longitudes.

There's a Persian story, Netzer knew, of a flock of birds that fly through the Seven Valleys of Adversity, overcoming all obstacles, in search of God. When they reach the end of the last valley and the uplands of peace, they cannot see the God they sought. But on looking about, they find they each have merged into the One and are indistinguishable from It and from one another.

It was like Project EAGLE. In the fullness of time, all the subparts would come together.

There was one other photo. It showed Kiani as a cadet in

the military school in Tehran. The photo was full-length. He was standing stiffly in uniform. His chest was thin. He was stocky and short. He had thick black hair and there was that same curious hook in the left eyebrow and the ironic smile turned up on the left side of his mouth that Netzer had seen in the other photos. The left eye was friendly, but the right, even then, was cold and steely. He held his right hand behind him.

It was Kiani's face that floored Netzer. Knocked the breath out of him.

2

Ronald Earl Smith, known to his friends—and they were a crew—as Smitty, had a duck's ass haircut. He was wearing a T-shirt, and the haircut and the shirt made him look like a kid lying stretched out there on his mattress, an old GI visored cap down over his eyes. He had a plastic bong that gave off a sweet hashish aroma. He inhaled slowly. The water gurgled, and there was a low, implosive thud when he took his thumb off the hole. And again. And again.

Smitty's vast apartment was room after room without furniture. He had one expensive stereo. He was playing rock-abilly on it when Jim found him.

"Thought we might do some business, Smitty."

"Business?" The bong gurgled and thudded, and Smitty held his breath for a time and then exhaled, coughing. It was like grass, Smitty said, only better. "Business," Smitty said again, as if turning it over in his mind. "Yeah. Business."

"I was thinking of you, Smitty. There's stuff to do."

"Yeah? For business? Shit, I'm always ready for business. Shit, yeah. So what kind of business?"

"It's kind of private."

"Yeah?" Smitty's visor was down, resting on his sunglasses, and he laughed a little, one of those laughs where nothing is funny, but you want the time to seem pleasant.

Smitty's girl had left the room when Jim came in. She was young and pretty and had on a short, plaid skirt, the kind that closed in front with a large brass safety pin and looked like a Scots kilt, and a white blouse with a frill running up the buttons, which closed at the neck.

Smitty. Jim had run across him first in Saigon. Smitty was flying out of there into strange places in Laos and Thailand, provincial airports so-called (scraped earth and bonfire markers, most of them) for Air Indochina's courier service. Gold and opium, people thought, but Jim never knew.

When Jim ran across him again it was in Jidda. Smitty had an Ethiopian woman in tow. He had married her in Asmara in a temporary marriage that was legal there, and he had bribed their way into the Kingdom. Her name was Ruth. She was beautiful. Smitty had an old white Cadillac convertible, and he drove her around in that with the top down. He took her to company cafeterias and let everybody get a good look at her, and then he started renting her out.

On the side, he produced *sadiki*, the local name for white lightning, mostly ethyl alcohol, in a home-built still and sold it by the gallon jar. It looked like plain water.

He ran a bit of gold from the *souk* in Jidda to places like Bombay and Karachi, where the prices are high, and once in a while to France. But mostly he flew Saudis around the Kingdom in light planes, "Tabuk to Khamis," as he put it.

He drifted out one day, as they all do, and his company was glad to get rid of him, maybe even engineered the departure. Jim never knew, but leave he did.

It was Fiscarelli who had tipped Jim about him. They'd been talking about old days and strange people and the talk drifted to Ronald Earl Smith, who'd made his way to Iran because the place was a magnet for every jerk weirdo flying ace from Nam. They poured in with their heads fucked over and full of whatever, because the shah wanted an air force and let the money run like torrents to get one. Hence Smitty.

He was a concern to Fiscarelli. Smitty had distinguished himself one evening by driving a motorcycle around the Shah Mosque in Isfahan—up those low marble stairs, sharp turn to the left, then hard to the right and around the ablution pool and the enormous courtyard and around and around again and again, tear-assing stoned and mean and yelling like a madman and back down the stairs screaming who knows what all the way to his compound. He got a reprimand from his American company; the Iranians shipped him out.

"He's around again," Fiscarelli said. "Still flying."

"Flying what?"

Fiscarelli smiled. "Used to be Air Uganda." He pronounced it "Yew-Ganda."

"You're kidding—there's an Air Uganda?"

"Hell, yes. Spades and ordnance. Whatever Big Daddy wants, wherever he wants it. Shotguns, handguns, silencers, high-velocity ammo, hollow-point magnum stuff, telephone scramblers, exercise twisters—the works."

"Exercise twisters?"

"Uh . . . sort of like handcuffs. You put 'em on a man like one arm twisted behind his head and the other arm twisted around into the small of his back, see, then you use an exercise twister and hook 'em up. Then you tighten it. Then you leave the man sit. They start screaming after a while. It's an attention getter.

"Anyhow, that was his last regular job. Didn't like Big Daddy, and it was mutual, see, so he got out. Good idea." Fiscarelli was into his tequila and licked at the salt on his glass. "He flew Globe Charter off and on."

"What's that?"

"Who the fuck knows?"

"The name's got a familiar ring to it, Pete. You sure you don't?"

"Nope. If it's Company, I don't know it."

Sure, Jim thought. He figured Smitty indeed had done some of that Indochina flying for Fiscarelli, who just smiled at the proposition.

Smitty flew off and on for Globe Charter for a time, then came back to Iran, said Fiscarelli, to Arya Flight. Arya Flight— here Fiscarelli got a confiding tone in his voice and Jim let him go—flew funny stuff in the south and around the Gulf.

"They fly charters. Dubai, Abu Dhabi, Kuwait, Bahrain. Local service in and out. Bring the sheikhs up for the hunting and stuff."

"Hunting?"

"Yeah. Mountain goats and wild asses in the desert. They love it. Some of the fuckers use machine guns."

"Just to make sure, huh? Swell. Anything else?"

"Whatever's convenient to go in and out down there and best not handled through regular customs."

"Gold, dope."

"That's the rumor. Dope out, gold in. The southern run. For our Gulf friends. Arya Flight's a quasi-military outfit. The quasi part raggy pilots take over. Otherwise, maybe Iranians fly it, maybe not. Sometimes sweet-smelling babies like brother Smith fly it."

Arya Flight, Fiscarelli did not know and Richard Levesque did, chartered into France and flew cargo out for Rochant Frères and Ingénieurs Rolands. Sometimes to Bushire.

Now Jim was in Smitty's enormous and empty apartment.

"Arya Flight. How many planes has it got?"

"Four, five. Some choppers, too."

"Where are they flying these days?"

"You need a ride somewhere?"

"Maybe."

"Is that the business? Come on, man, that's no business. Take a bus, leave the driving to us, man." Smitty stretched back, observing, and pushed the cap back on his head and took the sunglasses off.

"You got a run south, Smitty? Like Bushire? Like the coast?"

"Hey, Morgan." Smitty smiled and smiled. "Hey, Morgan."

"Yeah?"

"Like there's a forty-five right under this here pillow. You know?" He looked at Jim. His eyes focused normally but were dilated, and he had that gun. He pulled out the .45. It was heavy for him. He held it turned ninety degrees and parallel to the floor and flat. "Maybe you want to leave?"

"Hey, I'm right in the middle of talking business, Smitty, and you pull a gun."

"No, man. Business is over. You're just fucking around, man. Jiving." Smitty had stopped grinning. "What the fuck you want, man, say it."

"The southern run."

"What about it?"

"Some friends want to know, Smitty."

"Know what?"

"About it."

"That's cool."

251

"Yeah, could be."

Smitty relaxed. He brought the gun down. That grin again. He had a kid's face. "Friends?"

"Need some information. The real, good stuff."

"Like back in Nam?"

"Yeah."

"Yeah." Smitty rubbed his eyes. "Like back in Nam."

"Sure. Try it. Let me pass on a little. If the bucks are okay, we can do it some more."

"Where's it going?"

"Uncle. Who's flying?"

Smitty eyed Jim. "Business dudes, some military."

"Got any names?"

"Nope. I don't ask, they don't say."

"Like a bus driver."

"Yeah."

"Could be worthwhile."

"Okay."

There was a field. Close to Bushire, Smitty said, as if he shouldn't be saying, as if they ought to cut a deal first. But he came alive anyway, thinking about things. As when Jim asked him what the field was like.

"Field? Man, that's no field. That's just a flat place on a rock."

"Hairy?"

"The worst. Downdrafts like a son of a bitch. It's just this ravine, see, up in a mountain and the wind comes down, but not all the same way. Sometimes you get these crosswinds, very bad ass. Altitude's ten klicks. There's no radar and there's snow in the winter. The fuckers are crazy."

"You ever get off the field?"

"Up there? Nah, man, they'll gun you down up there first thing they do. They're all packing fucking Uzis. It's in and out. Fuckers are crazy."

"What do you do it for then?"

"Little Whore-eeta over there and I'm getting my shit together. It's a living for now, man."

"Not too permanent?"

"Nah."

"The girl speak English?"

"Nope. Just fucks."

"The stuff that's going to the mountain, Smitty. How about a list?"

"Can't get a list."

"No way? Big bucks."

"Can't. Might not be a list, and it's off limits anyhow."

"The flight manifests, logs, transfer docs. Anything like that. Uncle'll pay."

Smitty eyed Jim again. The bong thudded. "Maybe."

Why not? Netzer wondered. Why not Kiani? Why not kill him? He sank into thought as a chilly wind swept off the Mediterranean and beat against his suburban windows, which were no match for it. Netzer's time in Israel had led him to think little about winter, though it gets cold even there. He never expected winter, and every year when it arrived, it came as a great surprise to him. Why, it's cold, Netzer would exclaim.

Why not kill Kiani?

At Ha Qiryat, Halperin looked at Netzer impassively when Netzer made the proposal. Halperin's round face and flat, pushed-in features were made for it, Netzer thought. The room was soundless except for Halperin tapping the table with his pencil, letting the eraser end fall like a little pile driver, raising it, letting it fall again.

"Why?"

"He's the key, Joel."

"Nonsense."

"No—sense. He is. He's the program, not the shah."

"Craziness. Kiani is no scientific genius. He's a bureaucrat. Like me. Like you. If he dies, the program will go on. These things have weight, momentum."

"We should kill the shah? No, no, it's enough to send a message to him. Kiani's death will be it, the message. The shah is a coward and a weakling, yes? He'll read the message, Joel. He'll understand it. He will."

In Netzer's temple, a vein, blue under his white skin, beat slowly as he gazed into Halperin's eyes. "God, how I loathe inaction. Why are we not acting? Does the government expect someone else to do it, yes? The Americans, maybe? Is that it? Is that why we're backing away?"

"I don't know. It's possible. They don't say."

"You know, Joel, the Americans are afraid of the *shah*. It's a joke—he's terrified of *them*, after all—but they are. And so they should be. They have much to lose. Their presence in Iran is massive. They're everywhere. All through the military, the economic planning, the development programs. They're advisers, trainers, weapons suppliers, contractors.

"And they're running an electronic intelligence program that is unbelievable. They survey the Gulf. In the north they listen to the Soviets talk to themselves. A cosmonaut catches cold, they know it. They count the rivets on Russian missiles. And through this link they dominate the Gulf, dominate the Iraqi lowlands, survey the very steppes of Russia. Do you think they want to endanger this?

"And think of the nuclear contracting. The shah's building this big peaceful program, yes? He's working deals with the Russians, with the Indians, the South Africans. Spread all over the map he is. Reactors from the French, the Germans, maybe the British, and a big, big lollipop, Joel, ten billion dollars in contracting on this stuff, for the Americans. And why? Why so much for the Americans? So maybe the Americans will waffle and fudge and overlook a few ambiguous and questionable matters here and there. Ten billion dollars, Joel—it's an American-sized bribe. To turn their heads. Maybe that's why we don't understand the Americans on this, why their reactions seem so indulgent, yes?

"And further, Joel, if we tip the Americans on this, they will wonder how we learned. They'll want to know. And they'll figure something. Maybe they'll figure Givon's operation. You want that? You want that blown?"

"All right."

"Not 'all right.' Why aren't we moving?"

"Ari—"

"*Why!* It makes me sick."

Halperin had made discreet inquiries around the PM's office, where he knew some people. Disturbing rumors, he'd let on. Problems in Iran, he'd said. Something funny. Should he know something? he asked them. Should he be told? Strictly as a professional, he asked.

They'd equivocated, looked away, shrugged, shuffled their feet, pulled at their earlobes. He knew all the signs: the distinguishing marks of politicians.

They'll hold back, he told Netzer. They'll find reasons. The relationship is too good, they'll say. Too close. Don't queer it. We've built it up over the years with infinite work. Iran is a major piece on the chessboard. Think of that. And the Jewish community, too. Think of them. There is time. There are other ways. That's what they'll say.

"Ah, Joel, Joel, *Joel*, we know what they're doing. Givon got there, Joel. It was brilliant work, the best we've ever done. Givon went through all the twists and turns, down all the dark corridors, past all the empty rooms, to the center, Joel, where they're hiding it. We know things even Kiani's own engineers don't know. His engineers, they just work on the pieces, all they know are fragments. We know the whole. We know how they'll work it. The shah signs every nonproliferation treaty in sight, brings in inspectors, keeps everything on the up and up, cooperates fully—sure—till one fine day they reach a critical mass of technology. And then, Joel, some time, and it will be a time of their own choosing, they move. And everything's ready.

"They're managing it through one secret place, one office that no one can penetrate, no one can see or hear or even sense. Deep in a mountain, Joel, even literally, yes? We know all this, we know it because Givon got there. And they killed him."

"What do you want, Ari? Why this lecture?"

"I just wonder why we fought in '48 and '49. They were good years, the best years of my life, I think. Now look. A man is murdered in the streets. He was fighting the worst threat we have ever faced. And they say, 'Don't react, keep calm.' What kind of men are these? What kind of fools? Are they crazy?"

"Politicians, Ari."

"Yes, sure, and they have 'higher policies.' The world could burn and they would put out White Papers on it."

"The decision is to go slow on this, Ari. They believe the evidence."

"Do they? *Do* they, Joel. That's nice."

255

"No sarcasm, please."

" 'We believe, but we mustn't act.' "

"What do you want?"

"Hoseyn Kiani."

Halperin shrugged. "This other one, this Jandaqi? This group Shohada? They're all terrorists."

"Sure, Joel. And we'll take them all, but it was Kiani every bit as much as Hoseyn Jandaqi who killed Shlomo Givon. Kiani's death would be justice for Givon, and more: a message, Joel, I'm telling you. A message for the shah, God preserve that bastard's throne. He'll know he has no secrets on this. He'll know that if necessary . . ." Netzer let it trail off, then said, "Kill Kiani, kill the program."

Halperin began tapping with his pencil again. "How?"

"He comes, he goes, Joel. These messages are a tip-off. He inspects. When he does, they make a check-out. They notify Military Security. They go in. They look at things. Make sure it's safe. He's been to the VE docks in Bushire. He'll go again, maybe to see his beloved hotbox."

"And that little matter—the hotbox?"

"Let it go through."

"You're crazy! If they break through anywhere, it's over. We might as well regroup on Masada and commit suicide."

"Let it go through. Evaluations Section swears it's not the end if it does. They don't even have a reactor in place. We'll get it later. We know the precise location of everything. Let them think we don't. The hotbox, Joel, it is cheese for the rat. Let it go. We'll decapitate the program."

"We've never succeeded in getting close to this man, Ari. How can we do this?"

"Anyone," said Netzer softly.

"Sorry?"

"Anyone," said Netzer. "We can get anyone at all." Netzer was almost talking to himself. "We can."

"And again I ask you Ari, how?"

"Set him up. Invite him to a party, maybe. Like Givon."

"You know his social calendar?"

"We know his telephone number, Joel."

"So you'll give him a call?"

"We'll listen in, Joel. No one will ever know. We'll run our own operation, Raful and I."

Then Netzer went into it.

Bushire, Netzer said. His voice was cold and monotonous. He had the whole thing figured. Bushire is on a peninsula. The peninsula juts up north and forms a bay on the east side. The west is sea wall. The bay isn't worth a damn; it's all muck. The town is on the very northern tip of the peninsula. The peninsula is maybe fifteen kilometers long and five kilometers wide. There's a single main road that goes up the middle, cuts it in half. The VE jetty is south of the town, beyond even the airport. There's a feeder off the airport road. It runs by the airfield, right where the road turns north. The VE docks are down there. But you can't get ships up to the dock. Too shallow. Everywhere it's too shallow. The ships lie out in the Gulf and off-load to small vessels. VE has two of its own lighters.

"Our assets there?"

"We know it well. We have Bienfoie. Bienfoie has a house. It's close to where the road turns north. We can bring in others. We monitor SAVAK radio there. We've cut into phone lines. We've got a man in the municipality." A cheap liar, drunk and traitor, Netzer thought, but did not say. "Once a schoolteacher, once a communist."

"Jewish?"

"Yes."

"Reliability?"

"He's worked before. Besides, he's secondary. I mention him only to show we have assets. We know the town, Joel. We have control. No problem. Don't worry."

Kiani's done it before. Bienfoie's seen him. He pulls into the dock area, gets out, and pays his visit.

He comes down, Netzer told Halperin.

"How?"

"Range Rover. We can track him now, Joel. We can get him."

"The explosive?"

"Picrate, hexogen-enhanced. You can direct it. A shaped charge. It'll all direct upward. Magnetic detonation. Manual if necessary. Put another ahead of it for a rainy day."

"Place it where?"

"In the road, close to the feeder."

"And wait?"

"And wait."

He'll show at the turnoff. It's narrow there. There's a flag and a traffic sign. That's all. So we cover each side with mines and detonators. Both will blow when either is tripped. Chaim will surveil. He'll control the trip. If something funny happens—another vehicle, too much protection, whatever—Chaim will handle it. Call off the operation, if necessary. We'll control Chaim from Bienfoie's place. Chaim will be close enough. He'll be well armed. "If the blast doesn't get Kiani, Chaim will."

Halperin's face hadn't changed. "The withdrawal?"

"The *Argos Supreme*. It's off Oman. Very routine. Give it five days sailing, tops."

The *Argos Supreme*, or whatever it's called now, is a Mossad ship with a multiplicity of uses—port surveillance, radar checks, transport of sensitive cargo, and, when necessary, exfiltration. It flies a Liberian flag. It is registered nowhere.

"It's eleven hundred meters to the beach. The speed boat is up and running. It's circling. When the thing goes, the boat comes in. We rendezvous on the beach. Then Bienfoie, Chaim, Meir—we all head for the deep, blue water, to the *Argos Supreme*.

Halperin's pencil tapped. His face hadn't changed. "The reaction to this, Ari. The Cabinet."

"Terrorists, Joel. It will be terrorists, don't you see? The terrorists learned he was running a group. That he had them wired. That's the way. It won't be hard. A few documents here and there. A call to a Beirut paper. An Iraqi group did it. Not hard, Joel. That's the easy part. It's routine. We do that every day. But Joel, Joel, *Joel*, we've found EAGLE. That was the hard part, Joel. The hard part's over. Now all we need is will. That's all. Will."

Kiani, Kiani, Netzer thought, sitting again in his drafty rented room. A dead man with any luck. Netzer had had a good meal. He had dined alone at the Nes Ziona off Ben Yahuda, where no one recognized him, and had endured a banal revue at the Strella next door, put on by university students who thought they were social activists.

Netzer thought of the picture of the young Kiani, the cadet in military school. He hadn't told Halperin, but the young Kiani in that picture was the spitting image, one to one and point for point, of young Hoseyn Jandaqi. That same curious hook in the left eyebrow, the smile turned up on the left side, the cruelty in the right eye. Could have been shots of the same boy.

God is a comic, thought Netzer, a jester of real talent, infinitely funnier than all the self-satisfied university students who had ever lived.

Were Kiani and this boy father and son? he wondered. Uncle and nephew? Did it matter? They were both on the same payroll.

Smitty said the flight log was honest and top secret. True stuff. The real. Dropped off by a raggy pilot. Up from Bandar Abbas to Kangan, where there was no airfield known to the mind of men—just a flat place in the stones. Then up to Bushire, then down to Chah Bahar. A long day's journey. The transfer documentation listed "parts," which was funny.

"Pretty anonymous, Smitty. What kinds of parts?"

"Boxes of them."

"Don't know what was in them?"

"Didn't ask."

"Want to ask next time?"

Smitty laughed a short, contemptuous puff of air. "Dangerous. They don't like questions. Don't answer them. Might be the end if you fuck around asking questions. Might be the end."

"Find out. Uncle'll make it worthwhile."

"Don't be pushy. I'll handle it, you know? The shit down there's for me to decide. So don't be pushy."

Smitty had also said, "I don't fly the Honcho. No stinking foreigners can fly the Honcho. Just raggies. Raggy pilots."

"Who's the Honcho?"

"Shit if I know. But he's big. He's big and he flies into Bushire, and only Iranians fly him there."

"On scheduled flights?"

259

"Naw, you can't tell. They vary it. No way."

"Out of where?"

"The mountain, usually. When the Honcho comes to town, everybody salutes, and I get the fuck out. Orders."

"Important guy."

"Yeah. Doesn't like foreigners. Doesn't like to be seen. Not a whole hell of a lot he does like. Comes and goes. They pull in security like nobody's business. Guys with grease guns, guys with radios, put them in the trees, on the rooftops. Under the fucking bushes for all I know."

Which meant something. Jim once sat in a disco across from three of the four generals of the army entrusted with defending Ahwaz, an unpleasant but important town in the southwest. The generals just drove in and sat down, followed by not so much as an aide. They sat drinking beer and watching Persian girls do Persian dances to American music. Nobody followed them around. So the military and its sense of security. The Honcho was different.

And would Smitty get pics?

Smitty wasn't crazy about the idea. Smitty, in fact, was fucking fearful. Jim, eyeing Smitty, considered the hint of a threat. Smitty was in deep. Could be his neck, right? Got to keep the supply moving, Smitty, can't let up now, right? Or else, Smitty? Or else? And Jim thought about the girl, too, in her Scots kilt with the big brass safety pin. A little weakness there. Might make him move.

But in the end, it was the money that led Smitty down to it. Jim told him there was more. Jim wanted to know about the Honcho and the Honcho's movements.

Smitty was subdued when he took it. Fiscarelli's money, greenbacks cash, was in his hand, the thick paper, and Jim knew the smell and feel of it had him. Smitty just looked at Jim. That kid's look of his. "What the fuck," he said.

It was on the street. He was young and thin and he had this look in his eye as if he were unaware of anything but Jim, how Jim would move. He brought the gun up flat and sharp in one hand like part of his arm. He was ten feet away, maybe less, and his eyes were right on Jim, targeted like the barrel of the

260

pistol. Jim hit the pavement backward, rolling, as the first shot went off and kicked the gun high with a snap.

The young man could not control it. Jim didn't hear a ricochet. Maybe there wasn't any, or maybe they were too close and the gun was too loud. Jim, rolling fast over the pavement, scratched from the cement, got to a line of double-parked cars and went under. The barrel was down again and the boy's eyes were on Jim, who caught a sight of the barrel from the side of his vision, and the shot rang close again. The bullet tore through the door of the car. Jim was wedged now between hood and bumper, down low, where he could not see the barrel or the young man, and he looked for a way, any way, out, and scrambled for the sidewalk.

The young man now—where was he? where?—scrambled over the hood of a car down to the street and was scanning for the target, way too close to Jim without knowing. Jim caught him. He was skinny and light. Jim hit him full on with his shoulder and got one hand on his throat. The kid twisted down, his chest heaving, but he still had the gun. Those eyes again found the target and he brought the barrel up to squeeze the trigger. Jim shoved it up fast. The kid was panting and wild now, and the gun jerked away and out of his hand. Jim threw the kid from where the pistol was lying, and lunged for it as the kid scrambled up and away and under the wheels of an oncoming truck, and a sound like a thump came from the truck's tires as they left the pavement and came back down. The kid was off to the side. Jim was down on the pavement with the gun, coat sleeves torn, his hand numb and bloody from scraping on the pavement. His head had gotten banged good and proper at some point—on the sidewalk or a bumper?—and his ears were ringing. He felt nauseous. He held the gun loosely and realized the kid in the middle of the street would never move again.

And when Jim began to think, he felt very, very stupid.

"You killed an Iranian," Fiscarelli said.

"A truck killed a guy who was trying to kill *me*."

"Might get you deported."

"Holy shit!" echoed down the hall and rattled the ambassador's secretary, but, like most of Jim's statements, didn't get through the ambassador's door. "Jesus Christ!"

"Hey, don't shout, you know?" Fiscarelli put up his hands. "A little calm here, okay? The marines will come in firing. Who needs it?"

Then he smiled. "The cops are good and pissed."

"*They're* pissed?"

"Hey, be cool. They're trying to cover it up, keep it all under wraps. It's not so easy. We're pulling for you, Jimmy. Fix it up so it's just an accident, you know? No witnesses. That'll do it. If things get out, could mean you'll have to take a walk. So just cool it, okay?"

"Who *was* the fucker?"

"They're looking."

"Hard? I mean, I'd like to know, all right? The man came at me with a gun."

"Never happen before? *I* never sweat it. You can figure on it, Jimmy, you're in a bad trade. The cops are working on it."

"Who the hell was he?"

"No ID, no papers, no nothing. They're checking prints and photos. Don't look for great criminology. If some asshole bumps into something, maybe we'll know, maybe not. Otherwise, not. Who'd want to kill you, Jimmy? You been up to something? What have you been sticking it into?"

"Stuff."

"Uh-huh." Fiscarelli licked the salt from the rim of his glass. "What stuff?"

"Stuff."

"Who was it?"

Could be anybody, Jim thought. Who got Gordon? Could be Mossad. "I don't know."

"Maybe they're coming from all directions, Jimmy." And at all hours of the day and night, he might have added. Makes for lively thoughts.

What had Michel said? "When someone looks you in the eye and says he's going to kill you, it means nothing. But when you hear it indirectly, that's different."

"Watch it," said Fiscarelli. "They're watching you."

"Everybody's watching me and not talking about it. I'm a very popular guy."

"Uh-huh."

Jim told the whole story to an apologetic police lieutenant, and repeated it three times to an ever-expanding committee of Iranians he correctly took to be security officers, who were most concerned, appalled even, at Jim's close call and were highly impressed with his courage and skill. They were joined ultimately by an older gentleman with a sad smile, who quoted verse and who, Fiscarelli said, was a major general. Fiscarelli intimated Jim should be proud of the interest the Iranians were showing.

Jim got the sneaking feeling, though, like a cat's claw at the back of his neck, that maybe they were interested because they wanted to know what the hell they'd done wrong, and if they could figure that, they'd do better next time. Jim's happiness with P. F. X. Fiscarelli as protecting genius was finding its limits.

The ambassador, a new man and very businesslike, listened to a rendition and had his own reasons for being interested.

And so, finally, Jim wondered, Who's gunning for me? The Israelis? Al-Jihad? The Iranians? That raised the question, Which Iranians? At that point, Jim came pretty close to it.

Pari liked big bands. Stan Kenton, Woody Herman—or Nat King Cole alone sometimes for the smoothness—and she'd dance by herself, a little tipsy. Jim could be persuaded, though, clumsy as he was, and she'd let him lead and they'd shuffle slowly cheek to cheek.

They'd had steak and wine and the lights were out, just a glow on them from a lamp in another room, and her left hand was up on the back of his neck, smoothing the blond hair that needed cutting. She was dressed to go out, but they wouldn't.

"Hey, My Man Morgan. Time to go. Hey, okay? Time to split. I'm tired of it."

"I'll have to get out of here before Zimmerman prints it, Pear."

"To where?"

To bigger and better wars, he wanted to say. Like Gordon. That was Gordon's prescription for human happiness. But he

263

didn't with that warm face buried in his neck.

"Jeem Khan," she called him. Jeem, she said, was the third letter of the Persian alphabet; it was shaped like a fishhook and she was caught on it. An old poetic wheeze, she had told him, a one-thousand-year-old cliché. And his neck was damp.

"No problem, Pear. I'll get my man and make tracks. No problem." Except maybe the man would get him first.

"When I fall in love," Cole sang, "it will be forever." The man's satiny voice.

Some bad-ass characters were gunning for him and maybe for the Pear. That wasn't being a war watcher anymore, that was war, and it felt different from the old feeling, whether finessed with whiskey or not. No fun now. And he felt guilty beyond the telling for maybe bringing the same shit down on the Pear.

He talked Pari into going back to England. He would meet her there, he said. He would head south. He wanted to get a look at the place, see it with his own eyes. They bring it in through Bushire, he told her, and he wanted to check the place out. Maybe find the Honcho. She would close down the apartment and leave. Lucky her. She had more time than Jerry's girl friend, Lisa, anyhow, he said, smiling ruefully, and then was gone.

Pari stared out the window. One of the shah's helicopters was circling the neighborhood, searchlights casting cones of light down onto the flat rooftops, the rotors making strange slapping noises in the cold night stillness. It went away finally.

The green-eyed man, she knew, would go up the mountainside. She decided to cancel her ticket and move in with friends.

Gone. The horse-faced man didn't know what to make of the departure of the two of them; Ali Aqa for once had nothing to say. They'd left a UK forwarding address with the landlord, a nonagenarian ex-ambassador and Kurdish aristocrat, who spent his time shooting grouse and pheasant in the foothills of the Alborz and had no time or use for police of whatever sort.

264

Jim found Bourachide in new splendor in Le Sapin, rechristened Le Boogie.

"I need a U.S. passport."

"You have one."

"Don't be funny."

"When?"

"Right now."

"Day after tomorrow. You have photo?"

"Yeah."

Bourachide's people did a nice bicentennial number, deep blue with red and white Liberty Bells inside.

Jim encountered no fuss at passport control or customs at Mehrabad and with the usual trouble got a cab into town, changed cabs there, picked up Bucephalus from Alice's place, and left a thank-you note under the gate, not signing it or seeing if Alice was there or not.

And headed for the mountain.

3

They had no easy way to watch Kiani's house. The streets were patrolled. To watch, to loiter, or even to park a van briefly was not possible. Police units eased through the neighborhood and kept everyone moving. Everything was known to them. The phone lines were watched, too, and the high brick walls of the surrounding villas cut everything off.

Levine finally put an observer on the roof of a building 500 meters away, who shot pictures of the man's gate through the naked tree branches and complained about the cold.

The place was active, all right, with servants coming and going. And women. Were they family? A wife? Daughters? No one knew. No way to know. But the man himself never showed. Raful could attest that messages arrived in his office for him; answers to them went out over his name. But he never showed.

Snowflakes fell, soft and powdery in the northern suburbs, where the man lived, sodden in the city itself. Where was he? Icicles formed on the legation gutters. They melted and fell in time, whole groups of them like teeth from a rotting mouth, and broke on the ground below. Kiani was not in town.

To light the space heater, Jim ran a puddle of kerosene into the belly of the thing and tossed in burning Kleenexes until it caught. Pari had taught him the technique: you hold back on the flow and keep it dripping slowly till the chamber gets very hot and can burn more kerosene. But knowing is not doing, and Jim produced a series of rhythmic explosions, which deposited soot all over the cabin and scared the daylights out of him. When the explosions subsided, he put a teapot on the top grill for the moisture (another instruction from the Pear). It started bubbling after the flame got blue, and the chimney pipe got so hot he couldn't touch it and the room warmed up.

Outside, the wind yowled and rattled the windows and scuffed the snow, which lay powdery on the ground. The day was clear. The sun was high. Jim saw the old persimmon tree again. It had dark orange fruit now and its leaves were dusted with the white snow.

Operate from here, he thought, staring out the window at the white. A three-month visa. No complications. No papers. No permits. No surveillance. You are the lone player. They know nothing now and that gives you all the freedom in the world.

You've got a photo of young Hoseyn, bank deposit slips out of Beirut, and solid tracks in Munich. You've got the companies traced through France and half of Europe, and you've got them tied together in Tehran and photos of the documents. You've got pics of Haj Amin, hennaed hair blowing in the wind. You've got Hushang Razavi blown to pieces and you've got the Pars Imports–Ingénieurs Rolands connection.

You've got an installation somewhere in the mountains above Bushire. You've got a weird SAVAK airline that brings stuff in and out.

And there's the Honcho. Who Smitty does *not* fly around. The Honcho is not to be seen by mortal men. The Honcho runs this show. Bet on it.

Jim turned from the window. He'd wait for a time, maybe get a report from Smitty, maybe turn up the Honcho. Then head for Bushire.

He knew his lead already: "The Iranian government, with a massive and largely clandestine technology-purchasing program, is seeking to produce nuclear weapons. The program has been bedeviled by mysterious deaths in Iran and Europe. . . ."

And after, it will write itself, he thought. Inspiration from God. He would expose the Iranian government's shifty nuclear program. He would expose the U.S. government's ham-fisted sins of omission and commission.

He thought of Dave Gordon. "He came too close to them," Michel had said. Michel figured it was al-Jihad, the fuzzy-wuzzies on the Green Line, who did it. Maybe. But it was an

267

Iranian government operation. They killed Gordon, who wanted the truth and got it: that photo of Hoseyn Jandaqi. In Beirut the truth will make you dead. And they wanted to make even his death a lie. It's their way.

Maybe you will lose everything, he thought, and disappear from the face of the earth, a box of bones delivered to the south Tehran garbage pits, compliments of the Iranian government. He thought of Pari and the smell and taste of her. A bullet through his brain would put an end to all that.

In the evening he heard howling that wasn't from the wind, and stood at the window. Dogs are around all villages, some of them wild, some domestic. They run together. At night they come into the towns and ramble through the gutters and feed on garbage. Sometimes tear up a kid.

Then Jim saw him, a gray shape in the moonlight. He moved from shadow to shadow, his ears peaked. He ran fast over the snow and was gone. He had a long, sharp muzzle and loins thinner and shoulders higher than a dog's. As he moved, he was quiet, just a soundless pass of gray.

It's wintertime, Jim thought, and they have to come down out of the cold stones. Were there others? Jim watched for them. The Primus lamp, down and smoking, made no reflection in the window glass.

In the morning, Jim checked for tracks and found only the one set, almost obliterated by the wind. They disappeared down a slope and led to bare rock. He was headed down, alone.

Engineer Emile Bienfoie gazed from the seaward side of Bushire. The town is elevated on a promontory of natural stone, which rears up at the north end. Off to the southwest were ships waiting for the lighters.

The *Argos Supreme* was out there somewhere, he knew. Netzer had arranged it, Netzer the old master. They'd send the boat in when Netzer signaled. Kiani would appear at the VE project, then inspect the VE docks. It would work.

The esplanade by the water is narrow, and the buildings here crumble from the salt air. On the landward, the south, side of town, runs the old defensive wall, overgrown with buildings now. Bienfoie strolled past the Ministry of Justice, once the British Residency, the old Anglican church behind it unused. The church was a simple, square building, white, with a small cupola over the double front door. There was a bell in the church, Bienfoie knew, that never rang, inscribed "Political Resident 1865."

It had rained a cold rain the night before, and the winding old streets were sewers of mud because of it; the trenches running down the middle of each were clogged.

Bienfoie liked Bushire in a perverse way, liked exploring it. The old merchant families of a time when the city was a power in its own right were mostly gone. Their houses remained, though, graceful structures of shell and coral stone of a light, delicate gray. The houses had shuttered balconies stained blue, which rattled in the wind, and sometimes ladies' eyes peered down at Bienfoie through the slats as he passed in the deserted streets. The ladies, when they came out, wore face masks, nosepieces projecting like sandpiper beaks, blue tattoos on their hands showing from under their long black sleeves. Others—gypsies—wore no masks at all and looked at him directly and showed their long black hair trimmed with silk in shimmering colors.

Bienfoie liked to walk through the old market, where the scent of waterpipes and burning charcoal—there are two coffeehouses nearby—always hangs thick in the air, and from behind the mounds of spice and motorcycle spares, Indian and Arab faces as well as Persian watch the passing life of the city.

Bienfoie lived fifteen kilometers south of Bushire, close to the VE project where he worked, in an old house left over from the days of the British. It was built in Anglo-Indian style, one-storied, with a deep veranda and a flat roof from which thin columns rose; in the summer they held deep canvas awnings. Banyan and acacia trees surrounded the place, and stone walls led down a driveway to the Bushire-Shiraz road.

Bushiri natives call the rolling landscape of the peninsula the *mashileh*. The *mashileh* was green now in the cool winter, and Bienfoie liked the soft roundness of the hills. They lay, almost feminine, from promontory to mainland.

The man Netzer knew as Chaim was walking, too—down there, in sight of the bungalow. He had no identifying documents whatsoever. His passport and residence permit were ashes now, scattered on the wind. His clothes were international: an Italian shirt, German trousers, English shoes. He had an American suitcase, scuffed and beaten by all the world's baggage handlers and ready to fall apart. His newspapers and paperbacks were in English. I'm a real cosmopolitan, he thought. He pretended to be Australian. Coming down from Tehran, he got his new documents and final word on the way out.

At night in Tehran he had picked up Kol Yisrael easily on the AM band, and he had listened very carefully to a program on a movement in abstract art. Crazy Yael Evron, her voice high and nasal, read the script in her preachy manner. She had no idea what she was really saying, he knew, and he liked the irony of it. Opening of the Sterner Gallery in Tel Aviv would occur on the tenth. Yael gave no street address, for there was no Sterner Gallery. The tenth, she had said. Yael made the announcement twice, and that was the call to arms.

Chaim had walked to the end of one of those jetties—there must be three or four—that lie unused and useless far South of the VE docks. A shape deep in the water glided slowly and rhythmically in circles. Ships bring lambs to the Gulf from Australia and New Zealand, and some of the lambs die; as they do, they are thrown overboard. Australian great whites follow these ships across the whole of the Indian Ocean. And here was one, penned in strange, confining waters, feeding on the debris and garbage from ships.

Superb strength, he thought, as he watched it, passing, passing.

He glanced at his watch. It was 5:00 P.M. A chilly breeze came in off the water and brought a hint of cold rain.

Raful had gotten an intercept. Top Secret. To Military Intelligence CinC from the Commercial Section M10. Kiani's office. Inspection of Bushire docks. Security people would check them out, then take over routine guard functions. No names. Date to follow. Raful, with a prim look on his face, handed it to Netzer. Raful had it all figured. There was something at the corner of Raful's mouth that showed it.

Netzer looked at the translation. Strange, he thought, how a piece of paper that means so much, that means a man's death, maybe more, that ends the greatest threat to the Jews that was ever dreamed of, strange how it's as light as any other. Just a slip of paper.

Now, thought Netzer. Strike now. He looked up over his glasses into Raful's face.

"All right, Raful," Netzer said, and Raful padded softly out of Netzer's office into the shadows. Netzer smiled and his eyes glinted in the old way, the cracks around them hard. He's coming in, Netzer thought.

4

The bus was crowded and a lemon scent from a dispenser hanging above the driver's left shoulder wafted through it. The boy they called *shagerd shofer*—the chauffeur's apprentice—pushed a plastic crate of soft drinks up the aisle—orange cola, Coca-Cola, some lemon drink—distributing them to the passengers, while a song on the record player with a faint Arab lilt sang of love for a schoolgirl: "O girl of the red shoes, O cousin, will you be my love?" The driver, who should have known better, was told to turn it off, which he did with a sigh, for this was no time for frivolous music. The time of mourning was at hand, and beyond that there was something in the air, just a vague sense of unease for most of the people on that bus, but they all felt it.

All were coming in to Qom now from the villages. The bus stopped here and there on the road to pick up passengers. It was a poor bus of a third-class company. The peasants who rode it carried a clutter of packages and bundles, and in, on, or under it, there was scarcely room for more paraphernalia. It was an inconspicuous way to travel. At one stop Hoseyn Jandaqi boarded, lost in the crowds of the poor.

It was Friday noon and almost warm. The snow had melted and the eaves were dripping with water, the streets and sidewalks wet with it. There was little traffic and the air was clean. Hoseyn caught glimpses of bright blue sky through a parting in the curtains.

His room was bare. A pot of rice simmered on a three-burner gas hot plate. He had put out the Aladdin stove; the hot plate was enough to warm the room. He wore a cheap tan sweater and green army fatigue trousers and boots.

On the inside wall, a wooden garderobe with walnut veneering contained an international arsenal—four Russian AK-47s, a Polish M-63 machine pistol, four American Browning 9-mm machine pistols, a Spanish Astra pistol, a Hungarian Tokarev pistol. The rounds for the M-63 were armor-piercing. In a footlocker, for ease of movement, were a radio, eight handy talkies, and an assortment of condensers, relays, integrated circuits, other electronic gear. The explosives were picrate.

Hoseyn knelt on a *gilim* on the floor. The *gilim* was blue with a yellow geometric pattern of diamonds worked through it. It was thin and not much protection from the cold of the tile slabs of the floor. He wanted to open the curtains for the heat of the sun, but did not dare.

On the *gilim* lay a VZ-58, a Czech version of the Kalashnikov, virtually the same gun. It is the weapon of choice for certain operations.

The stock was a metal bar that extended from the body with a butt that fitted into the shoulder. Without the extension, the gun is a virtual pistol except for the curved magazine. A clip holds thirty rounds, and Hoseyn had twenty clips. It's a reliable gun. Never jammed, they said, and as machine guns go, it was not heavy at all. Light as a feather, comparatively. The VZ-58's fire rate is faster than a Kalashnikov's—800 rounds a minute to the Kalashnikov's 600. The position selector—up for semiautomatic, down for fully automatic—is just above the grip on the right.

Hoseyn, thinking of Jim Morgan and Morgan's blond hair and reddish beard, absently worked the selector up, then down, then up, again and again, and felt a queasy sensation push through him like a hand kneading his stomach. It was fear.

There would be an operation. The operation would be large. Hoseyn would be a part. He'd killed last in the month of Ramazan. Now it was Moharram, and he would kill again.

"A key of incalculable importance and opportunity"— that's what they had called Givon in Munich. They'd been right. They wouldn't tell Hoseyn how or why, but thanks to the killing of Givon, these Israelis, Givon's accomplices, had revealed themselves. The killing had flushed them out, even this American who hadn't been expected, hadn't mattered, but who now would die, too. Hoseyn waited till night, then went out into the austere streets of the holy city.

Night fell, and at the meeting place known as the *tekiyeh*, drumbeats signaled the beginning. Sharp and measured at first, they pulled the crowd closer to the stage constructed there, a raised platform set up before the madraseh wall, back behind Qom's old bazaar. Canvas roofing, stretched over poles, covered the stage. In time, the drumbeats became sharper and faster, and the crowd, which had laughed and talked at first, became expectant, and as it did, the drumming became fainter but faster.

"*Hi!* Don't shove so!" a henna-haired old man called and poked in the ribs a boy, who was pulling along a chador-clad woman of a certain age, while a villager, struck dumb by the day's commotion, jostled forward, too, his cotton *givehs* no protection from the cold water lying in pools in the clearing. Hubbub rose from the crowd of old men and women, girls in black chadors, black-dressed young men counting their beads. Some in the crowd had splashed themselves with rose water. The fragrance of grilling lambs' kidneys came from a row of braziers somewhere off to the side, where the cooks constantly fanned the glowing charcoal. Children were everywhere in the cold air, with shaven heads and little padded coats over their pajamas and rubber boots over bare feet in the chill. Hoseyn was there, too, by the kabab seller's brazier.

The drumming stopped suddenly, and the crowd went silent, ringing the stage, filling the clearing. A mullah entered, wearing the green turban of a *seyyed*, a descendant of the Prophet (there are so many in Iran). He was young and his voice was deep. He began to intone: "O ye faithful, give ear! And open your hearts to the wrongs and sufferings of his highness the Imam Ali, the vice regent of the Prophet and let your eyes flow with tears. And give heed to the sufferings of the Imam Hoseyn, beloved of God, and his struggle."

The audience listened eagerly, and the old man with the red hair stared, transfixed, at the young priest, and the mother and her son forgot that their arms were linked and the children grew silent, round-eyed. Hoseyn, rubbing his hands absently

274

against the cold, looked across the crowd and studied their faces.

Torches guttered in the wind, and black kerosene smoke drifted up. The audience began to sway in time with the mullah's words, which were a kind of sung poetry, not precisely metrical but fluent and rhythmic. As the priest went on, almost singing, the people swayed and marked time with the words. And the old man who had seen and heard all this many times, recalled the truth of it—the fearful suffering of humanity's best and justest, the cruelty of governments. The truth struck him as a pain in his heart that suffused his whole body, and he sobbed.

"*Voy, voy, ya Ali!*" he cried, "*Ya Hoseyn.*" Others knew the same truth, and they cried, too, as they swayed together, and they brought their hands to their chests, fingers linked, striking and pounding, the strokes in time with the words and the swaying of their bodies, and they cried out in a rhythmical wail, "*Ya Ali! Ya Hoseyn! Ey, Hasan!*" The keening gathered force and became a chorus, forceful, insistent, and uncontrollable.

As it gained, the young priest held his right arm high, and nodded to the side to a chorus of mourners who had formed below the stage. They began chanting a metrical version of the story of the martyrdom, and the audience gradually quieted to listen. The poetry seemed to sing itself, and the audience was silenced in the wonder of the words and the ancient deeds—the green riders, the horses, the red pennants, the flashing lances. Actors now came forward and brought the stage devices up before the coffin. One would portray Hoseyn ibn Ali, another his brother Abbas, and how they died fighting tyranny in the palm gardens of Karbala. The month when they died was Moharram, the year 680 in the Western calendar.

The mullah strode forward now and mounted the stage. His eyes were intense, and he looked into the faces of the people. When he spoke, what he said was utterly different from anything the crowd had heard before. " '*Ey, Hoseyn, ey, Hoseyn,*' we cry. But enough of the crying. I do not say the crying is useless, for it has kept Hoseyn's pure name alive through the

275

years, through all the centuries. But now, O friends, the time has come not to weep for Hoseyn, but to *be* Hoseyn."

"*Allaho akbar!*" someone in the crowd cried, probably a plant, and the phrase sprang from others in the crowd and from all sides in the open space by the madraseh wall. "*Allaho akbar.* God is most great."

"Let us be mindful," the young mullah went on. "Hoseyn was outnumbered, but he chose to fight. He knew that by dying he would show that the regime was godless, because he was the grandson of the Prophet and only the utterly impious could commit such an act as killing *him.* And he knew his death would inspire countless generations of Moslems to come to fight against unjust authority. Human history, O brothers, is this ceaseless struggle."

The young mullah sang rhythmically now, and his hearers were caught up in the tones of it.

"Let us be mindful, oh, let us be mindful. The shah is the Evil Yazid. He is a usurper. Oh, let us be mindful. He has desecrated the time of prayer as Yazid desecrated the time of prayer. Oh, let us be mindful. He has desecrated the haj, as did Yazid. Oh, let us be mindful. He denies water to women and children. In the fullness of time, the Shah Yazid will perish, O brothers and sisters, and he, too, will be cursed on the earth and consigned to the flames of hell. And we, O brothers and sisters, we shall fight the correct battle and we shall win. *Allaho Akbar.*"

"*Allaho akbar!*"

"God's blessings on Mohammad and Ali and their families, all of them."

"God's blessings."

"Oh, let us be mindful. For now it is a time to act. Now is not to fear for our own lives. If we do not care about our own lives, we do not make calculations. We act. When we are so unhappy that nothing matters anymore, not even victory, victory is not necessary. And that means that we are not afraid anymore. The shah's guns make a happy death. We say, 'We are independent, beholden to no one. We don't need material things because we are going to die. And if we are going to die, we will fight the shah's men, because it doesn't matter what they do. They can shoot us, but we're going to die anyway.'

"So we speak, we of the Pure Earth of Iran, defiled by an agent of the foreigners. But this year, O friends, brothers, sisters, we do not weep. Oh, no. To weep, to ask for gifts from the Imam Hoseyn, is no longer appropriate. This year we become Hoseyn, we are Hoseyn, we are Hoseyn! *Marg bar shah!* Death to the shah!" And the mullah sang:

> It is the eve of Ashura
> Karbala is inflamed
> Ah, the sands of Karbala!
> 'Tis the last night!

The crowd sang with him and some put lighted candles in the niches of the *tekiyeh*. A breeze caught the flames, and the candles guttered and burned quickly, and the thick wax, black with soot, dripped down the walls, the flames like a field of staring eyes.

Hoseyn held back as the crowd moved toward the bazaar. The mullah had held back, too, and gestured permission for Hoseyn to approach as the torches were taken down. The minarets of Hazrat-e Ma'sumeh, dark against the starry sky, towered over them in the cold, as the mullah told Hoseyn the message and blessed him with a kiss. Hoseyn would remain for a time.

The *dasteh* wound through the *kuchehs* back of the bazaar, and the crowd grew. Runners on each side carried torches soaked in kerosene. The young men dressed in black pounded their chests, not shouting. The only sound was their rhythmic pounding. Each linked his fingers, thrust his arms straight before him, then brought his palms back hard against his chest. Their marching was cadenced with the beating, their footfalls adding to the rhythm. Most had their hair cut short and, though the wind was icy, they were bare-chested. Then came the chants, of a sort not heard for years:

"Who took our oil?"

"America!" *Ahm-ree-kah.*

"Who took our gas?"

"Russia!" *Roo-see-eh.*

277

"Death to the Pahlavi family!"
"Death to the Pahlavi family!"
"Cannon, tank, machine gun, they have no more effect."
"The shah is a donkey, lead him away in chains!"

Soldiers had formed up in the municipal square, their trucks parked in rows. The *dasteh*, they knew, was winding from the bazaar in the old city, from the *kuchehs* around the Jom'eh Mosque, and would come across the bridge by the Mosque of the Imam.

They were young, their faces tense under their helmets. Their officers, unsure and unknowing, paced back and forth and cast worried looks at one another, at the gathering crowd, at their men, at the *dasteh*. One soldier went berserk with a rubber truncheon. "Get back, get back, get back!" he yelled at bystanders and flailed the air, his eyes wild, turning from person to person. "Get back, get back . . ."

Merchants were pulling steel grates down over their glass windows. A pottery seller there on the Isfahan Road across the dry stream from the golden dome of Hazrat-e Ma'sumeh and the A'zam Mosque, hurried to get his breakables off the street and into his shop, flower pots and urns and opium pipes.

The prostitutes had cleared out, too, they who would marry for half an hour, *sigheh* ladies, they were called, who would sit in the *kuchehs* with their shoes off and placed before them as the invitation to wed. With them had fled the priests, who would marry them and duly stamp the notary public's vast marriage records.

The bazaar was closed down and ready for trouble, the troops and police in the old city afraid to enter the narrow ways made ghostly in the shadows cast by Primus lamps. In a passageway, accompanied by flutes, a bearded dervish sang in trilling quarter tones and Eastern modalities:

> *Yea, again I've become mad,*
> *Where are thy chains?*
> *I'm God's own Hoseyn,*
> *Callest me disbeliever?*

The dervish wore goatskins and carried a begging bowl. His eyes were wide and they focused on nothing.

There'd been no word from Smitty, because Smitty was dead.

So said Alice when Jim called her from a station in Saltanatabad. It was the third week. The receiver was frigid in Jim's hand, the wind whipped around the fragile Plexiglas shelter, and snow kicked at his legs as Alice went on about a flying accident just reported out of Bushire. Made the wires. Jim said, "Sure, Alice, wow, okay," and wondered if Smitty had gotten those pictures. Lethal commodities, pictures.

That old feeling took him. Move into it, ace. Will they get you? Maybe. Will you get them? Maybe.

"You like war? You actually like it?" Pari had asked. And he had told her there was nothing more exciting. After you've known that kind of fear, he had said, what else is there?

He filled the gas cans at a pumping station south of town and topped off his tank. A day later, he was south of Shiraz, with the Salt Desert, cold and running endlessly to the east, behind him.

The air was chilly and the sky hung gray, low and mute. Jim had the road to himself except for an occasional truck or van, sheep loaded in the back; or a smoky country bus, *"Tavakkol be Ali"*—"Put your faith in Ali"—painted fore and aft; or a lone motorcyclist, perhaps, on one of those contraptions you have to pedal up hills to supplement the motor.

The wet curves of the hills led south past tumbled-down turquoise cupolas of *emamzadehs*—shrines of local saints— long abandoned by whatever village folk had built them.

The road snaked through collections of mud-walled, mud-roofed dwellings that huddled together like animals against the cold and wind.

Mists hung low on the roads now, and few people were out. As the way rose into the mountains, the dwellings disappeared. Off the road and up a rock incline was one final shepherd. He wore a thick, brown cloak and had a hood up over his head. He walked slowly with a crook in his hands, moving his sheep, the lambs almost grown now, their tails huge sacks of fat. They moved together as a few goats romped outside the herd. Then there was nothing. No life. Just the vast jagged shapes of cold, wet stone, colored strangely with minerals, wave on wave of them, rocks leaping up and falling away at crazy angles.

Two days after he left Tehran, Jim could see the old town far away over the muck. He had come down from the plateau.

It was twilight. The beach on his left was shiny in the dim orange light; a few sandgrouse still skipped beside the easy, lapping tide. The Gulf. He was bone-tired by that time, and Bucephalus was spattered with half of Persia. He had his Mamiya-Sekor and plenty of film.

Jim passed the turnoff twice, snaking back around, and ached to drive down it. In the old days, he would have. He'd simply bluster his way into the VE office. He had the knack. In the streets in Tehran, he'd get caught up in other people's affairs—a wedding procession, say, or a circumcision ceremony—and make it known that he was a newshound (everybody loves the press, he'd tell everybody, including everybody who didn't love the press) and he'd become a strange but honored guest.

The turnoff was plainly marked: "Vereinigte Energiewerke GmbH Energy Project." There was no guard just there. In a heart-shaped triangle where the road branched, some idiot had planted strange southern shrubs that Jim couldn't recognize, with red flowers like cylindrical brushes. Traffic went around the heart.

Down the turnoff—200 meters? 300?—was a wire fence and a gate and guardhouse, and beyond that Jim saw floodlit aluminum buildings. Warehouses? Maybe some offices? The buildings were long and high with triangular roofs. Rotors on the ventilation stacks sat motionless in the winter wind. Probably tightened down.

Here's where they bring it in, he thought with cool wonder. Here. Pars Imports. From Rochant Frères, from Hushang Razavi before the Israelis got him. And from here the funny stuff goes to the mountain where Smitty found the Honcho.

How to get in? Maybe get a boat? Sure. Hang out? Find the foreigners and get an invite?

He looked around as he had a dozen times. No place to hide. Just rolling mud flats. The air smelled of decay. Far over the flats stood isolated buildings, distant from the road. There was no cover. A tough one. Sit here? And get looked at, get hauled in. Patrol the road? And get stopped.

He drove north toward Bushire.

Netzer, Meir, and the others were in Bienfoie's bungalow. They kept the lights dim. The damp cold of the *mashileh* filled the old house, and a wind came down the Gulf and intruded everywhere.

You can't heat these houses, Meir was thinking. There's too much space in them. They're too open. And the waiting—that was always the difficult part. When would Kiani appear? In a day? Two days? Three?

Netzer was staring from the window. Far off in the dark, mercury arc lamps lit the VE docks with a brittle blue glare. Netzer looked back at Meir. Neither spoke.

Netzer had a Beretta Para, standard issue in the IDF—and in the Egyptian army, too—which lay beside him on an empty chair. The Beretta is a light, single-action automatic, and it takes a 9-mm bullet, the kind that Givon caught in the back and that blew his head away.

That first British boy, who stumbled on the cobbles, had thrown his hand in the air, Netzer remembered. He may have cried out, probably did, but Netzer hadn't heard it over the shot and his own excitement.

Odd, Netzer thought. Cold, wet stone and darkness there and now here, too. A draft passed along the wall from old windows that would not close.

Would they make it out? Maybe not. He would hold till the operation was over, then try to get to the boat. If not, not. There were worse ways to die.

They had taken care with everything, even with the tires on the Range Rover, which they had changed on the asphalt drive that led to Bienfoie's bungalow. From there to the main road there was no muck to drive through and leave tracks.

The plant was outrageously easy. They'd done it in the night. The thing was primed. Bienfoie knew the car. They

281

would spot it from the house. A signal from the radio would activate it. After that, anything made of heavy metal passing near it would detonate it and get blown to daylight. Fantastic stuff, picrate, enormous power. Chaim was the expert. Netzer, Meir, Bienfoie—they were mere amateurs at this game. Chaim was patrolling the road and would follow Kiani in. He had an Uzi and a grenade launcher for a coup de grace.

It was 1,100 meters from the turnoff to the house over mud flats. They'd timed it. It took sixty-five seconds. It was 1,400 meters from the house to the muck by the sea. That took ninety seconds. The ship, Netzer knew, was out there now. It would move in.

Meir watched Netzer, with that hint of a bullet in his left leg, pace off an intricate arabesque on the carpet, following the repeating lines as they arced toward the edge and were cut by the boundary at the margin. The repetition signifies the infinity of the cosmos, Netzer had told him. The pattern repeats itself forever and ever to the ends of the universe.

That year the month of Moharram stretched into January in the Western calendar, and bitter cold winds whipped through Qom. Toward the end of Moharram, after the passion plays of the ninth and tenth of the month, the shah's government, in arrogance and delusion, had set holidays to celebrate the liberation of women ("False," said the mullahs) and land reform ("Spurious," said the same mullahs). And just then, too, the semiofficial newspaper *Ayandegan* published an attack on Ayatollah Ruhollah Khomeyni. *Ayandegan*'s editorialist said the ayatollah was in the pay of the British and a homosexual.

They marched now from the Fayziyyeh. There were 4,000 of them in their black robes and white turbans—priests and their students—and they moved ten abreast across the bridge and into the main street toward the center of the new city. They had demands and they had placards listing them: implementation of the constitution, separation of powers, freedom for political prisoners, reopening of the Fayziyyeh.

As they marched, one began chanting, "*Ey, Hoseyn, ey, Hoseyn,*" and another took it up, and a third, till they all shouted it in unison, their feet marking time in the thin

282

coating of snow in the street. The flakes cut into their faces, for the wind was fierce. As they rounded the Isfahan Road, they saw the police vans, their canvas sides drawn up, the reserves sitting in them. They were far away. "We are Hoseyn," one shouted. "We are Hoseyn, brothers."

The rest took up the chant then, as monitors formed the line and directed them to the square. They were marching toward the vans.

When the police opened fire, at least 50 marchers died and 500 others were cut down. Kindly old Ayatollah Shari'at-Madari, the least political of men, declared the shah's government un-Islamic. The revolution was on.

5

Jim felt an edgy alertness, which was the old way fear worked on him, and he knew and liked the feeling.

He had slept ten hours, heavily, in the Bushire Palace, a large, old hotel of many additions, mostly brick, the multiple floors of which never quite matched up, which backed on the sheltered quays of the Khor Soltani and fronted on Bushire's old market street. When he went out into the bright, chilly morning, he was groggy from too much sleep.

His passport number would go to the police. So would Bucephalus's plate number. They'll put them on a list to file, forgotten already, which is fine. That sense of being observed, though, dogged Jim still, even as he started Bucephalus. He wanted to take a walk, cut around, double back, look for little men who were looking for him.

But he didn't. He would head for the VE docks. He would get some shots. Mail them back to Alice so they don't get confiscated, then make a return trip and head in.

The place is crawling with foreigners, right? That makes it safe as Sunday school, right? Sure. Then do it. Drive right down the feeder. March right in and say hello. Only way. Get a look at things. Have a powwow with the boss.

Bushire's old market street was strangely silent and empty when he nosed Bucephalus out of the hotel courtyard. The shops and stalls were closed, and the byways running off it, deserted. Police trucks, their canvas sides down, sat in two orderly rows on each side of the entrance to the bazaar. Their backs were open. They were filled with armed men.

Right. Moharram. Bazaar's down.

When a rock banged off Bucephalus's hood, Jim could make out only one young man in the empty street, a driver of a three-wheeled pickup vanette, who leaned against his vehicle, flipping his key chain, just gazing at Jim. His face was a blank.

Away from the market, in the newer parts of town as Jim drove through them, life went on and people were about, busy in the morning. But something had happened.

Jim took Bucephalus through the old city wall, leaving the Meydan-e Chahar Borj and the quays. Dhows and lighters lay at anchor, motionless on the Khor Soltani. The marsh flats beyond were green with plants that waved softly in the winds, and far over the flats he saw land. A few motor launches were easing between the Khor and those other docks somewhere on the mainland on the other side. There, he knew, somewhere, they would put in a reactor. There, he knew, they would have enough brackish water to cool their reactor even if they were cooking plutonium.

He was cold and he shivered as he drove down the rolling fifteen kilometers south on the peninsula road, green marsh far to the east of him and the blue of the Gulf to the west, and the smell of decay everywhere in the wintry sunshine. The sun was high now off the far foothills, the mountains behind them just the hint of darkness on the distant horizon.

Traffic was light—a few gas tankers, country buses, trucks hauling earth from somewhere—and he drove fast, Bucephalus's gearbox whining.

He thought of Smitty and the fearfulness in his kid's eyes and he wondered what Smitty had done and how they'd caught him and what they'd done to him. Had he gotten pics of the field? Of the Honcho? Who *was* the Honcho? Had Smitty told them anything of one James Morgan, newshound? He wondered, too, about Smitty's girl, how Smitty'd found her, how he'd treated her, where she was now.

War, sport.

It took Jim ten minutes to reach the VE turnoff. Not far from it, up the main road and off to the side, was a parked Range Rover. A man was sitting in it on the passenger side, reading something, very nonchalant, and didn't look as Jim passed. Jim didn't like that, the thing parked and waiting there and all. Police? Security?

The Range Rover was a light cream color and very clean

285

and stood high off the road. Jim watched it warily in Bucephalus's mud-spattered rearview mirror. The Rover didn't start up, just shrank in the mirror.

What'll they do? Throw you out? Or hold you? Or maybe you'll turn up missing. Maybe they'll float you out the Gulf.

He drove far down, past the heart-shaped intersection, past the feeder leading to the docks, down where a network of dirt tracks ran off the main highway and laced between it and the water of the Gulf. He eased Bucephalus over them—some had been washed out by the rains of years back and never repaired—and circled to the right, to the deserted brown beach, where he parked.

Hoseyn's arm throbbed and he felt faint. Gendarmes with peasant faces and peasant clumsiness had stopped him in his jeep at a roadblock on the Bushire highway. He had gotten one. The boy fell away, a look of mute astonishment on his face as his body snapped backward and his cap flew from his head, but the other had caught Hoseyn in the arm, and a dull pain kept the arm against his body, though he could move his fingers.

He'd gotten to the city and had disappeared into the safe house in a workers' suburb, where they worried about his arm. But he'd insisted and they let him pick up a car, an expendable old blue Peykan, though they knew a search was on.

Hoseyn could see the Land Rover far away. The American had left it under a rise where the peninsula pulls up sharply from the muck of the beach. Where was the American? Why did he leave the machine?

Hoseyn pulled the keys from his own car and loped toward the far off Rover, cutting through reed beds that filled small hollows, where wind and water had made incisions in the *mashileh*. The sand under his feet gave way softly as he ran, his shoes filling with it, and he took them off and threw them away.

He kept his gaze on Morgan's Rover, a way not to think, a way to concentrate. When he reached a stand of palms, six frail trees, one of them dead and rotting, he fell to his stomach, panting and thirsty, his head light.

He reached to test the action on the VZ-58, though his

fingers were light and uncontrolled. He pulled the curved magazine out, ejected the cartridge, and brought back the bolt. When he eased the trigger back, the bolt snapped forward. A classic gun. He felt for the other clips at his waist. Were they there? Had he dropped them? One was gone. Two others, heavy, bit into his side.

He looked at his arm. The bandage was professional, but had worked loose, and the blood was dark on his tan sweater. A coat of many colors, he thought. I am Joseph, he thought, and smiled to think it.

A sandstone ridge lay to the right, the sea to his left.

The sea. Like Lebanon. The shimmering sea road that led to all the world. "His love is a sea and we are drowned in Him."

Then Hoseyn moved again toward the Rover across the trackless beach, cutting through reeds and keeping to the low, rolling rise, the gun set on semiautomatic, the safety off now.

Ahead on the rise, low huts—fishermen's? pearl divers'?— lay off the beach and a squat stand of palms lay before them to the south. Was Morgan there in those huts?

Hoseyn, on his belly now, the Rover just ahead, crept up the rise, where sand had collected around the beach vegetation, and inching forward, he moved into the palm stand. He could see the huts now, their old walls half collapsed, and somewhere among them, he caught movement, the hint of a man's shape passing.

Then he heard the sound of engines from the main road, a lazy, far-off hum, carried through the cool air. Concentrating on the huts now, yet aware of the gun in his hand, he listened to the sound and wondered about it as he watched the huts for movement.

Was it the others? They who would strike the Israelis? They were near. They were ready.

Or gendarmes?

That thought made his heart pound as he snaked forward through the thick palms, still close to the edge of the sea, where soft waves broke gently with a hush on the dark sand. The water was a brilliant shining blue.

His face was close enough to the sand for him to taste the grains, and again that feeling, a queasy sensation like a hand

kneading his stomach, pushed through him, making him half
sick. To admit fear, he thought, and then act despite it is
bravery.

Hoseyn saw Morgan among the huts. The gun barrel
trailed in the sand as Hoseyn crept forward.

Seashells and smashed pottery with geometric designs and
dashes of blue-green glaze covered the floors of the deserted old
buildings. There might have been ten of them, abandoned long
ago by whoever had lived there. The buildings had all fallen in.
An *emamzadeh*, with a tall, white cupola, built like a sugarloaf
and leaning crazily, stood outside the cluster. Gulls rested on
its concentric circles of brick. A spur of land, covered by shells,
kicked out into the Gulf.

Far back, just off the Bushire road, on Jim's right, stood a
lone bungalow, weathered and gray. Thin columns on the
bungalow's roof reached up to support nothing. It was as
deserted as the village. Before the bungalow, closer to the VE
turnoff and not that far from Jim, sat that cream-colored Range
Rover.

Jim, crouching in the shadow of a crumbling mud-straw
half wall, looked back to the VE docks, where a lighter bobbed
slowly. Another offshore—the distance seemed a mile, but
might have been more—moved toward a vessel, rare in the sea
road down there, that lay far out. Even through his telephoto
lense Jim couldn't see the flag or the ship's name. It was small.
He squeezed off shots (they'd be lousy), then studied the docks.

Two jetties. Two warehouses end to end. A helipad between them. A chopper on it, its rotors motionless. The warehouses had docks for forklifts on the sea side, truck loading
docks on the inland. Security check at the one and only gate
and a single good road stretching up to the Bushire highway.
Big Mercedes-Benz trucks painted up like Russian Easter
eggs—the Iranian way—stood idle in the truck yard. Cleared
area around the ten-foot-high chain-link fence. Thick loops of
concertina wire over the fence. Heavy.

On one of the docks, a lone yellow forklift puttered from
stack to stack, shifting pallets, like some methodical insect
doing idiotic work.

Jim got shots of the pallets, of the docked lighter, and through the wire-fence boundary, shots of the helipad, the chopper, the warehouses, then shots of the concertina wire strung over the fence.

Jim heard the choppers before he saw them. They came rolling in low, mean and roaring from behind, and when they passed over, the sound was deafening. They were Cobras and they spat rockets, each two at a time, that hissed in flat trajectories in the air. The Range Rover went over, tipped like a child's toy car, a wraith of fire playing over it, and then the thing burst with high orange flames and black smoke, and the gasoline went off with a rumble.

He could see the driver there flat in the muck by the side of the road. Sand spit up around him as the choppers wheeled, holding, almost dancing in the chill air over the sodden *mashileh*. Jim's stomach turned as he watched. There was the driver, the anguish on his face like a gash torn across it, rolling on the ground as sand shot up around him, fountains blown into the air by 50-caliber bullets. His expression was more hopelessness than physical pain, which clearly he no longer felt. Some bullets caught him still and he rolled slowly. There was almost a balletic grace to it; when the firing stopped, the man lay motionless as the Cobras lifted higher, banking and swinging back over the VE jetty.

In the Mekong Delta, Jim had seen A-4s streak down once and strafe a fishing boat, blasting its left side to pieces and shredding the hull and deck. The lucky ones were overboard as the planes came back for another run, and it made Jim sick then to see the wood fly and the water spray up and the men there in it as a bit of the craziness of the war engulfed them.

Here was more craziness. He'd stumbled onto it.

Meir couldn't stop him. Netzer, madness in his eyes, had flung him aside and burst through the double doors out onto the veranda screaming, "No, no, no, no!" He shook the veranda's flimsy wooden railing in rage as he watched the flames and smoke rise away from Chaim and the vehicle. "No, no, *no!*" he yelled again and banged his hands against the railing, which finally broke away and pitched forward crazily.

Meir was with him now. Netzer had stopped yelling. He was panting, his eyes fixed on Chaim's vehicle far over the flats, overturned like rubbish.

Meir lifted his hand as if to touch something. "A land of dreams and illusions," Netzer had said. "All you see is the blur."

Netzer turned and their eyes met. They knew the boat was useless.

The Cobras swung back from the jetty now, flying low and fast again toward where Jim was, and again opened fire, criss-crossing and raking the turnoff and everything there, then wheeled away abruptly toward that far bungalow. They circled the building, spat cannon into it, and collapsed half the old structure, then dropped to land. Unmarked Land Rovers were streaking over the flats toward them.

It was over.

Jim got up off the ground finally and stood gaping without a thought in his head except why the fuck hadn't he gotten pictures? When he turned, dazed, to look around, he saw a young man not ten yards away, who was as stupefied as himself, and they stared at each other for a time. Jim recognized him finally—it was the hook in the eyebrow—as Hoseyn swung the gun up, faster and better and surer than that other kid in the street in Tehran.

" 'I called the whole world His dream,' " sang Alice to herself, her husky voice slurring the syllables. " 'I looked again, and, lo, His dream was Himself.' " Though noticing the cold only intermittently, she'd pulled her blanket around her in the night.

A luminous orb surrounded her, light on light, golden and green, the colors merging and withdrawing from one another. The subtle organism of the light, she thought as she saw it. Over the light is a mountain, under which Man is prisoner. Tranquillity is *fana*—annihilation—as the Sufis have it and which they seek, and even if man desires to keep it off from himself, they say, its nature is such that he cannot, and he gives up the body and goes to the world of Divine Majesty, and his ascents reach the high spheres, whence he may look back upon himself and discern there the radiance of God's light. Alice looked back, and looking saw herself curled on a *takht* by a kerosene heater that had gone out long before.

Alice, in short, was high as a kite with her infrequent toke of opium. A languid curl of smoke still rose from her pipe, and the feeling of heaviness she knew well lay on her, the sense that motion requires too much effort, when the ticking of a clock becomes infinitely interesting. From her record player— how many times had it repeated itself as Alice lay there?— came the lowing of a flute and the spare notes of a *tar*, the three-stringed instrument, and the crackling *zarb*, a drum open at the bottom, whose metal sides the player strikes with the ring finger, mixing metallic clicks with thuds on the skin. After a time a woman named Butterfly, *Parvaneh*, sang in throaty alto:

Asheqi peydast az zari-ye del *("Love is manifest
from the grieving of the heart")*,
Nist bimari chu bimari-ye del *("There is no
sickness like the sickness of the heart")*.

Stutely was gone. Alice feared the future. Though they didn't believe her at the *FT*, Alice could feel it, she told them, could sense the tension of the earth as before a quake and feared it would swallow her.

The bazaaris, she'd told James before—poor James—the biggest of the big, the oldest of the old, are fed up. Money's pouring out, to Khomeyni, to others, all of them raising Ned. The government is very stupid. The heart of the country's been torn out.

"End coming, Alice?" Jim had asked her. "King business not what it used to be?"

"Look for trouble, luv." Her eyes were large and round when she said it, wondering even then what would become of herself.

The massacre in Qom, Alice knew, which they're trying to keep a lid on and not succeeding, was just the beginning. The mullahs'll wait forty days and then have a mourning parade and there'll be another bash. A good one if the mullahs can manage it, and that will require more mourning. So every forty days a guaranteed fracas. The bazaar was alive with the possibilities.

This very day, Alice, kerchief over her blond hair, coat over a shapeless dress and sensible shoes on her feet, had made her way through those twisting, secluded *kuchehs* to the south and west of Tehran's great bazaar. The smell of cardamom, coffee, and rose water was in the air, and charcoal embers lifted the smell of roasting beets and the pungence of broiling lamb and chopped onion, and from the windows of houses came the scent of fenugreek and lemon and saffroned rice. She entered that city within a city on the oblique, as it were, and moved through the lesser passageways in the general direction of the *timcheh*, the storehouse, of one Haj Mohsen.

The *khareji* woman was known in the endless byways here: Alice had wandered for years down these paths amid the banging of the coppersmiths, among the porters yelling, "*Yal-lah!* Out of the way!" in their baggy pants and felt caps, as they carried chunks of ice or carpets on their porters' back hitches or shuffled crablike under refrigerators. Alice had marveled at this at first. She had wandered as young boys pushed past her, running trays of tea endlessly up and down the smooth flagstones of the bazaar from the teahouses or trays of lunch from the cookhouses, steaming rice and kabab sprinkled with tangy sumac. She knew the spice merchants' quarter and the scents there of ginger and turmeric and had a nodding acquaintance with the bearded hajjis who sold books, sewing machines, drugs, and whatnot on the main passage from there to the carpet merchants' quarter. Now and then she would encounter a *khoncheh*, a gazebolike structure, all of light, erected at a crossroads in the old bazaar in memory of some dear departed. Or a tank of drinking water put out as a kindness by one of the faithful and on top of it for good fortune the Hand of Fatemeh, whose five flat brass fingers pointed forever to heaven.

Some of the bazaaris eyed buxom Alice with other than

piety of course when they said, *"Ey, Khanom, be omid-e khoda!"* "Ay, Lady, in the hope of God!"

Through all this, as often before, came Alice. But it was a different bazaar. She felt the tension, knew it in the looks and gestures of the men and boys in their stalls and the women looking away, as when Mostafa Khomeyni was killed in Qom.

It was coming.

When she arrived at the *timcheh* of Haj Mohsen, his servant, Akbar Aqa, seeing her, scampered nimbly to the old man, who had dined on bread and cheese and tea and was even then thinking of his pallet in a side storage room off the *timcheh*. But the arrival of the *"Englees mahdahm"*—that's how he said it— cast the thought from his mind.

"Ey, Khanom, befarmaid! Please, please!" he said and gestured weakly with his old hand to his accounting office and didn't bother to call for tea since both he and the *mahdahm* knew it was already on its way.

Haj Mohsen had a wide grin and not quite the requisite number of teeth, dental care in Haj Mohsen's youth being on the improvisatory side, and such as were left were tea-stained.

His *timcheh* lay back off the main route of the bazaar and away from its din. It was high-domed and cobbled, and over the paving stones lay pile after pile of carpets, a meter high each.

The arches around the *timcheh* pointed upward with Persian grace, and above them soared domed filigrees of brickwork in intricate patterns of what for Alice was pure geometric thought. Somebody had actually worked it out, she knew. High up in the windows stone grillwork in a cloverleaf pattern circled the dome and pointed to the central octagon of light at the very top, through which streamed sunlight, softened by the dust and the gray stones.

Haj Mohsen, as always, wore patched, grubby pantaloons, ancient shoes with the heels turned down and crushed in back (transitional from the sandal stage), a white shirt smudged with graphite and ink, its thin collar buttoned up tight around his throat; as always, he had vast, amber globules of prayer beads in his hands. Haj Mohsen was a millionaire many times over, with sons in Hamburg, Rome, and Washington, who sold the carpets Haj Mohsen sent them. For Alice, he was a source

293

of wisdom, even erudition, on the ways of the bazaar.

"We see you so little, *mahdahm*. Today you have brought your nobility and today we are fortunate."

"Ah, Haj Mohsen, this servant lacks the wisdom to come more often, and besides, onerous duties prevent the pleasure," Alice said, smiling.

"Are you well? Are you healthy?" Haj Mohsen asked three times (it was the initial burst—he would ask again), and Alice praised God three times and said, *"Ey*, Haj Mohsen, tell me of your condition."

"Ey, praise God, *mahdahm, salamati*. Health. I still draw breath."

"If you are well, then God favors us all."

And so it went as Haj Mohsen, smiling, dipped a bit of hard sugar struck from the funnel-shaped sugarloaf first in his tea and then placed it between tooth and jaw and ran tea from his saucer over it.

He leaned forward finally, the amber *tasbih* in both hands, and said, "A carpet, *mahdahm!* Consider well this Isfahani."

Haj Mohsen pointed to a magnificent *farsh*, silken and gleaming, with a crimson field and a tracery of pure white and blue shot through it.

"For you, *mahdahm*, 10,000 tomans, for we are old friends."

"Ey, Haj Mohsen, would I had the money."

"Credit is easy." He smiled. "Our arrangement stands yet: pay over a year. If you bring the carpet back, all your money—all—will be refunded. What better guarantee?"

"I can't afford it. I've been foolish enough these last years, Haj Mohsen." And she had. Her house was filled with carpets of the most fantastic variety, for Alice had an eye.

"Buying such masterworks is not folly, *mahdahm*. How can you say so? And I am not like the Jews on Ferdowsi. They are all named Georges-morzh and Charles-marl"—Haj Mohsen pronounced the names in the French manner—"which latter sounds very like 'charlatan,' I think. Oh, yes, if you buy from them, the result is regrets." He studied Alice carefully, for he had perceived she was indeed not on a shopping errand. But if not that, what?

The *Englees*, Haj Mohsen knew, were a most clever people and in his youth had been a power and might still be. One could learn much of the purposes of the world from a personage such as the blond *mahdahm*. And, truth to tell, Haj Mohsen suspected that the *mahdahm* cultivated him for more than his carpets and that the wisdom he told her found its way to the great city of *Landan* and the councils there of the powerful. He was, of course, bang right.

This time it was for the sake of the infidels of the *FT*, skeptics all, that Alice had come wandering through the bazaar to talk with Haj Mohsen. She drank her tea there in Haj Mohsen's *timcheh* and talked of this and that. Her talk rambled and was indirect, but she kept coming back to the subject of the bazaar as Akbar Aqa deferentially refilled her tea glass, to the guilds and the syndicates and the merchants down there. She touched carefully on the matter of the religious devotees and their circles, on the denizens of the houses of strength, on the mosque endowments and those who funded them. Alice was fishing. What she wanted was the cash outflow from bazaar to the reverend clergy. How much? To whom? From whom? Overseas? For what purpose?

She got nowhere.

Haj Mohsen, a store of information of a high specificity, who more than once had shared surprising tales with Alice, smiled weakly through all the talk this day and replied in kindly generalities, caressing his shining prayer beads, which he held now and again to the side of his head and rubbed in circles on his short whiskers. Akbar Aqa nodded drowsily in a corner, looking at the two of them from under sleepy eyelids, as if wondering when the *mahdahm* would leave and he could clear away the tea things and lie down.

No go, Alice thought. And I reckon I don't blame him. Nope. Wrong bloody time to talk to foreigners.

Suddenly, Haj Mohsen leaned forward (his legs were curled under him in the chair), cocked his head, and looked at her closely with one eye. " 'The hour approaches,' " he said, quoting the Koran, " 'and the moon is rent asunder.' A happening, *mahdahm*, long before. When the idolators of Mecca persecuted the faithful, the moon split in two as a sign. The idolators were astonished by the appearance of the two moons, but in their ignorance persisted. And then they were lost. 'We loosed upon them a raging wind on a day of constant calamity. It swept them away as the uprooted trunks of palm trees.' "

Haj Mohsen knew a thing or two.

"Hullo, Pear."

"Hullo, Ace."

"You didn't go."

"No."

They were in the yellow and blue-tiled reception hall in the embassy, she in her raincoat.

"You bloody bastard."

"Hey."

Arms around his neck now. "Oh, you bloody, bloody bastard." He stumbled when she hung on him.

Civilians, large men with helmets and Uzis, had shot Hoseyn by the palm stand. The same civilians had picked Jim up and he had gotten good and violent, kicking and screaming in fact, when they did, but they knocked him around and kept him awake for two days and a night in the Bushire Municipality, then flew him to Tehran, where they deposited him, dirty, hungry, and hallucinating, at night at the embassy, in care of Peter F. X. Fiscarelli. Jim looked pretty much like a spook. When he saw Fiscarelli, he said "Jesus."

They took him to Fiscarelli's villa in Elahieh, where they bathed him. He fell into a sleep and dreamed of soundless gunships floating in the air and A-4s, of long mountain roads that led down to endless plains of mud and decay. As he tossed, the Pear stayed awake.

The next morning, Fiscarelli was in a state. "Sons of bitches. Sons of *bitches*," he yelled. "They won't talk." "They" were the Iranians and the Israelis. "*Air* strike. I mean, they use *choppers* for God's sake. What the fuck did you *see?*"

The natives were restless, said Fiscarelli. Trouble in Qom, trouble in the bazaars, trouble nationwide. Now this.

The announcement—the Israelis had to make one—was short and came out of Jerusalem, preceding by a day Jim's ghostly advent at Henderson High: "Iranian terrorists have shot two technical advisers in performance of their duties in Iran. Families have been notified." That was it.

Names were furnished quietly to "interested foreign diplomats," including Fiscarelli. The names meant nothing to Fiscarelli, who, like other interested foreign diplomats, had no easy time keeping track of the Israeli contingent. Uri Gellerman, stone-faced, in a quiet session swiftly arranged, told Fiscarelli the legation had no definite information on the attack, that they were awaiting a police report. The victims had been agronomists.

The Iranians confirmed the attack publicly. Further, said the Iranians—this to an astounded Fiscarelli at a brief meeting with him and his underlings at Henderson High and not at all public—they'd gotten Hoseyn Jandaqi. The young lieutenant who told them, whose name was Ebrahimian, had been quite proud.

A case solved, Lieutenant Ebrahimian said. The Givon shooting, Mr. Fiscarelli would recall, of last summer.

Mr. Fiscarelli did recall it.

This Jandaqi, the lieutenant said, had been implicated and had been the only one of the immediate terrorist gang to escape. A report was pending and would be shared with foreign security and intelligence services. The possible connection with the deaths of the Israeli advisers was being investigated. The report would address this issue.

"SAVAK got their man," said Fiscarelli.

"Can't be SAVAK. Hoseyn was working for them."

"Fuck off. You ready for this? Story is, a gendarmerie patrol stops him, just this routine roadblock, right? And he panics, they say, because the jeep he's driving is fucking loaded with ordnance. But they don't know this at first. So he shoots a gendarme, who later dies, and he jumps and runs.

"But they wing him, okay? They wing him as he runs, but they don't catch him. Lousy police work, but what do you want, the boy's got a gun. Smarter guys in SAVAK know where to look, though."

Inconspicuous colleagues of those men in civilian suits who carried Uzis tracked Hoseyn to a cheap apartment on the fringes of Bushire. They watched him, they followed him out, they tailed him in his blue Peykan down the Shiraz road.

"Then they dropped him. Right there by the palm grove. End of story. End of Hoseyn Jandaqi, boy hero."

Jim shook his head. "Shit."

"Yeah. He was after you. How'd he know you'd been chasing him?"

"Dozen ways. Beirut's a sieve."

"Uh-huh." Fiscarelli sipped at his morning whiskey.

"Goddam-it, it was *something*, Pete. Down there. It's the nuclear thing."

"Maybe."

"Givon, Hoseyn, Bushire, these Israelis. Technical advisers, my ass. It's all connected." As Jim said it, he was wondering in God's name how.

"Everything's connected, Jimmy. The world's complicated." Another sip at the whiskey. "So anyway, I raise the issue with Ebrahimian, who's not a bad sort of guy, after all, and his friends. I say there was some action with Cobras. I say we got an eyewitness here, our own young Jimmy. What the fuck was *that*, I say. Then they get sly, see. They say, no, no, no, that's *different*. He saw something *else*. But they don't say what else. They're checking, they say, right? They're checking and will tell me. Shit. For the tenth time, Jimmy, did you see something *else?*"

Jim shrugged. "It was an action."

"Sure. Fuck." Lifting his right leg with his hands, Fiscarelli put his feet up on his coffee table, a six-foot cable spool turned on its side, varnished shinily, of which Fiscarelli was very proud. He slipped his shoes off. "They use choppers for all kinds of things, Jimmy. They use choppers against smugglers. They use choppers against tribes that get uppity. We're not supposed to know about that, by the way. Ma Derian gets apoplexy. 'What about their human rights?' says Ma Derian. Fuck it, I say. *I* think it's just fine."

Fiscarelli rubbed his head. "Maybe they're not lying? Sometimes they don't."

"They're lying. It's beautiful, Pete. We're so close you can

298

smell it and taste it in the air. It's there, Pete, oh, shit it is. We'll get it."

Fiscarelli was uncomprehending at first, then made a face of disgust when he realized what Jim meant.

"You're a good boy, Jimmy, but dumb. You're here illegally, somebody's gunning for you, and you've been real close to one of *those* things. You're going on a plane."

"*Bullshit.*"

"Don't bullshit me. The Iranians are putting you on a plane. They want you to take a bath first and get all rested up so you're nice and beautiful when you step off in Europe somewhere, that's all. Figure tomorrow. Maybe the next day. Tough. Don't cry on my shoulder."

It didn't matter. As Fiscarelli talked, Jim had already thought of ten different ways of getting back into it, all of them doable, with or without Iranian cooperation. The story. It was beautiful. Zimmerman would knight him.

"You know, Jimmy, you've spent ten thousand four hundred and seventy of the taxpayers' dollars for fuck-all."

"Sue me."

"What do I tell Langley?"

"Tell them it's gambling debts, Pete. Tell them you're sorry, tell them you'll pay them back."

"I'll tell them I spent it on a whore. Which I did."

Right.

The Israeli announcement spurred the press in Tehran to make inquiries of the government, which were ignored.

In Jerusalem a storm threatened. In the face of it, the Foreign Ministry maintained a strict public silence. Spokesmen, off the record, talked of "national security issues" and would say no more. Fiscarelli assured Jim that in private the sons of bitches at the ministry were negotiating an end to the thing with the establishment papers, that the left-wing rags would go on to other scandals.

Whatever, the news ended, reminding Jim of the way the whole business had gotten started. Including a reporter getting chucked.

*   *   *

299

Pari and Jim walked in Fiscarelli's garden, their breath hanging before them in the air. The garden's high stone walls were made from turquoise-colored rock from a nearby streambed. The sun was metallic in the wintry haze.

"My Man Morgan." Her eyes were shining. "Hasn't ended, has it."

"No."

"Even though you found him."

"He found *me*, Pear. Now he's dead. Who was he?"

"Who knows?"

"Yeah. The Iranian question."

"Jeem Khan, you'll never stop." Her hand was up, the back of it on his cheek and reddish beard. The green-eyed man. "But it's all right. It *is*."

"What is?"

"You know what. The quest. Running about, here and there. *And* running in circles. You certainly do a lot of that."

"Hazards of the trade."

"Right. Well, anyway, I've thought about it. The running about, I mean. It's all right."

"Pear."

"It's all right. It's you, and I love you. So it's all right, mate. I mean I think I can put up with you, you bastard. Got that? I mean I think I can, you bloody bastard. Oh, you bloody, bloody bastard. Right." Her face was on his chest now, buried in the army jacket Fiscarelli had dug up for him, which was printed with jungle camouflage. Out of Vietnam, like Jim. The war-watcher. Pari shook in his arms, and he wondered why on earth he mattered to her. Never could explain that one, he thought.

At dusk the haze cleared.

Fiscarelli's cook made a *polow* with chicken breasts and currants and served dry Qazvin wine. In bed, they tasted the fragrance on each other's lips.

Cold moonlight cut through the night like a diamond and fell on Pari, whose long black hair lay spread on the pillow as she slept. Jim's bourbon was smooth over the ice. Fiscarelli kept a bottle of Early Times in every room of his villa. The room was frigid.

The Iranian guards around the property hadn't impressed Jim. He could see them from the window, shivering in the night at the far reaches of Fiscarelli's garden. They were more to keep Jim in than anyone out. The Pear lay on her side, face to the window where Jim stood. The long, slender neck and Nefertiti nose. She was wearing the moss agate necklace. When she sighed softly in her sleep, Jim thought of what would happen if someone came in shooting.

The night was clear and hushed. Snow had blanketed the garden and brushed the branch tips of Fiscarelli's tall cypresses. Glinting in the moonlight, the trees marched in stately parallel lines to the high wall edging Fiscarelli's grounds.

Jim still had the picture of Hoseyn. A boy. SAVAK had killed him. Which made no sense.

Jim stared out at the moonlight.

Fact: Israelis were down there.

Fact: Israelis were killed.

At the VE docks. By the government. Jim had seen it.

The Iranians must have known, must have been watching the Israelis. Count on it. The Iranians set them up. Maybe they'd figured out who was going after their nuclear program. Somehow. Maybe had even lured them out to it. Had they lured Givon out that early morning? Maybe the Israelis thought they were going to find the Honcho. And maybe the Honcho—whoever he is—found *them?*

What had Michel said? "In a game of chance, look around to find the fool. If you do not find him, you're the fool."

Then it came to him, seized him, as when the IBEX connection appeared to him clear and sharp out of the dust and haze.

Hoseyn Jandaqi was killed by SAVAK by the side of a palm grove. That means he wasn't a government worker.

Right.

But those phony companies in Europe, the purchasing schemes, the shipments, the project down on the Gulf, and Hushang Razavi, God rest his soul, as Farfar would say, that sure was a government program, wasn't it? And Hoseyn was in on it, wasn't he? Did its bidding, didn't he? He kills Givon. He follows these other Israelis down to Bushire, and he's carrying an arsenal at the time, follows *me*. So he *was* a government worker. Had to be.

But this is a funny government program.

For this swell government program, who's the courier? Suleyman Chemissa, Libyan, Qaddafi messenger boy, overseer of arms flows.

And whose bank do they use, for God's sake? Al-Jihad's, the fuzzy-wuzzies'. In Beirut. Maybe all this isn't just protective coloration.

Suppose . . . suppose the government's not a government. Suppose the government's split in two. Suppose there's the SAVAK side. And suppose there's the other side.

"The security forces are not so bloody secure," as Alice said and everybody knew. Right.

"The Iranian People's Martyrs have the capability to monitor SAVAK communications," said Fiscarelli's report. Right.

And fat old Haj Amin, the bazaari, with his hennaed hair? "Bazaar's boiling over," said Alice. "They're fed up." Right.

The Libyan connection, then? Friend Chemissa? Suppose the Libs want a bomb of their own and this is how they think they'll get one. They think they're running Shohada. They think they'll connect that way.

It works.

And suppose . . .

The Honcho who's running the nuclear thing—maybe he's somewhere in the security forces. But maybe also the Honcho's ties with the frizzy-haired types are pretty good? No maybes there, sport. The Honcho was running Hoseyn Jandaqi.

Then maybe the Honcho's on both sides of the street? Maybe if the shah goes, the Honcho will stay? With his bomb. No maybes.

Before they left—for London as it happened, Pari radiant— Jim tried it out on Fiscarelli. Fiscarelli didn't want to hear it. Fiscarelli laughed and waved his hand to dismiss the idea. But that didn't bother Jim in the least.

He was Onto Something, all right. A secret war. He knew it. He knew he'd be back. He knew he'd find the Honcho.

Zimmerman held him out, miserable, for a time, figuring to let things cool down. "Things" were going to hell in Iran, but better for the paper, better for Jim, that he stay out temporarily. They'd arrange it. Jim would go in on the up-and-up.

Then came Khomeyni.

Acknowledgments

Thanks first to friends in Tehran and Beirut, who in various ways had much to do with the shaping of this book. I hope you see better times.

My thanks, too, to the journalists covering the Middle East—Jim Morgan's noble colleagues—whom I've encountered professionally and otherwise over the years. Some of you are in here, of course; I hope my affection and respect for you come through.

Three scholars kindly gave me permission to quote from, and take minor liberties with, their remarkable work on revolutionary Iran. To them I owe special mention: Ervand Abrahamian's *Iran Between Two Revolutions* (Princeton University Press, 1982) is the source for the speeches of the underground leaders, Rahmani and Baharlu. The glassy-eyed dervish and the crowd toward the end of the present work are nicely agitated by the chants and songs that Michael Fischer wrote down in his *Iran: From Religious Dispute to Revolution* (Harvard University Press, 1980). And the young mullah who leads the passion play and sends Hoseyn out to kill Jim gets some of *his* lines from an Iranian villager Mary Hegland talked with in "Aliabad"—not its real name—a small town in southern Iran, where Mary spent much of the revolution. Her article from that time, "Two Images of Husain: Accommodation and Revolution in an Iranian Village," appears in *Religion and Politics in Iran*, edited by Nikki R. Keddie and published by Yale University Press (1983). It goes without saying that Ervand, Mike, and Mary should be wholly absolved of any sins I commit in the book.

I've made use of other scholarship on Iran too voluminous to cite here. Specialists will recognize what I've stolen and from whom. I would mention with thanks, though, Farhad Kazemi's *Poverty and Revolution in Iran* (New York University, 1980) for its description of Tehran's South City Pits. They're real, as are the whores and the opium smokers down there, if any readers doubted it.

I'm grateful to Philip Bruno, a French attorney working in Washington, for advice on French commercial and governmental procedure. That I've simplified things is no fault of his. Philip also vetted the names of Hushang Razavi's phony French companies and made sure they all sounded properly Gallic.

I am indebted beyond words to Ann Harris of Arbor House, who showed enormous patience, skill, and caring throughout in editing *Finding Hoseyn*.

Finally and mostly, to my wife, Shokoofeh, who put up with a lot and never failed to give encouragement, my warmest love and thanks.